& Son

Sooty Feathers
Book III

Also by David Craig

Lucifer & Son

Sooty Feathers
Book III

David Craig

Elsewhen Press

Lucifer & Son
First published in Great Britain by Elsewhen Press, 2024
An imprint of Alnpete Limited

Elsewhen Press, PO Box 757, Dartford, Kent DA2 7TQ
www.elsewhen.press

British Library Cataloguing in Publication Data.
A catalogue record for this book is available from the British Library.

ISBN 978-1-915304-66-7 Print edition
ISBN 978-1-915304-76-6 eBook edition

Designed and formatted by Elsewhen Press

This book is dedicated to
Emma, James and Ben.

Contents

Dramatis Personae

Wilton Hunt — A university student studying the natural sciences; body snatcher; heir to Baron Ashwood's title and estate, and the Browning Shipping Company. Son of the Devil.

Kerry Knox — Formerly a struggling actress, now Lady Delaney's apprentice, dedicated to fighting demons and the undead.

Lady Caroline Delaney — A middle-aged widow whose husband was Possessed by the demon *Beliel*, who killed their children. She has spent two decades quietly fighting the undead in Glasgow. Is allied to the Templar Order.

Wolfgang Steiner — A Swiss Templar Inquisitor based in London. He previously fought Glasgow's undead with a band of Templars, though only one survived.

Terrance Gray — A Templar marksman. African American, he was based in Edinburgh though resides in London for the moment. Aside from Steiner, he was the only Templar to survive their springtime mission in Glasgow.

Bishop John Redfort — Corrupt and opportunistic, he has risen through the ranks of both the church and the Sooty Feather Society. He is now the Second Seat on the Council. Redfort is also secretly a dabbler in necromancy, a branch of magic forbidden by the undead.

Richard Canning — Hanged for multiple murders, he is now a vampyre serving the demon *Arakiel*.

Amy Newfield	A ghoul loyal to Regent Margot Guillam; the Eighth Seat on the Council.
Tam Foley	Hunt's friend and a pharmacist. Since becoming a werewolf, he now resides with others like him near Loch Lomond.
Margot Guillam	An Elder vampyre, Lord Fisher's Regent, and First Seat on the Council.
Roddy McBride	Patriarch of the McBride crime family, and Seventh Seat on the Sooty Feather Council.
Johnny McBride	Roddy McBride's younger brother.
Edmund Crowe	Elder vampyre and owner of the Heron Crowe Bank. Fourth Seat on the Council.
Magdalene Quinn	One of Glasgow's leading magicians and the Fifth Seat on the Council.
Bartholomew Ridley	A magician sworn to *Arakiel.*
Police Superintendent Edwin Kenmure	Possessed by the demon *Maridiel*, and working for *Arakiel.* He has been directing the police against the McBrides.
Cornelius Josiah	A magician serving *Arakiel.* As a Demonist, it was he who Summons demons as required by *Arakiel.*
John Henderson	Possessed by the demon *Arakiel*, who was once a *Grigori* known as Erik Keel. He ruled Glasgow for centuries until Niall Fisher started a rebellion, slaying him. His ultimate goal is to be resurrected in his *Grigori* flesh.

Niall Fisher — A *Dominus Nephilim*, the reclusive ruler of Glasgow. For most of his two hundred year reign he has lived in his Crypt, fearing treachery. He rules through his Regent, Margot Guillam.

Neil MacInesker — Has recently inherited the Dunkellen estate and a number of mills. He is the Sixth Seat on the Council.

Bresnik — A vampyre sworn to *Arakiel.*

Khotep — An ancient necromancer whose soul takes refuge in a soul receptacle. Upon the receptacle making contact with a person, the soul will then Possess that person, similar to demonic Possession. Khotep previously Possessed Dr Essex, until that body was slain by Lady Delaney.

Yates — Khotep's valet. Is entrusted with finding an appropriate Vessel for Khotep's soul upon death.

Lewis Hunt — The 6th Baron of Ashwood, owner of the Browning Shipping Company, and father of Wilton Hunt. He is Possessed by Lucifer. In previous incarnations in the north of Scotland, Lucifer inspired or influenced legends of Cernunnos and Lugh.

Dash Singh — Lord Ashwood's valet. He is also *Kariel*, a *Seraphim* instructed by *Mikiel* to keep an eye on Lucifer and his son.

Glossary

Grigori — One of two hundred rebel angels, Lucifer among them, who survived his failed insurrection. Exiled to Earth a long time ago, they manifested as the first vampires. Unknown if there are any Grigori still in existence.

Ghoul — The first stage of undeath. A ghoul is Made when a human dies within a day and night of drinking a vampire's blood.

Nephilim — A vampire. What a ghoul transitions into, either within three years, or after eating the heart of a Nephilim.

Elder Nephilim — An old and powerful vampire. A status either transitioned to after centuries, or attained by eating the heart of an Elder.

Dominus Nephilim — What an Elder Nephilim becomes should they eat the heart of a Grigori or Dominus Nephilim. Very old, very strong and very rare. Perhaps only a score in existence.

Demon — A fallen angel. One of a hundred million angels who sided with Lucifer but fell during his failed insurrection. Exiled to Hell. A slain Grigori becomes a demon. Can only return to Earth if Summoned by a Demonist, Possessing a human vessel.

Seraphim	One of the one hundred million angels loyal to Mikiel who perished during Lucifer's failed insurrection. Spread to different worlds. Several thousand are bound to Earth, reincarnated time after time, sometimes remembering what they are and details from past lives.
Demonist	A magician who can Summon demons from Hell, placing them into a human vessel.
Necromancer	A magician who can commune with the dead and control corpses.
Jinn	A master necromancer who has fashioned a Soul-Repository to store their soul upon death. Upon the Soul-Repository coming into contact with another person, the necromancer's soul will then take over that body, displacing the original soul. Sometimes known incorrectly as a lich.
Soul-Repository	A receptacle prepared by jinn to hold their soul upon death. Sometimes known as a phylactery.
Diviner	A magician who can track certain objects, e.g. find a person if in possession of some of their blood.
Puppeteer	A magician who can use body parts and their own blood to animate a doll or puppet.

Werewolf	A person bitten by a werewolf is likewise infected. During any full moon, a wolf will manifest and grow within that person, bursting out from their flesh and growing to full size within a minute. Come the dawn, the person will manifest within the wolf and likewise burst free from inside, swiftly resuming their original shape, size and features. As time passes, a werewolf will retain some measure of control while in their wolf form, and eventually may be able to transform at will. Vulnerable to silver.
Scribe	A magician who can tattoo spells onto customers.

The origins of Demons and the Undead

Millennia ago in Heaven, the Archangel *Samiel* led one hundred million angels in a rebellion against the Archangel *Mikiel* and two hundred million loyalists, ultimately losing. *Samiel* and around two hundred of the rebels survived, and they were exiled to the physical realm, manifesting on Earth. They appeared human but were not in truth alive, their sex and appearance random. Known as the *Grigori*, the sun proved lethal, killing many. Others warred amongst themselves for territory, using the primitive humans as slaves and soldiers. *Samiel* was scorned by the others who blamed him for the Fall, mocking him as Lucifer, the Lightbringer.

In time, the *Grigori* learned that humans who drank their blood and died within a day became undead, giving them another weapon in their conquests. Newly Made undead were known as ghouls, who rotted and went feral if deprived of blood. Within one to three years, a ghoul would Transition to *Nephilim* – a vampyre – able to extend their canine teeth into fangs, manipulate the memories of people, and enjoy increased strength. A *Nephilim* who survived centuries would in time Transition to an Elder, made even more powerful. If a ghoul ate a *Nephilim*'s heart, or a *Nephilim* ate an Elder's, they would Transition up immediately. The only means by which an Elder could become as powerful as a *Grigori* would be to eat the heart of one, becoming *Dominus* or *Domina*. The *Grigori* became all but extinct, though an Elder can Transition up by eating the heart of a *Dominus* or *Domina*. As to date no Elder has Transitioned up through the passage of years, there will only ever be a handful of the Master vampyres, and every time one is slain without their heart being eaten sees the number reduced permanently.

The hundred million of Lucifer's rebels who perished in the War were exiled to Hell, becoming demons. Demons can only appear on Earth when Summoned by a magician known as a Demonist, who will have the demon Possess a human. There is no way to exorcise the demon save by killing the Vessel, and upon being Possessed, the victim's soul is cast out to whatever awaits after life.

Slain *Grigori* are also exiled to Hell, but if their mortal remains are found, a Demonist can resurrect them through a ritual, so long as they have the heart of either another *Grigori* or a *Domina/Dominus Nephilim.*

Mikiel lost half of his two hundred million loyalists in the war, and those angels manifested in the physical realm as newborns. They were spread out across different worlds, several thousand trapped on earth. Those on Earth are doomed to be reincarnated in human bodies, sometimes retaining their memories, other times living entire lives unburdened by the knowledge of what they were. They are known as the *Seraphim.*

Demons, *Seraphim, Grigori* and *Nephilim* can 'Unveil', revealing who and what they are. Mortals will feel a cold fear upon experiencing an Unveiling.

Resurrection Men recap

Body snatchers Wilton Hunt and Tam Foley exhume a recently buried Amy Newfield, only for her body to disappear while they're filling in the grave. They can find no trace of it, nor are there any reports of her being found wandering the city. Hunt is studying the natural sciences at Glasgow University, to the ire of his parents. His mother owns a prosperous shipping company, and his father is a lawyer, and is also the heir to the Baron of Ashwood's title and what little remains of the Ashwood estate in the Highlands.

Convicted murderer Richard Canning is visited in prison the night before his hanging by the Elder *Nephilim* George Rannoch, offering him an alternative to death. In the morning, he is hanged, and Hunt and Foley convey his body to Professor Miller, for whom they exhume recently buried corpses. The next morning the professor is found dead, murdered in the same manner Canning did for his victims, and Canning's body is gone.

Bodies start to turn up near where Newfield disappeared, and John Grant, a police friend of Foley's, confirms that the circumstances are being covered up, and that this is not the first suspicious death dismissed as natural or accidental. Amy Newfield is not among the bodies found near the cemetery.

Hunt and Foley return to the streets surrounding the cemetery, separating to cover more ground. Hunt is attacked by a gaunt and feral Amy Newfield, who is taken away by a mysterious woman arriving in a carriage. It seems clear to Hunt and Foley that Newfield is responsible for the recent deaths in the area, though the how and why escapes them. The signage on the carriage reveals it is owned by notorious crime boss Roddy McBride.

In a bid to reconcile with his parents, Lewis and Edith, Hunt visits Dunclutha House with his parents, the home of Sir Arthur Williamson. Among the guests are the

Gerrard family visiting from France; Hunt is attracted to their daughter, Amelie.

Templar Inquisitor Wolfgang Steiner arrives in Glasgow from London, sent to investigate the undead rumoured to rule Glasgow. He is to command twelve Templars sent from Edinburgh and starts meeting his contacts in the city. Among them is Lady Caroline Delaney, a widow whose husband was Possessed by the demon *Beliel* twenty years earlier, who tortured her and killed their children before she got free and killed him. Since then, she has been secretly working against the undead in the city and those who serve them. Delaney names the man who betrayed her family all those years ago, Benjamin Howard, and tells Steiner he may find him at a theatre he patronises.

Another visited by Steiner is the Reverend John Redfort, an ambitious minister who is part of the Sooty Feather Society, a secret society at the heart of the Black Wing Club. Seeing an opportunity, Redfort tricks Steiner into going after Glasgow's bishop. The bishop is killed by one of Redfort's henchmen, the blame falling on the Templars. Redfort then schemes to become the next Bishop of Glasgow.

Following a lead, Hunt and Foley infiltrate a local theatre, hoping to identify the mysterious B.H, who hired the carriage used to take Amy Newfield. There, Hunt meets Kerry Knox, an actress sent by Steiner to spy on Benjamin Howard. On the opening night of the production of *Doctor Faustus*, Hunt plays Lucifer while Steiner and Delaney abduct Howard. Howard is tortured by Steiner, revealing that there is a Crypt of ghouls – undead yet to Transition into *Nephilim* (vampyres) – in and beneath a house next to the Under-Market.

Hunt and Foley speak with Professor Charles Sirk about the strange circumstances they have recently encountered, and he tells them of demons and the undead. He agrees to help them, and just before dawn they follow George Rannoch from the Carpathian Circus to the

Under-Market, where the city's magicians ply their trade.

While there, the Templars launch a brutal attack on the Under-Market, killing the undead and destroying the house used as a Crypt. Innocents and a few Templars die in the chaos, but Hunt, Foley and Sirk escape unharmed, as does Rannoch. Redfort recovers one of the Templar bodies and uses necromancy – a branch of magic forbidden by the undead on pain of death – to learn where the Templars are hiding.

Hunt travels to Loch Lomond to spend a few nights with the Gerrards, learning that Sir Arthur Williamson and his cousin is there too. One night, Hunt witnesses an unknown guest at the hotel being abducted, and a dark ritual whereby the victim is Possessed by a demon called *Beliel*. He flees, not knowing who has been Possessed.

The Sooty Feathers attack the Templars, Steiner and Kerry Knox seeking sanctuary at Delaney's house, not knowing if any of the other Templars survived. Steiner is later captured, and Delaney and Knox make contact with the last three Templars still free.

George Rannoch attacks Hunt and the Gerrards on the return trip to Glasgow, Hunt the only survivor. He is taken back to Glasgow, the Sooty Feathers suspecting he may be working with the Templars.

As Hunt's absence continues, Foley and Sirk investigate, being taken by Roddy McBride and his men. McBride leaves them in the custody of his brother Eddie, only for Delaney and the Templars to rescue them. Eddie McBride reveals that Hunt and Steiner may be at Dunclutha House, where the Sooty Feathers are to meet. Eddie is then killed by one of the Templars.

Delaney leads Foley, Sirk and the three Templars, Carter, Gray and Burton, to Largs, where they infiltrate Dunclutha House. At the same time, men and undead from the circus attack the house, and George Rannoch kills Regent Edwards. Hunt is rescued but there is no sign of Steiner, and the demon *Beliel* is revealed to Possess Sir Arthur Williamson's cousin, Neil, only to be killed by

Delaney. The death of Rannoch's magician, needed to Summon the demon *Arakiel*, forces him to kill his own people, and play the hero, rescuing the surviving Sooty Feathers. Redfort escapes, but his secretary is knocked out by Rannoch's people during the attack. Richard Canning kills and eats the heart of a vampyre in Glasgow, Transitioning from ghoul to vampyre himself.

In disarray back in Glasgow, George Rannoch is accepted as the new Regent, buying time until he can find a new magician capable of Summoning demons. Margot Guillam is suspicious of Rannoch and betrays his location to Hunt and the others. Hunt, Sirk, Foley, Delaney and the Templars attack Rannoch and the last of his followers in the Necropolis, aided by Amy Newfield who was sent by Guillam to guide them to Rannoch's location. Steiner is rescued before Rannoch can have him Possessed by *Beliel*, but the Templars Burton and Carter die. Hunt kills Rannoch, but not before Erik Keel – the demon *Arakiel* – is Summoned into a human body. *Arakiel* was a *Grigori*, one of the original 200 Fallen angels who survived Lucifer's War in Heaven and manifested as the first vampyres. Richard Canning and Sir Arthur Williamson are the only allies *Arakiel* has, the circus having fled, most of the men dead. *Arakiel* plans to resurrect himself as *Grigori*, but he will need his remains, and the heart of Niall Fisher, the *Dominus Nephilim* who betrayed and slew *Arakiel* two centuries earlier.

Steiner shoots the undead Amy Newfield despite her helping to rescue him, not knowing the gun he uses shoots slightly to one side. Hunt, Foley and Sirk leave Delaney and the others on bad terms. Believing Newfield dead, Hunt and Foley attempt to rebury her in her coffin, only for her to disappear on them again. Delaney agrees to take Knox on as an apprentice, as Steiner and Gray return to London.

Arakiel and his last surviving followers, Canning and Sir Arthur Williamson, attempt to murder Hunt's parents in revenge for Hunt's interference, only for the Hunts to kill Williamson and injure Canning. Lewis Hunt is revealed to be Lucifer, and he and *Arakiel* agree to leave one another alone. Canning is shocked to realise that Wilton Hunt is the son of the Devil.

It is June, Glasgow caught in a long heatwave. Lady Delaney and her apprentice, Kerry Knox, kill a vampyre stalking Knox. Delaney and Knox learn that children working in mills are dying in unusually high numbers, and so decide to investigate.

Hunt's uncle, the 5th Baron of Ashwood, has died of old age, Hunt's father inheriting the title and what little remains of the Ashwood estate in the Highlands, near Loch Aline. Hunt and Foley travel north to spend the summer in the Ashwood estate, happy to escape the undead infesting Glasgow.

En route, Foley is bitten by a wolf – despite them being supposedly extinct in Britain – but survives, and the pair continue north once his wound has healed.

The recently Made undead Richard Canning is sent by the demon *Arakiel* to London to convince the necromancer, Dr Essex, to come to Glasgow to aid in the demon's bid to take over Glasgow. Essex reveals that he is no ordinary necromancer, having lived for thousands of years by having his soul transfer to a receptacle upon death, before Possessing a new body.

Delaney and Knox learn that the Imperial Mill has been buying orphans, some of whom are dying, and Knox infiltrates the mill as a worker to learn what is happening. She finds a Crypt of undead lurking beneath it, realising the undead are feeding off the orphans.

Bishop Redfort has risen to the Sooty Feather Council, but it is an uncertain time. Margot Guillam is the new Regent, taking the newly Made undead, Amy Newfield, under her wing. *Arakiel* is still loose and Sooty Feathers are still dying or disappearing. One of those killed by Canning was a senior police officer, and Chief Inspector Kenmure takes his place in the society. Unknown to the Sooty Feathers, Kenmure is in truth Possessed by the demon *Maridiel*.

Redfort tries to use his necromancy on the dead police

officer, only for the corpse to be briefly controlled by Dr Essex, who now knows Redfort is also a necromancer.

Hunt and Foley spend four weeks in Loch Aline, living in Ashwood Lodge with Hunt's parents. Hunt's ancestor, the 1st Baron, did not come by title and estate peacefully, and old grudges linger among some of the locals.

Canning and the necromancer, Essex, rob the Heron Crowe Bank, causing chaos for the Sooty Feathers who invest with it. One of the owners, William Heron, suffers further mishap when *Arakiel*'s people attempt to kidnap him, thwarted thanks to the intervention of the other owner, the undead Edmund Crowe.

Lady Delaney and Kerry Knox recruit Dr Sirk, currently running Foley's pharmacy in his absence, to help raid the Imperial Mill, where the undead are feeding off orphans. The three of them seize the mill, free the orphans and destroy the undead lurking in the basement level. Sirk learns Hunt and Foley may be in danger, and so arranges to travel to Loch Aline to warn them. Delaney and Knox decide to take the fight to Lady MacInesker, the Sooty Feather who owns the Imperial Mill.

Regent Margot Guillam, sends Roddy McBride to Loch Aline to force the Hunts to sell their shipping company for less than its worth, McBride viewing it as an opportunity to kill Foley, whom he believes killed his brother Eddie.

After an animal attack on livestock, Hunt and Foley help some locals track the beast down, only for a wolf to burst free from Foley, revealing him to be a werewolf, triggered by the full moon. Hunt climbs a tree, and at dawn Foley bursts free from the wolf.

Sirk arrives at Ashwood Lodge and warns Hunt and Foley, however Roddy McBride and his brother Johnny, allied with some of the locals, take Foley and the Hunts prisoner. Hunt's parents refuse to sell their business, and so the prisoners are taken deep into the woods.

It is revealed that the inhabitants of Loch Aline were

pagan, before the original Baron Ashwood conquered the area in the early 18th century. They seek revenge on the Hunts and so intend to make Hunt the vessel of the god, Lugh.

Hunt's father, Lord Ashwood, reveals himself to be Lucifer, whose time in Loch Aline centuries before either gave birth to, or influenced, local legends of the god Lugh. Roddy McBride shoots Foley twice in the stomach and has him dragged away. Sirk and Lucifer's valet, Singh, arrive with guns, and a fight ensues. The full moon rises, and the dying Foley is saved by his transformation into the wolf. Roddy and Johnny McBride escape, believing Foley to be dead.

Singh the valet is revealed to be *Kariel*, an angel reincarnated again and again since the Fall, tasked by the Archangel *Mikiel* to watch Lucifer and kill him if need be.

Hunt learns that Lucifer was Summoned into Lewis Hunt almost thirty years before, witnessed by Hunt's mother. The son of the locals' chief, a Sooty Feather studying Law in Glasgow, had revealed to those present that their 'god' was actually a demon – the Devil in fact – and they turned on one another. Hunt's mother escaped with Lucifer – newly Summoned into Lewis Hunt – and in time they married, and gave birth to Wilton Hunt.

To prevent any further Sooty Feather attacks on them, the Hunts, Foley and Sirk travel to Dunkellen House near Glasgow, where Lady MacInesker is hosting a summer ball. Most of the Sooty Feathers are attending, along with Bishop Redfort and William Heron. Lady Delaney and Kerry Knox are present too.

Redfort learns that three of his fellow councillors in the Sooty Feathers are in fact Possessed by demons allied with *Arakiel*. The demons try to have Hunt Possessed with *Beliel*, however Lucifer, Singh and Redfort intervene.

A sorcerous illness inflicted on a nearby village by Dr Essex kills its victims, who arise as *zombis*, under the control of Essex. They attack Dunkellen House, killing most of the guests. William Heron dies, as does Lady MacInesker. Hunt's mother dies protecting her son, and the *zombis* are only defeated when Lady Delaney kills Dr Essex.

Among the few Sooty Feather Councillors to survive, Redfort is now second only to Margot Guillam. Amy Newfield, Roddy McBride and Edmund Crowe join the Council.

Foley leaves Glasgow to find the werewolves near Loch Lomond, to learn about his condition.

Hunt refuses to move in with his father, still unreconciled with being the son of the Devil. A new anatomy professor – in truth now Possessed by the soul of the necromancer previously known as Dr Essex – engages Hunt and Sirk as body snatchers.

Lilith, the oldest human vampyre, receives a letter from *Arakiel* while living in Marrakesh, inviting her to Glasgow. The letter reveals Lucifer is there, who Made Lilith undead. Eager to send Lucifer back to Hell, Lilith prepares to travel to Glasgow.

Prologue

The City of London
Late November 1893
The Day of Lord Ashwood's Introduction
to The House of Lords

"I don't know why *you* look so damned nervous, Lord Durford," said the Garter King of Arms with an air of insolence as the four men waited in the robing room. "Lord Ashwood is the one being introduced."

Baron Durford's body was tense, his face grim. "Something I ate last night."

"Or drank, maybe," Turbridge teased. "Very generous of you, Lord Ashwood, to gift Durford and myself a bottle of such very fine scotch." With December mere days away, nothing beat a good, blended whisky for keeping the winter chill away.

"A token of my gratitude for your both acting as my escorts, Lord Turbridge," Lord Ashwood said. There something in his eyes that Turbridge *did* find off-putting. *A cold fish*, he had said quietly to Baron Durford while Ashwood was busy putting on his parliamentary robes. It was tradition for new peers being introduced to the House of Lords to be escorted by two existing peers of the same rank.

"I recall when … your uncle, yes? … was introduced to the House," Turbridge said. Almost thirty years ago that had been. Turbridge vaguely recalled that Thomas Hunt, the 5th Baron, had died a bachelor but outlived his older and younger brothers, so his heir must be a nephew. Maybe a cousin?

The new Baron Ashwood made no reply, too busy adjusting robes made from scarlet cloth and lined with taffeta. Two rows of ermine spots on each shoulder identified his rank as baron. Turbridge and Durford wore identical robes, although theirs were worn with age.

He remembered the shabby state of the 5th Baron's robes, decades old and inherited from the 4th Baron. The family had been poor back then, Turbridge recalling the grins on the faces of some of the assembled lords upon that Introduction, the whispered mockery afterwards as some joked that the impoverished Scottish lord might be forced to walk back home barefoot to preserve his shoe leather. That baron had attended the House of Lords only sparingly.

This Lord Ashwood wore new robes made from the finest materials, the family's fortunes having taken an upturn through marriage. He was the owner of some Glasgow shipping company, and while those lords from old money would mock the commercial association, much of that 'old money' was running out.

Horatio Biddell, the current Black Rod, entered the robing room. "It is time, my lords."

The Garter King of Arms straightened his tabard of red, blue and gold, holding in his right hand a silver gilt sceptre, and in his left Lord Ashwood's patent of creation. Black Rod led them out of the robing room towards the main chamber in single file, the Garter King of Arms behind him. Next was Lord Durford as the junior peer, then the new peer, Lord Ashwood, and at the rear was Turbridge, the senior peer of the three. He loved the ancient solemnity of these occasions.

Carrying their cocked black hats in their left hands, the three barons approached the Bar of the House, the new Lord Ashwood holding his Writ of Summons in his right. Turbridge followed Durford and Ashwood up the temporal side of the House to the Cloth of Estate, to which they bowed, Turbridge feeling a sharp pain in his back as he did so.

So far Lord Ashwood had made no mistakes, and the

new peer and his two escorts bowed to the table where the clerks sat, and to the judges. The Lord Chancellor waited for them at the Woolsack, where Lord Ashwood knelt before him, presenting the letters patent of his creation. Silence reigned as the Lord Chancellor raised his black tricorne hat to the kneeling Lord Ashwood, and accepted the papers which were given to the Reading Clerk who slowly read them aloud to the House.

Turbridge listened as the Writ of Summons was read out, irritated to note that Lord Durford's digestion still seemed to be troubling him, the man edging away from the House's newest peer. The Reading Clerk finished reading the Writ of Summons, authorising the new Lord Ashwood to take his seat in the House.

After that, Lord Ashwood read the Oath of Allegiance and signed the Test Rolls that dated back to 1695. Turbridge remembered signing it himself all those years ago, his excitement at the occasion marred by the lingering grief he felt for his father, dead some months before. This was the part he was not looking forward to, his knees too old for such exertions. He and his two fellow barons rose and sat three times, doffing their hats to the Cloth of Estate, and Lord Ashwood shook the Lord Chancellor's hand.

Upon the ceremony's completion, the three barons returned to the robing room where they removed their parliamentary robes. "You did well, Lord Ashwood," Turbridge said. "Didn't he, Durford?"

"Yes," was the terse response. Thus de-robed, the three quietly returned to the main chamber and took their seats, Lord Ashwood sitting a short distance from his two escorts.

"What *is* the matter with you, Durford?" Turbridge whispered. "If you are so ill-disposed after last night, you should think twice before attending the Earl of Easdale's ball tonight. It would not do to make a fool of yourself in front of Her Majesty."

"Her Majesty will be there?" There was a taut fear in Durford's voice. "You are sure?"

Really, what was up with the man? “Quite sure.”

Durford hissed out a breath. “And Ashwood is still attending? Will be granted an audience with the Queen?”

“I should say so. I hear she is attending specifically to meet Lord Ashwood. You know how much she favours Scotland.”

“Dear God…”

Turbridge frowned at him. “Really, man! He is a Peer of the Realm, not a lord of Hell.”

“A lord?” Turbridge didn’t think he was meant to hear Durford’s near-hysterical laugh and muttered reply, but hear it he did. “He’s the bloody prince!”

Chapter One

The City of Glasgow
Early October 1893
Seven Weeks Earlier

Kerry Knox watched from a distance as men hurriedly unloaded barrels from a slim schooner onto wagons waiting on the quay in the heart of Glasgow. Contraband of some sort was her guess, given the late hour and the number of men keeping watch in case the city's constabulary came to investigate. Among other, more dangerous threats.

A man Caroline had named as Roddy McBride oversaw the unloading, standing to one side with thick, folded arms, a stocky man with a hard, pitiless look about him. The McBrides were a family notorious for crime, extortion and violence. He also served the Sooty Feathers, a secret society who acted as proxies for the undead ruling Glasgow – for the moment – and that affiliation explained the presence of so many enforcers, as well as the attendance of McBride himself.

Spying from the shadows, Knox knew one mistake could lead to discovery and death. Roddy McBride was a ruthless, suspicious man at the best of times, and these were not the best of times for anyone aligned with the Sooty Feathers. A secret, bloody war for Glasgow itself had seen the city beset with death and violence – more than normal, and that was saying something. The proxies of the vampyre lord, Niall Fisher, opposed those of the demon, *Arakiel*, in a war that had already seen much death. Knox herself was among the few to have survived a *zombi* attack on the Dunkellen estate on the city's southern outskirts. Lady MacInesker had invited many members of Glasgow's high society to her home, including most of the Sooty Feathers, herself a leading member. They had come for a summer party and instead found horror.

That slaughter, unleashed by the necromancer Dr Essex, had seen many Sooty Feathers slain by animated corpses. With too many innocents among the victims. Wilton Hunt's mother, Lady Ashwood, was counted among them, sacrificing herself to save her son. Knox's mentor, Lady Caroline Delaney, had ended the nightmare by slaying Dr Essex, which cut the sorcerous strings controlling his dead.

The McBrides traditionally held sway mostly in the Gorbals and other areas to the south of Glasgow, but in recent months their activities had spread out across the city, piquing Caroline's interest. Had recent losses forced the Sooty Feathers to turn to the McBrides for muscle, in exchange for help expanding their criminal enterprises?

The last of the barrels was loaded onto the rearmost of the three wagons, two men climbing atop each. McBride and two of his men entered a carriage waiting nearby. Whips spurred the horses into motion, the carriage and all three wagons moving quickly away from the quay, heralded by a rumble of hooves and wheels running across cobbles.

Time to follow.

Knox ran to Caroline and the buggy concealed nearby, hoping her mentor was up to the task of following the wagons and carriage to wherever they were bound.

*

Richard Canning watched as the carriage and wagons left the quay, the cargo unloaded from the moored schooner. He would have liked to have introduced himself to Roddy McBride and his rogues as the cargo was unloaded, but his orders were clear; let them leave. *Let them live, more's the pity.*

He slipped slowly down into the freezing water and climbed the far side of the schooner, unaffected by the cold.

Dying was the best thing that ever happened to me.

He was now immune to disease and the passage of time. Only sunlight or violence could send him to Hell; a cellar protected him from the former, and he was well-practiced in the latter.

His fangs extending as he grabbed the closest sailor, needle-sharp teeth breached soft flesh and released blood into his waiting mouth. The dying sailor barely made a splash as he hit the water, once Canning was done with him. Other victims waited. This crew and ship had delivered its last illicit cargo to the Sooty Feathers.

*

"I'm curious as to the contents and destination of those barrels," Caroline had told Knox as they discreetly followed the wagons and carriage from the Broomielaw to High Street. The destination proved to be near the Under-Market, the rundown, ramshackle hub of Glasgow's supernatural community, buried beneath a railway bridge obscured by slums that should have long ago been demolished.

"Bootlegged whisky?" Knox suggested. There was always a market for that.

"Or perhaps weapons. We will know soon enough."

Knox had grown up in nearby Duke Street to working class parents from Ireland who had struggled to pay rent and put food on the table. She had reckoned her family poor, but the poverty she found in these slums shocked even her. The only respite these people had from misery was cheap alcohol, funded through theft and prostitution.

Caroline perhaps sensed her thoughts. "Some sell their blood here, to the undead in the market. With a war on, and newly Made ghouls in need of sustenance, I suspect some who do so find themselves simply snatched and bled white. So tread carefully."

The Under-Market itself lay beneath the squat, wide railway bridge, but the three McBride wagons and carriage were parked a short distance away, outside what appeared to be a shebeen – an illegal drinking den. Only one window was visible on the crumbling structure, and that had been boarded up.

Three barrels were unloaded from the first wagon by the three drivers and six accompanying men, who thereafter rolled the barrels round the corner to the tavern's entrance. One driver stayed to guard the wagons and remaining cargo.

"Now," Caroline breathed as she surged forwards, Knox following. As agreed, she walked slowly down the street, distracting the guard while Caroline circled quietly behind the wagons. There was a muffled cry as the driver was pulled backwards, followed by sounds of a gradually diminishing struggle.

On joining Caroline, Knox caught a whiff of chloroform, relieved that her mentor hadn't simply stabbed the man to silence him. The undead, demons and Sooty Feathers were fair game, in her book, but there was no reason to believe this man knew he was involved in anything beyond smuggling.

Caroline climbed up onto the wagon and stabbed a blade into the nearest barrel's top, prising it off. She reached a hand inside and sniffed it before giving her finger a careful lick. "You were right," she said with an unnecessary note of surprise. "Whisky of some sort."

"Told you so," Knox said smugly. "You forget I worked in a public house for a while. Lot of money to be made in illicit spirits. This was likely sailed down from the north." She joined Caroline on the wagon bed and scooped out some whisky with her hands before tasting it. "This is good!"

"You wish to take a barrel?" Caroline asked in amusement.

"No, I mean, it's good quality. Too good for this shitehole."

A man's gravelled voice spoke before they could consider what that meant. "The three barrels taken inside are from a lesser distillery. The Thistledown regulars couldn't afford what's in the barrels out here."

A shard of fear stabbed at Knox as she turned to see that Roddy McBride and his men had quietly returned, all armed with either a cudgel or shotgun.

"Then we are grateful to have sampled from the barrel we did, Mr McBride," Caroline said, as unruffled as ever. This wasn't the first time Knox's mentor had been on the wrong end of a gun, but she had to know sooner or later it would be the last.

"If you know who I am, then you know what happens to people who steal from me," McBride rumbled.

Caroline ignored the threat, something else drawing her attention. "Miss Newfield, a surprise seeing you here, in such company."

Knox saw her, the only woman with McBride. The last she had seen of the undead girl had been Hunt and Foley loading her body onto their wagon after the Templar, Wolfgang Steiner, shot her in the chest. She had helped them rescue Steiner from George Rannoch and been thanked with a bullet, there being no compromise in the Templar's soul.

"A surprise seeing me here, or seeing me alive?" Newfield asked coldly.

"Alive? Do you think of yourself as such, ghoul?" Caroline asked, a bite in her voice. "Mr Hunt told us how you disappeared as he and Mr Foley attempted to bury what they thought was your corpse."

"Fate spared me," Newfield said.

"My spare derringer shooting slightly off to the left spared you," Caroline corrected. "Which Hunt forget to warn Steiner of upon giving him that gun."

"You two have been poking your noses in Sooty Feather business since spring," McBride said. Anger and fear had crossed his face on hearing the name 'Hunt'. He had crossed paths with the Hunts, Professor Sirk, and Foley days prior to the horror that befell the Dunkellen estate. Wilton Hunt had been vague on the details, but evidently his parents, Lord and Lady Ashwood, had firmly rebuffed McBride's bullish attempt to force them to sell their shipping company for a fraction of its worth.

Knox had fought alongside Lord and Lady Ashwood at Dunkellen against the plague of *zombis*; a formidable pair. Just prior, Wilton Hunt and Tam Foley had spent time on the Ashwood estate in the Highlands, helping the new Lord and Lady Ashwood deal with the aftermath of the previous baron's death. It had been there that McBride had attacked the family. And been somehow thwarted.

"Miss Guillam may prefer to speak with them first," Newfield said.

Falling into the hands of an Elder vampyre was not how Knox intended for tonight – nor, indeed, her life – to end. "What should we do?" she muttered.

"Push," Caroline said quietly, hands pressing against the open barrel nearest the end of the wagon as those of McBride's men armed with guns raised them.

Knox helped, praying Caroline had more in mind than spoiling McBride's whisky. The barrel was heavy but slowly started to tip, the pair's efforts aided by the wagon facing uphill. For a moment Knox feared they would fail, just as the barrel toppled over and crashed onto the cobbles below.

A cry of outrage from McBride followed as whisky spilled from the splintered barrel, filling the gaps between the cobbles. There was a flare of light as Caroline struck a match and held it to her handkerchief.

Which she let go, the burning cloth fluttering to the ground…

*

Newfield threw herself to one side as the ground ignited into flame with a *whump*, a river of fire flowing downhill.

Those men caught in its path screamed, silhouettes performing a frantic dance of agony. Those lucky enough to avoid it beat at the flaming legs of their comrades with jackets, some of which caught fire too. Shotgun shells in their pockets exploded, causing further mayhem.

Still yet to transition to full *Nephilim*, Newfield's vision was nevertheless better in the dark than her living associates, but even undead night sight could be ruined by fire, and as she squinted into the darkness, she knew Delaney and Knox had made good their escape.

"Fucking bitches!" McBride raged. He had escaped the fire, but valuable cargo had been burned, and worse, his pride stung. Newfield had to admit to a sneaking admiration for Lady Delaney and her Irish companion. Bishop Redfort had warned the rest of the Council that they were a formidable pair.

"Forget them for now, we have business to attend to," Newfield told him to pre-empt any demand that they hunt down the two women. For a moment he stared balefully at her before perhaps recalling who she was, *what* she was, and who her mentor was. "Aye," he grunted as his unburned men tended to the less fortunate. "Ned! Load the wounded onto a wagon and get a doctor out his damned bed."

Chapter Two

The Thistledown's taproom stank of piss and vomit, even hours after closing. "This is the foulest place I've ever had the misfortune to visit." Newfield glanced at McBride. "And I include the time spent in my own coffin." Though admittedly, she had not yet completed the Transition from death to undeath until Messrs Hunt and Foley had exhumed her from it. But it sounded good, and it reminded McBride just what she was.

"If you want to get cleaning, don't let me stand in your way, Miss Newfield," McBride said as he opened the lantern.

She surveyed the stained floor and dirty, broken tables and stools. "I would not know where to start. I am not one to tell a man his business, but as the new owner of this establishment, you would do well to take action before it simply rots away."

"I would, but our little war takes up most of my time."

"Since joining the Council, you've expanded your business interests across the city, surely you can afford to hire a factor to look after them," Newfield said. Her father was a factor for a block of housing. Or at least, he had been when she died. How her family had fared since was a mystery, a half-healed wound she was minded not to open. Her uncle's profession as a stone mason explained how they were able to get a gravestone for her so quickly.

McBride wiped a stool with a handkerchief before sitting on it. "Since joining the Council, I've had Keel's hired men as well as the fucking constabulary interfering in my business."

Keel. Erik Keel.

That was how the Sooty Feathers preferred to name their enemy. In truth, he was the demon *Arakiel.* Thousands of years ago Keel … *Arakiel* … had been among the two hundred or so of Lucifer's rebels to survive the War in Heaven, being cast down to earth where they became the *Grigori*, the original vampyres.

Maybe seven hundred years ago, *Arakiel* had led his House to Glasgow, perhaps the loser in some undead war elsewhere in Europe, the Fallen angel by that time content for his name to be bastardised to Erik Keel. Almost three hundred ago, he had involved his House in an undead war for Bucharest, a war that dragged on for decades. In the end, many of the Elder vampyres of his House – his lieutenants in Glasgow – travelled to Bucharest and slew him and his loyalists. Three Elders survived the coup: Niall Fisher, Margot Guillam and Thomas Edwards. George Rannoch supposedly turned coat during the battle, a Keel loyalist who slew and ate the heart of his master's last Elder to become Elder himself. Fisher was the one to eat the defeated Keel's heart and thus became a *Dominus Nephilim*, ruler of the House of Keel.

Perhaps fearful of suffering the same fate as Keel, Fisher had become a recluse in the two hundred years since, letting Edwards rule as his regent. Until April, when Rannoch, secretly still loyal to Keel, slew Edwards and seized control of the House. He had been slain in turn by Wilton Hunt atop the Necropolis, but not before his Demonist had Summoned back Keel. When slain, a *Grigori* became a demon, joining its fellow Fallen in Hell.

The creak of the door opening returned Newfield to the present, and she turned to see Magdalene Quinn entering the tavern, her face crinkled in distaste. She was prominent among the secretive magician community, and like Newfield and McBride, she sat on the Sooty Feather Council.

"A good evening to you both," Quinn said as she joined her fellow Councillors.

"And to you, Miss Quinn," Newfield said. McBride just nodded.

"A far cry from those nights we met in the Council Chamber in the Black Wing Club," Quinn said.

"When Keel is in the fucking ground, we can return there," McBride growled. "Until then, pinch your nose if the smell gets too much."

"You are in a fouler mood than usual, *Septimus*," Quinn said, using his Council title. A reminder, perhaps, that he was junior to herself; *Quinta*, the Fifth Seat. Newfield was the junior-most member, *Octavia*. The Eighth Seat. Not that seniority meant much; all but three of the Council had been inducted on the same night, to replace the two slain at Dunkellen and the three revealed as demons.

"Lady Delaney and her companion followed us here, setting alight a barrel of whisky to cover their escape," Newfield said.

"That explains both your mood and the burnt ground," Quinn said.

"How fare the magicians, has Keel recruited many?" Newfield asked.

"Some, but who can say how many secretly work for him. There are scant few I trust anymore. The Under-Market does well, with Artificers selling protective charms, and Scribes tattooing spells to enhance speed, strength, or to protect against a *Nephilim*'s Mesmer. The richest Sooty Feathers have been spending a fortune on tattooed Wards to prevent demonic Possession."

"Expensive, aye?" McBride asked. Like the other non-undead on the Council, he had been tattooed with such a Ward upon his joining it.

"The ingredients are very rare and expensive," Quinn said. "I have offered no objection to this Ward being sold, so long as sufficient reagents are maintained for Council use."

"Silver has become scarce in the city," Newfield said. It was a metal undead were particularly vulnerable to.

"Those who know what's going on know that both

sides are Making a lot of ghouls.," Quinn said, with a shrug.

"We need to find Keel's Crypts and burn his ghouls before he sets them loose," McBride said.

"Warborn ghouls require a *Nephilim* to keep them in line, and Keel has no more than a few," Newfield said, repeating what Miss Guillam had told her

"What of our own ghouls?" Quinn asked.

The tavern door banged open before Newfield could answer, a group of burly policemen barging inside with truncheons in hand and shouting that no one was to move.

Newfield froze, too taken aback to act, the old instinct to defer to authority taking over. Not that she had any choice; undead but not yet Transitioned to full *Nephilim*, she was no match for six men.

Quinn sat still, too, surprise on her face. If she had some magical means of dealing with the policemen, she exercised restraint. Anger reddened McBride's face and he tensed as if to stand but thought better of it. He, at least, was likely no stranger to clashes with the constabulary.

"If you're wanting a drink, you're too late. The tavern's closed," McBride said.

"We are not here for your hospitality, if I may use the term loosely. Are you the owner of this place?" A seventh policeman entered the tavern, the others deferring to him as he looked around. Superintendent Edwin Kenmure. For weeks he had hounded the Society, deploying the constabulary against them.

That constabulary, once controlled by the Council, had become a weapon wielded against them. Now Possessed by demons loyal to Erik Keel, Lord Smith of the High Court signed warrants while Kenmure executed them.

"No. I am delivering whisky," McBride said heavily. When McBride had bought the tavern, he had done so under another name, a man supposedly living in England. Newfield suspected the man in question had been quietly killed and buried. A lawyer and the bank handled all official matters.

"And you are?" Kenmure asked, an amused glint in his eye as he played his game.

"Mr Roderick McBride."

*

Inspector John Grant had to admire Superintendent Kenmure's guts. The McBrides were not a family to cross, rumoured to have murdered policemen and politicians who interfered overly much in their business.

"And those are your wagons outside?" Kenmure asked.

"They are."

"Is the cargo yours?" Kenmure asked. "Spirits, aye?"

McBride glowered at him. "Whisky. Not mine, I'm just being paid to deliver it here."

"Do you have the documents confirming all duties have been paid on it?" Everyone in the tavern knew those barrels contained bootlegged whisky, likely from the Highlands and islands.

"I'm just being paid to deliver it," McBride said again.

Kenmure shook his head. "Then I'm afraid we'll need to seize it until the owner can present the proper paperwork." He motioned for everyone to follow him outside the tavern.

"Do what you want, I don't care." The anger in McBride's voice gave the lie to that. "But those wagons are mine, so I'll be taking those back to my yard."

"We'll be taking them back to the station, but you can pick them up after." Kenmure let McBride have that small victory before striking another blow. "Earlier, a check with the city council revealed no licence for this establishment. I'm afraid we'll be closing it down until the owner can resolve that matter also."

McBride jerked his shoulders in a shrug. "None of my business." He was a poor liar, but Kenmure didn't press him on the matter. Grant hadn't worked with Kenmure until a month prior, but those colleagues who had now muttered that promotion had changed the man. Made him colder, harder. Obsessed with finishing the McBride family. At the cost of his own, some whispered. Kenmure's wife was said to have fled Glasgow with their children.

"Sergeant Johnstone, leave a man here until that door is boarded up." Kenmure looked around the decaying slum, one of Glasgow's worst shitholes. "Two men," he amended.

"Aye, sir," Johnstone said.

"Inspector Grant, let's get this illegal whisky back to the station where it can be kept as evidence," Kenmure said. His wink suggested that he would not be averse to one of the barrels being 'damaged' while being rolled into the station and its contents having to be 'disposed' of among the men.

"Superintendent," Grant acknowledged, still uncomfortable in his new rank. That promotion in itself was a sign of a change within Kenmure, coinciding with his own promotion after the death of Superintendent Silas Thatcher. A staunch member of the Orange Order, Kenmure had until then favoured likeminded policemen, seeing them promoted into the best roles. For him to give Grant, a Catholic, the vacant inspector post, had raised more than a few eyebrows.

Not that Grant was complaining, him with a young family to provide for.

Once the tavern cellar had been emptied of all illegal whisky, the door was locked, and McBride reluctantly handed Kenmure the key.

Satisfied that McBride looked like he would behave himself and was watched by enough constables to restrain him if he didn't, Grant approached the two women they had found in his company. Neither were dressed like prostitutes, certainly not like the ones who haunted the sunless lanes and alleys of this shit-covered slum. One was barely more than a girl, eighteen at most and maybe not even that, her dark hair tied up. Both wore jackets over dark dresses, the older one shivering slightly, her breath misting in the cold autumn air.

The younger showed no such signs of the cold, the

hairs on the back of Grant's neck rising for some reason. Something was off about her, but he couldn't put his finger on what. He pulled out his notebook. "Can I have your name, ma'am?" he asked the older one.

"Miss Magdalene Quinn," she replied. Between thirty and forty, if she was not married by now, she probably never would be.

"Miss Amy Newfield," the other said unbidden, and then bit her lip as if she had said something she shouldn't. Grant paused, that name vaguely familiar to him, though he could not recall from where. Her face was familiar, too.

"Inspector Grant, the women are of no interest to us and can go about their business," Kenmure called out.

Miss Quinn gave Kenmure a small ironic bow; Miss Newfield just stared at him a moment. Both women turned and began to walk beneath the railway bridge in whose shadow this tavern lay.

"You're letting them go off unescorted?" Grant asked, alarmed to see the two women disappear into the darkness alone. This was not a safe place to walk at night – or indeed during the day – for anyone, least of all for women, and those two looked to be ladies of moderate means. The gin-wasted thugs lurking in the shadowed wynds would be on them in minutes.

"We will be quite safe," Miss Quinn called out from the darkness.

Kenmure stared after them, the look in his eyes disquieting Grant. "Those two have nothing to fear here," the superintendent said quietly. McBride also showed no concern over the ladies who had been in his company for no good reason Grant could think of. The distaste on his face mirrored that on Kenmure's, and Grant wondered at the secrets the two men shared.

Tam Foley … now he recalled where he had heard of Amy Newfield. His old friend had met him in the spring, asking about mysterious deaths near the Southern Necropolis cemetery. Foley had asked if any of the dead had been called Amy Newfield, which they hadn't. *What was her involvement?* Certainly, she looked alive and well, albeit in unsavoury company.

He caught Kenmure giving him an impatient look. "Up on the wagon, lads," he was quick to shout. Kenmure sat next to McBride, hot words seeming to pass between them. Grant did not know what they were discussing as the wagons jolted away from the tavern, but there was clearly no love lost between the two men.

None of my business.

Chapter Three

Hunt raised his guard just in time to block the punch, the blow almost numbing his arm. He replied with a swift jab that struck home, his opponent answering with a thundering punch he was too slow to block.

As his vision cleared, he found himself lying on the floor, the man who'd sent him there standing over with muscled arms folded. His face was a map of battles past, his ears torn, his florid cheeks and lips ragged and scarred, his nose misshapen from old breaks. Jock "Smiddy" Smith was not a man anyone preferring their brains unscrambled picked a fight with.

"Better," Smith allowed as he pulled off his gloves and helped Hunt up. "You're getting better, Mr Hunt."

Hunt shook off his dizziness. "High praise from you, Mr Smith."

Smith grinned, revealing a mouth missing several teeth. "I didn't say good, I said better."

"I will settle for better." For two months now Hunt had been a pupil of the pugilist, learning how to throw and take a punch. He held few illusions that it would avail him much against the undead; even Smiddy Smith would not last long against a vampyre.

Of more practical value was the shooting club he had joined, allowing him to practice his marksmanship with rifle and pistol. Purchasing a licence permitting him to carry his pistol in public had been a simple matter.

Hunt unlaced his gloves and entered the changing room, inclined towards a swim before meeting Dr Sirk for tonight's job. As well as providing a gymnasium floor, where Mr Smith did good business teaching pugilism to the gentlemen members inclined towards a bit of fisticuffs, there was also the large pool for swimming in. Just over twenty years old, gas lights somewhat illuminated the interior.

Built by and home to a private gentleman's club, there were no women allowed inside, and so Hunt and the few others enjoying the pool at this time did so naked. The cool water was almost pleasant, and he swam from one end to the other slowly, reluctant to further strain muscles already punished by his session with Mr Smith.

After perhaps half an hour, Hunt pulled himself out of the water, shivering as he headed to the changing room, taking care not to slip on the white tiles. He dried himself briskly with a towel and changed into a shirt, dark-grey tweed trousers and lighter grey waistcoat. He tied a floppy maroon bowtie around his neck before pulling on his black lounge coat and collecting his bowler hat from the hook.

A naked dark-haired man standing a few inches shorter than Hunt entered the changing room, his eyes widening on recognition, water dripping onto the floor. "Good evening, Mr Hunt."

Despite the cold, he appeared to be in no hurry to dry and dress. Hunt hesitated before deciding to reply. "Good evening, sir, but you have me at a disadvantage…?"

The man's face and chest were pale, almost as white as the tiles surrounding the pool. He neither shivered from the cold nor breathed heavily from his swim. *Nor breathes at all, that I can see…*

Their eyes met, the man's pale lips twitching in a smile as Hunt's face betrayed the revelation that had come to him. "Mr Fredds," the man introduced himself as.

Fear dizzied Hunt as he stood alone with the man he now knew to be undead. "I must apologise, but I do not recall a prior meeting, Mr Fredds," he managed.

"No need to apologise." Fredds dried pale, necrotic flesh. "It was just prior to your conveyance to Dunclutha. I escorted you to your carriage."

Meaning Fredds had led a blindfolded Hunt from his cell to the barred wagon that had taken him from Glasgow to the Dunclutha estate near Largs. Foley, Dr Sirk and Lady Delaney, among others, had rescued him from death or worse that night.

"An interesting event," Hunt said. That was an understatement. Armed men and ghouls working for the Elder *Nephilim* George Rannoch had attacked the country house, killing many and taking the rest prisoner. From what Hunt had gleaned, his accidental killing of Rannoch's demon-summoning magician had thwarted the plan to Summon *Arakiel* that night, forcing Rannoch to instead slay his own followers and 'save' the Sooty Feathers to buy time to recruit another Demonist. The Society believing him saviour rather than foe, Rannoch had replaced the leader he had slain as Regent.

Until Hunt had shot him in the chest and head some days later atop the Necropolis, a killing he still struggled to believe he had been capable of.

Anger simmered in Fredds' glinting dark eyes. "So I heard."

"You swim?" Hunt asked. The penny dreadfuls he had read when he was younger led him to believe the undead lurked in tombs and other dark places.

"An enjoyable pursuit, I have found. Marvellous, these indoor baths. As a child I enjoyed afternoons by the sea, but my present circumstances prevent such indulgences." Meaning the sun would burn him. Hunt had seen an undead suffer such a fate, once. *Would that they all shared it.*

"And now you return … home?" Hunt asked. Did Fredds call a forgotten hole beneath the city his Crypt, or did he enjoy the comforts of a basement flat? The membership fees of this club were not small, marking the undead as a man of some means.

Teeth glinted beneath parting lips. "First, I would sate my hunger. Can you recommend a restaurant nearby?"

They both knew it was not food the undead craved, and Hunt knew some poor unfortunate would be found either dead or weak from blood loss in the morning, spared only if Fredds' thirst for blood was sated before his victim died. In such a circumstance, the *Nephilim* would Mesmer that victim to forget all about the encounter.

A derringer lay in Hunt's coat pocket, a silver bullet in its single chamber. Enough to end this undead. If he shot true. If he chose to involve himself.

But he did not.

Nor did he answer, backing away from the door, knowing better than to take his eyes off Fredds lest he choose to make Hunt his victim, quietly struck agreements be damned.

"Do not judge me, you of all … people," Fredds said.

Hunt did not answer, though he felt his face flush.

"I know what you are, Mr Hunt," Fredds added with a sneer of disgust.

Hunt fled, not just the vampyre in the changing room, but the demon inside himself.

*

"How fortunate Professor Mortimer chose tonight for us to recover his subject," Sirk opined from the side of the grave as Hunt dug deeper. "A night prior, and we would have been required to break the frozen ground with picks."

"As if someone's smiling down on us," Hunt gasped as he threw out another shovel-full of mud, racing the increasingly heavy rain to get to the coffin before the fresh grave became a pit of sludge.

"I'm getting quite wet standing here, have you reached the coffin yet?" Sirk asked.

I may leave you in the damn coffin. His shovel struck wood beneath the rain-pelted mud before he could articulate this reply. "Yes!"

"Excellent." The doctor slowly lowered himself into the grave, carrying two crowbars as Hunt cleared enough of the muck surrounding the coffin to get access to the lid. Aware of rain pooling around the coffin, he took a crowbar from Sirk and quickly worked it beneath the lid on one side, the doctor following suit at the other.

"Now." As one they pushed down on their crowbars, Hunt using his weight to force the lid up, hands threatening to lose their grip on the rain-slicked crowbar handle. The top of the lid came free, and the two men moved to the bottom of the coffin. It too yielded to their efforts, and Hunt pulled the lid off to expose the body within.

In thc days when he had body snatched with Foley, one of them had remained in the grave to struggle with the corpse while the other waited at the top to pull it up once sufficiently raised. Sirk had shaken his head at that and suggested an alternative.

Hunt placed a noose round the body's ankles while Sirk tied another around its torso, beneath the armpits. He helped Sirk out of the grave before being helped out in turn, after which they each took hold of a rope. In deference to Sirk's greater age, Hunt took the rope tied round the torso.

"As one," Sirk said as they pulled the body out of its coffin, mud staining the burial suit. Not that it mattered; Mortimer was interested in what lay within the corpse, not what covered it.

They stripped it, mindful that while a body could not be legally considered property, clothing was. If they were caught, a wrathful sheriff would be sure to prosecute such larceny to the fullest severity of the law. If a mob didn't beat them to death first.

The clothing was dropped back into the coffin, the corpse wrapped in sacking and the grave hurriedly refilled. Hunt had insisted on leaving the corpse on the other side of the grave, so that he could keep an eye on it while they shovelled the mud back into the pit. Sirk, aware that one such exhumed corpse, Miss Amy Newfield, had completed her Transition to undead before slipping off into the night while an unaware Hunt and Foley reburied her coffin, did not argue.

Sirk led the way, lantern in one hand, tool-sack in the

other, as Hunt pushed the wheeled barrow holding the corpse of Mr Bernard Stall. Newer than some of Glasgow's other cemeteries, such as the Necropolis and Southern Necropolis, the Craigton Cemetery nonetheless had a fair number of occupied plots, owing in part to reburials from the Blackfriars Churchyard. Even the dead were fair game for eviction, it seemed, when the City Council gave the nod for a railway extension.

Mud-spattered and soaking wet, Hunt was nonetheless grateful to the rain for obscuring their furtive passage through the cemetery to its entrance on Berryknowes Road, where Foley's horse and wagon waited. Body snatching was commonly thought to have ended at least half a century earlier owing to the Anatomy Act, however Hunt and Foley had resumed the practice the year prior on behalf of the late Senior Professor of Anatomy, Angus Miller. Resurrected the practice, as it were.

All the same, two men seen carrying a man-shaped sack out of a cemetery at this ungodly hour would raise suspicion, and if the rain reduced the chances of such an encounter, then all the better.

*

"Dr Sirk, Mr Hunt. You are welcome, if somewhat late," Professor Mortimer said from behind his desk as his valet led them into the study. "Thank you, Yates."

The valet bobbed his head before giving the visitors a look verging on rudeness. Hunt was well-used to his attitude and ignored it. It was for Mortimer to answer.

"The weather, Professor," Hunt said, not minded to offer an apology.

"No matter, I keep late hours. You recovered Mr Stall, yes?"

"Recovered, most assuredly," Sirk said.

"As dependable as ever, gentlemen." Mortimer's accent was unplaceable to Hunt, as if the man had lived in so many places that nowhere had really settled on him. An amusement always seemed to ignite in his eyes upon looking at Hunt, as if relishing a secret only he was privy to. Maybe it was having a lord's son and heir reduced to stealing corpses for him.

This house, part of the university's medical college, was not unknown to Hunt. He had stood in this very study when Professor Miller had been the senior professor of anatomy. Miller had been slain in the nearby mortuary late one night, while inspecting the just-hanged corpse of notorious murderer Richard Canning.

The man had risen as undead, attending to the professor with his own surgical instruments before leaving the mortuary. Having been 'gifted' with his own scar at the killer's hands, Hunt could only hope the other undead of Glasgow had attended to him. By all accounts a murderous bastard alive, being undead would only drive Canning to greater atrocities.

"Do you wish us to bring the cargo inside?" Hunt asked out of politeness.

"No, Yates and I will attend to that," Mortimer said as Hunt expected. The professor and his servant had removed the body from the wagon on each delivery, carrying it into the medical school themselves. Spared the smells and sights of the mortuary, Hunt offered no complaint.

As he stood, Mortimer handed Hunt and Sirk £10 each. Something about the man put Hunt on edge, but at least he paid well for his bodies, allowing Hunt to continue studying the natural sciences. Sirk had until recently been one of Hunt's professors, however his dismissal had been the result of his association with Hunt and Lady Delaney, levied by the powerful members of the Sooty Feather Society. Sirk now earned a living by running the absent Foley's pharmacy and stealing the occasional corpse.

The rain still fell heavily, Mortimer and the sullen Yates wasting no time in lifting the sackcloth-wrapped corpse from the back of the wagon.

"I will let you know when I require your services again," Mortimer called out. "I bid you a good evening."

"The professor and his man appear to be well-practiced

in the moving of corpses," Sirk said as he watched the two men carry the late Mr Stall towards the building.

"They do," Hunt agreed. "Good for us, yes?"

"For my back, assuredly."

*

Hunt and Sirk sat in the sitting room of Foley's flat, each with a whisky in hand in what had become a post-exhumation ritual of sorts. Sirk would sleep in the armchair, Hunt knew, in part to save walking the short distance home only to have to return to the pharmacy below the flat later in the morning. There was another reason, known to both, that was left unspoken. Both men knew what emerged after dark, stalking the streets of Glasgow.

Hunt had changed into a tatty pair of tweed trousers in need of mending, and a shirt missing two buttons. Nothing he would be seen wearing outside, but suitable replacements for the clothing soaked and muddied earlier. Sirk had changed into the clothing he had left in the flat earlier, in anticipation of not returning to his own home.

There were guns loaded with silver bullets within the flat, though to date the pair had been given no cause to use them. A message from Father had offered an assurance that both sides in the war had been warned against attacking Hunt.

My father. Lucifer.

Whisky burned his gut. Hunt lifted his glass level with the oil lamp lighting up the room, watching as it gave the whisky a golden glow. He took a long swallow, feeling the familiar fire in his mouth and throat as the liquor slid down.

"I cannot say I enjoy our nocturnal excursions and exertions, Hunt, but I must confess to looking forward to a convivial whisky before retiring to bed for the night," Sirk said.

"Yes, Doctor." In truth, Hunt 'enjoyed' a whisky almost every night, usually to cap off an evening spent in the nearby public house, drinking ale before moving on to the stronger stuff. Sleep was slow to find him, haunted as he was by the dread truth of his paternity. And when it did, inevitably he would be throttled awake by nightmares spawned by the horrors he had witnessed and endured.

Sirk had given him laudanum to take each night, warning him against exceeding the specified measure. Dutifully, Hunt never took more than the doctor recommended, instead rendering himself further insensible through drink. He had once wondered why Foley and Sirk sought solace in the opium-based drug. After Dunkellen, he knew.

"Have you reconciled with Lord Ashwood?" Sirk asked.

Lord Ashwood. Yes. Better not to dwell on the name of the demon inside him. "No. Aside from the letter he sent assuring us of no further attempts on our lives, we've not spoken since my mother's funeral."

"Is that altogether wise? If either side realise you are estranged, they may decide that Lord Ashwood's protection – already a thin shield – no longer applies." Sirk took another sip of his whisky.

"Lord Ashwood – Lucifer – *my father* – may be a fallen archangel, the seed from which grew countless dark legends, but recall that he is in the body of a mortal man. His powers are scant, and he is no less vulnerable to a bullet in the head than we are."

Sirk regarded him, his bushy eyebrows furled. "Then why is he so confident that his prohibition on our lives will be honoured by demons, undead, and their human servants?"

"Because, Doctor–" Hunt took a swig, the strength of the whisky no longer making him gasp. "–The undead and humans suspect Hell is their destination, the Devil's domain. If you feared an eternity in such a place, would you dare vex its ruler, to make enemies?"

"And what of the demons? *Arakiel*, those Possessing Kenmure, Lord Smith and whoever else?"

"I do not know. My father intimated that the legends and gospels placing him upon Hell's throne as absolute ruler are … exaggerated. He had a hundred million companion angels Fall with him, fellow archangels among them. If Erik Keel … *Arakiel* … has ordered his followers to leave us alone, then it may simply be that he wishes to deal with Fisher and the Sooty Feathers before making more enemies."

"Or he may simply not care," Sirk said.

"Or he may simply not care."

A brief silence fell, broken by Sirk. "'Vex its ruler, to make enemies,' you said. Enemies, plural? You mean hellish allies of Lucifer?"

Acid burned in Hunt's gut. "I mean, there is apparently some … speculation … as to what will become of me when I die."

"You fear your demonic heritage will see you condemned to Hell?"

Hunt watched the flame dance on the candle. *Fear? Dread, more like.* "It is a concern. My life has not been so virtuous that I can see the angels in Heaven troubling themselves to raise me up."

"Nor are you so steeped in vice that you should condemn yourself so quickly," Sirk chided. "There is another possibility?"

"Heaven … Hell … I was unaware there was a third destination," Hunt said.

"Consider the *Seraphim*."

The *Seraphim*. A third of the angels had died fighting for Lucifer before being exiled to Hell. A third died fighting for Michael, likewise lost to Heaven and fated to manifest on … worlds. Some were exiled to Earth, born in a human body, death sending their essence to Purgatory before being born once again. Sometimes with memories of what they were and of past lives lived, other times blessedly ignorant and living a normal human life, albeit always childless.

"Consider them considered," Hunt said, slightly cheered. Being doomed to live life after life until the End of Everything was not precisely appealing, but better that than an eternity in Hell, ruling the Damned by his father's side.

"If you do reconcile with Lord Ashwood, I would be obliged if you would ask him about how the werewolves came to be," Sirk said.

"I will do what I can," Hunt said. "Perhaps Foley will learn more."

"Have you heard from Mr Foley again?"

"Not since he wrote me his address, confirming he had found a community of werewolves and would stay with them for the time being, to learn how to control himself," Hunt said. Two such creatures had attacked Foley and himself in the summer, one biting Foley before being shot and killed by Hunt. At the next full moon, Foley had become one of them. He had written little else, save that the attack upon them had been unintended, two younger werewolves having gotten loose. He wrote that they held no grudge against him for the death of their fellow. Whether they extended that consideration towards Hunt, the werewolf's killer, was not said.

"The same dreams?" Sirk asked, eyeing the almost empty bottle of whisky.

"The same," Hunt affirmed.

Dreams of his mother sacrificing herself to save him from a *zombi* in Dunkellen House. That the necromancer had died shortly thereafter at the hands of Lady Delaney was of scant relief to the guilt.

Chapter Four

"Should you be here, your Grace?" Captain Harrison asked with a quiet deference.

Bishop Redfort wore dark grey trousers and a cheap overcoat, a flat cap pulled low over his face. Not at all how he usually dressed in public, but then, that was the point. "'Sir' will suffice, Harrison. I would prefer you did not announce my identity to all and sundry." *Dolt.*

"Aye, sir. My point is, this will be dangerous and I can't guarantee your safety." Harrison had been an army captain until spiralling drink and gambling debts destroyed his career. He was now owned by the Sooty Feather Society, body and soul, figuratively speaking. He had acquitted himself well during this war, and should that continue, he would be offered the opportunity to pledge his body and soul literally, to Regent Guillam.

Redfort's position as Bishop of Glasgow made him too public a figure to become undead, though he had been assured that should his service warrant it, then that fate was his as his life neared its end. Upon dying and Transitioning, he would be sent away from Glasgow until a generation had passed, and then he would return under a new name.

Likely, he *would* accept a *Nephilim*'s blood and become undead. His vices were many, his virtues few, and his ascent to Bishop was due to murder and intrigue rather than divine selection.

"Too many of our undertakings against the enemy have failed, Captain. I would oversee this one personally."

"Aye, sir." If Harrison held an opinion of a clergyman with no martial service supervising tonight's operation, he wisely kept it to himself.

Most of the warehouse's windows had been pitched black, but Redfort had spied glimmers of light shining out of some that had been missed. People were inside, suggesting that the intelligence received regarding this place was accurate.

Someone from the far corner waved. "Everyone's in position," Harrison said. He had the flushed face and yellowed eyes of an alcoholic, but tonight, at least, they were bright. A silver whistle rose to his lips and after a moment's pause issued a piercing shriek.

A burly man took an axe to the door, splintering it with four heavy blows. Harrison's men rushed inside, maybe half armed with a pistol or shotgun, the rest carrying knives and clubs.

"Enter last," Harrison told Redfort as he followed the first half of his men inside, a Webley-Pryse service revolver in hand. Muffled shouts and gunshots sounded as Sooty Feather soldiers forced entry to every door leading into this Bell Street warehouse. Erik Keel's forces had put a stop to a Sooty Feather whisky smuggling operation and shut down a tavern; raiding this warehouse was the response, and Redfort would ensure that he received credit for its success.

It was a mixed force that raided the warehouse, thanks to two months of attrition that had seen the Council forced to hire thugs and mercenaries to replace the slain. Police Superintendent – and Sooty Feather Councillor – Silas Thatcher had ensured that the police unknowingly did the Society's bidding, but he had been killed in the summer, and his replacement Edwin Kenmure had been Possessed by a demon serving Keel. The police were no longer a Sooty Feather resource.

A half-dozen of Roderick McBride's thugs reinforced Harrison's men. McBride had offered a further six, but Redfort had declined, wishing to minimise his fellow Councillor's involvement in this operation. After the

Thistledown farce, McBride would be wanting to claim something to his credit. *Find your own victory against Keel. This will be mine.*

Redfort entered the warehouse shortly after the last of Harrison's men, revolver in hand, with a derringer lying in his coat's pocket. The tension that had gripped him all evening eased as he saw that his information had been accurate.

Seizing this warehouse and the legal whisky it held was but a secondary goal of tonight's action. Like the Sooty Feathers, Keel relied on a plentiful supply of thugs and mercenaries to carry out his war, and Redfort's spies had reported a large number of men congregating around this warehouse.

That in itself was not overly suspicious, but this warehouse was owned by Mrs Carlton. Like Kenmure, Mrs Carlton had been a Sooty Feather recently elevated to the Council upon death emptying a seat. And like Kenmure, she had been Possessed by a demon in order to manipulate and spy on the Council for Keel.

Redfort kept low as he proceeded deeper inside the warehouse, scattered lanterns providing light. There was a smell of whisky and unwashed bodies, some of whom now lay dead. Mercenaries brought into the city by Keel and sheltered here by Mrs Carlton – or rather by the demon Possessing her.

Men fought. Redfort was pleased to see that few of the fallen wore the red armband marking his people, and that Keel's people were retreating further into the warehouse. Not that it mattered, they would be hunted down and killed.

"Captain," Redfort called out.

After a moment Harrison appeared. "Sir?"

"Deploy your men to any possible exits."

The man frowned. "You don't want us to pursue the last of the enemy? You're giving them time to regroup, a mistake."

Redfort bit back an insult, mindful that Harrison might answer it with a bullet. "Just ensure that none of the enemy can escape. It is time to let Miss Kelp's wards off their leash."

"*Secundus*," Theresa Kelp acknowledged, addressing Redfort by his Council title. He sat on the Second Seat, senior to all save Regent Guillam, the *Prima*.

He eyed the *Nephilim*, wondering how old she was. "Your ghouls, Miss Kelp, are they ready for a little bloodletting?"

"They are," she affirmed, with a certain reserve. Many ghouls had been lost in the destruction of the Under-Market Crypt in spring; others slain at Dunclutha by George Rannoch's circus-folk and undead. Lady Delaney, her Irish girl and an unknown man had more recently discovered the Crypt beneath the Imperial Mill, using explosives to destroy both.

Ordinarily, the Regent would have had perhaps two-score ghouls to deploy against the enemy in this war, the survivors Transitioning in time to *Nephilim*. Instead, she was forced to rely on hired thugs while her *Nephilim* Made new ghouls and let the Thirst wither conscience and humanity. All the while, Keel's *Nephilim* doubtless Made ghouls of their own.

"Then see your charges blooded and well-fed," Redfort said, though carefully. He was in charge, but always in the back of his mind he knew that *Nephilim* such as Miss Kelp answered directly to Regent Guillam. And Lord Fisher, should he ever stir himself from his reclusive existence.

Miss Kelp led her three ghouls past the stored casks of whisky, giving this lot their first taste of battle. Ghouls Made as troops for battle – the Warborn – were treated harsher than those Made in peaceful times in order to destroy any lingering hesitation to kill, any residual humanity. Such ghouls were common in undead wars, when both sides 'recruited' indiscriminately, Making ghouls from anyone they could snatch, starving them so that they would kill and feed without hesitation, and then unleashing them on an enemy. Few would survive long enough to Transition to *Nephilim*, and those that did were particularly feared.

Gunfire resumed, Redfort estimating from the sound that no more than one gun was possessed by the enemy that remained. Screams followed, lingering on and sounding almost bestial. He could imagine what was going on in the bowels of this warehouse but preferred not to.

A short time later Harrison approached, keeping his distance as Miss Kelp led all three ghouls – two men and one woman – back. All were bloodied, a slight flush now showing on once-pale cheeks. Miss Kelp had not denied herself either, Redfort saw.

"Sir, the warehouse is almost clear," Harrison said.

"'Almost'?"

"There is a basement level, padlocked."

Redfort nodded in understanding. "Wise, to leave it for last." Perhaps Mrs Carlton housed more than just hired killers in her warehouse, or perhaps a Crypt of ghouls awaited below. Cheered at the thought of how such a thorough victory would raise his stock with the rest of the Council, Redfort permitted himself a smile. "Report."

"We lost three men dead, six wounded though only two seriously. There were twenty-three men and one woman in here, as well as a large stock of rifles, pistols and ammunition. Eight prisoners, including the woman."

"Take me to the prisoners," Redfort said.

Harrison led him through the shadowed warehouse. Most of the prisoners were wounded, with a fearful look about them. Whatever money Keel had promised them, suddenly it was entirely too little.

Redfort recognised the woman, a tinge of fear tainting his satisfaction as he approached. "Mrs Carlton, how good to see you again. When was it we last met …? Ah, yes. In Dunkellen House's kitchens, that night you thought to have Lord Ashwood's son Possessed. Forgive me, I never did catch your true name, demon."

The demon glared at him through the eyes of a middle-aged, grey-haired woman. "*Ifriel*, Bishop Redfort. You know that Keel's Demonist will simply Summon me back."

"Yes, no doubt, but he will have lost the monies and assets of J. Carlton & Co."

"Managing the company was an irritation," the demon said, its mouth twitching in a smile that gave Redfort pause. "With that distraction gone, I can devote my energies to finding and punishing you, Redfort."

Damn you. He shot her in the head. Another enemy made, but at least he could report to the Council that not only had he emptied a warehouse of men, ghouls and weapons Keel had yet to deploy against the Sooty Feathers, but he had also deprived Keel of the company that owned this warehouse, among others.

Now, to deal with the ghouls, if indeed there are any, lurking beneath us. It was after dark, meaning they would be … awake. And wanting blood.

"The other prisoners?" Harrison asked.

"Kill them," Redfort said, his attention already on that locked basement hatch.

Harrison joined him at the hatch while his men dealt with the last survivors. "Will Miss Kelp and her … people deal with any undead below?" he asked.

Redfort wasn't deaf to the hopeful note in his voice, but the Regent's undead were rarer and more valuable than Harrison, his men, or McBride's thugs, who were busy looting the dead mercenaries. "No, I think you and your men dealing with them will be a valuable experience."

Harrison gave a terse nod and shouted for his men to gather. Regular bullets were replaced by those cast from silver. Miss Kelp and her ghouls stood nearby in case any enemy undead escaped the basement.

The padlock was smashed off, the hatch lifted open, and those of Harrison's men armed with guns were the first to descend into the basement.

Gunshots sounded, a lot of them, confirming either the presence of undead or more mercenaries. Likely the latter. Redfort held his own revolver as a precaution.

After perhaps ten minutes Harrison climbed back out of the basement, breathing hard. "Eight undead below … dealt with. Sir."

"You have confirmed that?" Miss Kelp asked quietly.

Harrison nodded, tensing at being addressed by the undead. "We beheaded them all just to be sure."

"How did your men perform?" Redfort asked as Miss Kelp nodded her approval.

He hesitated. "We slew all the undead, we took only a few injuries."

"But…?" Redfort pressed, sensing more.

"Discipline was wanting," Harrison was forced to admit.

"Your men fired indiscriminately," Redfort guessed. "Had your men been using non-silver bullets, or in a less confined space, or against a greater number, or indeed against *Nephilim*, you might have been overrun."

"Aye, sir. We'll do better next time."

Time for the carrot. "Of course you will! Excellent work, Captain. I will commend you and your men to Regent Guillam. Enemies slain, a demon and undead among them, and a valuable company now lost to Keel. What a good night's work."

"Here, this one's alive," one of McBride's oafs shouted while rifling the pockets of one of the fallen.

Redfort frowned, displeased at this apparent carelessness. "I trust your men were more diligent in attending to the undead below?"

Harrison hurried over to the body McBride's man claimed was alive. "Probably just a reflexive move," he called back to Redfort as he knelt down. "Shotgun took him in the chest, his heart and lungs will be minced–"

The corpse's hand shot up and gripped Harrison around the throat, the captain struggling in vain to free himself. The man who'd called him over backed away, making no move to help. A familiar dread fell over Redfort, a sensation he had not felt in two months.

God, no. But he knew from bitter experience God would play no role in what was to follow. "Shoot the bodies in the head," he commanded with a shout.

Men either stared at him in confusion or gaped in shock as their captain's throat was ripped out in a spray of blood.

Most of the dead mercenaries rose jerkily to their feet, barring those whose brains had been destroyed by bullet or bludgeon. *A necromancer's work…*

"Undead!" someone shouted. In error. A fatal one, as those men who recalled their training stabbed or shot the risen enemy in the heart or head. Those corpses shot in the brain fell back down, but those struck in the chest kept moving towards the panicked soldiers.

Zombis.

Redfort had faced them before, at Dunkellen. Those who were killed rose en masse to attack the living, the slain in turn becoming *zombis*. An army of hundreds, a feat of necromancy that had left Redfort awestruck. A nightmare he had barely survived, and only because Lady Delaney had killed Dr Essex, the necromancer responsible. Lady MacInesker and almost all her guests and staff had died that day.

Had Keel found another necromancer willing to work for him? Unlikely, as it was a dark art few dared study. To Raise a score of *zombis* was no mean feat, well beyond Redfort's meagre ability. There were screams from elsewhere in the warehouse, where the prisoners had been executed. A few men had been charged with searching the bodies.

The architect of this calamity could be pondered later, after he escaped. "Stand your ground and aim for their heads," he ordered. "Miss Kelp, hold them back!" A *Nephilim* and three ghouls should be enough to slow the *zombis* long enough for Harrison's men to put bullets in their heads.

The dead prisoners arrived, armed with guns taken from the men they had killed. Guns loaded with silver, Redfort realised with dawning horror. Before he could shout a warning, the *zombis* turned their guns on the four undead, firing repeatedly. A necromancer could not directly control too many dead at once, usually issuing a few basic commands such as 'go here' and 'kill everyone'. In this case, the necromancer kept a more direct control over those carrying guns, firing shotguns and revolvers at the undead.

There was no precision aiming involved, the *zombis* too clumsy for that. Instead, they ignored the living, concentrating their fire on the undead. The three ghouls were the first to fall, followed by Miss Kelp. She was not yet done, no bullets having struck her brain or heart, but even a *Nephilim* could only withstand so much damage, especially from silver.

"Kill them!" Redfort shouted, firing his own revolver into a *zombi*'s head. Most of Harrison's men were too busy fighting with the unarmed *zombis* attacking them, but two followed Redfort's example. By then it was too late, none of the ghouls moving. The last *zombi* with a gun stood over Miss Kelp, an awareness growing in its eyes as it became the focus of the necromancer's attention. Its revolver roared one last time, a hole appearing in Miss Kelp's head.

Redfort shot that *zombi* and returned his attention to the bloody melee surrounding him. Already more than half of his men had been overcome by the mercenaries they had just killed. Two of McBride's men hacked hysterically at a *zombi* with knives, not knowing it was in truth a corpse and felt no pain. They would tire and fall. Already Harrison was getting up, his corpse now under the control of the necromancer.

Redfort shot the *zombi* closest to him in the head, missing. He fired again and again, finally doing enough damage to the brain to 'kill' it. Now his own revolver was empty, and there were too many *zombis* blocking the nearest escape route.

He pulled out his derringer and looked frantically for the best *zombi* to shoot, for a possible escape. It held but one bullet and he would have no time to reload. The last of his men was wrestled down to the ground, trying to scream as dead hands tightened around his throat.

A *zombi* shuffled over to Redfort while the others stood their ground, dead eyes fixed on Redfort. *And so it ends.* Redfort's hand trembled as he raised his gun, pointing it at his own head. *Better a bullet than to be mauled to death.*

Like the *zombi* who had executed Miss Kelp, an *awareness* seemed to grow in the eyes of this one, and his lips turned up in a smile. "Bishop Redfort, a pleasure to meet you again."

"Who are you?" he asked hoarsely. *It cannot be Essex, he was killed.* A student, perhaps, who had been told by the late Doctor that Redfort was also a necromancer.

"You know who I am, your Grace. Who I was, rather. I am impressed that you survived Dunkellen. And in such diabolical company."

"Dr Essex," Redfort managed through numbed lips. *How?*

"Indeed, though no longer."

"How?" *How did you cheat death?*

The necromancer ignored that question. "When I came to this city, I was surprised to find a necromancer here. Few dare embrace that school of magic."

"The ruling *Nephilim* prohibit it here," Redfort said, happy to talk if it meant the *zombis* weren't attacking.

"Mr Keel has a more tolerant disposition, for the moment. Who was your master?"

"Aaron Holdfast. The Council discovered he was a practitioner early into my apprenticeship and burned him."

"Self-taught thereafter?"

"I inherited his grimoire," Redfort said. "It has been added to over the centuries."

"Who started it?" the necromancer asked.

Redfort paused, trying to recall the author of the earliest pages, now a faded ink whose writings had been copied into later chapters. "There was no recognisable name in the original text, however copies made later in the tome attribute it to a 'Bahiti'."

"Bahiti … one of my apprentices. She died before fully mastering the Art. The grimoire you possess began as scrolls written some thousands of years ago, passed on by one of her own apprentices."

Redfort recalled Holdfast speaking once of what those who mastered necromancy could achieve; a mastery of death itself. The name came to him. "You are a *Jinn*." One who returned from death but not as undead. A few tomes who dared mention them used the term 'lich', but Holdfast had disliked that term, it being an old word for 'body'. A *Jinn* did not return in their own body but rather Possessed someone else's.

"Indeed. Death is but an inconvenience for me."

"How?" Ever since Holdfast's death, Redfort had spent little time with necromancy, focusing on his more worldly ambitions. Now, his eyes opened to what he might truly achieve, his long-dormant ambition to master that darkest of the magical arts was awoken.

"When one has mastered necromancy, one may prepare a receptacle for one's soul, a Soul-Repository, sometimes called a phylactery. If successfully bound to the necromancer, upon their death their soul will reside there. Should someone come into contact with the receptacle, the necromancer's soul will then evict that person's soul and take up residence."

"Then you were not born, Dr Essex."

A hissing laugh escaped the *zombi*'s lips. "Theodore Essex was but one in a very long line of bodies I have used. He was a young doctor of middling talent when I became him, my own anatomical knowledge allowing me to quickly establish myself as one of London's foremost physicians."

"How old are you?"

"Very. I was alive when the *Grigori* Fell to earth."

Redfort moistened dry lips. "And whose body do you occupy presently?"

"That would be telling." That reticence was a relief; had the necromancer intended Redfort's death, there would have been no reason not to disclose their new identity.

"Will you kill me?" Redfort asked, now reasonably confident they would not.

"I would have you reconsider your present allegiance in this war, Bishop."

Or you will betray my secret to Regent Guillam, who

will have me burned to death. "Will you take me on as your apprentice?"

"I have no interest in teaching."

But I suspect you have your own grimoire, perhaps with instructions on creating this ... Soul-Repository. "I will consider it."

"Consider quickly." The *zombi* stepped aside. "You may leave."

None of the other corpses moved, so Redfort quickly made his way to the exit, skin crawling as he half-expected the necromancer to change its mind and have him snatched back and bloodily killed.

That didn't happen, and Redfort found himself outside the warehouse, a light drizzle of rain falling on him.

As he walked briskly through the streets of Glasgow, he wondered at what to do. Firstly, he must report both stunning success and dreadful failure to the Regent. A demon, undead and mercenaries employed by Keel had been slain, and the demon had lost any claim to the Carlton company assets. On the other hand, a *Nephilim*, ghouls and soldiers had been lost.

He could honestly report on the return of the necromancer who had unleashed a necromantic plague in the Dunkellen estate, to the south of Glasgow, but that risked the revelation that Redfort too dabbled with necromancy.

Turn coat and join Keel? It had merit, though if Niall Fisher took a direct hand in the war, then Redfort would bet on him prevailing over the demon.

No. The necromancer must be killed, fully and finally killed, his soul's receptacle destroyed. But I will need allies and can trust none of my fellow Councillors with this information. Who, then, would be motivated to help me...?

Chapter Five

Once, the Council of Eight had sat along an old oak table at the head of their chamber in the Black Wing Club building off Buchanan Street, the true masters of the city. The inner circle of the Sooty Feathers, usually numbering twelve, counting among them many of Glasgow's richest and most powerful, would come to hear the will of the Council and receive instruction. They, in turn, would issue orders to the rest of the Society that would eventually filter down to those who believed the undead to be the stuff of myth and penny dreadfuls.

Now, the Black Wing Club was closed for 'renovations.' Amy Newfield had been Made undead about seven months ago; of the eight Councillors who had ruled the city and Society back in the spring, only Margot Guillam still lived – so to speak. The previous regent had been betrayed and killed by George Rannoch at the Dunclutha estate near Largs, one Elder *Nephilim* against another.

Between the disasters at Dunclutha and Dunkellen, many of Glasgow's rich and powerful citizens were dead, gutting the Sooty Feather Society. Some that still lived had fled the city. Those nobles sworn to the Society who had decamped to London for the Season remained there, in no hurry to close up their London townhouses and return to their estates in and around Glasgow. Many who had returned in July had been slain by *zombis* at Dunkellen, the Society now hoping to recruit their heirs. The Society's control over almost every institution in Glasgow had ended. Some were now controlled by those loyal to Erik Keel, such as the police and high court.

When Miss Guillam had taken the newly Made Newfield in, there had been fifty full members of the Sooty Feathers, made up of the mortal Councillors, the inner circle and junior members. With around fifty Initiates being groomed for full membership, whereupon they learned who they truly served, and that demons and vampyres were real. That the Society ruled Glasgow from the shadows was no secret to the Initiates; that it in turn was ruled by vampyres was, and those who had trouble with that revelation were quietly disposed of.

The Council now met in a different location each time. Tonight, Neil MacInesker hosted them in Dunkellen House's dining room, a pointed choice. Lady MacInesker had died during the slaughter, though Neil, her son, had been fortunately visiting London.

The house had been locked up, abandoned until tonight. The mortals present looked uncomfortable, especially Bishop Redfort.

Some walls and carpets were still black with blood, and the house screamed of death. Most of the Sooty Feathers had died within these walls or trying to flee the grounds.

In the two months since, the Council was marking those who had moved into the vacant positions of wealth and power, either by inheritance or initiative, with a view to recruiting those deemed of use once the war was over.

Newfield felt an imposter sitting on the Council, aware she only did so because Regent Guillam wanted a trusted face in the Eighth Seat. Unlike many of the others, Newfield had no prior Sooty Feather involvement or patrons. Her allegiance was solely to Regent Guillam and Lord Fisher. And she was among the very few to have met the reclusive *Dominus Nephilim*.

Neil MacInesker had been present at that meeting too, where he had learned that he was among the last known descendants of Fisher. For two hundred years a MacInesker had sat on the Council, the *Dominus Nephilim* favouring what remained of his progeny.

MacInesker was not much older than Newfield, and looked no more comfortable than she felt, though he at least had inherited many valuable assets, land and houses. Newfield was but a sixteen-year-old Made undead by Rannoch, intended to be nothing more than another disposable ghoul to be thrown at the Sooty Feathers. Seventeen, she amended, recalling her birthday had been in August. Though she would forever look sixteen and supposed she must deal with that sooner or later.

Miss Guillam, Regent and Council *Prima*, sat at the head of the table. Her accent still held a hint of what might have been French, though she had dwelt in Glasgow for almost six hundred years. Guillam was the only one entrusted with the location of Niall Fisher's Crypt.

"Lord Fisher is dissatisfied with the lack of progress in this war. While we suffered significant losses to Rannoch's treachery, Keel's subsequent demon infiltration of this Council, and his necromancer's bloody sorcery here, since then we have at best managed a stalemate and *must* do better."

"Maybe 'Lord' Fisher should come show us how it's done?" McBride asked, a note of scorn in his voice. "I've lost too much money and too many men to this 'war'."

McBride was a man feared across the city, but Miss Guillam showed no fear of him. "He employs *us* to attend to this business. If he feels it necessary to take a personal hand, he will. Perhaps first attending to those whose performance has dissatisfied him."

"If there even is a 'Lord Fisher'," McBride muttered.

A chill fell over the room as the Regent Unveiled. Newfield saw her power, as no doubt did the other undead present. Some of the mortals paled or shivered. To them, it would have felt like being in Death's shadow.

"Speak plainly, McBride," Regent Guillam said in a deathly hush. "But carefully, as they might be your last words."

The criminal patriarch swallowed but refused to back down entirely. "For years, you and Thomas Edwards have made a big deal about representing this old, scary vampyre lord. But I've never fucking seen him." He looked at Fredds and Crowe. "Have you? Has anyone?"

No one answered. Newfield had, in fact, met Lord Fisher, not an experience she was keen to repeat.

McBride dared to look at Miss Guillam, a hesitant challenge on his face. Bishop Redfort watched the exchange with a calculating silence.

"I have met him," Neil MacInesker said quietly. Miss Guillam gave Newfield a warning look to hold her tongue.

"Mr MacInesker was hooded, the route circuitous, so he does not know where he was taken, nor how far Lord Fisher's Crypt is," she said. "None of you will question him regarding Lord Fisher. Consider the topic … closed."

She stared hard at McBride. "Am I understood? Or will I bind you and throw you into a Crypt of hungry ghouls, and hope that one of your brothers will serve the Council better?"

"You're understood," McBride managed, taking a shaky sip of water.

"Excellent. Now, you will all report in turn." The gaze she turned on the rest of the table suggested her patience should be tested no further. "Bishop Redfort? You reported the possibility of a decisive victory against Keel's forces." During Edwards' reign, the Councillors had worn ceremonial half-masks. Now, such formalities had been abandoned.

Redfort was the Council's Second Seat, its *Secundus*. Miss Guillam had warned Newfield not to underestimate him, a man whose ruthless ambition had seen him rise through the ranks of both the Sooty Feather Society and Church. The respect he had won for surviving Dunkellen was somewhat tainted by the revelation that the demon Keel – *Arakiel* – had been beneath his nose the whole time, Possessing his secretary, Henderson.

Redfort cleared his throat. "Yes, Regent. Captain Harrison and I led men to a warehouse owned by J. Carlton & Co. The result was … mixed."

Dead eyes stared unblinkingly at Redfort. The Regent's tolerance for 'mixed' news was nearing an end. Her continued restraint was an acknowledgment that if she 'shot the messenger', her nights of receiving accurate reports would be at an end. "Continue."

"Yes, well. Mrs Carlton was Possessed by a demon calling itself … *Ifriel.* That demon is now back in Hell." He forced a note of optimism in his voice. "Keel will no longer be able to utilise the assets of that company. The newly arrived mercenaries were killed to a man. And I am pleased to report that a Crypt of ghouls was found and destroyed."

"Three successes, Bishop. Well done. Why, then, do you say, 'mixed'?"

"Because he led three of my men into a bloody slaughter," McBride growled. "None of them returned." That explained his ill mood. He had joined the Council expecting to find wealth and the trappings of respectability. Instead, his opportunities came with a price.

Regent Guillam held up her hand, silencing McBride. "Bishop?"

"I regret that I was the only survivor. Captain Harrison and his men, Mr McBride's men and … and Miss Kelp and her ghouls were all lost." Newfield could almost sense the fear coming from Redfort. Good news balanced by bad. Which way would the scales tilt?

"How many ghouls accompanied Miss Kelp?" Fredds asked, grey eyes fixed on Redfort.

"Three. Fewer than Keel lost," the Bishop hastened to add.

"How did you survive? Scampered off while brave men died, eh?" McBride spoke scornfully.

Redfort met his eyes. "I do not answer to you, McBride. You may have the drunks and pickpockets in your thrall, but you are no longer squabbling over scraps in the gutter or in taverns reeking of piss and shit."

"How did you survive?" Guillam asked before McBride could retort. Had the Society not suffered so many losses recently, Newfield suspected there would be one or two seats becoming vacant. Not that anyone's survival was by any means assured. McBride had still to report his own recent debacle.

Redfort's hesitation suggested a hesitance to answer honestly. "We had won decisively. And then the dead rose, like they did here. It was chaos, with many of our people fighting the *zombis* as they would undead, too panicked to heed my words as their efforts failed. I alone had experience fighting a necromancer's thralls, and I barely escaped." He looked around the room. "Judge me if you will, but there was no saving the others."

Regent Guillam studied him for a moment before nodding. "I am curious how Keel – whose release from Hell is recent – was able to recruit not one, but two necromancers of skill."

"This century, we have uncovered only one necromancer before Dr Essex," Fredds said. "And Aaron Holdfast was burned to death."

Magdalene Quinn spoke. "A necromancer recruited from outside Glasgow, like Essex? Perhaps an apprentice of his." It was in her interests that suspicion not fall on Glasgow's magicians, lest the undead burn out the Under-Market.

"I will seek out this necromancer and deal with him as Dr Essex was dealt with," Redfort promised.

"Do so," the Regent instructed. "All of you, spread the word to be vigilant for signs of necromancy. We can ill afford another Dunkellen." She gestured to a stain which darkened a broad swathe of the floor, MacInesker still had yet to cover up the bare floorboards with a new carpet.

There were murmurs of agreement.

"Mr Fredds, what have you to report?" the Regent asked.

Tertius was Reginald Fredds, a *Nephilim* who had little time for Newfield owing to her being a mere ghoul. Of course, he held little respect for most of the other Councillors, save for Miss Guillam. His position on the Council made him the third or fourth senior-most undead in Glasgow, after Lord Fisher, Regent Guillam and perhaps Mr Crowe. Not yet an Elder, his Transition to that state was expected to happen soon.

"We have twenty-three newly Made ghouls confined to two Crypts. A further fourteen ghouls are being mentored." Fredds glared briefly at Redfort before correcting himself. "Eleven ghouls, rather. Six are older than a year." Meaning they might Transition soon as, typically, a ghoul became a full *Nephilim* one to three years after being Made. The fewer generations separating a ghoul from a *Grigori*, the sooner the Transition happened. Newfield's Maker, Rannoch, had been Made by Keel himself; she expected to Transition within the next six months. If she survived the war.

"With Theresa Kelp dead, another *Nephilim* will be needed to take over her Crypt and mentor her remaining ghouls," the Regent said, looking at Fredds.

"Me?" He did not look happy at the prospect.

"You." Her tone did not invite further discussion.

The Fourth Seat, *Quartus*, had been given to Edmund Crowe, an Elder *Nephilim* in charge of the Heron Crowe Bank. Only nominally associated with the House, his bank had nonetheless handled all House and Society accounts. The bank's human partner, William Heron, had died in the *zombi* attack, and Guillam had tightened the bond between Society and bank by offering Crowe a Council Seat.

Fredds had been a *Nephilim* in Fisher's House for a long time; Crowe was an Elder and more powerful, but new to House and Council. And so Regent Guillam had, in part, cancelled out the two potential rivals who might seek to replace her as Regent. A mere ghoul, Newfield was no threat at all.

While Fredds wore a modern dinner jacket, Crowe's wardrobe contents were decades out of fashion. The undead banker wore a black short-fronted tailcoat over a grey waist coat and white linen shirt. His trousers were grey and wider than those worn by men these days.

He spoke with a dry, raspy voice, his hair less greying than normal. Suggesting he had fed recently. "Our account turnover has been high in recent weeks. Many heirs of dead members have closed their accounts, I suspect largely due to disquiet over our lack of liquidity in the summer." Which was his way of referencing the robbery: Keel's people had deprived the Heron Crowe Bank of a third of its cash, leading to a panicked flood of customers trying to withdraw their money – too much money to be accommodated at the one time.

Redfort stirred. "Have assets the bank has invested in been sabotaged?"

"No. But many of our investments are outside the city, indeed some are overseas," Crowe said. "Historically we made a large fortune investing in the transportation of slaves from Africa to the Caribbean plantations."

"And how would Keel know what and where your current investments are, eh?" McBride asked.

"He'll know, he will have spies in the bank," Redfort said. "A demon, perhaps."

Crowe nodded, his expression grim. "The possibility has occurred to me."

"If Keel has made no efforts to further weaken the Heron Crowe Bank, then…" Redfort rested his chin in his hands, his sentence unfinished.

"He expects victory soon. Soon enough to surrender the advantage he would gain by financially crippling the Society now," Miss Quinn said. "He intends to take over the bank and use it as we have. The demon wants to take over a prosperous city, not one crippled by financial ruin."

"Half of my mills have been put out of business," MacInesker objected.

"Mills owned by the MacInesker Foundation, not the bank," Guillam said. "And as I recall, the Foundation has taken out loans from the bank."

"Hence why you still have half of your mills," McBride said with an ugly laugh.

MacInesker did not look happy at McBride's tone, but he was clearly intimidated by him. "So that I can continue to repay the loans? Not with only half of them operating."

"It is so that when you default on the loans, the bank

can seize the mills," said Crowe. Meaning he would seize the mills.

MacInesker went red. "That would not happen! Would not be permitted to happen, Mr Crowe." His defiant tone faltered as he recalled who he was speaking to. Favoured by Lord Fisher he might be, but Fisher was not here. All the same, if Edmund Crowe tried to seize MacInesker's assets, Fisher would like as not intervene.

Miss Guillam gave MacInesker a look that quietened any further outbursts from him, looking displeased at him hinting at a well-kept secret.

"If Keel has defeated us and claimed the bank, then the fate of your mills may be the least of your problems, Mr MacInesker," Edmund Crowe said.

"He may defeat us – may – but surely he does not expect Lord Fisher to permit him his victory?" Quinn asked.

"Erik Keel – *Arakiel* – intends to become *Grigori* once more," Guillam reminded her. "To do that, he needs Fisher's heart. We can expect that the demon will seek to goad Lord Fisher into revealing himself."

"The question, then, is how does a demon with perhaps a half-dozen *Nephilim* – none of whom are Elder – and perhaps a score of ghouls, expect to defeat a *Dominus*?" Redfort spoke quietly. "To *kill* Lord Fisher, yes, that might be done through ambush, with a lot of guns firing a lot of silver bullets, with explosives. But to take Lord Fisher alive and restrain him long enough to remove his heart…?"

Regent Guillam nodded slowly. "And the heart will remain viable for minutes only after its removal for the Demonist to complete the ritual to restore *Arakiel*."

A brief silence fell before Guillam looked at the Council's sole magician. "What have you to report, Miss Quinn?"

"There is a lingering discontent after I had all reagents necessary for demon summoning seized, but no open insurrection," Quinn said.

Her position as *Quinta* had become significantly

shakier of late. The Heron Crowe Bank relied upon her Wards to warn of intrusions, and her *geas* prevented employees from sharing certain knowledge – whether they wished to or not, whether they were tortured or not. However her domain was the Under-Market, and it was in chaos as the city's magicians chose their sides.

"Has there been any sign of Cornelius Josiah?" the Regent asked.

"None. The bounty on his head has been increased, but he is the only remaining Demonist in Glasgow. Keel will be keeping him safe to conduct the ritual that will return Keel as a *Grigori*."

"Why would Keel need a Demonist to return as *Gri... Grigori*?" McBride asked.

Quinn looked at him. "*Arakiel* is currently Possessing Harold Henderson, Bishop Redfort's former secretary. In the improbable event Lord Fisher is taken, his heart removed, and *Arakiel*'s *Grigori* remains recovered, the demon must be removed from Henderson's body and then Summoned back from Hell to inhabit its restored remains. Hence the Demonist."

"Do we know where Keel's remains are?" Redfort asked.

"We do," was all the Regent would say.

"Should we not, then, destroy them to prevent any possibility of Keel returning as a *Grigori*?" he asked.

"The body was kept as a trophy. It has since been burned to ash. However, there is no way to truly destroy it," Regent Guillam said.

"Can we not scatter the ashes?" Quinn asked.

"His remains are in a safe place," the Regent said. *Lord Fisher has them*, Newfield decided. Which meant, if he was found and defeated, Keel would have all he needs for his restoration.

"Do many magicians side with Keel?" Redfort asked.

"There have been posters printed in support of Keel. Attacks at night. But who leads them, we do not yet know," Quinn admitted. "There is a lot of suspicion, and few travel to and from the Under-Market alone these days."

"*Sextus*, report," Miss Guillam said.

"As I said earlier, half of my mills are no longer operational," Neil MacInesker said. An air of defeat surrounded him, weighed down by the responsibilities inherited from his mother. He sat on the Council not due to any competence or skill on his part, but merely because Niall Fisher was a distant ancestor. And he knew it, even if few others did.

"I can have some of my men guard your remaining mills, MacInesker," McBride offered.

"I would be greatly obliged," he said, sitting up.

"Your foundation owns the mills wholly, aye?"

"Yes, though I own most of the foundation's shares. Most of the other shareholders died during … during…" He swallowed and raised his hands, his meaning clear. They had been killed by *zombis* in the summer.

"Get me the details of your dead shareholders' next of kin, and I'll have my lawyer buy those shares. Which mill is your least profitable?"

"I … don't know." MacInesker had gone pale, and little wonder. McBride was making a move to become the second largest shareholder of the MacInesker Foundation, the recent closures of half its mills no doubt meaning he would get them for a fraction of what they had been worth a few months earlier. When another mill ceased operation, those who had inherited the shares would be all too eager to sell them, and those who still refused would doubtless face another form of 'persuasion' to sell.

"Find out. I'll pay the next loan instalment due to the bank as a sign of … good faith. You can repay me with the equivalent value of your shares." McBride might end up a minority shareholder of the foundation, but he clearly expected to bully Neil MacInesker into doing his will.

"Yes, Mr McBride."

"Once this war is over, those closed mills will be restored and reopened," McBride said in a tone of certainty. If he thought to take over the foundation, he would be in for a surprise. Newfield certainly wouldn't be surprised if Lord Fisher had Regent Guillam deal with McBride once matters were settled, the shares returning to the MacInesker family. What remained of it.

Oblivious to Newfield's suspicions about his fate, Roderick McBride prepared to speak again. He was *Septimus*, the Seventh Seat. Like Crowe, he had been an ally of the Society for years though not truly a member. Membership and a council seat were given in recognition of the power he wielded throughout the city, though that power had been threatened in recent times by the constabulary.

"I understand you, too, have suffered losses, Mr McBride," the Regent said, an impatient bite in her voice. "Can you at least mitigate your losses with a dead demon and a destroyed Crypt of ghouls?"

McBride took a breath. "No, Regent. That bastard Kenmure took my bootlegged whisky and closed down the Thistledown tavern."

"Unfortunate." She let the word linger. "I believe your ship caught fire that same night, none of the crew surviving."

"Aye. But I got my wagons back from the police," McBride said, scowling at the titter of laughter that tiptoed around the room.

"I understand that Lady Delaney also took an interest in your dealings that night," the Regent said. She didn't bother to say that she already knew everything that had happened thanks to Newfield.

"She was skulking around, aye, cost us a barrel which we would have lost anyway," MCBride said. "I'll deal with that fucking–"

"Language. And you will exercise some restraint. Wilton Hunt has thus far distanced himself from our affairs, and I would see his lack of involvement continue, lest his father get involved. Lord Fisher has reiterated that he does not wish Lucifer drawn into our affairs and that no harm should befall the son."

McBride said nothing. His telling of his encounter with Lucifer in the Highlands had been a subdued one, his attempt to force Lord Ashwood to sell his shipping company a failure. Lord Fisher had passed on an instruction that no further attempt was to be made.

"You are also to continue to refrain from killing Dr Sirk, for now," Regent Guillam added. "Be content with shooting Thomas Foley."

Newfield caught Redfort stirring. She had been present when the bishop had confided to Regent Guillam that Foley had been present at Dunkellen, alive and surprisingly well for a man shot twice in the gut mere days before. But the pharmacist had not returned to Glasgow, and for now Guillam was content to let McBride believe he had partly avenged his slain brother.

And that leaves Octavia. *Me…*

*

Redfort watched the young ghoul, Newfield, nervously update the Council, not that she had much to say. McBride's misadventure was fortunate; Redfort could at least balance his losses with some success.

Having survived the meeting, he could now turn his attention onto identifying the necromancer's new identity and killing it as Lady Delaney had managed. More, he must locate the necromancer's Soul-Repository so that once the body was killed, the soul would be trapped. And Redfort could study it to learn how to fashion one of his own. And destroy it, to silence the necromancer once and for all.

Becoming undead was one path to cheating death, but as Miss Kelp had learned, it was death delayed, not avoided. Necromancy, on the other hand, offered a path to die not once but many times, over and over, with death avoided so long as one's Soul-Repository was intact. *Youth, recaptured.*

But first, Keel's necromancer must be found before Redfort's own dabbling in the forbidden magic was revealed. *I will need help, but I can trust none here.*

A wry smile touched his lips as the solution came to him.

Chapter Six

"Thank you," Knox said gratefully as Caroline handed her a glass of brandy. Three nights had passed since they had barely escaped Roddy McBride at the Thistledown tavern. The Glasgow Constabulary had subsequently closed the tavern down, and the schooner used to smuggle the whisky south had inexplicably caught fire and sunk.

She felt ambivalent about such setbacks. On one hand, she was pleased to see the Sooty Feathers suffer, on the other it meant victories for the other side, for the demon *Arakiel.*

"You are welcome," Caroline said as she sat on the couch, letting out a sigh. She held a glass, too. "My limbs ache."

"Mmm." They had sparred in the cellar Caroline had converted into a gymnasium, practicing unarmed fighting. After months of such training, Knox was now fitter as well as younger than Caroline, but the middle-aged woman had the benefit of experience, and could still best Knox more often than not.

There was a knock at the front door, and a minute later Ellison entered the sitting room, wide-eyed and a little breathless. "Excuse me, ma'am, but His Grace, the Bishop of Glasgow, is here to see you."

Knox exchanged a look with Caroline, reassured that her derringer was in her reticule purse. Evidently done with subtlety, Caroline placed her own derringer on the table. "We'll receive him, Ellison."

"Yes, ma'am." Her eyes widened. Ellison was well-used to her employer's eccentric ways but receiving a bishop with a gun on the table was a breathtaking breach of etiquette.

Knox took a sip of brandy, hoping Caroline didn't see her hand tremble. "You're not going to shoot him, are you?"

"Let us see what he has to say for himself, first."

The door opened again, Ellison leading their guest inside. "His Grace, the Bishop of Glasgow."

Bishop Redfort entered, his clerical collar showing above a black evening coat. He offered Caroline and Knox a brisk bow of his head, a wry smile touching his lips. "Good evening, Lady Delaney. Miss Knox. I apologise for attending without first sending a card."

"Your Grace. Take a seat." Caroline motioned to a vacant armchair.

Redfort sat, his eyebrows raising slightly on seeing the gun. "I do hope you don't plan on using that, Lady Delaney."

"Miss Knox believes I should not."

"Be a shame to ruin the rug or stain the floor," Knox said.

Redfort smiled politely, but he knew what Caroline was capable of. "I will take up no more of your time than necessary."

"You can begin by explaining what brings you here, Bishop Redfort," Caroline said. She made no offer of refreshment.

"Mr McBride was rather vexed with you both," Redfort said, though Knox sensed he had not come all this way to talk about a barrel of whisky set on fire, or a thug's loss of face.

Caroline's smile did not reach her eyes, which rested briefly on her gun. "I hear he suffered worse indignities that night, losing a ship, a tavern, and the rest of his contraband whisky. But if he wishes to discuss our encounter further, I am amenable to concluding our dispute."

"He has been instructed to stay away from you. For the moment," Redfort said.

"By Miss Guillam, or has the reclusive Mr Fisher stepped in due to the recent … indignities your society has suffered?"

"Yes," Redfort said without further clarification. "But be warned that such … tolerance has its limits. And memories are long."

"If Miss Guillam or Mr Fisher wish to discuss our activities, they too may feel free to call upon us," Caroline said.

Redfort leaned forwards. "I have the greatest respect for your abilities, Lady Delaney. If she does not get killed, Miss Knox may one day match you for daring. But rest assured, if Miss Guillam or Lord Fisher call upon you, you will both die."

"Is that why you came? To 'warn' us?" Knox asked. She knew he spoke truly. If Margot Guillam visited this house with murder in mind, they likely would die. That likelihood was a certainty, should Fisher come for them.

"No. I came to discuss another matter. You recall Dr Essex, Lady Delaney?"

Caroline's mouth twisted. "I rather doubt those few of us who survived will ever forget Dr Essex."

Knox certainly wouldn't. He had broken two of her ribs. Wilton Hunt's reckless bid to avenge his mother had ended as poorly, and ultimately it had fallen to Caroline to kill the necromancer.

Redfort let out a breath. "I regret that I must report that he … lives."

"Impossible," Caroline said. "I was most thorough in killing him."

"You did indeed slay Dr Essex. However, I recently learned that he was no mere necromancer, that he was … is … in fact, a *Jinn*."

"Explain," was Caroline's curt response.

"Necromancy is the study and manipulation of death. Such a magician can contact the souls of the dead, like a medium, and take control of the dead. As we saw at Dunkellen, Essex was no mere novice, unleashing a sorcerous plague that killed many of the locals, who then rose under his control. Those killed by the *zombis* also rose, joining that army of the dead."

Caroline nodded, her sharp eyes focused on Redfort. For a bishop, he seemed remarkably knowledgeable on this subject, Knox thought.

"You commendably killed Essex, and we believed the threat ended. Those few of us who survived that night. However, two nights ago the dead rose again."

"You know this for a certainty? It was not the undead?" Caroline asked.

He shook his head. "I saw, with my own eyes, the dead rise. I saw them unaffected by wounds that would slay the undead."

"Another necromancer?" Knox suggested.

"So believes Miss Guillam and the rest of the Council. But no." He took a breath. "The necromancer spoke to me through one of the corpses it controlled, confirming its identity."

"It said it was Dr Essex?" Caroline asked.

"It said as much."

"How?" Knox whispered. She still had nightmares from that dreadful day, and all that comforted her was the memory of Essex lying dead on the library floor.

"A master necromancer is capable of transforming an item into a receptacle for their soul. Upon death, their soul is stored within this item. And when some unsuspecting person comes into contact with the receptacle, the necromancer's soul possesses that body, evicting the original soul. Such a necromancer is known as a *Jinn*."

"You're saying Dr Essex is back, despite Lady Delaney killing him," Knox said, trying to get his claims straight in her head.

"I am saying, Miss Knox, that Dr Essex was the latest in what may be a very long line of bodies used by this necromancer – this *Jinn* – to avoid death. The *Jinn* has taken another body and works its foul magic once again. And you know what it is capable of."

"Jesus." Knox finished her brandy, the liquor doing little to chase off the chill in her gut.

Caroline looked sceptical. "And you came here to offer a friendly warning that this necromancer is back?"

"I came for your help in identifying and destroying the foul thing, Lady Delaney."

"As you were quick to remind us, you serve an Elder vampyre who in turn serves one even more powerful. Surely, with your secret society behind you, you can root out and deal with this … *Jinn*?"

"Miss Guillam and the others know a powerful necromancer still serves the demon Keel, but they do not know it is the same one from Dunkellen."

"You keep secrets from your own?" Caroline asked.

There was a hesitation that warned Knox that Redfort was not being entirely forthcoming with them. "I do not know who the *Jinn* now possesses, perhaps one of my allies. I do not know who among them I can trust, and so I am forced to confide in you."

"You expect us to work with you?" Caroline asked with a shake of her head.

"In this one matter, yes. I suggest we each attempt to unmask this *Jinn*'s new identity, and once done, join forces to deal with it once and for all."

"And just how do we do that, since Lady Delaney has killed it once already?" Knox asked.

"We must find and destroy the Soul-Repository. Then when the body dies, the soul will have nowhere to go but Hell," Redfort said.

"And do you know what this Soul-Repository looks like?" Caroline asked.

"No," he admitted. "It could be anything. But he will keep it safe. And he must have a means of ensuring that it will come into contact with someone, or his soul will be trapped within it indefinitely."

"And even if we destroy the Soul-Repository, we must ensure that the necromancer's death either precedes or very quickly follows it, lest it create a replacement receptacle," Caroline said.

Redfort nodded emphatically. "Yes. Indeed. You grasp the difficulties we face."

"Send a card should you learn anything of this *Jinn*'s new identity. We shall do the same. In this single matter, you may consider us allied, Bishop Redfort." Caroline's hard eyes met his as she stood. "But in time we shall have a reckoning."

"In time," Redfort said with a wry smile. He stood too. "A good evening, ladies."

Caroline showed Redfort out herself, perhaps preferring not to expose Ellison to the bishop again.

"Jesus Christ," Knox blasphemed again as Caroline returned to the sitting room, pouring more brandy into their glasses.

"Another who brought back the dead and rose from death himself, but not, I suspect, the one we seek," Caroline said.

"What do you suggest? The *Jinn* could be anyone, man or woman, and their … Soul-Repository could be anything."

"I will write Mr Steiner and see what assistance the Templars might offer," Caroline said.

"Bishop Redfort won't like that. He and the Templars don't exactly get on."

"Redfort's dislikes will cost me no sleep at night."

*

Redfort let himself relax somewhat as his carriage left Lady Delaney's street. All things considered, the meeting had gone well. He had considered calling upon Lord Ashwood – Lucifer – but feared Regent Guillam learning of it. Perhaps there might be a way to engineer a convergence of sorts, to draw the various players together and remove each other from the board in a manner that would not lead back to him?

The necromancer. Lady Delaney. Lord Ashwood. And not forgetting Keel's assorted allies. With some splashes of ink on fine paper, Redfort might bring about some mischief.

*

Amy Newfield climbed the hill occupied by the Necropolis, glad that it had not rained. The weather no longer troubled her, but all the same she had no wish to risk slipping in the mud as she ascended the hill in the darkness. Her eyes saw a little better in the night than they had while she lived, and she had been told her vision would improve further upon her Transition to *Nephilim*. By spring, perhaps.

But that still meant she must survive autumn and winter as the two factions warred over Glasgow. If she could eat the heart of a *Nephilim*, she would Transition then and there, but *Arakiel* had few *Nephilim*, and those he had were seasoned killers. She doubted they would stand by and let her feast.

Newfield navigated a forest of gravestones as she headed towards her destination, a large circular mausoleum secured by an oak door. There was what looked like a keyhole in the wood, however no mundane key would unlock it. She pulled out an iron rod prepared by Miss Quinn and inserted it into the hole, knowing that should anyone attempt to force the door or insert picks into that lock, the Wards prepared by the magician would trigger and alert the denizens below.

The door unlocked, Newfield looked around one last time to ensure she was not followed before entering the Poole Mausoleum. A collection of lanterns and matchboxes lay next to a hatch in the centre. Four plain, stone sarcophagi lay within, Willard Poole the first to be interred, in 1841. Sir Wilbur Poole was the last, interred two months ago. He had been the Council's *Secundus* before Redfort, the city's Lord Provost until he was butchered by Essex's *zombis*. And so ended the Pooles, a family with a long history in the Sooty Feathers.

Four sarcophagi but only three bodies. The night after his death half a century before, the stone lid covering Willard Poole's sarcophagus had been removed and the sealing lead cut open. The body of Sir Wilbur's great-grandfather was removed and taken into the catacombs below. Two days later, Willard Poole had risen as a ghoul. He had become a *Nephilim* of power and influence within the House, guiding his descendants from the shadows.

Newfield had only known him briefly, being among the undead killed at the Dunclutha Moot near Largs. The Poole family – both the living and the undead – might have ended this year, but their mausoleum still served, the hatch in the centre leading down into the catacombs below the Necropolis.

Before Keel's return, entry to the catacombs had been effected through the central tunnel beginning at the sandstone façade just across from the Bridge of Sighs. When the Necropolis had first been constructed in the 1830's, the intention had been to entomb the dead within large burial vaults below the hill, however the then-Regent, Edwards, had decided the catacombs would better serve the undead. Officially the hill had started to collapse in on itself and the vaults filled with water during the tunnelling, however in truth that had been a story concocted by the Sooty Feathers, one of whom had been involved in the Necropolis' excavation and construction.

Entry to the catacombs was to have been controlled by the large gates in the centre of the façade, to protect the dead from the body snatchers pillaging the city's overflowing churchyards. But by then the Anatomy Act had been enacted to provide the medical schools with sufficient cadavers, thus putting the resurrection men out of a job. The gates were now believed to cover nothing more than the central archway, while in truth they opened up to reveal a tunnel leading to a warren of catacombs honeycombing the hill.

Until the war. Now the gates were sealed. George Rannoch's betrayal doubtless encompassed this central Crypt of Fisher's House, but any of Keel's agents watching it would have seen no one enter or leave in weeks. The undead of the House who called the Necropolis their home now solely used the Poole Mausoleum's secret entrance atop the hill. Rannoch had been one of the House's only three Elders, but neither Guillam or Edwards had trusted him; it had been kept from him.

Newfield hoped. Regent Guillam had tasked Miss Quinn to Ward the door as a precaution, and so anyone seeking to invade the Crypt from above would find its undead waiting for them.

She put aside such thoughts as she struck a match and lit one of the lanterns before opening the hatch. She climbed down the ladder leading into the catacombs, the tunnel here kept deliberately narrow to force any invader through a bottleneck. The catacombs connected a series of stone vaults spread throughout the hill, home to many of Glasgow's *Nephilim*. Regent Guillam had dwelt here until her elevation to Regent and *Prima*. Now she lived in the 16th century Dumbreck Castle south of Glasgow, home to the MacInesker family before the construction of Dunkellen House almost a century and a half ago.

Thomas Edwards and other senior *Nephilim* had been granted permission by Lord Fisher to live in the castle upon his descendants moving out, a reward for support of Fisher during the original insurrection against Keel. Not that Edwards would have been aware of the connection between Fisher and the MacIneskers. Newfield recalled her meeting with Fisher, the location made a mystery by the thick curtain covering the carriage windows. Bags had been placed over their heads before leaving the carriage, not removed until their arrival at the door of Fisher's Crypt.

Privately, Newfield wondered if that Crypt lay beneath Dumbreck Castle, though to speculate aloud risked death at Miss Guillam's hands, favoured protégé or not. Scant few undead had met Fisher, and Neil MacInesker remained the only living Sooty Feather to have done so. And only because some measure of familial sentiment remained in the *Dominus Nephilim*.

Some dared to wonder when Lord Fisher would take a direct hand in the war against the demon they still referred to as Erik Keel. The many generations separating

Fisher and his Maker from an original vampyre – a *Grigori* – had made his undead body less 'efficient', requiring vast amounts of blood to maintain his full strength. As such, the Fisher Newfield had met had been a cadaverous figure with stretched, yellowed skin and straggles of white hair.

If the undead beneath the Necropolis had seen such a figure, they would not wager on his chances against Keel's followers, but Guillam had claimed that even in that state he still possessed a strength greater than that of an Elder. And so Fisher dwelt in seclusion with his books and thoughts, drinking enough blood to sustain the necessary strength to defend his station.

With her own Maker being Rannoch, Made by *Arakiel* himself, she knew she would enjoy a much greater efficiency, requiring much less to maintain her full strength. Should she ever become Elder, or perhaps even a *Domina Nephilim*, she suspected she would have no need to hide herself away.

Dangerous thoughts. For now, she was a ghoul still months away from Transition and in the midst of a war that had gutted the once-House of Keel in half a year.

Newfield's lantern chased the shadows back down the tunnel as she walked towards the main vault. Deep enough that there was little danger of the catacombs being compromised by any of the burials, Newfield had been assured that the walls and pillars were sufficient to support the hill covering the tunnels and vaults. Discreet ventilation had been built into the vaults to ensure some movement of air, not that the undead needed to breathe.

She entered the largest vault, her entry drawing several eyes. Candles and lanterns provided some light, enough for the undead present to read, write and otherwise amuse themselves. An adjacent vault contained an area to rest during the day, mostly coffins varying from expensive elm to cheap pine. Those without a coffin mostly rested in long, plain wooden boxes. Very few undead rested easily uncovered, though some were content to lie on blankets in a mimicry of life.

Miss Guillam believed the need to be covered was a memory of sorts passed on from the earliest vampyres, the *Grigori*, and their fear of the sun that had consumed many of them in those first desperate days on earth. Satan had not been cursed as Lucifer, the Lightbringer, lightly.

"Miss Newfield," Fredds said from the shadows. He was the senior-most undead present tonight, though she believed his own Crypt was in the west of the city. Newfield's presence on the Council and position as Miss Guillam's protégé meant most considered her the senior-most ghoul. Those who had been Made before her or had held high station while she was alive might have resented being usurped by a young woman of no great birth or heritage but, if so, they knew better than to vex the Regent with their complaints.

And besides, most had died at Dunclutha or since Transitioned to *Nephilim*.

"Mr Fredds, a good evening to you," she said, aware the other undead present were listening. Intrigue riddled the House, and Miss Guillam had suggested it to be a common undead trait the world over. Always the various Houses jostled and warred for power and wealth against one another, alliances that had lasted for centuries ending abruptly whenever an advantage could be seized.

Within the House, too, the *Nephilim* struggled for position, taking care not to overreach. So long as the plotting did not risk exposing the supernatural to the world at large, or interfered with the House's activities, or drew the ire of an Elder, a blind eye was turned.

I must not just contend with Keel's people but with my own, who may resent my rise or seek to supplant me. Once, she would have sighed. Was it any wonder that despite their seeming immortality, the House counted only two Elders among its numbers.

"Sir Kenneth and Lady Jasper are hosting a ball tomorrow, at their Ingram Street house. The Regent wants you there, to mark who attends. She also wishes to know if Keel sends anyone," Fredds said.

"Lady Jasper has sent me an invitation?" she asked in

surprise. In life, she had dreamed of attending such a ball, to wear a beautiful dress and dance with handsome, charming gentlemen, perhaps even meeting her future husband.

That dream was now being realised in part, it seemed, except that there would be no courtship or marriage; it was just another battlefield in an endless war.

"Per Miss Guillam's instructions. A dress is being prepared for you," Fredds said. "The necessaries will be delivered, and Miss Kerris will help you dress."

Newfield glanced at Ailsa Kerris, not blind to the flash of envy in her eyes. Kerris was *Nephilim*, and one who perhaps would have expected to attend the ball herself, a chance to impress Miss Guillam. Instead, she would help a ghoul attend to the matter. "That would be appreciated."

Chapter Seven

"Mr Hunt," Lady Jasper's butler announced as he led Hunt into the ballroom of Sir Kenneth and Lady Jasper's Ingram Street mansion. Lady Jasper's invitation had been a surprise and a late one at that, arriving an indecent five days before the party. The son and heir to Lord Ashwood, such invitations should have been arriving day and night for Hunt, counted among Glasgow's most eligible bachelors.

Indeed, perhaps such invitations did arrive at Lord Ashwood's West End townhouse, but if so, the father neglected to forward them on to his son. That such an invitation had arrived at Hunt's current abode, Foley's flat on Paisley Road West to the south of the city, made Hunt somewhat suspicious.

The dearth of such invitations had an easy explanation; word had passed down from Miss Guillam that the Sooty Feathers were to leave the Hunts alone; there could not be much left of that secret society after Dunkellen, but the survivors would have acceded to Miss Guillam's order, and the rest of Glasgow society would have interpreted that as a shunning.

Still, some of the young ladies present eyed him curiously while the young men regarded him as a double threat. Ashwood might be a remnant of its former self, an estate in the wild Highlands with a decaying house, but a title was a title, and Hunt was also heir to his late mother's shipping company. With the income from that prosperous company, the title was looking less of a joke than it had for a long time.

Hunt spotted Lady Jasper and walked over to pay his respects. His first invitation in some months, he had dressed his best: black suit complemented with a white neckcloth and light-grey gloves, and a white waistcoat and shirt. Aware that less was more in terms of jewellery, he contented himself with a gold watchchain attached to his pocket watch. A black top hat, now on Lady Jasper's hat rack, and a new pair of thin, enamelled boots completed his ensemble. If Mother was looking down from Heaven, she would have little cause for complaint. "Good evening, Lady Jasper. I am grateful for the invitation."

"Welcome, Mr Hunt. I am sorry Lord Ashwood could not attend." Lady Jasper was a little older than Hunt, maybe twenty-five. He recalled her being keen to establish herself in Glasgow society. "I am sorry for your recent loss, such a tragedy."

His mother. Sir Kenneth's parents had died at Dunkellen too, he and Lady Jasper inheriting this house. Hunt recalled Lady Jasper's thwarted ambition to host such events, to be a central figure in Glasgow society, and the deaths of so many that had allowed her to realise it. "Thank you, Lady Jasper."

"You were most fortunate to not take ill yourself, Mr Hunt." Her eyes searched his face.

Hunt became aware that she was keeping a certain distance from him. He had assumed that the Sooty Feathers were behind his social ostracism, but perhaps those not aligned with that secret society associated him with the 'plague' at Dunkellen, and that was part of the explanation for his barren social calendar of late.

Jagged memories of the dead overrunning well-tended gardens, rooms and halls; of the living being torn apart, of mutilated corpses rising in turn and clawing and biting at him, lunged to the forefront of his mind, unbidden and unwelcome.

"Very fortunate," he managed to say.

Hunt made his way to a side-room dispensing biscuits, sandwiches, coffee, tea, lemonade and wine. He was served a sandwich and a glass of red wine, suppressing the impulse to drink it in one go, to drown those fraught memories. If he could excise them, he would. Wine, whisky, ale and laudanum were the only cures that came to mind, and those he self-administered in liberal amounts, well aware they were a cure with a double edge.

On returning to the ballroom, he observed two young ladies exiting another side room, one Hunt assumed had been set aside for ladies to attend to their appearance, doubtless with looking-glasses and well-stocked with hair pins. Needles and thread too, if Lady Jasper was thorough, to repair any damage dresses sustained during the dancing.

He recognised neither lady, both younger than he, though the older woman chaperoning them looked familiar. Gentlemen made their rounds, inviting ladies to a future dance. Having been largely absent from the social scene for the past two years, Hunt recognised scant few of the younger guests, greatly limiting his choice of dance partners, unless he imposed upon Lady Jasper to introduce him to some of the ladies present.

Or I can loiter by the side and drink her wine.

A discreet glance at his pocket watch revealed the time to be almost half past ten, suggesting that even those who liked to be fashionably late had arrived. A study of the room revealed that Lady Jasper had made the common mistake of inviting too many ladies and too few gentlemen, which would force some of the ladies to dance with one another. That did, at least, mean the lady of the house would be well-motivated to introduce Hunt to some of those ladies to help address the imbalance. Having begun at nine, the ball would likely end just prior to dawn.

His chest tightened on recognising an older man among the guests, Lord Smith, the Lord Commissioner of Justiciary. He had been a family friend until the night he and three others tried to have Hunt Possessed by the demon *Beliel*. Hunt's demonic heritage had delayed the Possession sufficiently for Father and his valet Dash

Singh, along with Bishop Redfort, to arrive and intervene.

Lord Smith, it turned out, had been Possessed that summer by the demon *Asmodiel*. Erik Keel had arranged for three relevant Councillors to die or disappear, resulting in an unsuspecting Council elevating three demons to the vacant seats.

Superintendent Kenmure had been one of the other demons present, really *Maridiel*. The demon *Ifriel* had Possessed Mrs Carlton, though Hunt had been pleased to read of her recent death. A warehouse accident, it seemed.

There had been a number of accidents in recent weeks.

'Lord Smith' caught Hunt's eye and smiled slightly. Hunt waited until the demon had looked away before downing his wine. *Bastard*.

Bishop Redfort, at least, was absent. Hunt was in no mood for his sly insinuations and hypocrisy.

"Why, Mr Hunt, what a pleasant surprise to see you here," a woman said, her accent a blend of Glaswegian and Irish.

He turned to see Kerry Knox, wearing a white dress made from light material, its skirt a few inches off the ground, suggesting its wearer had come prepared to dance. Her silk gloves reached her elbows, and her chestnut hair was raised up, the bangs parted to each side. Makeup had been lightly applied, the light catching the freckles dotting her face.

Surprise held his tongue a moment before he recalled his manners. "Miss Knox, the pleasure is entirely mine. I trust I find you well?"

"Entirely well, Mr Hunt. And you?"

"Well enough, Miss Knox. You are accompanied by Lady Delaney?"

"Indeed. We were surprised to receive an invitation."

"As was I. It seems there is a … hesitation to invite those guests of Lady MacInesker who did not … succumb."

"Lady Delaney had surmised our being overlooked was

due in part to her long absence from society, as well as us being at odds with a particular club," Knox said.

"That, too." A suspicion formed. "A coincidence, then, that the three of us were invited tonight. My invitation arrived with very little notice."

"As did ours. Following which a list anonymously arrived of those guests confirmed to be attending," Knox said.

"Was my name on it?"

A shake of the head. "No, perhaps your RSVP had not yet arrived."

Hunt noted that the current set was nearing an end. "Miss Knox, will you honour me with your hand for a quadrille?"

"I would be delighted to," she replied.

He was out of practice and she was relatively new to dancing, but the quadrille was a common dance – one they walked through without mishap.

*

The months of practice Caroline had insisted upon paid off, Knox was relieved to note, as they danced. She made no missteps, and her dress was just raised enough to avoid the possibility of Mr Hunt stepping on it. During their brief acquaintanceship at Dunkellen, they been on first name terms, but that had been months ago, and she sensed a distance between them.

"How fare Professor Sirk and Mr Foley?" she asked.

"Dr Sirk, now. The university decided his services were no longer required. Mr Foley left Glasgow and has yet to return. Dr Sirk manages the pharmacy in his absence." Hunt's eyes narrowed. "That man Lady Delaney is talking to, Lord Smith, he is a demon."

"She is aware," Knox assured him.

"You both play a dangerous game."

"As you say, Mr Hunt. I had expected you to call upon us. Not immediately," she hastened to add, aware that he had been mourning his mother upon their return from the Dunkellen estate. "But we have crossed swords with the

Sooty Feathers on more than one occasion. And those who employed Dr Essex may decide to remove the last witnesses."

His face had lined since their last meeting at his mother's funeral. "Most of the Sooty Feathers died at Dunkellen. *Arakiel* and his … people are busy trying to kill the rest, those who have not fled. The Black Wing Club is closed, for now. Miss Guillam and *Arakiel* are, I believe, too busy fighting one another to bother with us."

"Another reason I had thought you might visit, to discuss how we could protect the city from this war. People are dying or disappearing."

"Every time I get involved, people I care about die," Hunt said. "George Rannoch killed the Gerrards. I killed him. Dr Essex killed my mother. Lady Delaney killed him."

He should know what Redfort told us. "Dr Essex is not dead."

His eyes, bloodshot and weary, widened. "Lady Delaney was thorough. Essex is dead, may Hell take his soul."

"Hell did not. Bishop Redfort paid us a visit." Knox took a breath and explained – as best she could – how Essex's necromancy had kept his soul on earth, and how he now Possessed another body.

A cold anger simmered in Hunt's eyes. "Who?"

"Redfort did not know. He claims he does not know who he can trust among his own people, which is why he visited us."

Hunt jerked a nod, and with a pang of guilt Knox knew he was back in the war.

*

The dance finished, though Hunt had carried out those last steps absently, reeling from Miss Knox's revelation. *Essex. I believed you dead. My mother's killer.* He knew he would hunt the man … the *thing* down. He could lie to himself and claim he wanted to destroy the necromancer to prevent another Dunkellen, to save people, but he knew it was guilt and vengeance that drove him, that goaded him back into a world he kept trying to leave.

I'm the Devil's son. There is no leaving that world for me.

Hunt forced himself to recall his manners, relaxing his face lest his anger show. "Do you wish a refreshment, or can I escort you back to the side?"

"Lady Delaney has a seat by the side, if you would be so kind as to escort me there?"

"Of course, Miss Knox."

"Mr Hunt, a surprise seeing you here," Lady Delaney said as they joined her.

"The pleasure is mine, Lady Delaney." Hunt, noticing Lord Smith watching them, lowered his voice. "Miss Knox assures me you are aware Lord Smith is a demon. We seem to have caught his attention."

"Yes. As Miss Knox is acquainted with him from Dunkellen, but so few others here tonight are, I asked if he might honour her with a dance," Lady Delaney said.

Hunt stared at her. "You believe that a good idea?"

"Yes, as it happens to be one of mine," she said with that damned unflappability of hers. Miss Knox looked surprised, betraying a slight grimace, but she voiced no objection.

"Miss Knox and I agreed that our being invited here is suspicious," Hunt said.

"Of course. Lord Smith is a follower of *Arakiel*, and there are also Sooty Feathers here," Lady Delaney said. "Looking for potential recruits, I imagine."

"Lady Jasper?" Hunt asked. That would explain the late invitations.

"Sir Kenneth, I suspect. His father was a Sooty Feather, which makes Lord Smith's presence curious. I daresay Sir Kenneth asked his wife to extend us invitations."

"Why?"

"The better question is on behalf of whom. I rather suspect Bishop Redfort's hand is behind our presence here," Lady Delaney said thoughtfully.

"Miss Knox told me about his visit. That he told you Dr Essex is back."

Lady Delaney flicked a displeased look at Miss Knox.

"Did she? It seems Bishop Redfort wishes this necromancer dealt with, and he wishes us to do his dirty work."

"I'll gladly kill this necromancer," Hunt said, taking care not to raise his voice.

"We must find him or her, first, Mr Hunt."

Hunt paused. "He … I mean, it, might be Possessing a woman?"

"This necromancer has been around for a very long time. They might be Possessing anyone," Lady Delaney said.

Lord Smith chose that moment to join them.

*

"Did he say anything of interest?" Caroline asked Knox after 'Lord Smith' had escorted her back from the dancefloor. He had taken a perverse delight in engaging Mr Hunt in conversation, the four of them well aware that *Beliel*, the demon he'd attempted to foist upon Hunt, had been the same demon who had Possessed Sir Andrew Delaney two decades prior. A young Lady Delaney had succeeded in killing the demon Possessing her husband, but not before he had murdered her children.

"Just some veiled threats and a kind offer to spare my life if I betrayed you," Knox said with a forced cheerfulness. Her skin still crawled from his touch, not that he had been inappropriate. Those eyes, though…

"I hope you weren't tempted," Lady Delaney said as she sipped lemonade.

"Told him I'd think about it," Knox lied with a smile. Hunt was watching Lord Smith walk off after reclaiming his glass of wine from a side-table. If looks could kill…

Knox was beginning to regret confiding in Hunt, at least so publicly. His anger was palpable, drawing attention from the other guests.

"Mr Hunt…" Lady Delaney tapped her dance card meaningfully.

He tore his eyes away from the demon and took the hint. "Ah, Lady Delaney, may I have the honour of dancing this set with you?"

"I would be delighted, Mr Hunt," she said with a smile as the other dancers began to take up their positions.

Knox watched.

"The Redova is fun," a woman's voice said.

Knox's heart quickened on seeing who had spoken, and her hand itched to reach for the derringer secured beneath the skirt of her dress. "You."

"Miss South," the young woman named herself as.

"Miss Newfield, is it not?"

"Not tonight. Amelia South when in public. A sixteen-year old newly arrived in the city. Not that I would ever expect to meet any family or old acquaintances in circles such as these," the undead girl said. Her dress was white, the flush to her cheeks telling Knox that the ghoul had 'fed' recently. *Don't want her losing control and attacking the guests.*

Knox fought to compose herself. "Are you enjoying the night? A more sociable occasion than our last encounter," she couldn't resist.

A smile that bared teeth. "Somewhat, though I have not been previously introduced to most of the gentlemen present, and those I am acquainted with have so far failed to extend an invitation to dance."

Meaning those who knew the girl calling herself Miss South knew she was undead and had no wish to dance with her. "Thoughtless of them. Though Lady Jasper has invited fewer gentlemen than ladies."

"Yes, I see some of the other young ladies are dancing together." Marbled eyes met Knox's, followed by a slight smile. "Would you do me the honour of dancing this set with me, Miss Knox?"

Her skin still crawled from dancing with a demon, but she saw the amused challenge in those dead eyes and felt the contrary need to answer it. "It would be my pleasure, Miss South."

"So long as you can refrain from trying to incinerate me with a barrel of whisky and a lantern."

"I will try to restrain my enthusiasm, Miss South." They were the last couple to reach the floor, the ghoul's hands cold. "Will it not vex you, forever looking sixteen?"

"As I am only seventeen now, the discrepancy is unnoticeable. In twenty or thirty years, we can revisit the question."

When my hair's greying and my joints ache, and you look then as you do now. For the first time, Knox caught a glimpse of what drew people to becoming undead, "If either of us live that long."

*

Lady Delaney danced well though with a slowness to her step. Hunt was reminded that she had held him as a babe after his Christening at St Mungo's Cathedral, the honours of which had been performed by a then-Reverend Redfort. Did God care that the Christening had been carried out by a clergyman steeped in immorality? That the child had been sired by the Prince of the Fallen? *Maybe my own sins stand sufficient to damn me.*

"Miss Knox should have told you of Dr Essex in a more appropriate setting," Lady Delaney said.

"I know now, and it is a revelation we must answer."

"We must identify both the body Essex has Possessed, and the object their soul is bound to. There is little to be gained in killing the body they currently Possess only for them to return yet again," Lady Delaney said.

"Do you have any suggestions?"

"None yet. It is a matter best set aside for now and revisited in private."

"As you say, Lady Delaney. Is 'Lord Smith' a matter to be set aside for now?"

She looked to her right, where the grey-haired man sat, holding his left arm. "Do not concern yourself with Lord Smith."

"*Asmodiel*," Hunt corrected.

She looked at him and nodded her thanks.

*

The Redova ended, the dancers returning to the side.

Knox and Newfield offered one another an ironic bow. Caroline and Mr Hunt joined Knox shortly after, surprise showing on their faces upon recognising Knox's erstwhile dance partner.

"What did she want?" Mr Hunt asked.

"To dance," Knox answered.

"She was not too greatly inconvenienced by our last encounter?" Caroline asked.

"She did not appear to be," Knox said.

"'Last encounter'?" Hunt queried.

"She and Roddy McBride caught us examining a cargo of bootlegged whisky some nights ago," Knox said. "We smashed a barrel off the ground and set it alight while making good our escape."

Hunt's eyes widened. "Jesus."

"Lord Smith returns," Caroline murmured.

"Come to ask me for another dance, Lord Smith?" Knox asked, but only because she was certain he hadn't.

"No, I fear this old body is done for tonight," he said with a grimace. "You mortals are so frail. I came to say good night."

"I am sorry to hear that, Lord Smith," Caroline said, making scant effort towards sincerity.

He looked her in the eye. "Shall I pass on your regards to *Beliel*?"

*

Hunt watched Lady Delaney's face pale, a mask subsuming any expression. She managed a smile. "A kind offer."

His heart clenched as Smith looked at him, knowing that the demon considered revealing Hunt's own secret. But it evidently thought better of it and walked stiffly away.

"With luck, God will strike that bastard down," Hunt muttered.

Lady Delaney's smile, if anything, grew colder as she kept her eyes fixed on Lord Smith. "God's proven

Himself unreliable in these matters, so we decided to show Him how it's done."

A clatter and exclamation of voices caught Hunt's attention, and he looked to see Lord Smith fall to the ground. Lady Delaney hurried over, an expression of concern painted on her face.

Hunt followed, Lady Delaney the first to kneel next to the fallen Lord Smith, his face turning purple. "By all means, *Asmodiel*, give *Beliel* my regards. And may you both burn in Hell forever," he heard her tell him quietly.

"How?" Hunt whispered.

"Poison in his wine, while he danced with Miss Knox," she replied, even quieter.

"Well done. But *Arakiel* may bring him back."

"Perhaps. But not as a High Court judge, I think."

*

Knox watched the commotion as men and women gathered next to the fallen Lord Smith. She looked up to see Amy Newfield watching her, the ghoul subtly raising an untouched glass of wine in salute.

Caroline and Mr Hunt rejoined her. "Time we were leaving, I suspect this party is over," Caroline said.

"Poor Lady Jasper, she did so want tonight to be a great success," Hunt said.

"Poor us," Knox said. "First Dunkellen and now this, no one will ever invite us to anything again."

He smiled at her jest. "I will call upon you and Lady Delaney soon, if that is agreeable?"

"It is," Lady Delaney said. "Bring Charles Sirk."

He bowed. "Lady Delaney; Miss Knox. A good evening to you." Though by now it was after midnight.

"Mr Hunt," Knox called out as he turned to leave.

"Miss Knox?"

"If we are to be working together, you may call me Kerry again, in private."

He managed a smile. "Wilton, then. Or–"

She smiled back. "Or Wil, if I prefer."

Chapter Eight

Hunt let out a breath as the front door opened, surprised to see it answered by his father's valet rather than the butler. "Singh! What happened to Smith?" The aging butler being no relation, he assumed, of the now late Lord Smith.

"Now employed by another on a part-time basis, Mr Hunt, owing to his age." Dash Singh was in his forties, dressed impeccably in a dark suit with a blue turban atop his head, his black beard immaculate. "I now attend to his duties." He stepped aside to let Hunt in.

"You've been well?" Hunt asked.

"Very well, Mr Hunt. Thank you for asking." He was properly deferential, but both knew that while Dash Singh was valet to Lord Ashwood, his true master was the archangel, *Mikiel*. Singh was, in truth, a *Seraphim*: an angel who perished fighting Lucifer's army, slain by Lucifer himself. Having 'died', he was unable to remain in Heaven, instead bound to Earth. When he died, his 'soul' lingered in Purgatory until it was reborn. For thousands of years, such had been Singh's fate. Or as he was truly named, *Kariel*.

Dash Singh might serve Lord Ashwood, but *Kariel* watched on behalf of the Archangel *Mikiel*, ready to send the Devil back to Hell should that be required. Hunt knew *Kariel*'s remit also ran to watching him, Lucifer's son.

If Lady Delaney and Kerry Knox learned *that* secret…

Singh led Hunt to the drawing room, Mother's favourite room. Its windows faced the morning sun, which would illuminate the white walls in spring and summer, but autumn had fallen, and the room had lost its lustre. Mother's books remained in the bookcases though the bowls lay empty of fruit and flowers. Hunt wondered if Lucifer had kept Mother's copy of *Paradise Lost*, one of her favourites. One couldn't help but admire a woman who favoured that particular book while married to the Devil.

"Mr Hunt, my Lord," Singh announced.

"Thank you, Singh." He sat on the three-seater couch in the centre of the room. Lewis Hunt. Lord Ashwood. Lucifer.

Father.

"*Kariel* may wish to stay for this conversation," Hunt said.

"I assume you are not looking for him to recommend a valet?" Lucifer asked.

"I am not." Hunt forced himself to look at that face with features so similar to his own, their pale blue eyes a match. In truth, they were Lewis Hunt's eyes, the man whose body Lucifer Possessed; in fairness to Lucifer, being Summoned from Hell into that body had been no fault of his. Almost two centuries earlier, Sir Geoffrey Hunt had brought an army to Loch Aline, using the Jacobite loyalties and pagan beliefs of the native Kail'ans as excuse to seize the land with fire and sword.

A surviving son of the Kail'an chief had anglicised his family name from mac Kail'an – son of Kail'an – to McKellen; a woman of his line married an unsuspecting Hunt and gave birth to Lewis Hunt.

Years later during a bad storm, the Ardtornish Point lighthouse's beacon had been extinguished and a false light lit to lure a ship belonging to the Browning Shipping Company onto rocks. Lewis Hunt's older uncle and cousins had perished, leaving Lewis the last of the family, save for his uncle, a bachelor.

Edith Browning, a young woman at the time, had also been aboard with her brother Ryan. They survived, and had allied with Lewis Hunt to investigate the wrecking, only to fall into the hands of the Kail'ans.

The druids had Summoned what they thought was the Celtic god Lugh into Lewis Hunt, using Ryan Browning as a sacrifice on the orders of Sir Hector McKellen, the Kail'an chief. Lewis' mother had been a cousin of Sir Hector's, conspiring in the drowning of her husband and faking her own death years earlier. She had returned, eager to offer up her son to become Lugh's vessel. Believing they had brought back a god, clothed in the flesh of the last son of the hated Hunts, the Kail'ans had not been pleased when Sir Hector's son Hamish – studying Law in Glasgow, and a Sooty Feather – had revealed the truth that their 'god' was in truth a demon.

Lucifer, in fact.

The younger McKellen had stormed away, angry recrimination leading the present Kail'ans to turn on one another. Only Hamish McKellen, Edith Browning and the Lucifer-Possessed Lewis Hunt survived the bloody ritual and its aftermath.

In time, Miss Edith Browning had become Mrs Edith Hunt and later Lady Ashwood. He still wondered why his mother had married *the Devil*, but so far as he had known, it had been a happy marriage. 'Lewis Hunt' had concentrated on his Law career while Edith managed her family's shipping company without spousal interference.

Hunt wondered how much of him came from Edith, Lewis, or Lucifer. How much of him was human, and how much demon. He could break a *Nephilim*'s Mesmer, having done so twice to recover memories the undead had wanted suppressed. And he had Unveiled, giving him the required ice-cold focus to shoot a shocked George Rannoch in the chest and head.

"You're keeping my valet from his duties," Lucifer said dryly. "While I am pleased to see you again, my son, I assume there was a purpose to this visit. Particularly given your choice to return to Mr Foley's flat rather than here, your home."

He took a breath. "I met with Lady Delaney and Miss Knox at Lady Jasper's ball last night. Our mutual presence was no coincidence, I believe, but rather arranged by Bishop Redfort."

"To what purpose, Wilton?" Blue eyes narrowed.

"Were you in any danger? I have made it *clear* to both Miss Guillan and *Arakiel* that any further attempts to involve us in their dispute will be answered."

"I was in no danger. Lord Smith, however, died."

Lucifer smiled. "Lord Smith died, in truth, some months ago when he was Possessed. I am pleased, however, that *Asmodiel* has been returned to Hell. Lady Delaney's work?"

"She poisoned his wine while he danced with Miss Knox," Hunt said. "Something for you … for us, to bear in mind should she discover who you are."

"Bishop Redfort arranged for Lady Delaney to be there so that she might remove one of *Arakiel*'s demons. That does not explain your presence, Wilton."

"Miss Knox told me that Redfort paid them a visit." He paused. "The necromancer responsible for Mother's death is not as dead as we believed."

Lucifer tilted his head. "Lady Delaney was most thorough in killing Essex. I examined the body myself."

"The necromancer spoke to Redfort through a *zombi* some days ago, its words confirming it to be the same one who had been Dr Essex," Hunt said, wondering if he was doing the right thing.

Lucifer said nothing, merely looking at his son.

Singh spoke. "A *Jinn*. We knew the necromancer was powerful, to raise so many *zombis* as it did, first with the plague and then raising those killed after. But if it is a *Jinn*, then who can say how old it is?"

"Khotep." The word was almost a growl from Lucifer's lips.

Singh cast him a sceptical eye. "There have been other *Jinn*."

"Fewer than you think. I suspect most are simply him, in a new body."

"Who is Khotep?" Hunt asked.

"A magician from Arabia," Lucifer said. "He lived around the time of the Fall, a young apprentice at the time, his mistress the queen of vast tracts of land. Much of which was seized by my fellow *Grigori*."

"Not you?" Hunt asked acidly.

"As the leader of the failed rebellion, I was not held in the highest regard by the others. My earthly kingdom was by necessity some ways distant from the others. Which we can discuss another time. This queen opposed the *Grigori*, just as the *Grigori* generally opposed one another. Wars were fought."

"She won or lost?" Hunt asked, wishing to move Lucifer's recollections in a more relevant direction.

"She lost most of her lands. However, Khotep delved deeper into the darker magics. One fateful day, as the army of … I cannot recall … a fellow *Grigori*, won the field, slaying this queen and most of her army. Khotep worked a spell, and the dead from both armies rose and attacked the living.

"After that, Khotep held a remnant of his queen's former kingdom, a land that became dark and fearful, ruled by him and his apprentices. His subjects who died became part of his army, sufficient to hold back the living armies of the *Grigori*."

"What happened?"

"Briefly? Once my kindred and I created armies of the undead, Khotep's small kingdom was swept away. He was slain, only to return in a new body and cause trouble on occasion. If there is one thing that unites the Fallen – aside from their antipathy towards me – it is a desire to end Khotep once and for all."

Hunt digested that. "This necromancer is thousands of years old?"

"Indeed. At times he has employed a mortal to ensure that his Soul-Repository comes into contact with a suitable person for him to Possess."

"We must find Khotep and his Soul-Repository," Singh said.

"Yes." The middle-aged man who had looked content sitting in his dead wife's drawing room had been roused to anger, the Devil awoken. "We will do what should have been done so long ago."

"What of *Arakiel*?" Hunt asked. Destroying his

necromancer would shatter any neutrality the demon had extended to the Hunts.

"*Arakiel* let me believe the necromancer who killed Edith was dead. He will rue that deception," Lucifer said quietly.

Hunt glanced at Singh, but the *Seraphim* simply gave a small nod of agreement. "Lady Delaney and Miss Knox are also hunting the necromancer's new identity," he cautioned. "If our paths cross, you should…"

Lucifer's lips twitched. "Mind my manners?"

"Recall that so far as they are aware, you are Lord Ashwood and his valet," Hunt said. "Lady Delaney will kill a demon as soon as look at it."

"I am no demon." Singh looked as though Hunt had just questioned his parentage.

"If she catches you Unveiling, you'll be dead before you can say '*Seraphim*'," Hunt said, in no mood for splitting hairs. "If you're lucky. She gut-shot *Beliel* and set him on fire."

"Worry not, Wilton, we will be discreet," Lucifer said. "But I will not sit by while your mother's killer walks this earth."

*

Magdalene Quinn awoke with a gasp, roughly forcing aside the vestiges of sleep. She had surrounded her flat with a layer of Wards that acted like a spider's web, with herself at the centre. And something had plucked one of the strands.

She rolled and fell out of her bed, landing painfully on the carpeted floor below, ignoring the pain. Her bed was in an alcove, leaving her with no escape should she be attacked while in it, knowing that every second counted if she wished to avoid becoming yet another dead Sooty Feather.

Quinn snatched a locket whose smelted silver had been mixed with a cat's eye and fastened it around her neck with shaking hands. She looked around, the Artificer-forged locket giving her better night sight than she would otherwise enjoy, darkened shapes coming into focus. Her bed was in the kitchen, the smells from her earlier cooking still lingering.

She saw no one, but nonetheless armed herself with the silver-loaded revolver by her bed. *Calming breaths.* She was a magician, the only one to sit on the Council, its *Quinta*. That the demon calling itself Erik Keel had sent someone against her was not a surprise, only that it had taken so long. *I should be insulted.*

If she lived.

Slowly she made her way out of the room she used as both bedroom and kitchen, moving into the hall. Quinn next entered her sitting room, hearing naught but her own breathing, though that meant nothing. Non-breathing undead served Keel, not to mention a necromancer who could send *zombis* after her. The sitting room bay windows were closed, a relief. Had a bird flown too close to the flat and triggered a Ward? Asleep when it had flared a warning, she could not recall which Ward had been disturbed.

She stood in the centre of her sitting room, gun in hand as she looked around, increasingly reassured that she was alone. *Not yet worthy of Keel's attentions, it seems.* Standing in her own home with a gun in hand, feeling increasingly cold, she conceded that she should not rush to attract the demon's attention.

Movement caught her eye. *A rat?* Perhaps. But she had bought charms from the Under-Market to keep pests away. Maybe just her imagination. She took a few steps closer and felt something on the soles of her feet besides carpet. Kneeling, she rubbed a hand across her left foot and raised it, sniffing. Coal. *Coal, on my carpet, but why?*

How… Fear clenched her heart as she realised not just how, but where the intrusion had occurred. *The chimney and fireplace.*

No man, demon or undead could have entered her flat by that method, but there were other threats. Movement caught her eye, and she saw a tiny figure emerge from behind the armchair and rush towards her. There was something in its hand, something long and sharp. A knife.

A puppet. Her enemy had indeed not entered her flat, instead sending a construct under their control down her chimney to murder her. *Bartholomew Ridley, you bastard!* He was not alone of Glasgow's magicians capable of manipulating puppets, but he was the only Puppeteer capable of this, and he was a known agitator.

Quinn's own magic offered no defence against the puppet, save for her Wards alerting her to the intrusion. It was down to her wits, now, and gun.

She was no marksman, and as she fired the first shot, she knew it was a mistake. All it accomplished was for the flash to ruin her artifact-gifted night-sight, the bullet not stopping the puppet even if it struck home. *Think!*

Puppeteers sewed a brain, spine, eyes and ears into their puppets, a distasteful branch of magic. Using animals was permitted, if one wanted an arcane pack of guard dogs that were less useful than real dogs, but using humans was forbidden by the Council, considered too close to necromancy.

That hadn't stopped Ridley – assuming he was the one trying to kill her – from creating a human puppet, sewing a dead child's brain, spine, eyes and ears into a construct of wood and cloth, and giving it a knife. The Puppeteer had full control over the puppet, letting the bastard watch her die without risking his own head.

Anger touched her. Ridley was a knave of the lowest order, and she was damned if she'd die at his hands. She jumped aside, hoping that the flash from the gun had blinded the Puppeteer as well as herself.

"*I still see you,*" Ridley's voice said from the puppet. Quinn said nothing, suspecting it was but a ploy to get her to speak and betray her location.

Her vision cleared in time to see the puppet leap, instinct swinging her arm up to deflect the knife with her gun. It proved a double-edged victory, both gun and knife falling to the floor. Quinn stumbled over a small table, wanting nothing more than to flee her home, but she quashed that impulse, knowing it would lead to her death.

Wood dug into her throat as the puppet tried to choke

her, both hands grabbing and squeezing. Sorcery animated the puppet, she knew, its strength coming from magic. With one hand she tried to fend it off while her other flailed around in search of her gun.

Failing to find it, she grabbed at the puppet with both hands and threw it back, feeling the skin of her neck tear. The puppet had greater strength than her, but its mass was that of its materials, and so it flew backwards. It went for the knife, she for the gun, fire burning across her face as the knife swung up.

Quinn forced back the impulse to fire blindly, instead taking aim at its centre – and pausing a heartbeat – before firing. The gunshot pounded her ears, the flash blinding her, but there was no further attack, no knife stabbing into her guts or legs.

Panting, she stepped back, blinking furiously to restore her sight, the gun re-cocked and ready to fire again. After a moment she could see a small shape lying on the floor, unmoving. Her shot must have struck its spine, magically prepared to allow the magician to manipulate its limbs.

"*Erik Keel will see you dead,*" Ridley said through his crippled puppet.

Quinn swallowed down her disgust, trying to ignore for now the agony that burned her face. "Do you think you will live to see it, Ridley?" She fired again, spreading wood and brains over her floor. *Best to be sure*.

The puppet was as dead as the poor child who had been harvested and blended with it. Ridley was too much a coward to come and attempt in person what his puppet had failed to do, but he was just one of Keel's servants, and Quinn knew better than to assume she was safe. She found matches and lit candles within her flat, grateful for the light despite the horror now visible on the floor.

By rights she should flee the flat but there might be killers waiting, too smart to assume Ridley's success. Instead, she smashed a small bottle on her desk, triggering a mystical alarm that would see her allies arrive soon.

And Ridley?

Dead. As soon as I can arrange it.

Chapter Nine

"Knight-Inquisitor Steiner, welcome." Grandmaster Sir Thomas Maxwell stirred his tea, holding court in the Cross Club's dining room, in London's Temple area.

"Thank you, Grandmaster." Steiner remained standing, cane in hand. Varnished mahogany tables and chairs were spread throughout the room, a cross carved into each. The Order had operated from the shadows ever since the undead had manipulated its downfall on Friday 13th, 1307, on false charges of heresy and witchcraft. Within five years scores of Templars had been burned to death and the Order officially disbanded.

But a remnant of the Order survived and continued its war against the undead, operating anonymously for the most part. This building, the Order's headquarters, was an exception, openly Templar inside. Many relics were proudly displayed, dating from both before and after the Order's official disbandment.

"Be seated," Sir Thomas said.

Steiner obeyed. Portraits of the Order's more notable members lined the walls, along with a few landscapes depicting significant battles.

"Coffee? Tea?" Sir Thomas asked.

"Tea. With a little honey, if they have it."

"They have it," Sir Thomas said. A waiter arrived and silently took the order.

Steiner held his tongue, knowing the Grandmaster of the Templar Order would not be long in getting to business.

Sir Thomas stirred milk into his tea. "You requested an audience."

Once, Steiner would have been received with greater enthusiasm, but his spring offensive against Glasgow's undead had seen every Templar bar himself and Terrance Gray slain. His requests to return to Glasgow with more men – his own men – to free that city from its demons and undead had been refused.

"Yes, Grandmaster. I wish to return to Glasgow."

"You have asked this of me several times." Sir Thomas sipped from his tea. "I have refused you every time. What has changed?"

Steiner pushed across an envelope. "Lady Delaney has been writing to me once a month, to keep the Order appraised of the situation there. This letter, received yesterday, tells that Dr Essex, the necromancer she killed in August, has returned."

"As undead? She should have made a more thorough job killing him. But as undead magicians lose their sorcery, I do not see why this merits your return, Steiner."

"He has not returned as undead." Steiner leaned forwards. "She claims that he now possesses another body."

Sir Thomas looked surprised, then sceptical. "She is certain that it is not just another necromancer? How did she learn of this?"

"She was visited by Bishop Redfort, a known Sooty Feather, who informed her," Steiner said.

"She associates with servants of the undead?" There was distaste in Sir Thomas's voice.

"No, she does not. Which suggests a desperation on Redfort's part in meeting with her. Lady Delaney wrote that Redfort claims he informed her of the necromancer's return owing to not knowing who among his own to trust. Demons infiltrated the highest level of the Sooty Feather Society, and evidently Redfort fears that the necromancer may likewise be among supposed allies."

Sir Thomas watched Steiner shrewdly. "You have your own history with this Redfort, do you not?"

"Yes," Steiner was forced to admit. "But my wish to return to Glasgow is not motivated by revenge."

"No? Ten Templars died under your command there. Captain Barker of the Edinburgh chapterhouse is unhappy at having lost half his men to your failed crusade. He is also not pleased that you have so far failed to return his American, Gray."

Steiner waited until the waiter served his tea and left. "Our losses were high but many undead were destroyed, including an Elder. We slew many of their mortal servants, too, and the demon *Beliel* was returned to Hell. Lady Delaney writes of a war between the Sooty Feathers and the demon, *Arakiel*. Many innocents are being caught in the middle. Now is the time for us to return, while our enemies fight one another. If we wait until one side prevails, it will quickly take full control of the city."

"I am not blind to the opportunity. But our resources are insufficient to answer every opportunity, and so as grandmaster I must decide where best to deploy them." Sir Thomas leaned back. "You were given eleven men in Glasgow. Why should I give you more? Why not send them to Edinburgh to replace their losses? To York, where magicians work their witchcraft? To Brighton, where the undead prey on unsuspecting visitors? In London alone, I could have ten times the soldiers I have, and still struggle to cleanse every borough of evil."

Steiner acknowledged Sir Thomas's words with a nod. "Indeed, Grandmaster. Many worthy crusades. Opportunities. But opportunities that can wait. York has a chapterhouse who can watch and take action. Edinburgh has eleven of our brothers remaining to keep vigil, their prior excellent work having kept the city mostly cleansed of the undead."

He took a breath, knowing the fate of a city rested on his next words. "Glasgow has no chapter, no Templars, only two women, one middle-aged and the other barely trained. There are demons and undead in the city. It took humanity thousands of years to send the *Grigori* to Hell; would you see one return? A *Dominus Nephilim* is abomination enough, but for one of the Fallen to reclaim its cast-out flesh?"

"Your demon would need an army to overcome this Fisher," Sir Thomas said.

"An army of the dead? Recall Lady Delaney's report on the events at the Dunkellen estate, where this necromancer unleashed an unholy plague to wipe out a village, who then rose to slay the living, who then rose in turn. Imagine, if you can, such necromancy unleashed in the heart of Glasgow itself… Necromancy, worked by a magician who has defied death for who can say how long. Even few among the undead will tolerate such a creature. Even for the damned, some sins are … too great."

Sir Thomas pursed his lips. "As always, Steiner, you speak well. I am not yet convinced to risk the scant soldiers we can muster. Continue your correspondence with this Lady Delaney and keep me informed."

"But–"

Sir Thomas raised a hand. "Those are my orders, Knight-Inquisitor."

Steiner had no choice but to bow his head. "As you command, Grandmaster."

"*Deus Vult*," Sir Thomas said. *God wills it.*

"*Deus Vult*," Steiner dutifully repeated. He finished his tea and left.

Terrance Gray was waiting outside – a black American, the son of freed slaves in Virginia, and thus hard to miss. He alone had survived of the eleven Templars sent by the Edinburgh chapterhouse to assist Steiner's Glasgow mission. Cool under pressure and an excellent shot with a rifle, Steiner had delayed returning him to Edinburgh. Aware of Steiner's intention to return to Glasgow, the American marksman had been content to stay in London, eager to be part of the force sent back to that troubled city. Steiner did not know what had brought Gray across the Atlantic to join the Templars and had not asked.

"Are we bound for King's Cross Station?" Gray asked in his distinctive drawl.

"We are," Steiner affirmed.

Gray looked surprised. "You persuaded the grandmaster? I'm impressed, Mr Steiner."

"I did not," Steiner said. "But we are going anyway."

"To Glasgow?"

"To Glasgow, Mr Gray."

"*Deus Vult*, Knight-Inquisitor."

Steiner nodded absently, his thoughts already turning to the battle waiting in the north. *God wills it.*

*

"What brings you here, Redfort?" Roddy McBride asked, his insolent manner putting Redfort's back up. He had gone to Walker's Bar to meet the man, though the bar's namesake and former owner had been shot dead by the late Lady Ashwood in the Highlands. McBride's confrontation with Lucifer had left the man shaken and quietly accepting of Regent Guillam's order to leave the surviving Hunts alone.

Fighting the urge to simply turn around and leave, Redfort threw him a hard smile. "That would be 'your Grace' to you, McBride."

The muscular, fleshy faced patriarch of the McBrides looked unimpressed, holding court at a table to the rear of the taproom. "We both sit on the Council, Redfort. Save your pious bullshit for those who don't know you like I do, you hypocritical bastard."

Ah, a lesson is required. Not unexpected, the preparations already complete. "Address me with such disrespect again, McBride, and you will swiftly regret it."

The cold, bloodshot eyes that regarded Redfort gave him the impression that his threat had failed to impress and that his prepared lesson was indeed required. "What are you going to do, pray I get the shits?"

It seemed to be common knowledge among the Council that Redfort had given the minister most likely to become the next bishop a mild poison to ensure he was too indisposed – not to mention incontinent – to conduct the last bishop's funeral, allowing Redfort to step in and impress the other reverends with an 'impromptu' speech. *So long as it is not common knowledge that I created the vacancy in the first place.*

He placed a small bottle on the stained and scarred table. “I understand you dined on ham for your supper. I do hope it was not undercooked, or I will have no *need* to offer a prayer regarding your digestive health.” He smiled at the expression on McBride’s face.

“You fucking poisoned me?”

“Bishops do not poison people, Mr McBride. Whatever could have given you that idea?”

“What is in that bottle?” McBride asked suspiciously, a hand resting nervously on his gut.

“Why, just a tonic to aid your digestion,” Redfort said innocently. In truth, it was water flavoured with several foul-tasting ingredients and some green colouring.

McBride wasted no time in drinking it down, grimacing at the taste. “That had better work, or my men will gut you,” he said ominously. In truth, Redfort had dispatched an agent to watch the McBride household to learn what they had dined on, anticipating this meeting and that McBride might be in need of being slapped down. With Jones dead, Redfort no longer had anyone capable of infiltrating a kitchen with poison.

He sat across from McBride, uninvited. The McBride patriarch kept a hand on his gut, looking a bit pale. As he had not been poisoned, Redfort knew any symptoms were down to the ale the man had drunk, and his imagination running riot.

“Why are you here?” McBride’s glower would give most other men motivation to leave the city as fast as a carriage or train could take them, but they both knew beings worse than the pair of them combined would not react well to one outright murdering the other.

“To do you a favour, though I cannot think why I should be so minded after such a welcome,” Redfort said with a feigned wounded sigh.

“Your Christian duty?” McBride suggested with a sneer.

Redfort ignored that. “I understand the death of your brother, Edward, remains unanswered. I would see your thirst for vengeance quenched.”

An old anger awoke in those cold eyes. "Charles Sirk is too close to that bastard Hunt, otherwise I'd have left him filleted on the street. But you know as well as I, we are to do nothing that might involve the Devil's fucking son in our business." *And thus, the Devil Himself.* Redfort was well aware.

"I speak not of Dr Sirk, but of Mr Thomas Foley."

McBride's frowned. "Foley? I gut-shot that bastard. Twice. He died slow and bad." That last was spoken with relish.

Redfort assumed a look of surprise. "Did no one think to tell you? Mr Foley was alive and well, last I saw of him."

"Last you – when…?" McBride's mouth remained open. Not unsurprising; for over two months he had believed one of his brother's suspected killers was dead.

"At Dunkellen. We fought *zombis* together. He survived, though he did not return to Glasgow." Redfort raised an eyebrow. "For a man who had been shot twice in the belly mere days before, he appeared to be in uncommonly good health."

McBride's breathing grew heavy. "How? I shot him! Twice!"

Redfort was curious about that too. "The fresh country air perhaps? They also say bathing in the sea can be most conducive towards good health."

McBride leaned forwards with an alarming speed. "Joke with me again, and we'll see if *you* can survive two bullets to the gut."

Redfort decided to put that threat down to McBride being understandably upset. "Do you forget that you left the dying Mr Foley in the company of Lucifer? Who can say what dark magic the Lord of Hell worked to save his son's dear friend?"

A ragged breath. "Maybe. Where is Foley now?"

"I cannot say," Redfort answered honestly.

"I will pay for that man's location," McBride said quietly. "Or kill for it."

Now to set McBride on his path. Redfort was playing a

dangerous game, but a necessary one. "I do not know, but I know who likely does."

"Who?"

"Wilton Hunt. He knows, I have little doubt."

"We can't fucking ask him, can we, or Guillam will rip our heads from our shoulders, and then his *fucking daddy* will roast us over a spit in Hell," McBride snarled.

"There are ways of asking, and ways of asking," Redfort said. He took a breath. "Here is what I suggest…"

Chapter Ten

Hunt tasted blood. Ignoring the ache in his jaw, he raised his guard in anticipation of a follow-up blow. A jeer sounded from the crowd as he blocked it, his opponent's glove scraping off his own. He countered with a jab, his opponent recoiling before answering with a volley of punches.

Hunt kept his guard up as he stepped back, good footwork keeping him on the move but still balanced. Before his sparring lessons with Smiddy, he'd have been down on his arse by now and not getting up. He gasped as a fist hammered into his lower gut, barely above the belt and leaving him winded. A follow-up punch to the side of his head left him stunned and on the ground, distantly aware of the crowd cheering.

The ones who've bet against me, Hunt thought muzzily as he tried to regain his wits and get back to his feet. He had almost succeeded when his opponent, a thickset bruiser with a flattened nose and scarred ears, punched him again.

Hunt lay on the ground, ears ringing and head pounding. Any disapproval from the crowd was lost on him, though after some time he was aware of them chanting the count that would declare 'Crusher' Jack the winner. Taking place in the large railway bridge vault joined to a South Side pub, with a small, pox-faced rat of a man acting as organiser and referee, Hunt didn't expect much enforcement of the rules.

Minutes before, Hunt would have accepted his defeat graciously, regarding the bout as another lesson. But that last blow awoke a cold anger within him. *He wants to cheat? I can cheat.*

He dug deep inside himself, clawing down to the darkest recesses, to the Wilton Hunt who had shot Elder vampyre George Rannoch in the chest and head with icy precision. To the one who had slain a werewolf with a derringer's single silver bullet near Loch Lomond.

I've done it before. Unveiled before, but never consciously. Never wanted to before, never wanted to have anything to do with his diabolic heritage. But the bastard had knocked him down while he was getting back up.

Had he been sitting in Foley's sitting room, mellowed after a glass or several of whisky, he couldn't have done it. But tonight, he had landed hard on cold stone, the vault filled with jeering onlookers who had mostly bet money on his opponent. His body ached and Jack was laughing, and most of the others were either laughing or shouting at him to stay down.

I'll show them. Show them the Devil inside.

He Unveiled, enveloped by a frigid darkness as old as time. His aches and pains lessened as his senses heightened, and the smiles and laughter died as the crowd sensed his Unveiling, feeling it as something cold and fearsome in their midst. An archangel's wrath once removed, tainted by Hell.

He got back to his feet, Jack making no move to strike him prematurely this time. Hunt's lips curled up in a smile and he invited Jack to attack. Still Unveiled. His father would feel it, he knew, their Unveiling identical and thus distance made no matter. Right now, he cared not, cared only about smashing this cheating brute into the ground.

A few in the crowd managed a feeble cheer, but most remained silent. Not knowing what they felt, unless they were undead, demon, or a Sooty Feather who had been in the presence of the former two during an Unveiling.

Jack's smirking confidence had gone, but he mustered just enough courage for one last attack, charging blindly at Hunt, fists raised and mouth roaring something incoherent.

Fear made him reckless. Hunt watched coldly, waiting. At the last moment he stepped aside and thundered both gloved fists into Jack's head in quick succession, his feet positioned perfectly to ensure each blow was delivered with the fullest power.

Jack sprawled to the ground. A groan issued from the crowd, some urging Jack to get back up. But there was little heat to their voices and not much expectation that Jack would oblige. The crowd, like Jack, had been cowed by Hunt's Unveiling. They could not put a name to what they felt, but feel it they did, the Devil winking at them.

Jack got slowly up after the count to ten had finished, Hunt declared the winner. Hunt's fists had knocked him to the ground, but fear kept him down.

There was little enthusiasm for Hunt's surprise win, save for the few reckless souls who had bet on him, but no one objected either, barring some quiet grumbles. Hunt took the victor's purse and headed to the adjacent tavern, confident no one would challenge him tonight, albeit aware of the stares that followed him.

He sat alone at the bar, a bottle of whisky and a glass before him. A few offered him congratulations, those foolish enough to have wagered on him. Hunt replied as briefly as he could without appearing rude, though after tonight, few would take offence save for the gravest discourtesy.

Fiddles played in the background, the din of music and conversation a welcome distraction as he drank himself insensible. *The Devil's son, I am, and so I proved tonight. Using demonic power to win a fucking fistfight.*

But it had been satisfying, to get back up and knock that cheating bastard down, and to see him stay down. Risky, though. It was possible someone in that bloodthirsty crowd might have recognised an Unveiling when they felt it. Would they bother to report it to either Margot Guillam or *Arakiel*? Would they know it came from him?

He took a long drink of whisky, accustomed now to the way it burned as it slid down his throat. *Fucking undead bastards. Fucking necromancer.*

Whoever the *thing* that had been Dr Essex was now, Hunt would find it and kill it. Permanently, this time. Every night he had nightmares of his mother sacrificing herself to save him from a *zombi*. A corpse Raised by that *fucking bastard!*

Time passed, and he drank. Undisturbed.

Finally done, the pub mostly emptied, Hunt's head spun as he slowly slid off the bar stool. Thanks to tonight's win, more than enough coin remained in his pocket to pay for a cabriolet home.

He staggered out the pub, almost stumbling into a wall as he struggled to navigate the pavement. A cabriolet waited nearby, its horses nickering impatiently. *My lucky night.*

He awoke with a jolt as the cabriolet stopped. "This the place, sir?" the driver called down.

Hunt peered out the window, smelling smoke. Sure enough, they were at the start of Paisley Road West, where Foley's pharmacy and flat were located. "Yes, this is me," he said, hearing the slur in his voice.

He paid the fare and half-fell out the cabriolet, wishing for nothing more than to find his bed and get some sleep. Smoke burned his nostrils, and he blinked to focus enough to recognise wagons from the Glasgow Fire Brigade.

The property on fire was all too familiar; the Foley Pharmacy, flames spreading up to engulf Foley's flat sitting above it. For a long moment he stood there helplessly and watched the fires consume what had been his home for nigh on a year. He felt sick and not because of all the whisky. *God damn it…*

Sobering a little, Hunt suspected the fire to be deliberate, a message from either Keel's faction or Guillam's Sooty Feathers. Not that he knew which, nor was he in a position to respond, regardless of who was responsible. He watched as men from the fire brigade fought to extinguish the flames, having arrived quickly enough to perhaps save the building and those adjacent, but not the interiors.

I'll have to write to Foley. His friend had inherited the pharmacy and flat from his father, not that he'd mourn the pharmacy much, if at all. Sirk had proven more successful in running the business. The flat's loss would be more keenly felt, both Hunt and Foley's belongings destroyed. Though even then, Hunt reckoned that none of the furniture had been bought by Foley. So long as the insurance had been paid, he suspected Foley might even secretly welcome tonight's destruction.

Was this perhaps aimed at me rather than Foley? An attempt to kill him, or a message? Hunt was unsure. *Sirk!* The doctor lived ten minutes away, and so Hunt broke into a staggering run, praying he would not arrive to find Sirk's home also on fire.

*

The door knocker banged several times, killing Knox's yawn just as it started. She and Caroline would normally be abed at this hour – save for those nights they were poisoning demons at balls, stalking the undead, or inconveniencing Sooty Feathers – but two acquaintances had arrived unexpectedly in the evening. After a wash and a quick meal of bread and cheese, those guests now sat in the sitting room, acquainting Knox and Caroline with their news.

"Another of yours, Mr Steiner?" Caroline asked.

Wolfgang Steiner stared at the sitting room door. "No, Lady Delaney. Gray and I came here alone. Absent permission, as I said."

"Colleagues sent to bring you back?" Caroline asked as she rose, taking a revolver from the table.

"Not so soon." He held his own gun, as did the American, Terrance Gray. "Sooty Feathers, perhaps? Undead?"

"Let us see, shall we?" Caroline was first to walk into the hall, killing Steiner's attempt to lead with a look. This was her house, and Steiner acknowledged that with a small nod.

"Are we all prepared to give our guests, whoever they might, an appropriate welcome?" Caroline asked.

They all affirmed that they were, Knox having retrieved a shotgun from the writing bureau, its barrels sawn off and its stock shortened. Both barrels were loaded with a cartridge filled with silver shrapnel.

Steiner frowned at her. "Do you know what you are doing with that, Miss Knox?"

She drew back the right hammer. "Just you look to yourself, Mr Steiner." When he had left the city before, Caroline had just agreed to train her, but that had been half a year ago.

"Miss Knox is a most capable student, Mr Steiner. Rest assured she has seen action." Caroline unlocked the door and rested her hand on the handle. "All the same, Miss Knox, do bear in mind the indiscriminate nature of that weapon."

Meaning don't kill everyone with one blast. "I'll do my best."

Caroline pulled back the revolver's hammer and opened the front door. After a moment she said, "Well, this is certainly a night for reunions." She released her gun's hammer and motioned for the others to likewise lower the weapons and return to the sitting room. "What brings you two here?"

"Let us in, Lady Delaney," Knox heard a familiar voice say as she led Steiner and Gray back into the sitting room, "and we will tell you." Dr Sirk. That likely meant his companion was Wilton Hunt, Knox wondering why that prospect cheered her.

A minute later Caroline escorted Hunt and Sirk into the sitting room, having divested them of hats and outer jackets. Hunt's eyes widened in surprise on recognising Steiner and Gray standing within, then narrowed. They had not parted on good terms; Steiner had shot Amy Newfield, despite her aid in his rescue. They had fought to the top of the Necropolis in time to free Steiner before

Rannoch could have him Possessed by the demon *Beliel*, but not in time to prevent the Summoning of *Arakiel* into another host.

"We are all acquainted, so there is no need for introductions," Caroline said.

Steiner bowed stiffly from the neck. "Good evening, Professor Sirk. Mr Hunt."

"Pleasure to meet you all again," Gray said, an ironic smile playing on his lips.

"Mr Steiner, Mr Gray. A surprise, to be sure," Sirk said as they all shook hands. "And it is Doctor Sirk now."

Anger had glinted in Hunt's eyes, followed by a brief flicker of fear, for some reason. "Mr Gray, the pleasure is mine." He shook the American's hand.

"I trust we can move past the events of our parting?" Steiner said, offering his hand to Hunt.

Hunt hesitated, then shook it. "Of course, Mr Steiner. Not least since you failed to kill Miss Newfield."

A frown touched Steiner's face. "Failed? I shot her in the heart." He looked at Caroline for confirmation and explanation.

"Not quite, it appears," Sirk said.

"I tasked Mr Hunt to arm you with my spare derringer as well as your new cane." Caroline glanced at Hunt. "He forgot to mention that the gun pulled to the left, and so your bullet missed Miss Newfield's heart. The silver was enough to incapacitate her for some time, it appears."

"For the best, since Miss Newfield was an ally who aided us in good faith," Hunt said. His tone was light but failed to mask the anger therein.

"There is nothing to be gained in revisiting the past," said the woman whose life these past twenty years had been dedicated to avenging the past.

"Perhaps I was … hasty in my judgement of Miss Newfield. As you say, she aided us, and as a newly Made ghoul, she offered little threat," Steiner said, in what was as close to an apology as he was likely to manage and offered more to keep the peace than from any genuine remorse, no doubt.

"Let us look to the future," Hunt said, his tone conciliatory.

"Be seated, gentlemen, and tell us what brings you here at this hour," Caroline said, already moving to her drinks cabinet. The new butler, Smith, had been relieved for the evening, as had Ellison.

*

Steiner studied Hunt and Sirk, their arrival a source of ambivalence, half-listening as a not-quite sober Hunt spoke of the Foley Pharmacy burning. Allies were to be welcomed, certainly, and Sirk's eccentric demeanour masked a ruthless and experienced undead hunter. In Edinburgh many years before, the Templar Ben Jefferies had fought alongside Sirk before a demon lured their small group into a trap. A broken Sirk had abandoned the war, fleeing to Glasgow. Jefferies had remained, allying with the newly arrived Templars and all but freeing the city of the undead pestilence. A chapterhouse had been established in that city, and Jefferies inducted into the Order.

Upon learning of Sirk's acquaintanceship with Jefferies from Gray, Steiner had written to Edinburgh requesting more information on the professor. Jefferies had been terse in his reply, perhaps bitter at the loss of so many of his comrades under Steiner's command, but he had mentioned that Sirk had been particularly close to a John Harris. A demon had Possessed Harris and led the amateur undead-hunters into the trap that saw only three survive. Jefferies had emphasised that the loss of Harris had broken Sirk: reading between the lines, Steiner suspected that Sirk and Harris had been closer than friends.

Hunt was the one who concerned him. Aged twenty-four and born to a wealthy Glasgow shipping family – not to mention heir to a barony – his privileged upbringing had not prepared him for the perilous, murky world he blundered into. Yet he had survived a fight where veteran Templars had not. Indeed, Hunt had been the one to kill George Rannoch. Steiner had been too busy duelling a female vampyre to pay much attention to Rannoch's end, but he had felt the creature Unveil, and thus had to grudgingly credit Hunt for aiming true despite that onslaught of fear.

Lady Delaney's report regarding the necromancy at the Dunkellen estate had praised Hunt, Foley and Sirk – and her apprentice, Miss Knox. Lord and Lady Ashwood, Hunt's parents, had acquitted themselves well, though Lady Ashwood had sacrificed herself to save her son. A choice Steiner bitterly wished had been given to him.

Experience, Steiner expected, would temper Hunt, and if he survived long enough, he would lose his absurd sentimentality towards the undead no matter how innocent they had been in life. The undead must be destroyed and demons sent back to Hell. Every last one of them. *God wills it.*

Until then, Hunt would bear watching. His eyes had oldened since the spring, but he was still a young man, given to a young man's impulses and foolishness.

"A regrettable incident, gentlemen," Lady Delaney spoke of the fire, sympathising. "You suspect either the Sooty Feathers or *Arakiel*'s faction were responsible, yes? Understandable, though surprising that they waited so long."

"I was seen in your company when Lord Smith died, returning *Asmodiel* to Hell," Hunt pointed out. "Lord Smith was an old friend of my family's, perhaps *Arakiel* assumed I did the deed? *Asmodiel* served him, after all, and he did try to have me Possessed by *Beliel*."

"Perhaps." Lady Delaney sounded doubtful.

Steiner stirred. "This *Asmodiel* attempted to have you Possessed by *Beliel*?" The vampyre Rannoch had intended such a fate for Steiner, thwarted only by Hunt and Burton's intervention. *Or did this demon perhaps succeed, and* Beliel *now watches us through Hunt's eyes?*

"*Asmodiel*, *Maridiel*, and … *Ifriel*," Hunt said with a shiver. "At Dunkellen the night before the *zombis* attacked, while Possessing Lord Smith, Police Superintendent Kenmure and Mrs Carlton."

Steiner watched Hunt's eyes. "You were most fortunate to escape before they Summoned *Beliel*."

Hunt met that gaze. "As were you, atop the Necropolis, Mr Steiner."

"You saved me that night," Steiner allowed. "Who saved you?"

"My father and his valet, Singh. And Bishop Redfort."

"Redfort?" The corrupt clergyman had proven himself Steiner's nemesis in the spring, and he intended to send him before God's judgement as soon as could be arranged.

"My father gave him little choice. And the 'good' bishop already suspected those three had been Possessed in order to spy on the Council for *Arakiel*," Hunt said.

"You came here to warn us of an attack here," Lady Delaney said, perhaps to prevent tempers flaring.

"In part." Hunt sounded rather furtive. "But also to ask if we might impose upon your hospitality, for the time being."

"While aiding you in your fight against the undead, Sooty Feathers and *Arakiel*," Sirk added.

"Your father lives not too far from here," Miss Knox said.

Hunt was slow to answer. "He does. However … we are not on the best of terms at present."

Despite him saving you from Possession and fighting at your side against the zombis? Steiner's curiosity was aroused, his suspicions not entirely allayed. Perhaps Lady Ashwood's death had come between the two men, or perhaps there was a more sinister explanation?

"You are both welcome to stay here. You both proved your worth in the Necropolis as well as at Dunkellen House," Lady Delaney said.

"We did not anticipate you already having guests. Do you have sufficient rooms?" Sirk asked, giving Steiner and Gray a wry look.

"We shall manage, I think," Lady Delaney said.

Chapter Eleven

There was an air of awkwardness as Hunt sat at Lady Delaney's dining room table, joining Kerry, Sirk, Steiner, Gray and the lady herself. The housemaid Ellison bore a harried expression as she struggled to serve breakfast to so many unexpected guests, and Hunt suspected the cook would have had words to say in the kitchen.

He had been surprised to find his parents' old butler, Smith, now working for Lady Delaney. Grey-haired and stooped, he had perhaps thought to find an easy billet here, serving just two women, but if so, he now found himself in a busier household. Smith showed no signs of being overwhelmed, his eyes alert and taking everything in as he stood discreetly to one side.

He had been standoffish upon being greeted warmly by Hunt, who had known the butler all his life. Perhaps he felt ill-served by the family he had served for three decades, though Hunt had understood the man to be approaching retirement. Perhaps Singh's foreign heritage had offended him, causing him to leave. Or perhaps Lucifer had decided he had no need of a valet and a butler.

Porridge, bread rolls and cold meats were served, along with eggs. Toasted bread and tea arrived shortly after. There was no resumption of the topics discussed the night before, the conversation confined to the trivial.

"Mr Gray and I will reacquaint ourselves with the city," Steiner announced. "Visit old contacts and allies of the Order, those that might remain."

"Yesterday you agreed to join Miss Knox and I for a

game of mixed doubles tennis," Lady Delaney said in mild remonstrance. "One of our regular gentlemen partners cannot attend, but I promised the other that I could provide a replacement."

Steiner hesitated, clearly having forgotten about tennis in his zeal to be about butchery. "My apologies, Lady Delaney. When Glasgow is free from both demon and undead, I shall put myself at your disposal for whatever activities you see fit. I did tell you at the time that I am not skilled at tennis."

"That's why we were so looking forward to seeing you play," Kerry said sweetly, drawing a laugh from Gray.

"I shall hold you to that, Mr Steiner," Lady Delaney said.

"Perhaps Mr Hunt could make himself available?" Sirk suggested with an arched eyebrow.

"Not you, Professor?" Kerry asked.

"Not I, Miss Knox," Sirk said firmly. "And it is 'doctor', as I no longer lecture."

"You no longer get *paid* to lecture, Doctor," Hunt said by way of retaliation for being volunteered for tennis. "Yet still you persist."

"Excellent, Mr Hunt, it is very good of you to help us out," Lady Delaney said, ignoring the minor issue that Hunt had, in fact, made no such agreement.

Seeing as she had given him a bed and food from her larder, a refusal seemed churlish, so he managed a smile. "Say no more about it, Lady Delaney, it would be my honour and pleasure."

Kerry's snort was less than ladylike. "It will be my pleasure to see you thrashed."

"What if we are on the same team, Miss Knox?" Hunt asked. He looked forward to demonstrating his skills, rusty as they were, to the cocky young Irish woman. "I should warn you, my father was a formidable player, and taught me in my youth."

"That will not be the case. In the interests of fairness, we pair youth with experience," Lady Delaney said. "You shall be paired with me, Mr Hunt."

"And who will Miss Knox be paired with?" Hunt asked.

Kerry smiled. "Your father."

Shit.

*

The morning was sunny, at least, easing the autumn chill. Wil wore old sporting clothes that had belonged to the late Sir Andrew Delaney, Knox and Caroline dressed in long white skirts and blouses. Learning that he was to play his father had quietened Wil, the pair estranged indeed given that he was unaware that Lord Ashwood and Lady Delaney maintained contact.

Knox saw that Lord Ashwood and his valet, Singh, were waiting for them at the Hillhead Sporting Club tennis courts. The former's sportswear was impeccably white, a credit to the latter, who was dressed in his customary starched suit and turban. Dark-skinned and black-bearded, Singh had been born in distant India. He gave her a slight nod, an acknowledgement of the bond between the five of them; they had survived the *zombi* horde, fighting side by side.

"Lady Delaney," Lord Ashwood called out on seeing them approach. "A brisk morning."

"Brisk indeed, but a set or two on the court will warm us up, Lord Ashwood." Their weekly bouts on the tennis court helped keep them fit and healthy, be it singles or mixed doubles like today. Caroline was still the more experienced player, but Knox's increased fitness and growing experience had seen her become the older lady's match.

They would face one another again this morning, though Knox fancied that their friendly rivalry paled to that between father and son.

"Wilton, a surprise seeing you here. I understood Lady Delaney planned to introduce me to a German acquaintance," Lord Ashwood said. His hair was dark where Hunt's was auburn, but otherwise they were much alike. “Her note last night suggested as much after I informed her that Mr Kettridge had to pull out at the last minute.”

“Mr Steiner is Swiss,” Caroline corrected. “And he has other business this morning, however I am sure you will meet soon. Mr Hunt kindly agreed to take his place.”

“Father.” Hunt’s tone was neutral. He looked at his father’s valet. “Singh, I hope you’re well?”

“Very well, Mr Hunt,” Singh said. Knox sensed an undercurrent of tension between the three. Still haunted by the ghost of Lady Ashwood?

*

Hunt swatted the ball back across the net, breathing hard. Kerry lunged to intercept, batting it back, long and high. He heard it thud off Lady Delaney’s racquet and saw it fly over the net, his father failing to intercept it.

The game was proving surprisingly balanced, tied at one match each for the moment, with Hunt and Lady Delaney now one set up. Hunt took a vicious pleasure in seeing his father struggling for breath, his will to win hampered by the middle-aged body he Possessed. Kerry was responsible for most of their points, her inexperience countered by youth and fitness. It seemed Kerry and Delaney played at least once a week, either against each other or in mixed doubles.

Lady Delaney spent her energy sparingly, using her greater experience to anticipate where the opposing team would send the ball so that she might position herself to intercept it without undue exertion. Perspiration running down all four faces, Hunt caught Kerry’s insolent grin to her mentor.

Hunt himself was tiring, even with his strength and stamina improved after months of swimming and pugilism. He cared less about answering the challenge in Kerry’s eyes than in beating his father. *In beating the fucking Devil.*

*

Knox lunged, knocking the ball across the net, too low to bat it back as Caroline calmly tipped it over the net with a well-satisfied smile.

"A fine game," Knox said between breaths as she straightened up.

"Or indeed, a fine game, set and match," Caroline said.

"Well-fought and well-won. My congratulations, Wilton. Lady Delaney," Lord Ashwood managed between breaths, as Singh came over with a towel.

"And you, Father. Miss Knox," Wil said, magnanimous in victory, the prick.

"Quite a journey for a game of tennis," Lord Ashwood said to his son.

There was a brief hesitation before Wil answered. "Less than you think. Dr Sirk and I are Lady Delaney's guests for now. Foley's flat and pharmacy were set on fire last night."

Surprise and suspicion cracked Lord Ashwood's urbane mask, momentarily revealing a hardness beneath. Knox might once have been surprised to see it, but no longer.

"An accident?" Ashwood asked.

"Unlikely, though chemicals stored in the pharmacy cellar didn't help." Fear crossed Wil's face. "I may not have been the target. Roddy McBride blames Foley and Sirk for the death of his brother back in the spring. If he's learned Foley … survived his bullets, then this might be him trying to finish the job."

"Or send a message," Singh said. Knox noted that Lord Ashwood did not chastise his valet for speaking out of turn, noting also the speculative look Caroline gave the pair.

"If it was McBride," Lord Ashwood said. He looked as if he might say more but thought better of it.

"I'll write to Foley and let him know. We should make no moves until we learn more." There was a furtiveness to Wil. Father, son and valet knew something they were not sharing with Knox or Caroline.

"Mr Foley seemed in good health at Dunkellen," Caroline said. "Not at all like a man shot."

"It's not relevant to what concerns us," Wil said. "In any case, he is away from the city and given no indication he intends to return any time soon."

Lord Ashwood nodded, a rare agreement between father and son. "Indeed. Has Bishop Redfort offered more news regarding the necromancer we knew as Dr Essex?"

"I see your son has confided in you," Caroline said.

"The necromancer is responsible for the death of my wife. I will see him repaid in full." Lord Ashwood's quiet words sent a shiver through Knox.

Caroline nodded slowly, her eyes fixed on the baron. "I anticipated he might, hence my wish to introduce you to Mr Steiner."

"And just who is Mr Steiner?" Lord Ashwood asked.

"Knight-Inquisitor Wolfgang Steiner, of the Templar Order," Caroline said. "I would invite you to dinner tonight, Lord Ashwood."

"An inquisitor. So, the Templars have sent you a torturer." Distaste showed on Lord Ashwood's face.

"A *Knight*-Inquisitor," Singh corrected. "Meaning he is no stranger to honest battle. My Lord."

Caroline's sudden regard of Singh told Knox she was not alone in her surprise at the valet's knowledge. He seemed to know even more of the Templars than his master.

"Steiner's a fanatic," Wil said. "Uncompromising, sees everything in black and white. After we rescued him from the undead atop the Necropolis, he shot a ghoul allied with us in cold blood. And the Templars did not send him, this time."

There was an odd warning in Wil's voice, and Lord Ashwood's answering nod suggested he was not blind to it. "I would be delighted to attend, Lady Delaney, and meet your Mr Steiner."

"Will you be bringing Mr Singh along, since he seems oddly knowledgeable of the Templars, Lord Ashwood?" Knox asked dryly.

A cold smile. "Singh has chores to attend to."

"Tennis-wear to wash," the valet said with a straight face.

*

Hunt sat at Lady Delaney's writing bureau with pen, ink and paper. A bath had soothed aching limbs, refreshing him. He kept his letter short and to the point, writing about the fire to Foley's property. The pharmacy was a gutted shell thanks to the chemicals stored within, and the flat above was not much better, though the building had survived. No one had died thankfully, and if the police or fire service had found evidence that it had been deliberately started, the malign powers ruling the city kept such findings quiet.

Foley was unlikely to be unduly troubled by the destruction of his property – so long as his insurance was paid. Indeed, he'd likely find freedom in it. For all Hunt knew, Foley was at peace in the north, with no intention of returning to Glasgow. His letter five weeks earlier had said only that he had found those he was looking for and had been welcomed into their group.

Six months ago, we believed ourselves ordinary men.

Hunt re-read the letter, deciding to write of his suspicions that the McBrides were responsible for the arson. He thought of warning Foley that the necromancer from summer had not died, instead moving their soul to another body, but decided his friend had enough problems to contend with. After folding the letter and placing it inside the envelope, he sealed it and addressed it to Mr Thomas Foley, care of the Inverarnan post office.

He met Kerry in the hall, her eyes catching the letter. "Letting Mr Foley know what happened?" she asked.

"As much as I know happened, yes."

"Leave it there," she pointed to a small wicker basket on the hall table, "and Smith will take it to the post office with the rest of the mail."

"Smith, not Ellison?" Surely it was a bit of a walk for the venerable butler.

A shrug. "He insists. Says the exercise and air will do him good."

"Thank you." He paused, recalling that hot, bright afternoon in the Dunkellen estate, when he and Kerry had found that pool and waterfall within the woods. Swimming therein before enjoying a packed luncheon and wine. Being together unchaperoned was cause for ruin.

Unknown to them as they swam naked and carefree, the plague afflicting the villagers of nearby Kaleshaws had reached its terrible conclusion the night before; those walking corpses had besieged the village and killed almost all, their victims rising in turn.

Hunt's memory of their lazy bathing in that pool of water was tainted with the knowledge of what had followed; a day of horror, capped with his mother's death. He had not sought Kerry out in the days and weeks that followed, wanting no part of Lady Delaney's war, wanting to avoid close attachment to Kerry Knox while she walked a path almost certain to end with her dying young.

Kerry watched him. "Good day to you," she said as she turned away.

"Good day."

He placed the envelope in the basket, noticing Smith standing at the kitchen entrance. The butler gave a reserved nod but said nothing, and so Hunt left without a word.

Chapter Twelve

Knox was unused to seeing Lady Delaney's dining table so busy. Indeed, the last time it had come close had been when the Templars Gray, Burton and Carter had visited in April. The rescue of Steiner from the Sooty Feathers had been the pressing topic that night, successfully done but at the cost of Burton and Carter's lives.

Typically of an evening, it was just Knox and Caroline sitting at the long, varnished oak table, congregating at one end. Tonight, they were joined by Lord Ashwood, Wil Hunt, Steiner, Gray and Dr Sirk.

The room's intimate lighting came from two wall-mounted gaslights and three candles on the table. Roast beef and gravy were served, along with potatoes, peas and carrots. Bottles of red and white wine had been opened by Smith. A veritable feast, but given what they fought, the possibility remained that it might well be among their last.

"It's strange to be served by Smith in another house," Wil said to his father when the butler had left the dining room to fetch something.

"Yes," Lord Ashwood said. "Given the additions to this household, I suspect he may decide to start his retirement even earlier than intended."

"I did ask if he wished to, due to the arrival of Messrs Steiner, Gray, Hunt and Dr Sirk," Caroline said. "He declined, assuring me he could manage."

Conversation was confined to the trivial as they ate. Sirk and Gray spoke of Edinburgh and their mutual acquaintance, Ben Jefferies. The two Hunts avoided talking to one another, the younger also avoiding conversation with Steiner. Lord Ashwood did speak with Steiner, and Knox watched as the two men gauged one another.

By the time the plates were all cleared away, Knox's head had been dizzied slightly by the wine.

Caroline leaned back in her seat. "Well, now that we are all fed…" she paused while everyone murmured their thanks. "… We can discuss matters of mutual interest." She glanced at the butler. "Thank you, Smith. That will be all."

He bowed his head slightly. "Lady Delaney."

Knox watched as the butler slowly left the dining room.

"My thanks for your hospitality, Lady Delaney," Lord Ashwood said. "As you've hired my former butler, I may reciprocate by stealing your cook."

"You are all most welcome," Lady Delaney said. "But you did not come here to be fed. We all share a mutual interest in freeing this city from the demons and undead currently plaguing it – so let us discuss how best to attend to our enemies."

*

Steiner watched Lady Delaney as she spoke, satisfied her resolve was as strong as ever. Not for the first time, he wished the grandmaster had sent him north with a dozen Templars. With a score, Glasgow would be cleansed in weeks.

"Agreed, Lady Delaney, so long as our enemies include the necromancer we knew as Dr Essex," Lord Ashwood said. Reflected candlelight shone in his shadowed eyes, a controlled wrath in his voice.

Based on his experiences with Wilton Hunt, Steiner had expected to find Lord Ashwood an older copy of his son; ignorant and lacking in the resolve required by this damned, bloody, endless war.

Instead, he had felt Ashwood's firm grip and seen a hardness in eyes that matched his son's in colour, and instinct warned him that Lord Ashwood was not a man to be taken likely. Verily, the same was true for the son, Steiner grudgingly admitted to himself.

"I remind you, Lord Ashwood, that Dr Essex fell by my hand. And if necessary, I will kill him again. But we must not only find the man but identify whatever unnatural object his soul is bound to, or he shall simply return again and again."

"I am mindful of your role in avenging my late wife," Ashwood said. "And of the challenges we face in sending the necromancer's soul to Hell. But I am not minded to sit and wait for Redfort to slip us whatever scraps of information he sees fit to."

"Bishop Redfort?" Steiner said sharply. That hypocrite of a clergyman had played a role in the slaughter that had seen so many of his men die. "We should be killing him, not relying upon him."

"Rest assured, I harbour no illusions regarding Redfort," Ashwood said in assurance. "But he can be an asset if properly motivated. He did help save Wilton from Possession."

"Was he properly motivated?" Gray asked.

Ashwood's smile was a cold one. "Lady Ashwood held a gun to his throat."

"Maybe this time, we'll try that," Gray said dryly.

Yes, and pull the trigger. "I would see the bishop dead," Steiner said.

"In time, once the necromancer is dealt with," Lady Delaney said. "He *is* the Bishop of Glasgow. Finding him will not present a problem, Mr Steiner."

"We have spoken of this necromancer, but he is not the only threat. What of the undead and their Sooty Feather Society? What of *Arakiel* and its undead?" Steiner demanded.

"We must map out the spheres of influence they each hold, and learn of their weaknesses," Lady Delaney said. "Both sides have hired mercenaries, to say nothing of Making new ghouls. Outnumbered, we must be careful. Manipulate one side into attacking the other, where we can, before falling upon the victor."

"We must take care not to allow one side to prevail over the other," Sirk said.

Gray swallowed some wine. "So, we've got two enemies, but we have to beat them both at the same time?"

Sirk gave him an irritated look. "I am not saying that we must pass up opportunities to strike a blow against either *Arakiel* or Fisher's factions, but we must be vigilant to ensure the other does not fill the gap and so become too strong for us to fight."

"Fisher's faction. What numbers does he command?" Steiner asked.

"Unknown," was Lady Delaney's succinct answer. "Far fewer than he did during your last visit."

"Does the Sooty Feather Society still recruit via the Black Wing Club?" Steiner asked.

"The Black Wing Club has closed its building off Buchanan Street, officially for refurbishments," Hunt said. "As to recruitment, I can't say."

"Though it is still collecting dues from its membership," Ashwood said with a wry smile.

Steiner looked at Lord Ashwood, his suspicions re-awoken. "You are a member?"

"Yes. As is Wilton." He met Steiner's gaze easily. "Many of Glasgow's elite share that distinction. Or did. The past year has not been kind."

"Does Fisher still rule Glasgow through the Council, and through it the Sooty Feather Society?" Steiner asked.

"The Council as it was in the spring and summer is surely all but gone." Ashwood said. "I daresay it has since been reformed. As for the Sooty Feathers itself, the Society is but a shadow of its former self. Some were lost at Dunclutha, and many more at Dunkellen. Some whom I believe are members have since left the city."

Steiner took some measure of satisfaction in hearing that the secret society had suffered. "Who now does Fisher employ to control the city?"

"Roddy McBride's criminal empire appears to work for Fisher, now," Lady Delaney said. "An army of thugs.

Miss Knox and I had an encounter with them some nights past."

"And how many undead?" Steiner asked.

"Unknown," Lady Delaney said. "We can assume both sides are Making ghouls indiscriminately. Bishop Redfort did claim to have destroyed one of *Arakiel*'s Crypts, only for the necromancer to Raise the dead to slay his force."

"And *Arakiel*, who follows him?"

"He wields considerable control over the local constabulary, through the demon-Possessed Superintendent Edwin Kenmure. He *did* have some sway over the High Court, until Lord Smith drank some bad wine, returning the demon Possessing him to Hell," Delaney said.

"Gwendoline Carlton was a third demon," Hunt said quietly. "But she died recently too."

"Killed by Redfort's people," Miss Knox said. "Before the necromancer sent the dead against them."

"Both sides have recruited mercenaries from outside Glasgow," Lady Delaney said.

Steiner considered all he had heard. "Fisher controls much of the criminality while *Arakiel* employs the constabulary."

"Two of *Arakiel*'s three demons are now back in Hell," Lady Delaney said.

"*Asmodiel* and *Ifriel*," Lord Ashwood named them. *Curious that he knows their names.* The elder Hunt knew a lot. Suspiciously so.

"It seems to me, we would do well to send the third demon on his way," Gray said. "And so deprive *Arakiel* of your constabulary."

"That has my vote," Hunt said.

"And mine," Lady Delaney said.

"The demon Possessing Kenmure is called *Maridiel*," Lord Ashwood said.

"We would also have to hurt Fisher's faction, to stop them taking advantage," Miss Knox said quietly. A far cry from the young woman he had unwittingly involved in this world in the spring.

"We could kill some McBrides," Hunt suggested, with an unexpected hardness to his voice.

"Did they also try to have you Possessed with a demon?" Gray asked dryly.

A humourless smile twisted his lips. "In a sense, yes. They took me to a group who tried to Summon Lucifer into me."

"You have acquired an unfortunate habit of vexing those who serve demons," Steiner observed. *As well they failed. Matters are dire enough in this city without the Devil walking amongst us.*

"The McBrides," Hunt repeated, ignoring that observation. "The Council would lose its army of eyes, ears and fists among the underbelly of the city."

"Killing Bishop Redfort would also aid our cause," Steiner said. The corrupt clergyman was responsible for much evil.

"Redfort is, doubtless by now, a senior Sooty Feather Councillor, but he commands no armies," Lady Delaney said. "We require a target whose elimination prevents Fisher from benefiting from our assassination of Superintendent Kenmure … *Maridiel*."

"I have no love for the McBrides, but if you kill Roddy McBride, a brother will simply take over. And if none prove adequate, the eldest surviving will simply be Possessed by a demon loyal to Fisher," Ashwood said.

"Then we kill every McBride," Steiner said. "Redfort too. Every man and woman who serves the Sooty Feathers. And those who serve the demon."

"That is quite the slaughter you have in mind." There was a mild alarm in Sirk's voice. But this was not a war that would be won with compromise.

"The Order did not liberate Edinburgh with timidity or sentiment," Steiner said. "We do not hold what we do of London through weakness or showing mercy to evil."

"The world is not black and white–" Hunt started.

"The world *is* black and white. Good and evil," Steiner interrupted. "And I am here to destroy the evil infecting this city. I will see the enemy's strongholds riven with fire and the gutters choked with their blood. With silver, steel and guns, we will prevail."

"And explosives, if we can find any," Gray said cheerfully.

"Dr Sirk created the explosives we used to destroy the Imperial Mill," Lady Delaney said.

"Nitro-glycerine, only more stable. Less so than dynamite, perhaps, but sufficient," Sirk said with a note of pride.

Steiner bit back hot words born from cold certainty. Explosives would allow him to destroy the infrastructure relied upon by those serving Fisher and Keel, such as McBride's carriages and wagons. These associates of Lady Delaney might lack the necessary commitment to the cause, but it seemed they were not without their uses. *And they will learn what must be done to win.*

Lord Ashwood spoke. "Let us discuss targets. Lady Delaney, have you a map?"

Chapter Thirteen

This return visit to Walker's Bar in the Gorbals, the heart of Roddy McBride's criminal empire, was not one Redfort particularly relished, least of all with his present company. Street toughs discreetly guarding the tavern made a poor job of playing at patrons, with ales barely touched and too-alert eyes watching every arrival.

A wise precaution. McBride's position on the Council might mean he had free rein to expand his enterprises across the city, but Keel's people were not making it easy. McBride was a small fish entering a larger pond, learning that he must grow quickly or be eaten.

Noticing Jimmy Keane turn towards the bar with a want in his eyes, Redfort grabbed his companion's shoulder. "Later. We have business to attend to."

"Aye, your Grace," the dishevelled magician muttered.

"'Sir' will suffice, I would prefer some anonymity, Keane."

Clearly expecting Redfort, the burly thug guarding the office door stood aside to let the two men enter.

Roddy McBride sat behind a scarred oak desk. "Welcome, Bishop."

Redfort ignored the mocking undertone. "Gracious as ever, McBride."

The up-jumped thug's eyes turned to Keane. "And who is this, your new bodyguard and assassin? He's no Sid Jones."

"Nor is he a bodyguard or assassin." Jones' death had proven most inconvenient for Redfort, and he had yet to find a replacement.

"A new secretary?" The insolent glint in his eyes was naked. "Hope you've had him checked, after your last one."

"Mr Keane is not here to take notes, McBride. He is here to deliver you to your sought-after vengeance," Redfort said.

Months-old anger twisted McBride's face. "He knows where Tam-fucking-Foley is?"

"No. But he can lead you to him. Should I so instruct him." *Now, perhaps, you regret taking your earlier tone with me.*

"How? I burned the bastard's flat and pharmacy as you suggested."

"How? Mr Keane is a Diviner. After you burned Hunt out of his abode, I had … an agent … watch him. He is currently a guest of Lady Delaney's. As expected, he wrote a letter to Foley, presumably appraising him as to the recent arson. My agent marked the envelope with a small amount of Keane's blood." Redfort hoped McBride would not question him regarding the 'agent' watching Hunt. That was part of the long game Redfort now found himself playing. *Small steps for now, I tread a perilous path…*

Sure enough, the expression on McBride's brutish face suggested a singular focus on finding Foley, uninterested in the details of how Redfort facilitated it. *Excellent.*

McBride jabbed a finger at Keane. "If your agent saw the envelope was addressed to Foley, then they know the address, so why bother with him?"

"Because," Redfort said slowly, "the address does not lead directly to Foley but to a post office where presumably Foley will collect it from. But regardless of where it goes, Keane can follow the letter to Foley."

McBride's grudging nod and lack of further argument told Redfort his point was well taken. "You've been as good as your word, Bishop."

"A fact I trust you will remember," said Redfort. "Mr Keane will accompany you or whomever you send after Foley."

"My brother Johnny was with me at Loch Aline when I shot Foley. He knows what the bastard looks like, he'll finish the job this time."

"Excellent. You should know, the letter is addressed to the post office in Inverarnan, near Loch Lomond. I'll leave Keane in your care."

"What's his price?" McBride asked bluntly.

"I've already paid his fee, but I daresay he would welcome the run of your bar until your brother is ready to depart," Redfort said. McBride's brother would be well advised to leave soon, before Keane drank the bar dry. "The letter was posted today, and so I anticipate its dispatch north in the next day or two. You should send your men to Inverarnan as soon as possible to precede its arrival. Lest Foley claim the letter and dispose of the envelope before Keane can track him."

McBride squinted at him. "What are *you* wanting in return, Redfort?"

"We'll get to that in time." Redfort ignored the omission of his rank. McBride could be given a pointed lesson in courtesy in due course. "Just recall who let you believe Foley was dead, and who is delivering him to you."

"*If* you deliver him," McBride said. But the seed had been planted. He was a Councillor, one of eight, yet Regent Guillam had not seen fit to tell him Foley still lived. And so he must wonder if he was tolerated solely for his small army of thugs, still regarded as up-jumped scum.

Which of course you are. But useful scum.

*

Canning crouched in the shadows, watching Reginald Fredds swim his lengths. The gentlemen's sporting club was otherwise deserted, the hour late indeed, and the *Nephilim* swimmer showed no signs of fatigue.

Canning's presence here was a response to recent losses incurred by Keel's Council. *Ifriel* had been slain, along with ghouls and a small band of thugs in a warehouse owned by the demon's Vessel.

Asmodiel, Possessing Lord Smith of Glasgow's High Court, had been poisoned at a social event, Lady Delaney the suspected culprit.

Keel as he preferred to go by until he reclaimed his *Nephilim* body, had decided that the loss of two Councillors required an answer.

Maridiel was to attend to Lady Delaney, but Keel had entrusted Canning with delivering a more pointed message to the Sooty Feathers. To Margot Guillam and Niall Fisher. *Do not fuck with us.*

It was a message Canning intended the recipients to receive without ambiguity, the object of that message being Reginald Fredds, *Nephilim* and member of Fisher's Council of Eight. Canning had suggested killing Margot Guillam, Fisher's Regent, but a scornful laugh had relayed Keel's opinion of Canning's chances against her. His pride had been stung, but in recent months he had been guilty of underestimating some opponents, and so prudence suggested he pick a lesser target.

Fredds. Canning supposed he could simply approach the pool and shoot him with silver bullets until he died, but he was minded to use a knife as the instrument of tonight's message. Silver, meaning to handle the blade directly caused him pain, but less than it would cause Fredds if properly wielded.

Which he was resolved to do. What good was immortality if one was killed? George Rannoch had stood in Canning's prison cell and offered him the opportunity to kill across the centuries. Faced with the hangman's noose the following morning, Canning had accepted both the offer and Rannoch's unholy blood, choking to death on the hangman's noose only to arise undead.

Rannoch was dead, but if Keel succeeded in overthrowing Fisher and restoring himself to his *Dominus Nephilim* glory, then Canning would rise with him.

But first, I must kill Fredds.

Finally, the vampyre exited the pool, naked and

dripping wet. Unaffected by the cold, Fredds walked towards the changing room. Canning followed, creeping barefoot across the tiles. Fredds, it seemed, had no qualms about swimming in the dark, and so the gaslights had been left off.

Canning drew his knife and entered the changing room, expecting to confront a surprised and naked Fredds.

Instead, he found the *Nephilim* waiting, revolver in hand and aimed straight at him. "Did you really think me unaware of your presence, of you following me here?" Fredds asked. "Your name?"

"Richard Canning," said he, slightly chagrined at having been spotted.

"An upstart ghoul barely six months old, and you think to defeat me?" The sneer in Fredds' voice was as naked as his body. He pulled the trigger–

The hammer fell on an empty chamber.

Canning opened his left hand, bullets falling to the tiled floor. "I found your gun while you were enjoying your swim." He had *expected* to surprise Fredds but had taken precautions anyway.

Fredds shook off the surprise from his face. "No matter. I'll still kill you."

Months had passed since Canning had killed his first *Nephilim*, the one whose heart he had eaten to Transition from a ghoul. *I cannot even recall his name, now.*

He looked forward to killing this one, too.

Fredds attacked, unarmed though he was, evidently believing Canning was still a ghoul. Canning almost trembled in anticipation at showing Fredds his dreadful error. But carefully. His opponent was no Elder, but Keel believed him not too many years from becoming one.

A chill washed over Canning as Fredds tried to grab his knife-hand, hoping to cow him by Unveiling. Instead, Fredds flinched as silver sliced his forearm open, black blood dripping onto the tiled floor.

Canning skipped back, enjoying the look of pain on Fredds' face, fangs bared as he lunged again. This time it was Canning who Unveiled, timing it just as they clashed to distract Fredds. Long enough for a knife to slash the naked man's abdomen, spilling blood and guts onto the ground.

Not a mortal wound for an undead, but Fredds still screamed, reflexively cradling that dreadful wound. Canning stabbed his knife into his enemy's chest, both of them falling to the bloody floor.

"You're *Nephilim*," Fredds gasped.

Canning rolled to his knees and looked down at the mutilated undead. "Very astute, Mr Fredds." Flashing his own fangs in a grin, he stabbed down again, this time driving the silver knife through Fredds' heart.

A job well done!

Canning collected Fredds' gun and bullets and exited the club back out onto the night streets. With luck, his path would cross that of some unfortunate, and he could feed.

*

Keane sat slumped on the wagon as it left Glasgow, his head pounding from the ale he had drunk the night before. Roddy McBride had let him drink his fill, Keane enjoying the novelty of drinking in a tavern several steps above the drinking dens he frequented these days, Walker's Bar stocking good ale rather than cheap swill watered down. And best of all, it had cost him nothing.

Of course, McBride had kicked him awake early the next morning in the taproom, telling him to get up before leaving him in the care of his younger brother, Johnny.

Two wagons were rumbling north, carrying eight men to Inverarnan, drivers included. Guns and ammunition had been secured in hidden compartments beneath the wagon beds, more than enough, in Keane's opinion, to deal with Tam Foley. Roddy McBride insisted the two shots to the gut he had given to Foley near Loch Aline should have killed him, but he conceded the normal rules clearly no longer applied. Regardless, Johnny McBride was determined to finish the job.

"Can you feel anything?" Johnny McBride asked over the clatter of hooves and squeal of wheels. Aged between thirty and thirty-five, he had dark hair and a moustache.

Keane quested out for the envelope bound for Tam Foley, stained with his own blood to allow him to follow it. Sure enough, he could feel it. "It's behind us, Mr McBride."

Johnny McBride nodded, his jaw clenched and eyes hard. "Good. If Foley thinks to hide in the middle of nowhere, we'll teach him different."

Keane plucked up the courage to ask a question. "Is it true your brother shot him twice?"

McBride spoke quietly. "Aye. Twice in the gut. Death would have been long in coming but come it should have. Maybe Lucifer healed him, or something. But this time, I'll make certain. Cut off his head and burn everything."

"That should do it," Keane acknowledged, feeling the bite of fear on hearing the Devil's name. He had met Wilton Hunt briefly in the spring, nothing about the young man suggesting he was the Devil's son, but nevertheless he was, his friends tainted by association.

No wonder I drink.

Nevertheless, Glasgow and its various monsters would soon be behind them, cobbled streets giving way to rough country roads, lined by trees instead of tenements.

Chapter Fourteen

Police Inspector Grant walked briskly down this well-to-do street in the West End of Glasgow, followed by a sergeant and seven constables, and personally supervised by Superintendent Kenmure. *Number fourteen.* On Kenmure's nod he banged the silver knocker three times, hard. The hour was early, all the better to take the occupants by surprise.

A grey-haired man answered the door, his face showing surprise on seeing so many policemen.

Kenmure spoke. "Police, let us in."

"Of course." The old man stepped aside to let Kenmure inside, and Grant followed with the other officers. He had known two of them for years, but the other six had been on the job only a month. Hard, cruel men brought in by Kenmure, and answering only to him.

Grant had half-expected only the household staff to be up and at their duties, the residents still abed, but to his surprise people were breaking their fast around the dining room table. His stomach grumbled upon smelling eggs and toast and bacon. Porridge had been all he had found time for, rising before dawn in order to help Kenmure execute this raid.

Four men and one woman sat at the table. One man looked to be in his forties, long, grey-speckled hair tied back in a tail, a well-kept moustache and goatee on his face. Instinct warned Grant that this was a dangerous man.

Another man was black, clearly a resident or guest rather than a servant, Grant was astonished to see. That man's eyes flickered to the first, evidently looking to follow his lead. What was an African doing here, guesting in this well-to-do townhouse?

The oldest was in his fifties, grey and gaunt, surprise showing on his face, a forkful of eggs hovering before his open mouth.

The youngest man was maybe in his mid-twenties with reddish-brown hair and cleanshaven. He looked to the lady rather than to the man with the goatee. The lady was maybe between forty and forty-five, her own hair starting to grey. Her seat at the head of the table suggested that the house was hers. Who, then, were these men? None looked to be a son, only one being young enough.

"What brings the constabulary to my house, and at this hour?" the lady asked, irritation in her voice.

"I am Inspector Grant. The reason for our … visit will be explained by Superintendent Kenmure, the senior officer present." Which was handy, since Grant truly had no idea why they were here, or even who these people were. Sergeant McPhail and Constable Bremner had stoic expressions on their faces, but Grant wasn't fooled. Neither were comfortable with this. He had hoped that the secrets and odd policing deployments would die with Superintendent Thatcher, but if anything, matters had got worse. Kenmure's promotion had turned him into a different man. Colder and more distant.

"I'll take it from here, Inspector," Kenmure said. There was an undeniable relish in his voice as he slowly entered the room and surveyed the sitting occupants. The youngest man's expression changed from surprise to fear. There was no fear on the lady's face, just a visceral hatred at odds with her apparent high station.

"Good morning, Lady Delaney. Mr Hunt." Kenmure studied the others sitting at the table. "You must be Dr Sirk. And you, sir, must be *Herr* Steiner."

Lady Delaney's eyes were fixed on the superintendent. "I am surprised that you know who Mr Steiner is."

Kenmure quirked a smile. "You underestimate the … Glasgow Constabulary at your peril, Lady Delaney. I assume the African is one of yours, Steiner?"

"American, actually." The black man spoke for himself, his accent strange. Grant could only take him at his word, having never met an American.

"These are dangerous revolutionaries, Inspector Grant," Kenmure said.

"As you say, sir." He saw nothing to justify such an accusation, just five people enjoying breakfast.

Kenmure was watching him. "You have your doubts, Grant? I admit, they do not look the sort to kill and maim indiscriminately, but Lady Delaney blew up the Imperial Mill in the summer. Along with an older man and a young woman. Speaking of whom, where *is* Miss Knox?"

"Not entertaining guests," Lady Delaney said.

Kenmure was amused rather than angry at her flippant tone. "We'll catch up with her. Won't we, Grant?"

"Aye, sir." Agreement seemed the safest course.

Kenmure didn't miss his reservations. "You want proof, Inspector?" One of Kenmure's own entered the dining room. "Unless I'm mistaken, you're about to see it. Martinson?"

"The cellar, sir." There was satisfaction on the man's brutish face.

"Show Inspector Grant what you've found. I'll be along shortly," Kenmure said.

"Sir, if you'll follow me," Constable Martinson said with just the faintest hint of insolence.

With no choice, Grant followed him. Two more of Kenmure's company entered the kitchen, revolvers in hand. They might be new to the constabulary, but they held the guns with a familiarity that Grant hoped betrayed a military background rather than one more nefarious.

*

"You were warned to stay away, *Maridiel*," Hunt said as the inspector left the dining room, confirming to Steiner that Kenmure was indeed the demon-Possessed policeman.

"Going to run and tell your *father*, Hunt?" Kenmure

asked with a twisted smile. To that, Hunt gave no answer, and Steiner sensed there was something left unspoken between the pair. Kenmure spoke freely in front of the two thuggish constables watching over them with guns ready, and Steiner assumed that they knew who and what they worked for.

"How about we kill you and you can tell *your* father, Lucifer, in Hell?" Gray suggested.

A laugh burst from Kenmure. "Oh, the irony. Eh, Hunt?" Neither chose to explain what he meant. "Where *is* Miss Knox?"

"Visiting family in Ireland," Lady Delaney said. In truth, she had gone out for a walk. If the demon here decided to seize everyone, Steiner was not confident in Miss Knox's ability to rescue them, but God willing she would have the wit to let Lord Ashwood know. Steiner sensed a capability to Hunt's father, a willing ruthlessness to do what was necessary. A kindred spirit, perhaps.

"Ireland. And just how long has Miss Knox helped Irish rebels? How long have you all?"

So that was Kenmure's excuse for this intrusion.

"What now?" Sirk asked.

"Now? After Grant returns, I will have you all detained and taken away."

"On what charges?" Lady Delaney asked.

The demon smiled. "Depending on what Grant finds in your cellar, I think we can manage to find any number of charges for you all. Treason and suchlike."

*

Grant looked around the cellar, too astonished to speak. He had feared Kenmure's visit here was born of excess zeal or madness, but sure enough this discovery justified the morning raid. Rifles and revolvers lay on two tables, along with a lot of ammunition. What looked to be explosives sat stored in boxes next to detonator cord, a homemade look about it. Part of the cellar was clearly used as a shooting range, paper targets pinned against the concrete wall.

Are they planning a damned revolution? He regretted doubting Superintendent Kenmure and was glad he had only done so in the privacy of his head. *I might get a medal for this.*

"Catalogue what's here," he said to Martinson. "After that, gather the guns and ammunition, but leave the explosives well enough alone, understand? God knows how stable it is."

"Yes, sir," Martinson said with his usual air of insolence.

Grant let that pass, too preoccupied with the contents of the cellar. *What is going on here?*

*

Hunt watched as a constable asked Sirk for some basic details such as his name, date of birth, place of birth and address. The two constables who had watched them the whole time seemed content to let this officer do the work. Hunt had half-hoped – or half-feared – that Delaney or Steiner would attempt to overpower the constabulary, but neither had, and the others had followed their lead. Kerry's morning walk had at least allowed her to evade arrest for now, though Hunt wondered what exactly she could do. Not least since Lady Delaney's arsenal had been seized. He regretted declining her invitation, but after drinking so much last night, his belly had craved bacon and toasted bread over fresh air and exercise.

The inspector from earlier entered the dining room. "Have you got his details, Billy?"

"Aye, sir."

"Take him out to the wagon. I'll deal with this gentleman."

Sirk gave Hunt a wry smile as he was led out the door.

"Your name, sir," the inspector asked. Grant, Hunt thought he was called. At least he was civil. Had he been otherwise, Hunt could see himself asking, "*Do you know who my father is?*" and feeling less of himself for not standing on his own two feet. *No, really, Inspector. Do you?*

"Wilton Hunt," he answered, noting Grant's eyes flicker in recognition. He was unlikely to be aligned with the Sooty Feathers, given he worked with *Maridiel*. Perhaps he served Keel through *Maridiel*, and simply recognised the name. If he did serve Keel, then there was a chance he might recall Keel's agreement with Hunt's father to leave the family alone. *Jesus, my only hope is that this man and his demon superior are scared enough of my father that they let me go.*

Though if Delaney or Steiner learned of his heritage, neither Keel's lot nor the Sooty Feathers would need to kill him. That pair would attend to it themselves.

"You're living with Tam Foley," Grant said, which was not what Hunt was expecting.

"Yes. Well, I was living in his flat while he's … away," Hunt said, taken aback.

"He's away?"

"Up north," Hunt said vaguely.

"You're keeping an eye on his pharmacy and flat, then?" Grant asked.

"I was, until they were set on fire the other day," Hunt said.

"What? Set, you say? Not an accident?"

"Foley got on the wrong side of Roddy McBride," Hunt said.

Grant shook his head. "No wonder he's left the city. McBride's a bad bastard."

Hunt recalled Foley mentioning a police friend, the one he had spoken to when Professor Miller was killed by the newly – and briefly – deceased Richard Canning, when Hunt and Foley were searching for Amy Newfield, whose corpse had disappeared on them. Followed by several murders in the vicinity of the Southern Necropolis.

Before we knew about demons and the undead.

"Foley met you some months ago," Hunt guessed carefully. How much did this Grant know?

"Aye, asked about a dead professor and about some girl called Amy Newfield. When next you see him, you can tell him the Newfield girl is safe and well, albeit mixing with bad company." Grant frowned. "Such as Roddy McBride. Is she the reason McBride is hunting Foley?"

"No." Hunt decided for some truth. "McBride believes Foley was involved in the death of Eddie McBride. He wasn't."

Grant whistled. "If I thought McBride held me responsible for the death of his brother, I'd be as far north, south, east or west as I could get. And be keeping my head down the rest of my days."

It was fear of himself, of what he became every full moon, that was responsible for Foley's self-imposed exile rather than fear of McBride, but Hunt just nodded. He wondered if he should be fearful of himself, of what he might become, given his demonic heritage. That was why he had not attempted to court Kerry Knox, despite his attraction to her, why he forced himself not to spend too much time with her. There was risk enough living in the same house as her and Lady Delaney, and it was an arrangement Hunt was resolved to end as soon as practical.

If she learns who my father is. If she learns what I am ... Not that *he* knew what he was. And Lady Delaney would not trouble herself pondering such questions. She would put a bullet in his head and hunt down his father. *Lucifer, King of Hell.*

"Your hands, Mr Hunt," Grant said, and Hunt saw he was holding handcuffs.

Hunt held both hands out and offered no resistance as the policeman fastened them around his wrists and locked them. He had expected to feel more fear, being taken as he was into custody by a demon, yet it was muted. Instead, there was what he might almost call anticipation, one thought rising above the others, to his disquiet: *Do you know who my father is?*

If they didn't, they soon would.

*

"Shit," Knox muttered to herself as she watched her friends being led out of the house one after the other by the constabulary, the men handcuffed. Caroline had been spared that indignity, an act of chivalry her captors might live to regret. Her gut tightened on recognising the policeman in charge; Superintendent Kenmure.

Torture and death were what Caroline and the others could expect to find in a demon's clutches. *I'm still free, I can save them.* But how? She was unarmed save for a silver knife and a derringer, along with whatever bullets lay in her purse. Hunt was the last one led out to the waiting barred wagons, two constables remaining behind to guard the house. *I can forget about getting to Caroline's arsenal.*

Even if she was armed, she did not know where the prisoners were being taken, nor had she the means to follow them.

Lord Ashwood, Hunt's father. She had visited the house after Lady Ashwood's funeral, and it was not too far, close to the Botanical Gardens. Carrying just enough money for a cabriolet, she flagged one down.

*

Singh answered the door, recognition showing in his eyes. "Good morning, Miss Knox."

"Not really, Mr Singh. I need to speak with Lord Ashwood urgently."

"Of course." He stood aside to let her in.

Singh led her through the darkened hall, several portraits watching her passage. He knocked twice on the door before opening it and entering.

"Miss Knox wishes to speak with you, my Lord, on a matter of some urgency, she says."

"Show her in," Knox heard Lord Ashwood say. At least he was up; her working class prejudices had warned her that the baron might still be abed.

Lord Ashwood was standing by the time Knox entered the white-panelled drawing room. "Good morning to you, Miss Knox. I assume this visit concerns my son?"

Straight to it. Good. "That demon copper led an early morning raid on Carol – Lady Delaney's house. Everyone was arrested except me."

Blue eyes narrowed in surprise. "You are sure it was Superintendent Kenmure?"

"Saw him with my own eyes. I was out the house, got back in time to see them lead everyone out in handcuffs."

Lord Ashwood looked past her to Singh. "He was warned. Warned, as was *Arakiel*, and yet they choose to test my patience."

Knox felt a prick of fear at the quiet intensity in Ashwood's voice. She was not sure why two demons would give two shits about warnings from the baron of some Highland estate, but at least he seemed of a mind to act.

"My Lord," Singh said, a warning in his voice. Perhaps reminding Ashwood that what he faced would not be cowed by an angry letter or title.

"What were they arrested for?" he asked.

"I don't know, Lord Ashwood. But Lady Delaney had a small arsenal in her cellar, which will surely give them an excuse."

"We will need to know where they are being taken," Singh said.

"Weapons, too. And perhaps an ally," Lord Ashwood said thoughtfully.

"An ally? Who's going to help us go up against the police?" Knox asked.

Chapter Fifteen

Steiner sat alone in the small cell, empty save for a bent metal bucket no one had bothered to empty. This was not his first time being taken captive in Glasgow, though at least the last time, he and his men had struck several blows against the Sooty Feathers before being undone.

On this occasion, he had accomplished nothing beyond socialising with Lady Delaney and her friends. And if this arrest was spurred by his return to Glasgow, then he had caused Lady Delaney, Dr Sirk and Hunt to suffer, too. And Gray, a brother Templar who loyally followed him.

A key scraped into the lock and turned, the door swinging open. The policeman who had led the raid entered along with two other men.

"Wolfgang Steiner of the Templar Order. I am Superintendent Kenmure."

"Demon."

Neither of Kenmure's companions reacted, both staring balefully at Steiner.

"*Maridiel*," the demon introduced himself as.

"What have you arrested me for?" Not that it mattered.

"Does it matter? You will not see the inside of a court," the demon said.

"You will kill me here, then." If that was his fate, so be it. *Deus Vult*. A small part of him whispered that it would be appreciated if He willed a Templar victory over the hellspawn, but it was not his place to question God or His Plan.

"Not at all. You will be returned to London." *Maridiel*

smiled. "You will even be hailed a hero, having struck several blows against the Sooty Feathers."

Horror gnawed at Steiner. He knew, now, what they intended, the fate he had escaped months before. "Rannoch intended to Possess me with *Beliel*. You intend this also?"

"*Beliel* is busy. However, thanks to Lady Delaney, *Asmodiel* is in need of a new Vessel. He was useful to us as Lord Smith of the High Court, but he will be equally useful to us in the Templar chapterhouse in London."

Steiner felt despair rarely, but today was such a day. If this demon had its way, the demon inside him would be free to spy upon the Templars and work against them. The Order had survived disbandment, exile and mass executions hundreds of years prior, its assets looted. Steiner was alarmed at the possibility that it might not survive the mischief wrought by a demon Possessing his body.

"You have brought your Demonist?" One of the demon's two companions, perhaps. Was one of his associates to be brought in as the Sacrifice?

"What? No, Mr Josiah is not here yet. *Arakiel* keeps him safe, being perhaps the city's last surviving Demonist. My men are about to visit your African, they will pass on your regards." *Maridiel* motioned for the two men to leave, which they did.

"What of the others?" Steiner asked.

"Lady Delaney has inconvenienced us for the last time, as an old acquaintance wishes the pleasure of killing her. Sirk's blood will be fed to our ghouls. Farewell for now, Steiner. I will return soon." The demon left.

Minutes later, Steiner listened grimly to Gray's muffled screams in the adjacent cell. He realised that *Maridiel* had made no mention of Hunt and wondered at the omission. *Intended as Vessel for another demon, or already dead?*

*

Panic almost overwhelmed Hunt as darkness washed over

him and threatened to drown him, as the walls fell in and buried him. Ragged gasps rasped through the silence, coming, he realised, from himself.

Every fear and dread from his time as a prisoner of the Sooty Feathers filled his veins like cold poison, a return to the nightmare. He could hear his heart thumping in his chest so loud and so fast he thought it must burst. For how long he had been locked in here, he couldn't tell, there not even being a window to let in daylight.

Hours. Hunt had fought back the panic, but the slow drag of time had drawn it over him, and he recalled being locked up for days during his time as a prisoner in the spring. *Days…*

He flinched as his own feral voice shrieked out, echoing off the brick walls enclosing him, part of him yearning to bash his head off that wall to find blessed oblivion.

There was another shriek, this time from the iron door as it swung open, lantern light filling the cell, held by a dark silhouette.

Hunt blinked back tears, praying his father had come to deliver him from darkness. *But my father is the darkness…*

No, he was Lucifer, the Lightbringer, and soul be damned or not, Hunt yearned for nothing more than the presence of the man who had raised and protected him.

"My, you can make some noise, Mr Hunt," came the mocking observation as the cell door opened with a rusty howl.

Maridiel. Whatever shame Hunt felt at his loss of control was small compared to the ambivalence twisting him now; relief at seeing light, and fear at what the demon might intend. He *remembered* that dreadfully long moment when the demon had been pulled from Hell and put *inside* him, the feeling of his own soul being evicted.

He had slowed the Possession by Unveiling, evoking his own demonic power. But that had not been enough, and bit by bit *Beliel* had claimed his body. Only the arrival of Father and Bishop Redfort had saved him,

Father's Unveiling joining with his own to cast *Beliel* back to Hell.

Now would be a fine time for Father to come. Hell, even he'd even welcome Redfort's arrival if it saved him from *Maridiel.*

"What do you intend for me? My father assured me he had struck an agreement with *Arakiel.*" *A misunderstanding, this can all be sorted out...*

"They agreed you were not to be harmed. And you have not been, which is more than can be said for Steiner's man."

Maridiel's words belatedly recalled to Hunt that he was not unique in his captivity, feeling a pang of guilt that he had forgotten the others in his own misery. "My associates, what have you done with them?"

"Lady Delaney is locked up but otherwise well. Conducting herself in a considerably more dignified manner than you, I must say. Gray endured the attentions of my men rather well. Insisted he wouldn't talk, not that we asked him any questions. We'll kill him soon, payment for the loss of George Rannoch and his people atop the Necropolis. Dr Sirk is unharmed for now."

"And Steiner?"

"I will pay him another visit and watch as my men amuse themselves while we await Mr Josiah's arrival." There was a shiver of anticipation in the demon's voice. "We'll have him Possessed and sent back to the Templars, there to bring about their ruin."

"*Beliel*, I suppose." Steiner had been the intended Vessel for *Beliel* that night in the Necropolis, until Hunt and his companions had intervened. *A fate both Steiner and I have escaped, though I fear it has found him once again.*

"No, *Beliel* is otherwise occupied and looking forward to a reunion with Delaney. But *Asmodiel* will welcome the opportunity to escape Hell again."

"And me?"

"You'll be my guest a little longer. Once your associates have been attended to, you'll be returned to *Samiel.*"

"Guest?" Panic filled him at the thought of being trapped in here for days, a small sliver of shame that he was more concerned for himself that for his friends who would endure worse than days in captivity.

Darkness swallowed the light as the cell door slammed shut. "Wait!"

*

Gray had fallen silent some time earlier, Steiner hoping that the demon's thugs had stopped short of killing him. Lady Delaney's fate particularly concerned him, Sirk and Hunt's to a lesser degree.

The cell door opened, Steiner blinking as light blinded him.

"Rested, Steiner? I hope so, as you are in for a long night."

Steiner recognised the demon's voice. "Whatever torment you have in mind for me will be fleeting compared to the eternal torment awaiting you upon the death of your Vessel. I will sit at the Lord's table in Heaven while you must endure Hell."

Two of the demon's men entered the cell and began beating Steiner, enough to hurt him without risking death or bodily impairment. *If the means to kill myself presents itself, I must take it.* And pray that the Lord understood and forgave such desperate action. *Better that than to allow my flesh to be corrupted by a demon and used as the instrument of my Order's destruction.*

Blows rained down upon him, bruising ribs and limbs and lacerating skin, his torturers efficient in their craft.

He spat out blood. "I will not talk. Just kill me."

"I have asked you no questions," the demon pointed out as Steiner lay bleeding on the ground. "I told you earlier, we will not kill you. At least, not your body…"

The beating continued, Steiner struggling to protect himself as *Maridiel*'s men did their work. Steiner was a Knight-Inquisitor of the Templar Order. The Knight designation marked him as a leader of men in battle, but his role as inquisitor meant he was no stranger to torture. He had broken a Sooty Feather Councillor during his last visit to Glasgow, the one who had tempted Sir Andrew Delaney to join the Sooty Feather Society, and later betrayed him to Possession by *Beliel*.

An explosion rocked the building, the expected blows failing to land as everything paused.

What tattered remnant of hope remained to Steiner was rekindled. This building was under attack, either by the Sooty Feathers or by Miss Knox and whatever allies she could muster. Regardless, it was an opportunity for escape.

"Get out there and arm yourselves," *Maridiel* ordered.

"What of him?" someone asked.

"Leave him," the demon said. "The Sooty Feathers will either use him as we intended or kill him. He will die soon, regardless."

Perhaps, demon. But Steiner had faced certain death before, and his faith in God had seen him survive. Perhaps the secret was to have nothing to live for, save for doing His Will.

And vengeance.

*

Fear made her nauseous, though she did her best to hide it, not wanting to look weak in front of her allies, two of whom had been enemies until this evening. She had not been happy at delaying the rescue until night, but the nature of two of her companions made it a necessity.

Amy Newfield, she had met thrice before, first when she had assisted in the rescue of Steiner from atop the Necropolis, second when Knox and Caroline had spilled a barrel of bootlegged whisky and set it alight, and third at Lady Jasper's ball. Newfield was a mere ghoul, and Knox had killed vampyres before. Newfield was not the worry.

The undead who led Newfield here tonight *was* a worry. Margot Guillam might look to be a smallish woman in her thirties with auburn hair, but in truth she was an Elder *Nephilim*; very old, very powerful, and she ruled this city in Niall Fisher's name. During the journey to the Necropolis in spring, Tam Foley had spoken of putting two silver bullets into Miss Guillam and achieved little beyond irritating her. A shot to the heart or head would have killed her, but she had cowed Foley, Hunt and Sirk; luckily for them, her visit had been to enlist them to deal with Rannoch, in exchange for the location of Steiner.

Once again, it was necessary to rescue Steiner from those loyal to *Arakiel*, only this time Caroline, Wilton, Sirk and Gray had managed to get themselves arrested alongside him. Wilton's father, Lord Ashwood, had somehow succeeded in persuading the Sooty Feathers to not only meet him, but to reveal which police station the prisoners had been taken to. And then he had convinced Miss Guillam herself to take a hand.

"Why are you both here?" Knox quietly asked Newfield. Caroline and the others had hurt the Sooty Feathers on at least one occasion and surely Miss Guillam would celebrate her death.

"Erik Keel has been controlling the police through *Maridiel* for months, directing them against our interests," Newfield said.

The hesitation before she answered made Knox suspect Newfield was not telling the full truth. "As you say, he's been a pain in your arse for months. Why now? Why not let him kill Lady Delaney, Steiner and the others, and then strike? Not to toot our own horn, but we've also been a pain in your arse. Almost cooked you with McBride's whisky not so long ago, didn't we?"

Anger stirred in the undead's marbled eyes at the mention of the Thistledown encounter. "Tonight's truce was agreed by Miss Guillam and Lord Ashwood. You should ask them." The fearful respect as she named Miss Guillam was expected, but oddly it was there too when she named Lord Ashwood. *Just who is Wilton's father to make deals with vampyres?*

In the summer, Miss Guillam had sent Roddy McBride to the remote Loch Aline area to force Lord and Lady Ashwood to sell their shipping company. That bid had failed, according to Wilton, with McBride losing a man and returning to Glasgow with his tail between his legs. And now Guillam was willing to help Ashwood rescue his son, among others.

"The explosives are ready," Singh called out. "The fuses set."

Knox and Newfield joined their three companions. "Are explosives not a bit much, for a police station and a bunch of coppers?" Knox asked diffidently. She had learned much from Caroline, but here, she sensed, she and Newfield were very much the novices of this little band. Even Singh the valet exuded an air of familiarity with such escapades.

"This is not an official police station. Money stolen from the Heron Crowe Bank allowed *Arakiel* to buy and refit this building with cells," Guillam said.

"What of the constables inside?" Singh asked.

"Thugs hired on by *Maridiel* since summer, wearing the uniform and forming his 'special' unit tasked to deal with gangs. In truth, they target Sooty Feather interests in general, and the only criminals they target are those working for Roderick McBride," Guillam said.

That revelation soothed Knox's doubts, somewhat, that they were not attacking regular constables just doing their job. She had no love for the polis, but neither was she wanting widows and half-orphaned children on her conscience.

"We are clear on our respective duties tonight?" Lord Ashwood asked, a warning in his voice. Knox had to admire his guts, to speak to Miss Guillam so.

"Miss Newfield and I find and deal with *Maridiel*, while you rescue your son and his associates," Guillam said. Her own voice hardened. "We have a truce for tonight, but I strongly suggest you convince your son and Lady Delaney to absent themselves from this city for a time."

"And Mr Steiner?" Ashwood asked, his tone suggesting detached interest rather than any real concern.

"Nothing short of death will end that fanatic's war against us. Ensure your son ends his association with the Templars, or he will likely share their fate, agreement or no agreement, *Lord Ashwood*."

There was a notable chill between Ashwood and Guillam, the former showing no fear of the latter. "Understood, Miss Guillam. Understand, however, that if my son is harmed by you or yours, I will go to war against you."

"Your last war did not end in your favour," Miss Guillam noted. Knox hadn't known Lord Ashwood had served in the army or navy, but then, she knew little about the family.

He gave her a wry smile. "The war you refer to did not end well for me, but that was not my last war."

"How then did your last one end?" Miss Guillam asked.

"Not in my favour." *What the hell does that mean? What war does he refer to?*

"The explosives? The fuses set?" Singh interrupted, his questions rhetorical. "Miss Guillam, do you no longer intend to enter beforehand?"

"Ready your weapons," Miss Guillam advised. She walked towards the police station entrance with Amy Newfield.

Lord Ashwood fixed Knox with a look. "Set aside mercy from your heart, Miss Knox, or it will see you dead. A cold, ruthless certainty, that is what you will need this night, if you wish to rescue our friends. And other nights, if you must stand by Lady Delaney's side."

She swallowed. "I'll do my bit, Lord Ashwood."

"Your talent for recruiting others to your cause remains undiminished," Singh said with an oddly sour note.

*

Newfield followed Miss Guillam into the police station, a sandstone building bought over by Keel. Some, Roddy

McBride most vocally of all, had questioned Miss Guillam's hesitance to attack this place, given that it was from here that Keel's people had caused much trouble for the Sooty Feathers in general, and McBride's criminal empire in particular.

There were whispers that Regent Guillam feared to attack it, that the Sooty Feathers lacked the power to remove this rook from the board. Newfield suspected that it was too public a target, that either the Regent or Lord Fisher knew to attack the police in such a manner risked the public learning of the secret society and the undead ruling Glasgow.

The capture of Lucifer's son gave Miss Guillam the reason she needed to take such a risk. It was a mystery why Lord Fisher was so adamant that Lucifer be placated, given the Devil had no army or intention to take over the city. Miss Guillam had hinted that Fisher's true interest was in the young man, Wilton Hunt, though the reason for such attention remained a mystery.

Miss Guillam approached the desk where a policeman sat. Unlike those Newfield had known and been wary of all her life, this one was unshaven, his uniform slovenly. *One of the demon's.*

"Aye?" he asked, not bothering to look up from his newspaper.

Anticipation tingled within Newfield as Miss Guillam addressed the poor wretch. They had not had the opportunity to feed before coming here. The promise of blood tugged at Newfield's self-control. "Good evening. I am here to see Superintendent Kenmure," Miss Guillam said.

The man looked up, a mocking glint in his eye. "Are you, eh? And who should I tell him is here?"

"Miss Margot Guillam."

Newfield watched the policeman's face as that name finally registered, as his mouth opened.

Miss Guillam reached over and yanked him towards her, her head ducking down to his throat, a spray of blood following thereafter.

Chapter Sixteen

Steiner's eyes darted around as he was dragged from the cell out into a bare brick and concrete corridor. "Remiss of you, to not establish an underground escape, demon."

"My men will deal with the intruders," *Maridiel* said. Steiner noted that the demon made no mention of taking a personal hand in the battle.

He was taken into a large cell intended to house a group where he was relieved to see Lady Delaney, Gray, Hunt and Dr Sirk. All appeared well, though Gray sat slumped on the ground, his face bruised and bloody. God knew what injuries were hidden beneath his torn and filthy clothing.

The cell door was shut and locked by *Maridiel*, who left without a word.

"Lady Delaney, you are well?" Steiner asked. She looked unharmed, at least.

"As well as can be expected after a day in such a place, with only a little water to sustain me," she said. "Otherwise, all I had to endure was the demon's mockery."

"I was ignored altogether, although upon seeing the attentions given to Mr Gray, I shall offer no complaint," Sirk said. Hunt said nothing though he too appeared unharmed. *The demon saved its ire for the Templars, it seems.*

Steiner knelt next to Gray. "How fare you, brother?"

Gray managed a smile. "Had the bastards on the ropes, sir. I'll be fine with a bit of rest. Assuming we get out of here."

"Do you know what is going on, Mr Steiner? I heard an explosion," Lady Delaney said.

"A rescue, perhaps."

"By whom? Miss Knox is a most capable young woman, but she is not capable of storming this building on her own, and in any case, our weapons and explosives were seized by the constabulary," Lady Delaney said.

"Perhaps she visited Lord Ashwood?" Sirk suggested, glancing at Hunt.

"A plausible explanation, and I have seen first-hand that Lord Ashwood is no stranger to battle." Lady Delaney then voiced caution. "However, we should be prepared for the possibility that this building is being attacked by the Sooty Feathers, and that in fact we may be slain alongside *Maridiel*'s men."

Better to die than to be Possessed and be made the instrument of my Order's downfall, was Steiner's opinion on that possibility.

*

Knox followed Ashwood and Singh into the police station in time to witness Guillam and Newfield feeding from dead constables. She held a shotgun loaned to her by Lord Ashwood, and part of her wanted to turn it on the two undead. Another, more practical, part of her recognised that tonight they were a necessary evil.

And that the shells loaded into her shotgun contained no silver and thus would serve only to enrage them.

Lord Ashwood stepped over a body. "I suspect my son and his associates will be in the cells below. We will effect a rescue of any who survive."

"Miss Newfield and I will attend to *Maridiel*'s people on this level and those above. With luck, we shall find the demon itself and send it back to Hell," Miss Guillam said.

"Good hunting," Ashwood said.

"And to you." She paused. "Lady Delaney and Steiner have greatly inconvenienced me and my people in the past. It would be best if our paths never cross again. Impress that upon them."

"I understand," Ashwood said. "Come, Singh, Miss Knox."

*

The cell door opened again, perhaps ten minutes after the demon had left. Two constables entered, both carrying revolvers. The look in their eyes alerted Steiner to their purpose.

"Sounds like you boys ain't having the best of this fight," Gray said from the ground. "Maybe would be best for you to leave for the day."

"Mr Kenmure's orders are clear," one of the constables said. His tone suggested murdering prisoners was just another job for him. The look the other constable gave Gray suggested that killing the black man would be a particular pleasure for him.

Steiner met Lady Delaney's eyes, reaching an unspoken agreement. Neither would go quietly or easily. The two constables raised their guns, and Steiner tensed in readiness to charge. He was the one they were most wary of, underestimating Lady Delaney as so many had in the past. If he must sacrifice himself to give Delaney and the others a chance to overwhelm their would-be killers, then so be it. *God wills it.*

Hunt spoke up. "You there, hand me your weapon."

Steiner stared at the younger man. A bold strategy, albeit one unlikely to yield results.

"You what?" one of the constables asked with a disbelieving laugh.

"Kenmure's orders were clear, were they not? Kill everyone in here, myself excepted. Yes?" There was a hint of a drawl in Hunt's voice, sounding almost like his father.

"Aye," one of them muttered. "But to keep an eye on you."

"Did he tell you why?" Hunt asked.

Silence answered that question.

"*Maridiel* – or Superintendent Kenmure, if that makes you more comfortable – wanted to ensure the process was completed. I assure you, it is."

"Eh? He said not to kill you, nothing about giving you a gun, lad," the elder said.

"'Lad'? You are confusing me with Wilton Hunt. I am the demon *Beliel*," Hunt said. "Kenmure and his Demonist Summoned me not an hour ago. I now fully Possess this body."

Twin snorts of laughter told Steiner that Hunt's bluff had not fooled their executioners, a flicker of resignation crossing Hunt's face.

"Aye, lad. Very good. And you've proof?" the older constable asked.

"I do," Hunt said quietly.

"Go on, then–" one of them began to say, as a dread chill fell over the cell.

A demon or undead has Unveiled, Steiner realised looking around. Too intense to be far, he decided.

"Is that proof enough?" Hunt asked.

It is true, he has been Possessed. Steiner stared at Hunt, or rather the demon Possessing him, in dismay. He must be killed, and the demon returned to Hell. Hatred sparked in Delaney's wounded eyes as she glared at the body of their companion, now hosting the demon who had Possessed her husband and murdered her young children.

"Christ, it's true," the younger constable breathed.

"Indeed." Hunt faced Delaney, wisely keeping his distance. "Lady Delaney, we meet again. For the last time, it seems."

"Bastard." The insult hissed from Lady Delaney's mouth. "Twice now I've killed you, I am willing to return you to Hell a third."

"Shooting me in the gut and then setting me on fire *was* rather unpleasant," the demon said. "I would return the favour, but time is short, alas."

There was no chance now, Steiner knew, of relying on Lady Delaney to attack the constables. Inevitably, her rage was focused on *Beliel*.

The demon turned to the younger constable, a haughty look upon his face. "As you have heard, my last parting from this woman's company was not … pleasant. Might I trouble you for your gun, to personally answer the insult?"

Beliel was still Unveiled, and the younger man handed over his gun without further question.

"My thanks." *Beliel* cocked it before looking Delaney in the eye. "Time to die."

Lady Delaney replied with a profanity.

Beliel winced. "That sounds most painful." He turned and shot the older constable before re-cocking the gun and shooting the younger.

*

Lord Ashwood and Singh kept a brisk pace as they ventured into the bowels of the police station, not hesitating to shoot at anyone who got in their way. Knox was yet to fire her own shotgun, still uncomfortable at the thought of killing the living. She couldn't help but wonder if any of the dead or injured men lying in their wake were true police constables simply unlucky enough to be here tonight, or if they were truly all mercenaries hired by Kenmure to put on the uniform and do his dirty work.

Most had been armed, at least, and shown no hesitation in attacking the trio, which was some consolation. Lord Ashwood stiffened suddenly. "He's Unveiled."

"Are you certain?" Singh asked.

A nod. "I have always felt it when he has, for obvious reasons. I fear it may not be well received by the others. Guard the exit, Singh, while Miss Knox and I effect a rescue."

Knox felt nothing, nor apparently neither did Singh, but Ashwood seemed certain and quickened his pace. *Who has Unveiled – Kenmure?* Lord Ashwood wasn't making much sense.

*

Steiner shook his head, half-stunned by the deafening gunshots in such close quarters.

"Nicely done, Mr Hunt," Sirk said as their hearing recovered.

"You're welcome, Doctor," the demon said. And paused, fear crossing his face. "Pray lower that, Lady Delaney, until I've had a chance to explain."

Steiner turned to see that Lady Delaney had recovered the other gun and now had it aimed at *Beliel*, cocked with one finger pressed against the trigger, hatred in her eyes.

"Hunt is not Possessed by *Beliel*," Sirk said quickly.

"He knew how I killed his last Vessel," Delaney said quietly.

"Yes, because I was there," the demon said, trepidation on his face, and justified too, now that it faced Delaney's vengeance. For a third time. "I'm not *Beliel*, I'm Wilton Hunt."

"You Unveiled," Steiner said coldly. "One demon or another, you are Possessed."

"That is not quite … true," Sirk said.

And what do you know of this?

"Explain," Lady Delaney commanded, her hand steady as she kept her gun trained on Hunt, or whatever Possessed him.

"He is my son," a new voice said from the door.

Pained regret crossed Lady Delaney's face as Lord Ashwood and Miss Knox entered the cell, both carrying guns. "Lord Ashwood, I am more sorry than I can say, but *Maridiel* has had Wilton Possessed during our imprisonment. He told those two dead men he was *Beliel*, before shooting them."

Which *was* odd, unless the demon had decided its allegiance was better placed with the Sooty Feathers.

Steiner spoke. "He now denies being a demon, however we felt him Unveil." *You know what must be done, Ashwood.* A pity that the man had arrived before the unpleasant, yet necessary, duty had been attended to.

"Wilton spoke truly, he is no demon," Lord Ashwood said. "He is my son."

"Lord Ashwood," Lady Delaney began.

Another chill fell over the cell, the same as before.

"Cease that," Steiner barked at *Beliel*.

"It is not him, it is me," Ashwood said. He let out a

breath and the chill passed. "I had hoped to avoid the need to disclose this, but circumstances dictate otherwise. My name is *Samiel.*"

"Lucifer," Gray said from the ground. Steiner, likewise, recognised the name, a chill tingling his body. *And I stand in his unholy presence.*

"The pleasure, I suspect, is all mine," Ashwood said dryly. "Lady Delaney, do lower that gun, and I will explain." His tone darkened. "Or, regretfully, I will shoot."

Sirk cleared his throat. "Perhaps we might declare a truce, leave here, and discuss this situation somewhere more comfortable? Or shall we all just shoot one another and save our enemies the trouble?"

*

Newfield found herself little more than a spectator to Miss Guillam's wrath as they hunted the demon. The Elder vampyre was unstoppable, tearing through *Maridiel*'s people with hand, teeth and knife. Stronger than most mortals, Newfield nonetheless lacked a *Nephilim*'s strength and fangs, and so carried a revolver, her task mainly to distract any armed enemies long enough for Guillam to reach them. And to kill the wounded with her knife, lest they recover enough to shoot them in the back.

Non-silver bullets had struck Miss Guillam, one even hitting Newfield, but none struck head or heart, and so the two undead continued their advance through the station. Blood stained the paper-littered floor, chairs and desks broken or knocked aside.

Maridiel's men were either dead or fled, there being no sign of the demon itself. An office window had been opened wide and Knox looked out to see *Maridiel* limping away on the ground below. "Miss Guillam!"

The Regent joined her, watching the demon's attempted flight. "Your gun."

Newfield handed it over and watched as Miss Guillam

took aim and fired. The gunshot was followed by a scream, *Maridiel* falling to the ground.

"Let us free the constabulary from Keel's grip," Miss Guillam said as she climbed out the window and dropped two storeys, landing without injury. Newfield was less certain of her own durability and so climbed out and lowered herself down, taking care that her skirts not catch on anything. She felt a jolt go through her from her legs upwards as she let go and landed, collapsing to the pavement. Another storey higher, and bones would have broken.

Miss Guillam approached *Maridiel*, the demon's Vessel crippled by injury. Edwin Kenmure had been a valued Sooty Feather, once, before being Possessed and used against the Society. Perhaps knowing that Hell awaited, the demon hauled itself along the cobbled street, desperate to delay its Vessel's death for as long as possible.

"You have caused us much trouble, *Maridiel*," Miss Guillam said quietly, her voice, face and eyes utterly devoid of mercy.

"It was my pleasure, Guillam," the demon said through gritted teeth.

"We have Summoned you time and again, since Keel's death, you, *Asmodiel* and *Ifriel*. Never before have you acted against us, making no issue of Keel's demise," Miss Guillam said as she stood over *Maridiel*. "So why now? Why not come to us when Keel … *Arakiel* … Summoned you? You have picked the losing side, and Lord Fisher will never again free you from Hell."

Pained laughter. "You believe you're winning? Tonight is a battle won, but by no means the war, and you have no idea what is coming for you. As for me, Keel will Summon me back, doubt it not."

"You call him Keel, not *Arakiel*," Newfield observed.

"He will not use his true name until Fisher is dead and he once again inhabits his true flesh," *Maridiel* said. Newfield wasn't blind to the envy in the demon's voice, that for Keel the possibility existed to return as *Grigori*.

Had *Maridiel* been one of the two hundred Fallen angels to appear on Earth as the first undead, or had he perished in Heaven and gone straight to Hell?

"Miss Newfield," said the Regent. "Send this creature back to Hell."

"It will be my pleasure," Newfield said, not entirely truthfully. An honour, yes, but if she was bound for Hell herself, best not to have enemies waiting.

Maridiel wasted no words begging, he just stared at Newfield through human eyes. She aimed her gun at his head and pulled the trigger.

"Well done. We should go," Miss Guillam said.

Newfield followed, wondering how Lord Ashwood's rescue had fared. And wondering just what the demon believed was coming for the Sooty Feathers. Nothing, surely, beyond the capability of a *Dominus* and two Elder *Nephilim*?

*

What in God's name happened? John Grant wiped the sweat from his brow as he stood among the dead. He had lost constables before, and felt their loss keenly; how was he supposed to feel about a score of such losses? Numb, for the moment. In truth, he and most of his colleagues did not regard these new men recruited by Kenmure as true constables, disliking their brutality and coarse natures. And now most of them lay dead in the building Kenmure had opened up as a police station. So far, every casualty was one of Kenmure's; Grant was relieved to see no true constables among the fallen.

Had he returned to the station five minutes earlier, he would be lying dead on the floor too. Instead, he had seen the two ladies enter the station from a distance, and by the time he had walked through the doors, the slaughter was already well under way.

He had caught glimpses of it, seeing the older woman butcher men much larger than herself, her strength not human. The younger he recognised as Amy Newfield from the Thistledown Tavern, witnessing her murdering the wounded with cold dispassion.

Kenmure's men had not died without a fight, a few rushing to the chaos after first arming themselves with guns. They too died, and Grant watched in disbelief from the shadows as bullets struck the older woman yet failed to stop her. Newfield had a gun of her own, firing back until her companion reached the hapless constables and cut them down.

Then both women drank blood from the fallen, their faces smeared with it, their quick movements betraying a thirst for it.

Any thoughts Grant had of confronting the pair had died then, a terror cutting through him. Whatever the two women were, they were no longer human, and so Grant quietly slipped away and hid in a storage room.

Upon exiting, he had found only corpses. Lady Delaney and the other prisoners were gone, either rescued by the two 'ladies' or by others.

How the hell do I explain all this? Upon leaving the station in a daze, he realised he had a further problem; who to tell it to? Superintendent Kenmure lay dead in the street.

Grant's first thought was to use the telephone to contact the South Albion Street Station, but caution stayed him. Suspicious deaths written off as accidental or natural causes by the procurator fiscal were not uncommon. There had always been rumours of a secret society – not the Masons – ruling Glasgow and with members promoted to high rank within the constabulary to control it. Dark whispers, too, of evil haunting the night-time city streets until dawn.

Tonight, Grant had seen proof of it. *No one knows I've been here since before … this.* To report it risked powerful people knowing he had witnessed tonight's slaughter, and silencing him. Colleagues had died under mysterious circumstances before, having reported strange occurrences.

No. He'd leave without reporting this horror and let

some other poor bastard on the night shift stumble across it. There was an ungodly evil in Glasgow, and Grant knew he must face it, but not alone and not blindly. *Amy Newfield ... Tam Foley asked about you months ago. Who is your companion, and what are you both?* He recalled now why her face had been familiar; she had visited the late Superintendent Thatcher in the summer. That had been the last night he had seen Thatcher; the superintendent had died in his sleep that night. *Aye, right...*

A pity Foley was away from the city, but Wilton Hunt might know where he was. Hunt and his associates were gone, and as Kenmure had kept the morning raid and arrests under his hat, Grant wondered if anyone would even know they had been arrested, let alone escaped.

Chapter Seventeen

"Explain," Steiner demanded. Lady Delaney said nothing, the gun in her hand her only communication, a promise of what would happen should she not like what Father said.

Father ignored him for the moment. "You are unharmed, Wilton? I made myself clear to *Arakiel* and Miss Guillam about the consequences should they target our family again."

"I'm well, Father." Hunt forced the words out. "My thanks for coming to get me. I was only taken because I was present in Lady Delaney's house. *Maridiel* claimed I would be released unharmed once he had … finished with the others."

"I'm well, too, Lord Ashwood, you will be relieved to hear," Sirk said dryly.

"Clever of you, to pretend to have been Possessed and to Unveil when your claim was challenged," Father said. He glanced at Steiner and Lady Delaney. "Even if you have exchanged one threat for another."

"*Maridiel* sent two men to kill the others, I couldn't let that happen," Hunt said pointedly. It couldn't hurt to remind everyone that had he not acted, they would have died. Kerry Knox stared at him as if he were a stranger, keeping her distance. The horrified disbelief in her eyes cut his soul.

"Let us hope your associates return the courtesy," Father said. He acknowledged the others for the first time since the fugitives had fled up a small, cobbled lane. "Margot Guillam and the Newfield ghoul were present, also. I suspect *Maridiel* has been returned to Hell and thus the Glasgow Constabulary is no longer aligned with *Arakiel*."

"I will not repeat myself," Steiner said quietly. "Are you truly the Devil?"

"I have many names, that title being among them," Father said. He briefly summarised the details of his Summoning and marriage to Edith Browning.

"And you claim Wilton Hunt is *your* son? Templar tomes on the subject are definitive that demon-Possessed bodies cannot breed."

A frown creased Lady Delaney's brow. "If 'Lord Ashwood' speaks the truth about the timing of his Summoning, then it precedes Mr Hunt's birth by a couple of years. And there can be no denying the resemblance between the pair."

"Wilton is indeed my son, conceived after I was Summoned into Lewis Hunt. I will not go into the full circumstances, save to say your information is correct, and that Wilton's heritage is unique."

"He looks like Lewis Hunt," Gray observed, obviously in pain as Sirk and Singh attended to him.

"Your body and soul are born of the bodies and souls of your parents," Father said. "My … essence … as you might call it, is part of Wilton. Part of me is part of his soul. Hence when one of us Unveils, the other feels it even from a distance. It is identical."

"And can he breed?" Steiner asked bluntly. Hunt took umbrage to being discussed as if he were absent, but decided that the hardened, killer eyes of Steiner and Delaney were better fixed on his father than on him.

"I expect so," Father said carelessly. "If your next question relates to what will happen to him after death, I cannot tell you. Can he go to Heaven, or is he cursed for Hell? Perhaps he is doomed to be reborn again and again like the *Seraphim*."

His father's almost academic speculation about his soul's fate did not quell the fear in Hunt's gut as Steiner and Delaney weighed his life.

"Perhaps we should find out," Steiner said, his uncompromising glare sending a spark of fear up Hunt's spine. The Templar would kill him without hesitation or remorse, so as well he was unarmed, however Lady Delaney held a gun and was at least as fanatical as Steiner where demons were concerned.

Lady Delaney spoke after a long silence. "I am grateful to you, *Lord Ashwood*, for rescuing us, however I find I cannot in good conscience allow the Devil to roam free." Unspoken were her thoughts on the Devil's son.

Both she and Father raised their guns in unison, and Hunt knew it would all end terribly–

An Unveiling fell over the group, Hunt recognising Singh. The valet, forgotten by the others, squatted on the ground next to Gray and Sirk, his shotgun aimed at Lady Delaney. "Don't do anything foolish."

"Another demon," Lady Delaney spat, her gun-hand twitching so much Hunt feared she would shoot his father without meaning to.

"Which demon are you?" Steiner asked, his mouth curled in disgust.

"I am no demon." Singh rose. "I am *Kariel*, a *Seraphim*. One of the many angels who fell fighting *Samiel*'s army in Heaven."

The quiet intensity in his voice quietened everyone, most perhaps having forgotten the Indian valet was there, dismissing him as just another servant. There was a difference to his Unveiling than Hunt had experienced from the undead and demons he had encountered, slight but noticeable. Untainted, perhaps.

There was no doubting his words, Lady Delaney even lowering her gun as they all stared at the man earlier dismissed as a foreign servant.

"You are truly an angel?" There was grudging awe in Steiner's voice.

"I am *Kariel*," Singh repeated. "Loyal to *Mikiel* and slain in Heaven by *Samiel*." He glared briefly at Father.

"You serve the Devil, who cast you from Heaven?" Steiner asked in disbelief.

"Perhaps you would welcome his return to Hell as much as we would," Lady Delaney commented.

"Perhaps I would," Singh agreed. "But I am bound to

my mission by *Mikiel*." That name was well-known, at least; the Archangel Michael.

"Your mission? To slay the Prince of Lies, surely," Gray said.

"To watch over him. Kill him if necessary. As he says, the birth of Wilton Hunt is a unique event," Singh said. "I know not if *Mikiel* facilitated it, permitted it, or simply has not yet ordered its termination."

"And so we must let the Devil run free?" Lady Delaney asked.

"He is in my custody," Singh warned, his tone offering no compromise. "I will carry out *Mikiel*'s orders and attend to him should it be necessary. Until then, the politics of Heaven and Hell are none of your concern."

What miniscule pleasure Hunt took from this conversation was in seeing the expressions on Lady Delaney's and Steiner's faces upon being chastised by Singh. They had found the Devil, were ready to send him back to Hell or die trying – only for an angel to tell them he had matters in hand and to back off.

Or earn Heaven's ire.

Hunt was unsurprised to see Lady Delaney lower her gun, and Steiner to be at a loss for words for once. Less satisfactory was the look in Kerry's widened eyes as she stared at him as if he was guilty of some vast betrayal. No one had any choice in their parentage, and if Hunt was guilty of evil, he was confident they were all minor ones.

I suppose from now on we will always be Miss Knox and Mr Hunt to one another and never again Kerry and Wil.

Hunt found his voice. "What will you do now? We're fugitives from the police, you cannot simply return home and ask Ellison to brew some tea. Even the most inept of Glasgow's constables cannot fail to find you at your own home."

"I daresay they might, if they were looking for us," Gray said. "As the demon's men beat me, they taunted me that our arrests had not been logged, letting them kill us without a judge asking what happened to us between cell and court."

"Then I believe it best if we return to my house and act

as if today never happened." Lady Delaney looked at Hunt. "I will have your and Dr Sirk's belongings packed and ready for collection." Not that there were many, mostly clothing purchased after the fire.

Her dismissal was polite, but a dismissal it was. Hunt and Sirk were longer welcome guests at her house.

He bowed stiffly, face burning. "Thank you for your hospitality, Lady Delaney."

"You are welcome home, Wilton, and you, Dr Sirk," Father said. He glanced at *Kariel*. "Singh, be so good as to see to the reclamation of their belongings from Lady Delaney's house."

And just like that, Lucifer and *Kariel* were once again Lord Ashwood and valet, a transformation surely not lost on the others.

"A good evening to you all," Father said with an ironic twist to his lips. "Miss Knox, you may keep the revolver I gave you."

Kerry said nothing, merely jerked a nod, a panicked look in her eyes at being addressed by Satan himself.

"Better to return it, Miss Knox, than risk being in the Devil's debt," Steiner said harshly.

Father smiled as she hastily handed him the gun, as if it might burn her. "If you insist." He handed it to Hunt, the handle still warm from Kerry's grip.

Hunt found his voice. "You know where we'll be, if you wish to work together again. Good evening." He paused. "I truly did not know about … this, until the summer, when McBride attacked us up north. My word." *For whatever that is worth to you now*.

"I understand tonight's revelations have come as rather a shock, and so I choose not to take offence," Father told the others. "Rest assured, I will always extend a welcome to you. Wherever I might be."

He didn't mean his Windsor Terrace townhouse, and everyone knew it, faces paling as they recalled his *other* residence.

"Don't tease them," Singh said. "We may need them again."

The group broke into two, Hunt looking back at Kerry Knox. She left without word or backwards glance.

*

Knox wanted to say it was good to be home, but in truth Caroline's townhouse felt violated. The guns and explosives had all been removed, leaving them only two revolvers and some bullets with which to defend themselves, beyond some silver kitchen knives.

Caroline's lady's maid, Ellison, and her butler, Smith, had both looked surprised at their return, the former looking relieved. Fortunately, the servants had tidied up the house, and there was sufficient food in the larder for the erstwhile prisoners to enjoy a late supper.

Afterwards, everyone decamped to the drawing room for some much needed brandy, Knox guessing she was by no means the only one stunned by the day's events and revelations. Caroline, Steiner and Gray might be veterans of this war, but tonight they learned that they had met *fucking Satan!* Not only met him but dined with him in this very house, and were now *indebted* to him.

Hell, Knox and Caroline had fought shoulder to shoulder with him against the *zombis* sent against Dunkellen House. And his valet was in truth *an angel* assigned by the archangel Michael to monitor him and his activities.

And then there's Wilton...

Knox had liked him, liked that he respected her as an equal and recognised that her position as student to Caroline meant she was better prepared than he was in this struggle. Most men, she knew, would expect that what dangled between their legs made them her better in this fight. Caroline had said as much, training her to use that prejudice to her advantage. Undead men had stalked her, mistaking themselves for the predator and she as the prey, only to die by her hand.

She had expected Caroline to break the heavy silence first, or perhaps Steiner, but instead it was Gray: "Are we gonna talk about what the *hell* just happened today, or just sit here and sip Lady Delaney's whisky?"

"Brandy," Knox murmured.

"Sorry, brandy. Not that I'm complaining if you all choose to do the latter, it's good stuff. Medicinal." He grimaced, his injuries including two broken ribs.

"You should be in bed, Mr Gray," Caroline said, a brooding look in her eyes.

"I should be in that cell being beaten to death, like the rest of you, but then Lucifer happened," he said.

"Should we have killed them?" There was a troubled look on Steiner's face. "Is that what God willed? Every Templar sworn to this fight would give their life to send Satan back to Hell should they find him here. And we let him walk away."

"The angel told us to," Knox said, fearful that Steiner would get to his feet and demand they go to Lord Ashwood's house and re-challenge Lucifer.

"If the Indian truly is an angel," Steiner said.

"You know he is, as well as I do. We all do. We felt him Unveil, and felt the difference," Caroline said quietly. "It appears Heaven wishes for Lucifer to remain on earth for now, under the eye of this … *Kariel*."

"And what of the abomination?" Steiner asked. "The Devil's child. The Antichrist, he can only be, born of the unholy union of demon and woman, and his name is Wilton Hunt."

"He was baptised, wasn't he?" Knox said, hoping to sway Caroline from accepting Steiner's as-yet unspoken suggestion that they kill Wilton Hunt.

"Evil men have been baptised for centuries. It did not turn them from evil," Steiner said.

"Mr Hunt was baptised by Bishop Redfort," Caroline pointed out. "Hardly an exemplar of the church."

"Redfort? That creature is long due a reckoning," Steiner said.

"Redfort, yes, Wilton Hunt, no," Caroline said. She reached for a recently framed photograph and studied it. "No. The angel has taken responsibility for the Hunt men. He will attend to them if necessary."

"And trust that God wills it?" Steiner asked, his mouth twitching as he realised his mistake.

Caroline gave him a sharp look. "I care not for the notion of 'God's will', since that would mean it was 'God's will' that my sons died, slain by *Beliel* while it Possessed their father, my husband. *Fuck* God. *Fuck* Him and His angels. *Fuck Kariel.* That angel was there for the *Devil's* son? Where was he when *my* sons died?"

Her blasphemous fury shocked Steiner and Gray, taking even Knox aback.

"That picture, it's of you and your sons?" Gray asked quietly of the framed photograph Caroline had handled.

"It was taken within Lord Ashwood's home address shortly after the Christening of his baby son. The two young boys sitting on either side of me are mine. The baby I'm holding is Wilton Hunt. Lady Ashwood spoke to me of this photograph and promised it to me when we met at Dunkellen House, the night before she died. Her husband kept that promise."

The four of them drank Caroline's brandy in silence.

*

Steiner sat at the writing bureau and wrote to Grandmaster Maxwell, detailing the situation in Glasgow. Sir Thomas had been reluctant to send men north to wrest the city free from the two warring factions, but now Steiner was able to write of the Devil himself in Glasgow. With a son. Surely, now, Sir Thomas would send an appropriate company of Templars to free Glasgow from darkness?

He prayed so. Lady Delaney and Miss Knox were competent allies, but they lacked the whetted edge of the Templars. There would be no compromise with evil, no surrender to godlessness. Lucifer would face Templar justice, and his son was an abomination who should never have been born.

Chapter Eighteen

"Incompetence!" Keel was coldly furious, causing unease among what remained of his Council. "Much of our good work over the past several months has been undone, by hubris and by stupidity. After a number of morale-sapping defeats, Margot Guillam and Niall Fisher now have some victories to crow about, not all of which they are entitled to take credit for. Three of my Councillors have been slain, and I have one Seat I am still to find a successor for."

Cornelius Josiah cleared his throat. "So *Maridiel* will be rejoining us after all, Master?" Josiah was the Demonist, recruited – unwittingly at first – by George Rannoch to bring *Beliel* and *Arakiel* back, but he had soon seen which way the wind was blowing and tossed aside his allegiance to the Sooty Feathers.

"No. After *Maridiel* told me of yesterday's fiasco, I had his new Vessel killed. He was only brought back to tell me in person what befell him. Let him suffer in Hell with *Ifriel* and *Asmodiel*, penance for their recent failures. When my anger has cooled, I may see fit to bring them back, but not any time soon. Understand me, Josiah? Leave them in Hell."

"Understood, Master," Josiah said.

Interesting. Canning noted that Keel had said there was still one vacant seat, but the loss of the three demons meant three. Josiah had assumed *Maridiel* would be resuming his seat in his new Vessel, meaning the Demonist knew who was to fill one of the seats. Keel had replacements in mind for two seats, but his three fallen demons were to remain in Hell.

Canning wondered if he was to be elevated, though there were a number of non-Councillors standing around the darkened room. He preferred murder to politics, but had learned in recent weeks that the latter facilitated the former.

Keel looked at every face seated around his dining room table. "Firstly, I will attend to the 'apologies' for those absent. For those unaware, *Ifriel*'s death lost us control over J. Carlton & Co. Losing that company's warehouses is a blow, mercenaries and a Crypt of ghouls further losses we can ill afford. Not a total defeat, as our necromancer was nearby."

"Necromancy," Bartholomew Ridley muttered with distaste. A magician, and one who could manipulate puppets. Why someone would want to send a construct to kill was beyond Canning's comprehension. The joy was doing it in person.

Keel fixed him with a look. "When I am so frequently failed by the living, it seems I must rely upon the dead to get anything done."

Ridley lowered his head.

Keel continued. "Lady Delaney poisoned *Asmodiel* at Lady Jasper's ball, losing us Lord Smith of the High Court. *Maridiel* learned of newly arrived Templars staying with Lady Delaney, and so had Delaney and her guests arrested. Good, yes?"

There was a cautious murmur of agreement around the room.

"It was, except that one of those arrested was Wilton Hunt. I was very clear that Lucifer and his son were to be *left alone*. Instead, the son was taken, and Lucifer allied with Margot Guillam long enough to free the prisoners, kill most of our men placed within the constabulary, and send *Maridiel* back to Hell. With Superintendent Kenmure now dead, we have lost our control over the police, and thus Roderick McBride will be free to expand his criminal enterprises on behalf of the Sooty Feathers." Keel drank some whisky. "Bresnik is still away on other business. *Gadriel*, report."

The demon Possessing Walter Herriot, a director of the Heron Crowe Bank that primarily did business with the Sooty Feathers, spoke. “The bank’s stability is still in doubt, after Mr Canning’s robbery and the closure of so many accounts after the Dunkellen incident. Many heirs to those dead Sooty Feathers had little confidence in the bank due to the robbery, and a number of current members have been quietly withdrawing money, perhaps intent on leaving Glasgow.”

“Is Edmund Crowe aware of this?” Keel asked. With William Heron among the dead of Dunkellen, Crowe had been forced to take a more active role in the management of the Bank.

“I’ve managed to facilitate the withdrawals whilst hiding the scale of them from Crowe,” *Gadriel* said.

Keel rested his chin in his hands. “Make Crowe aware of what is happening.”

“If I do that, I lessen the chances of the bank failing,” *Gadriel* objected.

“I do not wish the bank to fail. It will be useful to us upon our victory,” Keel said. “Set in motion your plans to remove Crowe.”

“You intend for me to replace Crowe in due course, once he is dealt with?” *Gadriel* asked. Not that it would be easy, with Edmund Crowe rumoured to be an Elder *Nephilim*. He had been somewhat unaligned until recently, though now he was part of Fisher’s Council.

“Yes. Mr Josiah, have you any news with which to inform us?”

Josiah shook his head. Keel demanded little of him, requiring only that the Demonist Summon a demon when required, and otherwise keep his head down until the time came to confront Fisher. And then the Demonist would be required to bring Keel back as a true *Grigori*.

“Mr Ridley.” The name was spoken slowly and softly, the magician’s early disdain for the necromancer neither forgotten nor forgiven by Keel. “You were to convince the greater part of the magician community to follow me rather than the Sooty Feathers. How does that progress?”

Keel's tone suggested he already knew the answer and it was not one to his liking.

The magician clutched his hands, Canning wondering if they'd get to see him killed. *Dinner and a show.* "Not well, I must admit. I sent a puppet to kill Magdalene Quinn, the Sooty Feather Councillor whom most of the magicians look up to. Alas, she survived." The last was almost a whisper.

Cold eyes fixed on Ridley. "Do better."

"I will," he promised, face red and sweating.

The eighth Councillor, the necromancer who had previously occupied the body of Dr Essex, was absent, Keel wanting his new identity kept secret for now. No one lamented his absence, necromancers hated by the living and undead alike. Quite why Keel had appointed him to the Council was beyond Canning's ken.

"How do you wish us to answer these setbacks, Master?" Canning asked boldly, aware he was not on the Council. A taut silence followed that question; most present had aligned with Keel because they believed he would win. Every defeat made it likely that his forces would quietly desert or defect back to Fisher.

"Before I sent him back to Hell to reflect on his failures, *Maridiel* revealed that he was killed by Amy Newfield. A sibling of sorts to you, Canning, as she was also Made by Rannoch."

"You want me to kill her?" Canning asked, eager to hunt again.

"Not her. The people living at this address." A note was passed around to Canning, who took it.

"Any preferences as to how I do it?" he asked.

"I leave that to your discretion. Make it … colourful. A message that relays to Miss Newfield my extreme displeasure."

Canning smiled. "It will be a work of art."

"Just get it done. I commend you, Canning, on your killing of Reginald Fredds. He was present in Romania when Fisher turned on me. A sore loss to Fisher and Guillam. For a *Nephilim* only months Made to slay one centuries old and nearly an Elder is impressive." Keel paused. "You killed one of Fisher's Councillors, so now you sit on my Council."

"I'm honoured, Master," Canning said with a bow. Now, he had a stronger voice in the doings of this House.

"I say again, that the Hunt family are to be left alone. Am I clear?" Keel looked around from face to face until he was evidently satisfied that his prohibition was understood. He motioned for Canning to take a seat at the table, which he did.

"What of the other two seats?" *Gadriel* asked.

"I have not yet decided on the eighth. The seventh, however, is to go to this man." Keel raised his voice. "Enter and take your seat."

Canning watched as the door opened and a middle-aged man entered, his identity resulting in gasps of breath and disbelieving stares. *What is this?*

The man affected a regal air as he took a seat at the dining room table, a bitter enemy to everyone here. He had played a part in George Rannoch's downfall, and he had led the group who slew *Ifriel* and a Crypt of ghouls. He was the senior-most mortal Sooty Feather, second only on the Council to Margot Guillam.

Bishop Redfort looked around the table and smiled. "Good evening."

*

"Good evening." Redfort took his seat at Keel's table, not blind to the hate-filled looks many of the others gave him. A minute ago, they had believed him an enemy to be killed, only to see him promoted above them. *Delicious.*

"What is this?" someone asked, breaking the stunned silence.

"It is the reward for success. For delivering the results I demand. For not being *fucking killed* by Lady Delaney, Guillam's pet ghoul, or the good bishop here," Keel said.

It still jarred Redfort that Keel Possessed his former secretary, though the demon no longer had to mimic

Henderson's mannerisms. Keel had also left Redfort to die in Dunkellen House, though his survival had impressed the demon, somewhat.

"Your necromancer invited me to meet with Mr Keel to discuss my future," Redfort said. *A meeting I had no choice but to attend, or the necromancer would have revealed my own dabbling in that forbidden sorcery to all and sundry, and Miss Guillam would have seen me burned alive.*

He had met Keel. And on agreeing to cross that Rubicon, he had resolved that he should do as well for himself with Keel as he had with the Sooty Feathers. Disappointingly, he had still to uncover the necromancer's new identity, but he was confident he would learn it in time.

"A fruitful meeting," Keel said. "Bishop Redfort may have inconvenienced us in the matter of *Ifriel* and the slain mercenaries and ghouls, however he has, in partnership with *Beliel*, worked to turn Roderick McBride to our side."

Redfort watched the surrounding faces as that revelation sunk in. If McBride turned against Fisher and Guillam, they would lose his army of thugs and cutpurses.

"How?" It was Richard Canning who asked.

"McBride lost a brother in the spring, last seen preparing to kill Thomas Foley and Dr Charles Sirk in Walker's Bar. Instead, Eddie McBride and his men were found slaughtered, and Roddy McBride wishes vengeance. He shot Foley up north in the summer and believed him dead. I told him Foley had been alive and well at Dunkellen House, among the very few to survive. Like myself." *Remind them I am a survivor.*

"That was all?"

Redfort briefly explained his plan, and finished with a smile. "McBride will join us."

This, though, was not the only reason Keel had appointed Redfort to his Council. Redfort's trump card had been revealing to Keel that he knew why the

MacInesker family always had a seat on the Sooty Feather Council; the name meant 'son of the fisher'. *Neil MacInesker is descended from Niall Fisher.*

Keel, of course, was already aware, having known Fisher before he became undead all those centuries ago, but he had been suitably impressed that Redfort had deduced it. *Finally, the Gaelic my father insisted on beating into me has proven of use.* If Fisher still favoured his family, then young MacInesker was a vulnerability, a means of luring out the reclusive *Dominus*.

Luring him out was one thing, defeating him was another. Fisher was among the most singularly powerful creatures in the world, and Keel's handful of vampyres, ghouls and guns-for-hire would barely inconvenience him. And given it was Keel's intention to capture Fisher long enough to cut out his heart and use it to regenerate his own *Grigori* remains, Redfort was not optimistic.

"What of Dr Sirk? Why has McBride not killed him?" someone asked.

"Too close to Wilton Hunt. The Sooty Feathers are likewise forbidden from harming the Hunts, per an agreement between Lucifer and Fisher," Redfort said.

"Margot Guillam still has more undead than us," Josiah pointed out. Months had passed since Redfort had seen the Demonist, Keel keeping him safe.

"She has perhaps two score *Nephilim* surviving, to our six. Five, if we exclude Bresnik while he is out of the city. She and Crowe are Elders, and Fisher is a *Dominus*. The Templars and Lady Delaney have accounted for two Crypts of their ghouls, and we have destroyed a further two." Walter Herriot looked at Redfort. "You can tell us the locations of other Crypts throughout the city?"

Redfort had been told Herriot was Possessed, though he could not recall the demon's name. "Not yet, however I will work to identify their locations." A destroyed Crypt would cement his position in this Council.

"Do so," Keel instructed. He met Redfort's eyes. "Be more loyal to me than you are to Fisher, or your church will need a new bishop."

"Mr Keel, this Council commands my first loyalty, be assured," Redfort said. He'd said much the same to Miss Guillam after Dunkellen House, and he meant it as sincerely now as he had then. With a foot in each camp, a piece on each side of the chessboard, he would win regardless of who prevailed, so long as neither realised he was playing one side against the other.

The look Keel gave him had a knowing glint, and Redfort belatedly recalled that Erik Keel had ruled an undead House for millennia.

He would not be easily played.

Chapter Nineteen

To breathe in deeply and no longer smell the perpetual reek of Glasgow still made Foley marvel. For years he had been used to the pervasive stench of human shit, horse shit, and the effluence from factories flowing down the Clyde, but in the hills and woods of Inverarnan, there was only nature.

He had lived here for about two months, accepted into this small community upon them learning he was one of them.

A werewolf.

He had only the vaguest recollection of pain, of searing agony, but Hunt had witnessed one such transformation and told him the gory details.

Maybe as well he couldn't remember the transformations.

Reborn again. Certainly, there were advantages, though Elder Archibald had warned that they varied from werewolf to werewolf. Every full moon his body would be torn apart by the moon-born wolf ripping itself from his flesh, reborn in turn in the morning as the man ripped itself free from the wolf. Diseases and cancers were gone. Foley had been heartened to realise he could drink as much whisky as his gut would hold, without fear of any damage carrying over into the following month. In a sense, he wouldn't even age, his body being reborn as it had been the day he had been bitten.

In a sense. And here was the problem. According to Archibald, every time a copy was made, there were small differences from the original. Every full moon a copy of himself would rip itself free from the wolf, ever so slightly different from his original body. For some the differences were tiny and so they lived a long, long time. For others, the differences were large and they 'aged' and died earlier than they might have done had they remained fully human.

A man already well on the path to liver destruction, Foley was happy to take his chances with lycanthropy. Of greater concern to him were the risks if he got loose. It was rare, the small community well-practiced in ensuring none could escape upon the full moon, but mistakes happened.

Hunt had shot and killed Ruaridh, and the second wolf, Barra, had fled. That wolf's flight had been a mystery at the time, and to the werewolves it was a mystery still, Barra having only a hazy memory of her encounter with Hunt and Foley.

He knew now why Barra had fled the pair. Hunt had unknowingly Unveiled, his demonic essence cowing the werewolf. Sirk had told Foley of how he, as a wolf, had fled from Lucifer, Hunt's father, upon his Unveiling in the Lewswood. There was a link between the Devil and the werewolves, according to Lucifer, though he had offered no explanation, and the werewolves knew nothing. *And I'm in no hurry to tell them I know the Devil.* He counted himself lucky they held no grudge against him for Ruaridh's death.

They accepted Hunt and Foley had no choice but to defend themselves, but that did not mean Hunt could expect to find a warm welcome here. Archibald was the laird of the insular estate, ensuring adequate game to sustain them in the fenced-off wolfswood. He and the other Elders, more aware than the younger wolves, kept an eye on the pack and – usually – succeeded in keeping them within the wood.

For most of each month, life was the same as on every other Scottish estate, the pack working to maintain the grounds and buildings, growing crops and managing sheep in fields separate from the wolfswood. Laird

Archibald Cowan was said to be over a hundred years old, yet he looked no older than sixty, his brown eyes and grey hair giving him an air of thoughtful wisdom.

But even he was not immune to the wild nature within, having led the pack to the Drover's Inn that night so that they might express their outrage at the death of Ruaridh. A warning only, Archibald had told Foley, who had been unconscious during the siege, but privately he wondered how the werewolves would have acted had they got inside the inn.

Foley lifted the axe and drove it down onto the logs, chopping up more firewood. Winter was coming, and Archibald wanted a good supply to see them through the cold months. *A good life. I could be happy here. I* am *happy here.*

Still, part of him worried after Hunt. Together they had exhumed and sold corpses, fought demons, *zombis* and undead, and somehow survived. *Stay out of that war, Hunt.*

Foley intended to.

*

Inspector Grant stood in the house and tried to keep his breakfast down. Two bodies lay in the master bedroom, torn and bloody. The killer had taken his time, killing them slowly and painfully, their faces frozen in agony. Had the killer not left the front door open, it might have been days before the bodies were found, the couple's son living in Stirling with his wife and child.

Neighbours had alerted the police, the attending constables finding the gory discoveries upstairs.

"Got an address for the son?" Grant asked one of the constables.

"Aye, sir. We're sending word to Stirling to have him notified. A Darren Newfield. The couple's daughter died in March, according to the neighbours," Constable Salter said.

Grant nodded absently. Then the name registered. "Newfield, you say?"

"Aye."

Grant looked around for photographs. Sure enough, he found one of the son and his family. And one of the daughter. He lifted the photograph, the hairs on his arms tingling as he recognised the young woman. Amy Newfield, who had died in March and yet was still somehow alive.

Part of Grant wanted to believe Amy Newfield's supposed death was all part of a deception, but another part of him knew that it wasn't. He had seen bullets do little more than slow her and the other woman, had seen the pair tear apart Superintendent Kenmure's thuggish recruits. Suspicion among some in the constabulary that something lurked in the bowels of Glasgow went largely unspoken, but it was there, and Grant was swiftly becoming witness to more than he could deny. *I need answers*.

And, unfortunately, he had an idea who might have them.

*

Jimmy Keane sat at the bar and drank contentedly from a tankard of ale, the Drover's Inn stocking a far better quality of ale than the Thistledown or any of the other drinking dens Keane frequented in Glasgow. More expensive ale, aye, but the McBrides were paying, and Keane was happy to spend their money.

His job was to follow his own blood. Redfort had taken some from him days before, whereupon by means and persons unknown it had been dabbed onto an envelope being sent to Thomas Foley. The letter had been addressed to the post office in Inverarnan, Keane guessing that every so often Foley would visit to check for any mail.

For two days now the letter had not moved, and while Keane had no objections to drinking ale all day before passing out in a guest room, Johnny McBride was growing increasingly restless. Roddy McBride's younger brother was becoming less and less convinced by Keane's assurances that the letter had not left the post office, going so far as to suggest he lay off the ale and whisky, lest it be limiting his Diviner talent. *A nonsense!*

At least he and McBride had rooms in the inn. The other six men drank in the inn, hard men the locals stayed clear of, but when the taproom closed, they were forced to sleep in the two wagons. So far, the nights had been cold and dry, but if it rained, McBride would either have to swallow the costs of hiring rooms for his men or face their rising discontent.

McBride stood next to him. "An ale."

"As you say." The landlord, Owen Dale, filled a tankard from the barrel. So far none of the tension between the visitors and the locals had turned to violence, but if they stayed much longer, it surely would. The wary suspicion in Dale's eyes when he looked at the visitors told Keane that the man recognised the group for what they were: trouble. Keane had expected McBride and his men to brawl with the burly farmhands who frequented the inn, but so far McBride had kept his men leashed.

McBride motioned for Keane to follow him to a table where the rest of their group sat, next to the fireplace. "Is it still there?" he asked for what had to be the hundredth time.

"Aye, Mr McBride, it's not moved," Keane assured him.

McBride swore under his breath.

Dale the landlord approached to clear away some empty tankards. There was a girl who worked in the inn, her red hair suggesting she was probably Dale's daughter. Keane had only seen her at the entrance reception and never in the taproom. Perhaps, he suspected, owing to the rough nature of McBride and his men.

"Mr Dale, a fresh round of drinks for me and my companions, and pour yourself one and join us," McBride said in a surprisingly friendly tone.

Dale blinked in surprise. "Very good of you," he said grudgingly. Minutes later he brought over the last of the tankards and took a seat. The taproom was otherwise empty, save for an old man nursing a pint. As it was after two in the afternoon, most of the locals would be hard at work in the fields or whatever industry employed them.

"A fine place, Mr Dale," McBride said. "We'll be sorry to leave."

"Aye, that it is. What brings you gentlemen here?" Dale asked. Doubtless a question he and the other locals had wondered and discussed at length.

"My family is involved in many businesses in Glasgow," McBride said. "We're waiting for a cargo of whisky being delivered from Aviemore, to take back to Glasgow."

"Ahh." Dale glanced at the group, maybe wondering why eight men were needed for two wagons, and how McBride would have room for both the cargo and his men, but he said nothing.

"This seems a quiet place, can't think you see much excitement here," McBride said.

Dale laughed, his guard lowering somewhat. "You don't think so, no? Well…" He leaned forwards. "In the summer, we were attacked by *wolves!*"

"Aren't they all dead?" one of McBride's men said with a frown.

"So we thought, aye." Dale leaned back and folded his arms. "Two young men staying here went out for a walk in the evening, and when they returned, one had been bitten by what they claimed was a wolf. Now, we thought what you did, that there are no wolves here no more. While the fellow who was bitten was being tended to in his room, we told the other one that it was probably a pair of dogs what had attacked them."

Dale spoke with a practiced ease, suggesting to Keane that this was a tale he had told often, a new local legend.

He lowered his voice. "And then they came that night. A whole damned pack of them, surrounding the inn. Luckily for us, I shouted on my boy to lock the doors, otherwise they'd have been inside and at our throats. All night long they circled the inn, howling bloody murder until the dawn came. And then they left. Wolves, not dogs."

"That's quite a tale," McBride said so that Dale wouldn't see two of his men exchanging smirks.

"All true," Dale insisted. "We searched the hills and woods for them later but found nary a trace. Gone. Still, sheep vanish on occasion. And only the brave or foolhardy walk the hills at night."

"Another round of drinks, Mr Dale," McBride said. "Yourself included, and you can tell us more about this place."

Chapter Twenty

John Grant drew his coat in around him as he loitered at the foot of the steps leading up to Lady Delaney's front door, the hour late. *What am I doing here?* Only days before he had arrested the occupants of this house. Bloody hell, they hadn't even been officially released, they had been *broken out!*

But despite the investigation into the slaughter at the Ingram Street Police Station, no mention had been made of the missing prisoners. The logbook held no record of their detention, nor was there any trace of the warrant issued to Kenmure to search the house. Most of the officers involved in that arrest had been Kenmure's recruits and were now dead, and Grant had cautioned Sergeant McPhail and Constable Bremner to forget all about their visit here.

Which I should do.

Instead, here he was, ready to walk into the lion's den. Amy Newfield should be dead, but instead of occupying a coffin she was filling them.

I should go home to my wife and children and leave this well enough alone.

Instead, he climbed the steps and removed his hat. A new bowler hat his wife had bought for him to celebrate his promotion to inspector. He knocked the silver knocker twice.

The butler answered the door, his eyes betraying recognition of Grant.

"Are you here with another warrant, Inspector Grant?" Lady Delaney asked dryly as Grant was shown into the sitting room.

Grant took a breath. "No, Lady Delaney. The warrant to search this house was lost with Superintendent Kenmure. The … items seized here did not arrive at the Ingram Street Police Station, nor at any other police station. No one knows anything about them, and Constable Martinson, who was tasked by Kenmure to transport them, is dead."

"Sounds like this Martinson, Lady Delaney, took your weapons and ammunition to his master," the black American said. "And my rifle too, God damn his filthy soul."

"What is the reason for your visit, then?" the older man, Steiner, asked. He sounded German.

"Not to arrest everyone again, I'm guessing," the younger woman said, Irish by her accent. Lady Delaney, it seemed, had friends from all over the world. She was the only one Grant didn't recognise, suggesting her to be the missing Miss Knox that Kenmure had asked about.

Grant took a breath. "I'm here because … I … I want to know what the *hell* is going on." He met Lady Delaney's eyes. "I'm up to my neck in something, and I don't even know what it is. I saw two women butcher a station's worth of coppers!"

Lady Delaney's mouth quirked. "Are you sure you want to know? You may find yourself sleeping better if you leave here and forget all about what you've seen."

"I'm sure," he said after a moment.

Lady Delaney pointed to a chair. "Then take a seat. Miss Knox, would you be so good as to fetch some glasses and whisky?"

"Of course," the young woman said. Grant wondered at her role in the attack on the station that freed her companions. Not alone, surely, even accounting for the other two women.

"Where is Dr Sirk and Mr Hunt?" Grant asked.

"No longer welcome," Lady Delaney answered, and Grant wasn't blind to the sudden tension caused by those names.

"Do you know a Tam Foley? We grew up together," Grant added.

"We know him," Lady Delaney said.

"He's out of the city, staying away from the McBrides." Miss Knox handed round glasses of whisky.

Grant nodded, accepting a glass. "Aye, I heard McBride was after him. Supposedly Foley killed Eddie McBride." The death of Eddie in the spring had seen Roddy McBride terrorise the Gorbals area in a bid to identify his brother's killer.

"Foley didn't. Eddie McBride's throat was cut by a man named Carter," Gray said. "A late comrade of mine."

"Why kill McBride?" Grant asked.

"Because I was done asking him questions," Lady Delaney said. "We came across Edward McBride and his men about to kill Dr Sirk and Mr Foley – which is why Roderick McBride believes Foley is responsible – and intervened. Young Edward had some information we needed. There was no need for him afterwards."

The calm coldness in her voice gave Grant pause, as did her familiarity with murder.

"We have strayed from Mr Grant's reason for coming here," Steiner observed.

"As you say, Mr Steiner." Lady Delaney met Grant's gaze. "You want to know the truth of Glasgow, the truth that haunts the world? Very well. What do you know about vampyres, Mr Grant?"

The others kept quiet while she spoke, telling Grant of vampyres and demons. Of the Sooty Feathers, a secret society of the rich and powerful that ruled Glasgow on behalf of the undead, and of the demon *Arakiel*, warring to reclaim both the city and his former power.

"How can we drive out such evil?" he whispered once she had finished, overwhelmed by what he had heard.

"You cannot. The Templars can. And will," Steiner said with an iron certainty.

"I thought your fellows were too busy with London to come up here?" Miss Knox asked with a slightly mocking air.

Steiner looked at her. "That was before I wrote to them that the Devil himself was here."

"The Devil is here? In *Glasgow*?" Grant asked, this being the least welcome revelation of the evening. *My family lives here…*

Steiner's cold eyes turned to him. "Indeed. He has Possessed Lord Ashwood for many years."

"Lord Ashwood…" The name was familiar.

"You met his son and heir earlier. Wilton Hunt. The Devil's son."

*

Tonight was Redfort's turn to host the Council meeting – the Sooty Feather one, this time – and it amused him to host it in the Cathedral. Certainly, the mood was funereal, save for Regent Guillam who appeared wrathful. Now a member of both this Council and Keel's, Redfort felt like a chess master playing both sides of the board. But he must be careful lest the Regent discover he also served Keel, and that Keel did not realise Redfort served chiefly himself. One side would win this war, and Redfort had taken steps to ensure he would be on that side regardless.

There were supposed to be eight on the Council, yet only seven sat around the table set out in the middle of the cavernous nave. Reginald Fredds was the missing Councillor, its Third Seat. Councillors dying was not unusual in these turbulent times, but Fredds was a *Nephilim* – one believed to be close to Transitioning to Elder.

"We are all gathered, so I declare this meeting open," Regent Guillam declared quietly. "When I ended our last meeting, I told you all that we need victories, and more of them. Yet you answer me with failures, one after the other!"

Her sudden shout echoed round the nave, and a startled Redfort feared the Elder vampyre intended to empty some more seats tonight. Perhaps all of them…

"Reginald Fredds was found dead within the changing room of his sporting club. Richard Canning 'signed' the killing, so to speak, so we know who was responsible," Guillam said.

"Who is to replace him?" Edmund Crowe asked, the only one who dared.

"No one." Dark angry eyes looked around the table. "The days of 'making up the numbers' are done. They have led to a Council of *failures!* Should a Sooty Feather prove worthy, I will elevate them to this Council. Until then the Third Seat will remain vacant."

Redfort glanced at Crowe, who would have expected to move up from the Fourth Seat to the Third, but he showed no reaction. Normally upon the death of a Councillor, the others would move up a seat as appropriate, the newest Councillor occupying the Eighth Seat. But no longer, it seemed.

Not that Redfort cared, being *Secundus*, the Second Seat. Regent Guillam would need to die for him to move up, and if that happened, he suspected Lord Fisher would emerge from seclusion to assume the First Seat himself. Or simply put Crowe in it. The First Seat had always been occupied by an undead.

"Report," the Regent said brusquely.

Meaning me. "I have nothing, Regent. My search for Keel's necromancer continues."

"Without success. Mr Crowe?"

"Confidence in the bank outside of Glasgow continues to recover after the summer robbery, however investment within the city remains slow. Too many of our investors have died in recent months," Crowe said.

"Find new investors. Miss Quinn?"

"The Under-Market remains officially under our control, though those magicians sworn to Keel continue their efforts to take it over. Frankly, trust is low."

"Mr MacInesker?"

"I have nothing to report," Neil MacInesker mumbled. Not that he had anything to fear either, given his family.

"Mr McBride?"

"Nothing." The criminal boss sounded rather more abrupt than Redfort would have liked. *Hide your discontent, at least, McBride!* If he aroused the Regent's suspicions, in her current mood she would just kill him, and Redfort had plans for the thug and his organisation.

"Really?" Regent Guillam stared at him. "I understand you sent your brother John, the Diviner Keane, and six men away from the city. Are they away on a holiday, perhaps?" Her voice dripped with sarcasm.

McBride reddened, anger sparking an angry response, one dampened by a healthy fear of Margot Guillam. "They're away on business, Regent."

"What business? I remind you, your business is *our* business."

An icicle of fear slithered down Redfort's back. If McBride revealed that he had sent his brother off to kill Tam Foley, then the Regent would want to know how he had learned Foley still lived, how he had learned where he was, and those answers led back to Redfort. And back to Erik Keel.

"Someone stole some of my whisky. After our recent loss, I want it back and so sent my brother to put the thieving bastards out of business," McBride said, revealing a gift for deception.

"Miss Newfield?" The Regent evidently accepted McBride's explanation.

Amy Newfield, the Council's *Octavia*, hesitated before answering. "I helped you send the demon *Maridiel* back to Hell. We also killed the mercenaries he recruited into the constabulary."

Redfort feigned a look of pleased surprise at this news, being already aware of it. Just as he was aware of Keel's retaliation for Newfield's involvement.

The Regent looked around the table. "After months of mostly failures, I have taken the fight to the enemy in person. With Kenmure and his thugs dead, Keel has lost a vital asset that he has used often against us, in particular one he employed against you, Mr McBride. With the constabulary no longer hindering the expansion of your enterprises across the city, I expect to see progress. Or I will see you dead."

"Aye, Regent," McBride answered.

But when his brother killed Foley and returned to Glasgow, Roddy McBride would owe Redfort a debt – and would learn that he also owed a debt to Keel for getting the Diviner Keane's blood onto the letter bound for Foley.

Enough to turn McBride? Not quite, but it would help him reach the proper conclusion when matters reached a critical juncture.

Regent Guillam continued. "We can expect a response from Keel, so I bid you all be wary."

"He has already responded," Redfort said, feigning a sympathetic tone and expression. "I learned earlier that Miss Newfield's parents were murdered last night, the killer scrawling 'RC' on a wall. The killings were … shall we say, brutal. Done in a similar manner to many of Richard Canning's previous murders."

Newfield's eyes widened as the news sank in. "My parents? … Was my brother there also?"

"Only two bodies were found," Redfort said.

Newfield's face twisted in rage. "Richard Canning will die," she promised. A ghoul against a full *Nephilim* well practiced in murder; Redfort knew who his money would be on should they meet. Of course, only he among this Council knew that Canning had Transitioned from ghoul to *Nephilim*.

"I am sorry for your loss, Miss Newfield," Guillam said, not that Redfort believed her. The long years had ground away such humanity from Margot Guillam.

"How could Keel know that Miss Newfield was involved in Kenmure's death?" MacInesker asked, a surprisingly perspicacious question from the rather useless young man.

"Kenmure was Possessed by *Maridiel*. I suspect Keel had him Summoned back to describe what happened and who killed him," Crowe said.

"Then Regent Guillam's victory was a fleeting one, if *Maridiel* is already returned," McBride dared to say.

"Not so," Miss Quinn said. "I doubt Keel appreciates

losing his influence over the police, so *Maridiel* may well have found itself returned to Hell. And if not, no matter what body it Possesses, it can hardly pretend to be Superintendent Kenmure."

"I too suspect *Maridiel* is languishing in Hell along with *Ifriel* and *Asmodiel*, until Keel decides they have suffered enough," Crowe said. "That was how he rewarded demonic failure in the past."

"Certainly, there has been no sign of *Beliel*," Quinn said.

"Not since Cornelius Josiah attempted to Summon *Beliel* in Dunkellen House, an attempt thwarted by myself and Lucifer," Redfort said, happy to remind everyone of his role in that incident. In truth, he knew where *Beliel* was, and who it Possessed.

"Let us take stock," Guillam said. "Keel has lost the police and has only a small number of *Nephilim*. Bishop Redfort oversaw the destruction of a Crypt of ghouls and a gang of mercenaries, albeit lost some undead and soldiers to *zombis*.

"We can assume that *Arakiel* still has some newly Made ghouls held back for a large offensive, and his necromancer has the ability to Raise the dead. Whether he has any thugs or mercenaries remaining, I expect they are also being held back," Guillam finished.

"Should this necromancer not be our priority?" MacInesker asked. "Dr Essex unleashed an unspeakable horror at my home. Had he managed a similar spell in the middle of Glasgow…"

A disquieting thought. "We can hope that this new necromancer is less skilled than Dr Essex was, an apprentice most likely," Redfort said, continuing the narrative that Essex was dead and gone.

"Are you *any* closer to identifying this 'apprentice'?" Regent Guillam asked pointedly.

"Alas, no," he admitted, truthfully. The identity of the necromancer's new body remained a mystery. "Fortunately, he or she is either unwilling or unable to practice their art overtly."

"Keel is saving them for one big fucking battle," McBride opined.

"Which may come soon, so *find* that necromancer, Redfort. And kill them," Guillam said.

"As you command, Regent," Redfort said with a bow of his head. *Change the subject!* "What of Richard Canning? That undead has been making quite the nuisance of himself."

"He will be dealt with," Guillam said.

"I want to kill him," Newfield said, candlelight glinting off marbled eyes that did not blink. What remained of Amy Newfield's humanity appeared to have died with her parents.

"You are no match for an undead as skilled at killing as Canning, Miss Newfield," Guillam said in sharp rebuke. "You are undead. Patience is our way, the patience of the dead. Your time will come, but not if you rush. Let Canning make enemies and take chances, and in half a thousand years, you will not even remember his name."

"Yes, Regent," Newfield said quietly.

"We have another enemy," Guillam said, as if they were not having troubles enough with Erik Keel. "Wolfgang Steiner has returned to Glasgow."

Bile rose in Redfort's throat. "How many Templars has he brought?" Steiner had cause for enmity towards him.

"One."

"*Maridiel* arrested both Templars along with Lady Delaney, Wilton Hunt and Dr Sirk," Newfield said.

"While we attended to the demon and his men, Lord Ashwood rescued them," Guillam said.

"Could you not have waited until *Maridiel* killed the Templars?" Redfort asked, hating the panicked edge he heard in his voice. "The last time there were Templars here, they destroyed a Crypt of ghouls. And that was while we were at our peak strength!" *And he greatly insulted me.*

"To say nothing of how Lady Delaney has vexed us," the undead banker, Crowe, said.

"Wilton Hunt was among the prisoners. Lord Fisher

has made it clear he wants Hunt alive," Regent Guillam said. "Or would you prefer the Devil enters the fray? Delaney and the Templars will be dealt with."

If the Hunts were with Delaney, then the good lady had passed on Redfort's message that 'Dr Essex' was not as dead as they believed. Would they still enlist his aid, should *they* learn the necromancer's new identity, or would they attend to it themselves with Steiner?

Redfort wondered. Certainly, Steiner would not ally himself with Redfort, and in any case, the Templar Inquisitor was ruthless. In April, Miss Newfield had helped Delaney and the rest of her motley companions rescue Steiner, only for him to shoot her once done.

No. Better to keep my distance from him.

He would prefer to take an active part in the necromancer's downfall, to find its Soul-Repository to ensure it suffered a lasting death – and perhaps learn the secrets of its 'immortality' – but so long as it could no longer betray Redfort's own dabbling with necromancy, then he would be content.

Chapter Twenty-One

"A large fellow," Sirk observed as they loaded the sackcloth-wrapped corpse onto the wagon. "Though I have misgivings taking a body from sanctified ground."

"You think *that* makes a difference?" Hunt asked as he pushed the wheelbarrow through the churchyard, struggling to steer the unwieldly barrow so as to avoid the silhouetted gravestones. At least Professor Mortimer had tasked them to recover a corpse newly buried in the West End, avoiding the need for them to travel across the entirety of Glasgow. They were presently living in the West End, as was the Glasgow University medical college atop Gilmorehill. Convenient, for once. *Exhume the late Mr Henry, deliver him to Mortimer, and then back home.*

And then…?

He was still studying the natural sciences at the university, his attendance markedly improved since his return home. Anything to get him out of the house he had grown up in, the house that still bore the indelible stamp of his late mother. Father – Lucifer – was rarely at home during the day, his attention turned to the Browning Shipping Company founded by Mother's family.

Hunt's cousin Neil Dearing occupied a senior position in the company, and during Hunt's parental estrangement he had clearly hoped that the company would pass to him rather than Hunt. Part of him wanted to meet Cousin Neil and tell the arsehole just exactly who his Uncle Lewis was. *Oh, his expression!*

One day, maybe.

Professor Mortimer was waiting for them. "Another successful recovery, I see. Excellent, gentlemen, excellent. Yates will show you into the mortuary."

Hunt knew where it was, having delivered corpses to Mortimer and his predecessor many times, but he said nothing as the sullen valet led them towards the cold, dark mortuary. From there, cadavers would be wheeled out to the anatomy hall for Mortimer to cut and slice and show his students the inner pieces of the human body. Hopefully seeing the dead would help them understand the living.

"Our thanks, Professor," Sirk said as Mortimer handed him their money.

"*My* thanks, Dr Sirk. You have both been very useful." A head tilted in consideration. "Perhaps I can have a word, in due course, into the right ear to see about restoring you here?"

"That would be greatly appreciated, Professor," Sirk said with a note of surprise. The pair returned to Foley's old wagon, Hunt's arms still sore from having to do more than half the digging. If he insisted Sirk do his share, they'd still be digging at dawn.

"Did you hear that, Hunt? My days of haunting your father's house may soon be at an end," Sirk said.

"I hope Mortimer succeeds in getting you your position back," Hunt said sincerely. Sirk's termination from the university had been a petty act of revenge orchestrated by the Sooty Feathers, owing to his association with Hunt.

"Yes. Your studies must be suffering greatly from my absence. I remain bemused by your inexplicable refusals to engage with my selfless offers to tutor you at home, Hunt."

"I find it easier to concentrate in the lecture hall, Doctor."

I can doze off less conspicuously in a crowded lecture hall.

*

Hunt sat in the sitting room, sipping from a glass of whisky, tired enough to sleep but not yet inclined to go to bed. Since his return, he'd managed to avoid the drawing room, where Mother had once held court. Sirk sat across from him, likewise occupied with a drink.

"This must be quite an eye-opener for you, Doctor, being in a house with matching furniture," Hunt said, recalling Sirk's haphazard décor.

"I assumed it to be further evidence of your family's diabolical nature," was Sirk's retort.

"Do you think Delaney and Steiner are preparing to attack us?" Hunt asked as he watched the contents of his glass glow golden.

"If they're content to wait, liver failure will save them the trouble," Father said, standing at the door.

"Maybe they want to kill you too, *Father*," Hunt said, the liquor loosening his tongue.

"They can join a very large queue," Father said with a wry smile. "Singh, get in here."

The *Seraphim* valet entered, a sardonic expression on his face. "You wish me to pour you a drink, my Lord?"

"Pour yourself a drink and sit down," Father said in an exasperated tone as he helped himself from the bottle. "I find myself vexed with my son and his mortal friend. At least with an old enemy I might find some sense."

After a moment, Singh obliged and sat down with his drink. "This would give the cook fits. She still talks … Slowly. And. Loudly. To me."

"Maybe if *you* had talked slowly. And loudly … my father might have not rebelled in Heaven, thus sparing the world from demons and the undead," Hunt said.

"The only one your father ever listened to was *Mikiel*, and then only so that he might do the opposite," Singh said.

"Just how many lives have you lived?" Sirk asked.

"I do not know. The earliest are mostly forgotten. I was a French woman during my last life. Sometimes, I only remember the life I am living." Singh paused. "I prefer those lives, where I am free to live as I am not knowing what I am."

Hunt emptied his glass, drawing a look from his father.

"You should drink less, as your mother would tell you," Father said.

"You're not her."

"No. But that fact will not stop the liquor killing you any less, Wilton," Father said. "You have come to the notice of dangerous people, and you would do well to keep your wits about you."

"I thought you had convinced Fisher and *Arakiel* to leave us alone," Hunt said, the whisky starting to fog his mind.

"Which they will, until they decide to kill us. In any case, I was referring to Lady Delaney and Mr Steiner, who are bound by no such agreement."

"I would recall you to Mr Gray's skill with a rifle, Hunt," Sirk said. "You could be dead before you hear the shot that kills you."

Hunt gave him a dirty look. "Thank you, Doctor. That's just what I need on my mind every time I leave the house. We need to convince them that we're not enemies."

Sirk gave a snort. "How? Steiner is a fanatic, one who could kill everyone in this house and lose not a minute's sleep. Lady Delaney has a particular hatred for demons. And that is before we consider *Lord Ashwood*'s reputation as the King of Hell and the Prince of Lies."

A daunting struggle, to be sure. "Singh, could you not convince them to give us the benefit of the doubt?" Hunt asked. "You are an angel, after all."

"An angel exiled from Heaven for thousands of years," Singh pointed out. "And my presence was the only reason they did not try to kill you both then and there."

"Delaney and Steiner are a problem for another time," Father said. "Our more immediate task is to identify the necromancer who killed your mother, Wilton. To uncover the *Jinn*'s new identity and discover what it uses as a receptacle for its soul. And then we must destroy the receptacle and kill the Vessel."

Hunt shivered at Father's words, not that he disagreed. "And after? What of the war between Fisher and *Arakiel*?"

"I care not who prevails," Father said as he sipped from his glass. "And I would encourage you to adopt a similar indifferent neutrality, Wilton."

*

"Be seated," Lady Delaney said as her guests were led into the dining room, where Steiner, Gray and Knox stood waiting. Steiner had hungered to return to this city with Templars, and while he was pleased that his last letter had convinced Grandmaster Maxwell to at last relent and dispatch some, the distant expression on Lieutenant Millen's face warned Steiner that his coming here against orders had been neither forgotten nor forgiven.

"Introductions first, yes? Tea and sandwiches are being prepared," Lady Delaney said as Millen and the two Templars accompanying him joined her and the others at the table. They had taken time to freshen up after their train journey from Edinburgh, but still wore their travelling clothes. "I am Lady Delaney, and this is my companion, Miss Kerry Knox. You are acquainted with Mr Steiner and Mr Gray, I assume?"

Millen was yet to see his twenty-fifth year, and if he had battled the undead, he had yet to distinguish himself sufficiently to earn the 'knight' appellation to his rank. "I am Lieutenant Millen of the Edinburgh chapterhouse. I'm acquainted with Gray, but this is the first time I've met Steiner." His blond hair was cut short, his moustache trimmed.

"Ben Jefferies," the grey-haired man to his right said, a mutton chops beard running down his weathered face, his spectacles catching the light.

"That name is familiar. You are acquainted with a Dr Charles Sirk, I believe?" Lady Delaney asked.

Surprise showed on the grizzled Templar's face. "Aye, Lady Delaney. Sirk and I fought the undead in Edinburgh many years ago, when we were young men. After … what happened, I joined the Templars. Always wondered what happened to the doctor."

The third Templar was a woman, aged perhaps thirty, a long scar on her left cheek tightening as she spoke. "Rhonda Jackson." Her brown hair had been tied up, and her accent suggested she too hailed from Edinburgh.

"You are well, Gray? You look ill-used," Millen said. Addressing the American Templar before the higher-ranking Steiner was a deliberate insult.

"A demon had his minions beat me, but I'll mend. Good to see you again, sir."

Millen turned to Steiner. "Grandmaster Maxwell sent orders that you are to be relieved of your duties and returned to London, Inquisitor."

Steiner straightened his back. "*Knight*-Inquisitor, Lieutenant. I will obey. But until I leave, you would be wise to heed my counsel."

"I will hear you out," Millen allowed. "But the decisions are mine."

"What of me, sir?" Gray asked.

"You will be disciplined in due course, but we are short of men and so you will remain here for now," Millen said.

"Gray accompanied me at my command, I take responsibility for his presence here," Steiner said.

"That will be taken into account, but desertion is not looked upon kindly," Millen said.

"How many soldiers did you bring?" Steiner asked.

"I brought four with me," Millen said. "The other two are conveying our luggage to our lodgings."

Four, five including Millen ... meaning nine of us against our enemies. Eight, in fact, since Steiner was being returned to London in disgrace, unless he could convince Millen to *delay* the execution of that order.

"Do you know what we face here, Millen? Two warring factions, each building an army of undead. Demons, vampyres, sorcerers and mercenaries. One side, until recently, had enjoyed great influence over the Glasgow Police Constabulary. There is a necromancer capable of unleashing a plague that gives him control over the *dead*." Steiner took a breath. "And as I informed

Grandmaster Maxwell, *Satan* himself lives in the city. With a son, who may be the Antichrist."

"Which is why we are here, Steiner," Millen said quietly, doubt visible on his face. Not of the claims, but of his ability to face these enemies, Steiner intuited. "And why the grandmaster has dispatched more of our brethren from London. Eighteen soldiers and weapons enough to purge Glasgow of these threats."

Excitement stirred beneath Steiner's breast upon hearing that. At last, the Templars were being sent here in force.

"I would ask, Knight-Inquisitor, why you did not send Satan back to Hell yourself," Rhonda Jackson asked.

Steiner paused. "I would have, but he was in the company of … of an angel, a *Seraphim*. This angel, *Kariel*, warned us that he watches Lucifer on behalf of Heaven. He acts as Lucifer's valet."

"You are sure it was really an angel and not a demon?" Millen asked, his tone implying that Steiner had chosen not to challenge Singh's claim, perhaps fearing a fight.

"He Unveiled," Lady Delaney said. She had been content to listen until then, perhaps deeming it Templar business.

"*Kariel*'s Unveiling differed from any I have experienced before, be it a demon, vampyre or even an Elder vampyre." Steiner met Millen's eyes. *I am not newly come to this war. I have fought in it since you were a young boy.*

"Differed?" Jackson asked.

Steiner struggled to find the words, but Gray saved him the trouble. "When a demon or vampyre Unveils, it is like looking down a dark bottomless pit. The *Seraphim*'s Unveiling was like looking up at the endless sky."

"As apt a description as any," Lady Delaney said. "Very poetic, Mr Gray."

Gray answered that with a grin.

"Let us accept, for now, that the Devil's valet is an angel tasked to watch over him," Millen said. "Satan's presence here is certainly reason enough for us to bring the Light of Holy War to Glasgow, but he is a demon, not greatly different to those we have sent back to Hell over the centuries." Millen paused as the butler, Smith, led two servants into the room with trays of sandwiches and a pot of tea.

"We will serve ourselves, thank you, Smith," Lady Delaney said.

The old butler gave the room a furtive look before bowing slightly. "Very well, Lady Delaney."

Tea was poured, and Steiner watched as the three Templars, hungry after their train journey, helped themselves to a sandwich each.

"You suggested it was not just Lucifer that brought you here," Miss Knox said once everyone was served with food and drink.

The lieutenant looked at her, perhaps unsure of what to make of Lady Delaney's young companion. Delaney, at least, was well known to the Templars, having trained and fought with them years before, but Miss Knox was new to this war. Would she prove boon or a thin reed that would break when the war turned bloody?

Millen put his teacup down. "The Devil's spawn. That is what troubles the grandmaster, and chiefly why he has sent so many of us to Glasgow."

"Wilton?" Knox said with a disbelieving laugh. The use of his first name suggested a closeness between the pair that Steiner had not observed. Miss Knox would bear watching.

"Mr Hunt has shown no sign of diabolical ability." A frown tugged at Lady Delaney's mouth. "Save for him Unveiling, which he did to save our lives in an attempt to convince our captors that he had in fact been newly Possessed on the orders of the demon…"

"*Mardiel*," Knox supplied.

"*Maridiel*," Gray corrected.

"You saw no other signs?" Millen asked, looking from face to face.

"If he has cloven hooves or horns, I have not seen them," Steiner snapped. "To my eyes he was a young man possessed of some courage but no great ability."

"In April, he killed George Rannoch, an Elder *Nephilim*," Lady Delaney said quietly.

"True," Steiner conceded. He thought back to that desperate night atop the Glasgow Necropolis, when he himself had been captive and minutes from Possession by the demon *Beliel*.

"Even an Elder vampyre can do nothing against a silver bullet in the head," Gray said.

"There was something," Steiner said slowly. "Rannoch had mortally wounded Burton while I fought the female vampyre. Rannoch Unveiled and ran at Hunt who had a gun. But then that *coldness* sharpened, and I chanced a look. Rannoch stumbled somewhat, shock on his face, and Hunt shot him."

"You believe Mr Hunt Unveiled, surprising Rannoch?" Lady Delaney asked.

"Now, I do."

"He told us he only learned about his heritage in the summer, when McBride attacked his family and forced Lucifer's hand," Miss Knox said.

"Maybe he lied?" Jackson suggested with a pointed look.

Miss Knox met that look. "I think not, Miss Jackson. When we met at Dunkellen, something clearly troubled him. I believe he learned the truth regarding his heritage when his family were confronted by the McBrides."

Old Jefferies spoke up. "Does it matter? Point is, he's the damned son of the *Devil!* The Antichrist, for all we know. At the least, we should seize him and send him to London."

Millen nodded. "Have him … investigated."

"And at the most?" Miss Knox asked. "Kill him? Kill the Devil?" She stumbled a little over that last bit. "Need I remind you all that he lives with an angel sent to watch over him by the *Archangel Michael!*"

"Miss Knox makes an excellent point," Lady Delaney said. There was reluctance in her voice, she not being one to shy from the opportunity to send a demon back to Hell. "Lucifer has lived in Glasgow for the best part of thirty years, and to my knowledge and dealings with him, he has *not* engaged in any diabolical plots. We fight Hell; shall we risk war with Heaven too?"

"But why would God oppose us sending His Enemy back to Hell?" Jackson asked.

"I have little time for God or His plans," Delaney said acidly, untroubled as her blasphemy widened the eyes of her guests. "But we have enemies enough to concern ourselves with."

"Knight-Inquisitor Steiner will be returning to London in the company of another Templar, in due course. A letter to Grandmaster Maxwell will go with them, and we will await the grandmaster's instructions before we take any actions against Satan or his household," Millen decided, to Steiner's grudging approval.

"As Lady Delaney said, we have enemies enough to occupy us," Jefferies said.

"Then let us discuss what steps we might take next, and plan our campaign against these enemies," Millen said. Steiner felt a gnawing regret that he would be absent from the coming battles. Perhaps he might convince the grandmaster to allow him to return here, and postpone any punishment until after Glasgow was cleansed?

Chapter Twenty-Two

Night fell swiftly as autumn tightened its grip, driving the sun from the sky quicker with each passing day. Richard Canning breathed in the cold, crisp air, from habit rather than need – save to speak – revelling in the greater freedom granted by winter's approach. There was a shiver of nerves, but what he felt chiefly was anticipation. For weeks this Crypt had been watched, the comings and goings of its denizens noted. This was believed to be the largest of Fisher's Crypts, and it would not fall easily.

Canning entered the Bothwell Street tobacconist shop, its door having been forced open. He had done many killings for Erik Keel, and finally the demon had seen fit to test his ability as a captain, leading a small force of ghouls and mercenaries to bloody Fisher's nose.

"All is ready?" Canning asked as the rest of his murderous, merry band entered behind him. The undead half were ghouls, all Made by him. As one of only six *Nephilim* in Keel's service, the task of 'recruiting' new ghouls for the war was one that fell to him as well. At first, he had resented the task, forced to share his blood with whatever unfortunates were dragged down to the Crypts, but now he rather enjoyed seeing his 'spawn', the living corrupted into undead. Once-good people corrupted into dark reflections of themselves.

His ghouls might be warborn, starved of blood and then allowed to gorge on the innocent again and again until the last of their humanity and conscience was crushed, but he rather fancied those *he* Made also inherited some of his own amorality and talent for violence. Certainly, they were traits he encouraged, and tonight he would show them the heady joys of killing.

Some would die, many perhaps, but the survivors would have proved themselves. And more importantly, helped Canning prove himself to Keel. Their hunger had been somewhat sated, enough to ensure that they kept their wits and obeyed orders, yet enough blood was withheld to goad them to violence when the order was given.

Having happily murdered even while alive, Canning needed no such prodding to awaken his own bloodthirst, and so he had drunk long and deeply from a young couple unfortunate enough to cross paths with him. Blood was strength, and his would be needed tonight.

"Mr Canning," Nash said as he and his five men entered behind the ghouls. They were some of Keel's mercenaries, armed with rifles, shotguns and pistols.

Canning consulted his pocket watch. "Jana and her group should be heading down into the basement now from the shop across the road." He noticed his lads and lassies moving towards the back of the shop. "Wait."

"Are we not to attack together?" a middle-aged woman asked. In times of peace, new ghouls were made from those who had served the undead well, the reward of immortality. In war, quantity was desired over quality.

"Let the other groups go first," Canning said. By minutes only but let them be the first to meet the Crypt's defenders. Nash gave a nod of silent approval; willing to fight for money, but preferring not to die for it.

None argued, silence falling over the fifteen ghouls and mercenaries as Canning led them down into the basement. The expensive façade on the shop floor gave way to exposed brick and pipes, a door lying closed at the far end. Most of the workers who staffed the shops, banks and offices of Bothwell Street toiled by day in blissful ignorance of the undead slumbering in the foundations and basements beneath them, connected by a warren of tunnels running beneath the streets and buildings.

Weeks of surveillance had revealed to Keel's people which buildings were most often used by the undead to access the Crypts below Bothwell, Hope, Gordon and Union streets, and Canning was confident that neither he nor the other three groups would be interrupted prior to descending into the foundations.

Five minutes later, he snapped his pocket watch shut and looked at the pale, half-wasted faces watching him, knives held tightly. “Time to get killing, my friends. No mercy!”

On his nod the door was forced open, Canning leading his band into a haphazard maze of tunnels and gaps separating the building foundations. A shotgun with shortened barrels hung from his shoulder, its shells containing gunpowder and silver shrapnel. In these confined spaces, he harboured no doubts that it would prove a most lethal combination when discharged into those undead lurking down here.

Onwards they moved, silent and swift. He carried a long silver knife, hoping to kill the first few undead they encountered silently. If the alarm was raised too early, if the undead of this Crypt succeeded in arming themselves and forming a defence, then the mission would end in failure.

A noise sounded ahead, and he signalled his followers to wait. He crept on, keeping low and moving slowly, knife ready. Darkness claimed this area, assuring Canning that he had not yet reached the heart of the Crypt.

He peered round a corner and spied a figure approaching. It was too dark even for his undead-enhanced eyes to discern whether it was a man or woman, not that it mattered where the undead were concerned. Canning waited until the scraping of shoe-soles against the ground grew louder, and then he lunged, driving his knife into the unwary figure’s chest.

His victim, a man, collapsed silently to the ground, dying – for a second time if they were undead. Canning was pleased to note his knife had found his victim’s heart, a strike which would kill Lord Fisher as quickly as it would whoever this had been.

He and his band advanced deeper into the Crypt, meeting no more sentries or stragglers. By now, the three other groups should be likewise approaching the centre of the Crypt, and Canning was of a mind to let them bear the brunt of the initial assault.

Sure enough, muffled gunshots echoed down the tunnels and gaps between building foundations. “Come on!” Canning urged as he increased his speed. Let the other *Nephilim* attack first, yes, but to dally too long risked them being either routed in defeat or victorious before Canning could join in. Neither would endear him to Keel.

The gunshots got louder, and by now everyone in the Crypts would know they were under attack. Canning and his troop found themselves flanking a group of undead rushing to the gunfire, Nash and his men slaughtering them with silver shot. As practiced, the ghouls then charged to finish off the survivors with silver blades and brute force.

Had the enemy been mortal, Canning knew that there would have been the risk of the Thirst overcoming his ghouls’ reason, but they would find no such sustenance from the fallen undead, and so there was little difficulty in restoring them to order.

More gunfire could be heard as the four groups converged, pushing deeper through the foundations of Bothwell Street. Guillam’s brief alliance with Lucifer had seen Keel lose control of the police, but tonight would see Fisher and Guillam lose control of the centre of Glasgow. Their warborn ghouls were down here, and Canning knew it would be a bloody bit of work taking this Crypt, but worth it to deal such a blow against the enemy.

“Move!” he snarled, urging his followers on. Nash and his hired guns followed, encouraged by their success so far.

A wounded Jana waited for them, reduced to an escort of three, all undead. “Canning.”

“Jana.” He made a show of looking around. “Where are the rest of your people? Chasing a beaten enemy, aye?”

She grimaced. "Dead. We are in heart of the Crypt. Ambush waiting around corner."

Her accent was strong, but Canning understood her. Worse, it was clear he was now expected to lead his group into the same killing ground that had done for hers. If he refused, Keel would not be happy. If he accepted, he risked being killed, and neither was an outcome he favoured.

I must attack. But who to send first? His first instinct was to sacrifice Nash and his mercenaries but after a reluctant consideration he decided his ghouls were a better choice. He quickly laid out his plan of attack, ignoring the looks of dismay on several faces. His ghouls knew him all too well by now, and better to risk likely death than face its certainty by disobeying his orders. Nash and his men had an air of fear about them, but they likewise knew what would happen should they disobey Canning and Jana.

On his nod, his nine ghouls and Jana's three charged an enemy hidden in darkness. Canning listened as guns fired before signalling Nash and his men to follow the ghouls.

Canning and Jana turned the corner, seeing bodies fall. The ghouls had borne the brunt of the assault, but every bullet that struck them was one less to kill the more vulnerable mercenaries, and Nash's men were competent. As Guillam's undead fired at Canning's ghouls, Nash and his men fired back, silver bullets striking home.

Howls echoed out as enemy ghouls charged, no doubt recently Made, sent out to slow the attackers, and so utterly consumed by the Thirst to be heedless of danger. Guns fired, Nash and his men well-trained in fighting the undead. Death had taken those slow to learn these past months.

Other shots could be heard as more of Keel's forces finally arrived, and the battle for the Crypt disintegrated into a chaotic melee. Canning decided it was time to enter the fray himself and took a rifle from the body of one of Nash's men. Lanterns brought by the mercenaries had been opened and left on the ground.

Canning knelt and peered down the corridor, raising his

rifle. A woman in rags was reaching for one of his own ghouls, so he shot her in the chest. He doubted his bullet had struck her heart, but silver was anathema to the undead, especially a blood-deprived ghoul, and so he trusted in his own to finish her off. Shouts and gunshots turned to screams as shotguns were emptied, and Fisher's surviving ghouls fell upon the mercenaries.

Canning dropped the rifle and unslung his own shotgun, pulling back a hammer as he moved forwards. Risky, yes, but to win meant taking risks. The first barrel he discharged tore apart two screaming ghouls with silver shot. The second barrel halted another howling charge of feral ghouls in its tracks, buying time for Nash's disciplined survivors to reload.

Three shotguns fired a ragged volley, and Canning felt a savage relief in seeing the enemy stagger back. He dropped his shotgun and drew a revolver, knowing he had six bullets and that he must make them count.

Which he did. His last shot fired, and his knife drawn, Canning gloried in the spilled blood as he stabbed and hacked, his joy slightly dampened by the fact that he was killing undead rather than the living. Again and again, he stabbed his knife into the guts of a *Nephilim*, raising it high one last–

"Wait!" Jana grabbed his arm, the interference sparking fresh rage.

"Unhand me," he growled, Unveiling.

Her eyes met his, uncowed, and he belatedly recalled that she was over a century old. "Let one of our ghouls feed on his heart," she said.

Canning paused, forced to admit the sense in that, giving Keel one more *Nephilim*. The battle was won, he noted, his victim being among the last defenders to fall. "Any ghoul in mind?" he asked as survivors slew any of Fisher's ghouls who still lived before tending to their own wounded.

Jana looked around. "Whichever of yours you feel fought particularly well," she said, not sounding as if she cared overly much.

Neither did Canning, in truth. “Merton,” he called out.

“Dead,” someone answered.

Canning looked around at the survivors, everyone gathered in the open space that served as the heart of the Crypt, now strewn with bodies and smelling of gunpowder and blood. Choosing a newly Made or unproven ghoul over one of the older ones would cause resentment. “Tessa,” he said, spying one of the first ghouls he had Made.

Most of the ghouls Made by both sides tended to be victims snatched off the streets, generally the homeless or prostitutes. Indeed, a local newspaper had commented recently on the fall in the number of prostitutes walking the streets, hailing it a sign of improving public morality. In truth, many had been snatched for their blood, and others were now undead, Tessa having spent six weeks as a ghoul being intermittently starved of blood before having victims thrown at her to gorge from.

He had not seen her fight this night, but she had survived and looked bloody. “You may take his heart.”

He ignored the barely hidden disappointment of the other two surviving ghouls. Tessa approached, a light in her eyes as Canning and Jana held the wounded *Nephilim* down. She stabbed her knife down into the man’s chest and pulled up shattered ribs to expose his unbeating heart.

Watching her pull it free and start to devour it recalled Canning to the *Nephilim* he had killed in the spring. Cooper, that was his name! Cooper’s heart had Transitioned him from ghoul to *Nephilim* mere weeks after he had become undead, saving him a year or more of servitude as a ghoul. Tessa was now Keel’s seventh *Nephilim*. Sixth, discounting the still

absent Bresnik.

The rest of the attacking force arrived, Keel himself accompanied by the *Nephilim* Klaus.

The demon looked around. “Report.”

Jana answered. “The Crypt is ours.”

“Excellent. Our losses?”

None of the four *Nephilim* who had led the assault had

fallen, doubtless a relief to Keel. Of the forty-odd ghouls who had entered the Crypt, eighteen survived, one now Transitioning to *Nephilim*. Twenty-eight mercenaries had accompanied the undead, sixteen suffering no or only minor injuries. The rest were dead or dying, and on Fisher's nod Jana and Klaus began feeding their undead blood to the badly wounded mercenaries, none of their fellows daring to voice any complaint. That done, any silver bullets were removed from wounds before each was killed in such a way as to not prevent their Transition to undead.

Canning stood over Nash's body, having fed the mercenary leader his own blood. A ghoul had stabbed him at the last, saving Canning the need to hunt around a wound for any silver, which pleased him. If Nash survived the Transition to ghoul, he would be a useful man in Keel's House.

"Master," a *Nephilim* called Uriah called out. "You should see this."

Canning followed them down a tunnel to a locked door with a viewing hatch that reminded him of his time in prison.

"Ghouls, Master," Uriah said. "Fourteen of them, recently Made, I'd say."

"Recently made," Keel repeated. "And thus with no loyalty to Guillam."

"We keep them?"

"Keep them. We took heavy losses capturing this Crypt and will need to quickly replace those losses if we are to hold it," Keel said.

That gave Canning pause. Margot Guillam would not let this disaster go unanswered. If it proved insult enough to draw Niall Fisher from seclusion, then a half-dozen *Nephilim*, two score ghouls and a small band of guns-for-hire would face the wrath of a *Dominus*, two Elders, and maybe two score *Nephilim*.

We would not survive that. What, then, was Keel's plan?

Chapter Twenty-Three

A Very Long Time Ago

Palm trees lining the bank of the river stirred as the hot breeze caressed them, the horizon a crimson blaze as the sun set, stars gleaming already in the night sky. Lilith filled her clay jug with water and stood, knowing to linger risked her falling afoul of the crocodiles that haunted the river.

Her second husband had been killed by one such creature, her first having died after a wound turned bad. Not uncommon, but the loss of two husbands within a year – the same year the rains had been late to fall, and children had sickened – had left the villagers regarding her with suspicion.

Lilith's father was an Elder in the village, respected enough that the others did not cast her out. All the same, her mother now looked after Tammuz while Lilith lived in a small hut just outside the village. Fear would pass, her father assured her, and she would soon be allowed to return to the village. Until then, she must tend to sheep and miss her infant son, shunned and lonely.

Her hut was built on the upper pasture, high enough to be safe when the river flooded and close enough to the vagabond sheep that she could watch over them. The Great War had left them alone so far, the gods battling it out to the west. *Yomiel*, who ruled this land, had gathered many of the younger men and taken his army to join forces with *Ramiel* and *Arakiel*, the three allied against a fellow god.

Lost in thought, Lilith had been about to gut some fish

she had caught earlier when she realised she was not alone. A tall, slender figure approached, silhouetted against the night. As they drew closer to Lilith's fire, she was surprised to see it was a woman. She had never seen a man stand so tall, never mind a woman. The stranger had long black hair, her skin gleaming grey by the light of Lilith's fire, and she bore several vicious-looking wounds.

"There is a healer in the village," Lilith called out, a fear going through her.

"I have no need of your healers," the woman said as she approached. She stood tall and beautiful, unravaged by illness, age or the burdens of life like Lilith and her fellow villagers. Even the wounds seemed to leave her untroubled.

"Who are you?" Lilith whispered, trembling as she realised she was in the presence of a god.

"I am *Samiel*," the woman answered.

The name was unfamiliar to Lilith, not that she spent much time pondering the gods. Her face must have betrayed her lack of recognition, for *Samiel* smiled wryly. "I am the one my kindred call the Lightbringer."

That name was infamous, this god a sworn enemy to *Yomiel* and many of the other gods. Such matters were well beyond Lilith, but travellers to the village claimed Lightbringer was the one responsible for the gods being cast out of their realm to earth. Given the village was forever forced to tithe crops and young men to feed the never-ending wars, that was reason enough for Lilith to hate this god.

"Can I get you something to eat?" she asked, her eyes lowered. *Yomiel* would not take kindly to one of her subjects helping a rival, but for the moment Lilith was more fearful of the god before her than the one in the west.

"In a moment," *Samiel* answered, something in her tone sending a chill of fear down Lilith's back despite the warm night. "My army was defeated four nights ago, and I have spent every night since running, every day hiding from the sun."

She stepped forwards and grabbed Lilith before she could react, mouth opening to reveal lengthening fangs as her head ducked down towards Lilith's throat. Lilith struggled, or tried to, her strength as nothing compared to the god holding her. Her neck burned as those fangs pierced her flesh. The gods needed blood to sustain them, and Lilith feared this one would require every drop it could wring from her.

A hand lay across her mouth, and in one last act of contrary defiance, she bit down on that hand, teeth tearing away flesh. Blood filled her mouth, sickly and vile, and she choked as it slid down her throat. She wondered if *Samiel* even noticed. Her head spun and a veil of darkness fell over her.

*

Awareness crept tentatively over her, her senses slow to awaken. There was no pain, though her limbs were grazed and bleeding. She was vaguely aware of having awoken earlier, consumed by a terrible thirst, of being in her parents' hut…

Lilith realised she lay on the ground, and that night had fallen. She was in her village. No moon or stars glittered above, clouds covering the sky. Nor did any fires burn, the village cloaked in darkness. But she could see, she realised, sufficiently to discern the dark shapes that littered the ground, unmoving.

The villagers, she realised in horror. Dead. Their throats had been ripped out, by *Samiel*, she assumed. Somehow, the god had spared her yet slain her people.

Lilith ran to her parents' hut, where her son lived. *No...*

Her family lay dead within. Likewise, they had been mutilated, though the wounds to them were more numerous. She fled the hut, fled the expressions of frozen horror on her mother and father's faces. Her son's eyes were closed, and she clung to the desperate hope that he had died sleeping.

Samiel was waiting for her. The god regarded her with

an intent curiosity. "I was not sure you would awaken again."

"You killed them all," she screamed. "Why did you spare me?" *Why!* Her son's bloodied body was burned into her mind.

"Them all? No. You killed some, starting with your kin. I believe the villagers found your body where I left it, taking it to your family." *Samiel* walked closer. "I returned here as night fell, for another to feed from, only to find the village in chaos. For you had risen as darkness fell, feral and hungry. You killed your kin first, and then those villagers who tried to stop you. I killed the rest, those who did not flee."

"I don't understand." Her head spun.

"I killed you last night. Tonight, you rose, hungry for blood and so you fed."

Flickers of memory came to her, of screams and people running, some towards her, others away. *No*. "I killed my son," she whispered.

"Yes," *Samiel* said flatly.

Only then did Lilith realise she drew no breath, save to speak. There was a stillness to her. "What am I?"

"Neither living nor dead. *Un*dead, like me and my kin, perhaps."

"How?" It came out as a whisper.

"You bit me and drank my blood. Blood formed from the stuff of Heaven, the stuff of creation. It changed you, revived your corpse, leaving you undead." *Samiel* spoke as much to herself as she did to Lilith. "Stronger than the living. With an army such as you, I might stand against those of my kindred who seek my head."

"I'm a monster," Lilith said, despair binding her.

"You might walk this world forever, the first of my army," *Samiel* said.

Lilith regarded her but said nothing.

You made me a monster. A monster that killed my child.

I will not forget.

And one day I will bring you down, Lightbringer.

Chapter Twenty-Four

"Bad news?" Barra asked.

Tam looked up from the two letters he had been reading, guessing their contents had drawn a frown.

"I suppose so. A bastard named Roddy McBride burned down my pharmacy and flat." That was what Hunt's first letter had said. There had been a second also waiting in the post office, telling of the police arresting Hunt and Lady Delaney among others. It seemed the Templars Steiner and Gray had returned to Glasgow. What had been of interest had been Hunt's revelation that Foley's old friend, John Grant, had been one of the arresting policemen. The letter had said little more, save to assure Foley that Hunt expected no further trouble from the police.

"You suppose so?" Barra's eyes had widened. "Your business and home are gone."

"It was my father's business and meant to be my brother's, God rest them. I inherited it but it was never really my calling," he said. His flat had always borne the stamp of his parents, all the furniture inherited from them. Living here felt like a new start, and losing the shop and flat just removed any lingering ties to his old life.

"Will you return to Glasgow and deal with this McBride?" Barra asked. She was twenty-six, but had only requested to be bitten the year before. Like Foley, it was too soon to tell how fast or slow she would age. Elder Anna had seen ninety-two years but looked no older than sixty. Eustace was not yet thirty but had the aches, pains and weathered look of a middle-aged man.

"Tam?" she said, breaking his reverie.

"Sorry! No, I see no reason to return to Glasgow," he said slowly. "My friends can attend to the last of my affairs there. They can deal with McBride if they want. Certainly, they've dealt with worse than that bastard."

Barra straightened at the mention of his 'friends'. One of those friends had killed her cousin in the summer, and Foley inwardly cursed himself for mentioning them.

Around thirty werewolves and forty non-werewolves, including children, lived and worked the estate, some staying in the main house while families lived in nearby cottages. Laird Archibald and Elder Anna led the pack and managed the estate, while Elders Rab and Veronica mentored the younger werewolves.

After a year or so, a werewolf would start to gain some measure of control and sense of self upon changing, and that could not come soon enough for Foley. An Elder could transform at will and maintained lucidity while a wolf, capabilities Foley envied. For the youngest werewolves, every full moon brought the risk of getting loose and spilling innocent blood, which Foley had already done near Loch Aline.

He had asked about children, wondering at the risks that posed, but he had been assured that lycanthropy was not an inherited trait. Upon reaching adulthood, members of the community would be given the choice of being bitten by an Elder or remaining fully human. Barra had initially declined to be bitten until the year before, along with her younger cousin.

Should a werewolf become pregnant, she would be given a Charm to prevent transformation. Foley had felt excitement on learning of this magic, but he had been told that the pack only possessed a handful of the precious charms and that they were kept either for women who were pregnant or were trying to conceive, or for anyone who might be away from the estate during a full moon, should there be any to spare.

Further, he had been warned that to prevent the transformation would delay his ability to gain control over the wolf. Better to let the transformation happen each full moon where there was no one to harm, where the rest of the pack would keep him in line.

A bell tolled, telling Foley that it was time for the evening meal, the hour so late that darkness was falling. They broke their fast early here, and dined late.

He took his place at the long, rough-finished table in the dining room. Candles illuminated the room, Laird Archibald seated at one end. Twelve of them sat at the table, including another two of the four Elders. Foley had rarely eaten so well since his mother had died, the table boasting bowls of thick, meaty broth, and platters of steaming vegetables and roasted meat.

Tankards filled with ale sat at every place, lively conversation passing back and forth. He was still an outsider, but for now he found himself content to observe the warm familial bonds shared by those around him, and dared hope they might in time snare him also.

"The first snows might fall early this year," Anna said.

The others nodded sombre agreement. Foley had never liked the stuff, and the others had spoken enough of winter for him to know it would be a hard season spent rescuing livestock from thick snow.

*

Johnny McBride's breath turned to steam as he spoke quietly. "Right. Let's get this done. Take Foley alive. If anyone else gets in your way, kill them."

Keane listened as the other six men muttered their assent, armed with a mix of pistols and shotguns. He held a shotgun, reluctant to use it. Not that the others cared overly much if he did or not. His job had been to find Tam Foley, and that he had done.

After days staying in the Drover's Inn, doing little else but drink, Keane had sensed the letter marked with his blood finally move from the post office. McBride had been told, and Keane had led two of the men to the letter's location, to this remote farming estate hidden by hills and woods.

McBride had casually asked around about the estate, learning that the Inverarnan locals knew little. The people living on it kept themselves to themselves, it seemed, not mingling with the locals. Which suited Keane, as it meant no one in the area would trouble themselves to investigate the gunshots, putting it down to hunting.

They're on their own. God help them.

Keane followed McBride and his six men, wishing he had been allowed to stay behind to drink his fill of ale and whisky in the Drover's Inn taproom. Creeping up hills and through forests was not how he wanted to spend his nights, least of all on a mission of murder.

Gunshots shattered the silence as the group met the first residents unfortunate enough to cross their paths. First contact made, McBride's men fired several shots at nearby cottages, the intent being to spread panic and prevent the residents coming together to form a cohesive resistance.

Men and women left their homes to investigate the commotion, silhouettes McBride's men gunned down without mercy or hesitation as they advanced on the main house. As screams pierced the night, Keane fired into the air. Best to let the others think he had taken part in this horror, or they might leave him here.

After the initial onslaught, McBride and his men rounded up the stunned survivors into the centre of the courtyard. No children, Keane was relieved to see, the families maybe living in the cottages and crofts on the edge of the estate. Lanterns were lit and placed down, illuminating the courtyard.

Johnny McBride stood before the prisoners, his rapid breaths condensing as he spoke. "Mr Foley. You're looking well for a man my brother shot twice in the guts and left to die."

"You've killed innocents just to get to me, you bastard. How did you find me?" There was a dread in Foley's voice. Maybe he feared Hunt had been tortured for his address.

"Mr Keane, here, used his talent to track a letter sent to you by your friend," McBride said. "We've spent days waiting for you to collect it from the post office, and here we are. You were involved in my brother Eddie's death."

"Eddie was killed by a Templar called Carter, who died on the Necropolis in April." Foley sounded resigned. "My friend and I were tied up, at gunpoint, by several men, one of whom had my gun. No way we were getting free and killing your brother and his men. The Templars turned up, killed your brother and his men, and freed my friend and I."

"How did you survive Roddy shooting you?" McBride asked. "You were set for a slow, painful death. No way you were surviving that. Magic?"

"Not quite."

An old woman knelt next to one of the dead or wounded, hate on her face as she looked up at McBride. "Leave here. If you stay, you'll find out how Tam survived his wounds."

"Shut your mouth," McBride snarled.

"How's Laird Archibald?" Foley asked.

The woman slowly stood. "Dead."

"I'm sorry, Anna." There was pain and guilt in Foley's voice.

"You did not kill him, Tam. Barra, how is Rab?"

A woman looked up, rage in her voice. "Dying, at the moment."

Anna turned to McBride. "Take your people and go. Now. Your last warning."

"We'll leave when we're done. In the morning. After we're done with Foley," he said, an ugly promise of violence in his voice. Keane knew Foley's death would be slow and terrible, and that none on this estate would be left alive to speak of it.

"So be it." There was a heavy finality in Anna's voice, and a promise that sounded an alarm within Keane.

The dying Rab, the one Barra tended to, began to spasm, his dying convulsions maybe. Anna fell to her knees, limbs jerking, agony written on her face. None of those present showed any sign of surprise, nor alarm. Barra smiled in anticipation.

"You want to know how I survived those wounds?" Foley asked. "You're about to find out, you bastards."

Anna and Rab screamed, their torsos exploding in blood and gore as something emerged from within each of them, tearing its way out of their flesh. Keane stared as the two bodies started to rot away, two growing beasts in their place. Too late he realised what they were dealing with.

"Werewolves!" he cried out. "Shoot them!"

Too late. A large shape flew out from the darkness, knocking over several of McBride's men, snarling as its jaws gripped Cammy Rowe's throat. As the third werewolf killed Rowe, fur sprouted from the other two beasts. McBride and his men were too stunned by the transformation and distracted by the attack to kill the two growing werewolves while they were vulnerable. Keane had never, to his knowledge, met a werewolf before, but some of his acquaintances in the magician community had, and had spoken of it. There was no full moon, meaning they must be … Elders? … which also meant these wolves were not feral.

The death of Rowe awoke the others to action, at least two guns firing as the other two wolves attacked, now grizzled and massive. One issued a piercing yelp as McBride emptied a barrel of buckshot into it, too late to save Caleb Tonner from having his throat ripped out. He pulled back the second hammer, but the jaws of another wolf closed around his arm and dragged him to the ground.

Keane watched as McBride pulled a revolver from his coat pocket with his free hand and fired it into the wolf's skull. His arm a ragged mess, face twisted in agony, he fired at the third wolf. Two of his men shot it, too, and it lay still on the ground.

By then most of the surviving residents had joined the fight, some falling as a couple of McBride's surviving men managed to fire before being overwhelmed and beaten to the ground. Keane did not think any of them would be getting up ever again.

He was distantly aware that he was carrying a gun, and

after moment's thought, let it fall from his hands. Johnny McBride was struggling to re-cock his revolver when Tam Foley kicked it from his hand.

"That's how I survived," Foley said, pointing to the first wolf McBride had shot, still alive. The other two weren't moving. There was the sound of breaking bone as something ripped the wounded wolf apart from the inside, and Keane stared as what looked like a blood-covered child crawled out, already starting to grow.

The girl, Barra, had run to the house as soon as the surviving werewolf began its transformation back to human, returning with a robe which she handed over to the naked woman. Keane recognised the blood-smeared woman as Anna, bearing none of the wounds she had suffered as a wolf.

"Rab … Veronica," Anna managed to ask.

"Dead, Anna," someone said. Neither of the other two wolves stirred.

Despite being clearly fatigued from transforming into a wolf and then back again, Anna walked over to where McBride lay on the ground. "Who is this man?"

"He's Johnny McBride, the younger brother of Roddy McBride, patriarch of a Glasgow family who run a large criminal gang," Foley said.

"They came here for you?" she asked.

His head lowered. "Aye. I'm sorry, Anna."

"You did not kill our friends, Tam."

There was fear and pain on the younger McBride's face. "My brother is–"

"Not here." Foley's voice was cold.

"What do we do with him?" someone asked. Most of the survivors had left the courtyard, Keane guessing to search for those killed and wounded during McBride's rampage.

"Hang him," Anna said. "Then have the bodies disposed of. Burned, and the ashes scattered. Not on our land, mind. I won't have Archibald's home tainted with the remains of those who murdered him and our people."

"What of this one?" Foley asked, pointing to Keane.

A blade of fear went through him. "I never shot anyone."

Foley regarded him. "His name is Jimmy Keane. He's a Diviner. He led McBride and the others here. A letter, aye?"

Keane nodded. "A letter from Wilton Hunt was marked with my blood, letting me follow it."

"You didn't know where I was until I collected the letter today?" Foley asked.

"No, but we knew the letter was bound for a post office in this area, from the address," Keane said, praying they would let him live if he cooperated.

"And it was Roddy McBride who had my pharmacy and flat set on fire?"

"Aye. To get Hunt to write to you," Keane said. Belatedly he recalled it was Bishop Redfort's plan, but he decided that made no difference.

*

Guilt and anger kept Foley's fatigue at bay as he helped the survivors take the wounded to the main house and tend to them while others gathered the dead. Anna was now the last surviving Elder, was now the leader of this gutted community. Men and women from the outlying crofts and cottages had arrived to help, but many were dead and others were wounded.

"Tam." Barra had survived, at least. "Anna wants us all in the barn."

Foley followed, noting that only werewolves were present.

"Tam," Anna said. She looked exhausted, Foley recalling that she was in her nineties, even if she looked younger. "We are discussing what to do next. How to answer … this."

Something tightened in Foley's gut. This had been a sanctuary to him, only now it had been desecrated. And worse, when Johnny McBride failed to return, Roddy would send more men, likely led by himself, and they'd tear this area apart hunting for Foley. *Twice I've come here and both times I've brought death to these people.*

"I will go to Glasgow and deal with Roddy McBride," Foley said reluctantly. "Or this will happen again. This is my mess and I will clean it up."

"Some of us should come with you," Barra said.

"Too many of the pack have died, and you don't know the city, Barra. I'll go and end this," Foley said.

"Agreed. I am too old for a war, Tam," Anna said. "And we will need you here, Barra."

"What of the estate?" Eustace asked. "We've been exposed here. If that man McBride left a message or sent a letter telling his brother of this place…"

"Our time here may be done," Anna said, regret heavy in her voice. "When those men fail to return to the inn or wherever else they may have been staying, and word spreads of the gunshots echoing out over these hills, local eyes will turn our way."

"Where can we go?" Barra asked. She had lived here all her life, Foley knew.

"We will find somewhere, Barra. After winter," Anna said. She looked at Foley, raw grief and anger in her eyes. "You will avenge our losses here, Tam?"

What choice have I? "Aye, Anna." He looked her in the eye. "My word. Roddy McBride will die, or I will."

"Thank you. Do you need anything?"

"One of your charms, if you can spare it. I'll likely be away during the full moon." He hesitated. "If I'm still welcome among you, would you send word of your new location to the Inverarnan Post Office, if you have to leave before I return?"

"I will," Anna promised.

"You'll return to us?" Barra asked.

"If I can."

Foley stepped outside the barn, breathing in the cold air. It was too dark for him to see, but he knew that Johnny McBride was hanging from a tree by the edge of the courtyard, Jimmy Keane decorating the tree next to him.

You wanted a war, Roddy McBride? You've damned well got one.

Chapter Twenty-Five

Redfort sat at his usual booth in the Albert Club, taking a sip of wine and thereafter clasping his hands together beneath the table to disguise their trembling. There were risks tonight, but Keel's recent success convinced him that giving the demon cause to doubt his loyalty was perhaps the greater risk.

At least the club was a public place, for whatever that was worth. As always, his derringer was within reach, a silver bullet within its single chamber. Though given the nature of tonight's guest, failure to strike either brain or heart would see his death follow swiftly and bloodily. Quite ruining the evening for everyone.

A waiter led the guest over to his table, a fresh tingle of fear going through Redfort. Edmund Crowe sat down as the waiter pushed the seat in.

"Mr Crowe, I'm pleased that you accepted my invitation," Redfort said. He turned to the waiter. "We do not wish to be disturbed."

"My pleasure, your Grace," Crowe said in his dusty, dry voice. As an Elder *Nephilim* and head of the Heron Crowe Bank he was the oldest and among the richest men in Glasgow. Indeed, the west of Scotland.

Man, indeed. For such a powerful creature, he had kept a remarkably low profile, keeping to the shadows while the late Mr Heron – and his forebears – had conducted the day-to-day business of the bank.

Such days in the shadows were gone.

Redfort cleared his throat. "I would offer you refreshment, however…" The *Nephilim* did not eat food or drink. A glass of wine lay before Redfort, already half-finished.

"Let us get down to business, Bishop Redfort," Crowe said.

"Of course. This has been a difficult time, Mr Crowe. Losing the Bothwell Street Crypt and the undead who dwelt there is a bitter blow."

"Indeed. A bold move by Keel. But then he was prone to such gambits." There was a familiarity in his voice when speaking of the demon.

"You knew him, then, when he was *Grigori*?" Redfort wondered if that bode well or ill for tonight's mission. "I did not know you were in Glasgow that long ago."

"I met him in London in the middle of the 16th century. He was leading an expedition to Bucharest, and my bank was based in London at that time," Crowe said. "Erik Keel and George Rannoch lingered in the city for a time disguised as Catholic priests, denouncing a painter called Henry … Henry Norman as a protestant."

Redfort frowned. "Why ever would they bother with such a triviality?"

Crowe's thin lips twitched in what was almost a smile. "Religion was anything but trivial to Queen Mary. I asked Rannoch, who claimed Norman was in truth a necromancer. In England at that time, witches were not burned, but heretics were, and so they accused him accordingly."

"A necromancer?" Redfort leaned back in his chair. An earlier incarnation of the necromancer latterly known as Dr Essex? If Keel had arranged for him to be burned to death, why would he now serve Keel? Had an agreement been reached between the two, where Norman had been burned while Rannoch found a replacement Vessel for his soul?

"So I was told. Several months after Norman's death, Keel and his expedition sailed to France," Crowe said.

That expedition's mission had been to ultimately wrest control of Bucharest from two warring undead Houses. For years Keel and his undead navigated the intrigues of western Europe before travelling east to Bucharest with the goal of seizing that city. Instead of a quick victory, he had found himself bogged down in a three-way war that lasted almost a century. The undead remaining in Glasgow, led by Keel's regent, Niall Fisher, found themselves increasingly dissatisfied with the absent Keel's rule, his demands for more money and undead to sustain his campaign.

Attrition had seen many of Glasgow's undead die in Bucharest, and those undead Made in Glasgow over eighty years to replace them had never known Keel, and thus their immediate loyalty was to Fisher. Keel commanding Fisher to lead reinforcements to Bucharest to help end the war once and for all proved the opportunity for Fisher to overthrow his master.

Having quietly secured a truce with the other two Houses in Bucharest, Fisher and his rebels turned on Keel and those loyal to him. Only Niall Fisher, Margot Guillam and Thomas Edwards survived, Fisher eating Keel's heart to become a *Dominus Nephilim*. He then led the survivors back to Glasgow.

That had been roughly two hundred years ago, and perhaps fearing he might meet the same fate as Keel, Fisher had largely hidden himself away, ruling first through Edwards, and now Guillam. Not an unreasonable fear, given Rannoch's betrayal this year.

Hence Redfort's meeting tonight with his fellow Councillor, Edmund Crowe. "Why did you relocate from London to Glasgow?" Redfort asked.

"Margot Guillam met with me upon her return from Bucharest after Keel's demise. Between the war in Bucharest and Niall Fisher's coup, the House was in dire need of money. I offered significant loans, and they offered a city completely within their control, a safe place to operate," Crowe said. "The subsequent tobacco trade with the New World proved this to be a wise decision."

"London was not safe?"

"Between rival banks operated by other *Nephilim*, and the increasing power of the Templars, London was becoming an unacceptable risk."

"Templars?" Redfort queried.

Crowe tilted his head. "Before becoming undead, I

worked for the Templar Order's London bank in the early 14th century. Upon it being declared heretic and disbanded by the then-Pope, I took much of its money and started my own bank. Many of the Templars were burned, others joined the Order of the Hospital of Saint John. The element of the Order who fought the undead fled abroad, quietly establishing chapters around the world.

"They returned to London just over two hundred years ago, though I do not believe they ever truly left. They knew who and what I was, that my bank was born from the carcass of theirs. My assets were attacked, forcing me to flee to Glasgow and merge what remained of my assets with Oliver Heron's to form the Heron Crowe Bank."

Redfort toyed with his wine glass, resisting the urge to down it in one. "How did you become undead?"

The undead banker offered a thin smile. "A tale for another time, your Grace."

"I look forward to hearing it one night," Redfort said, though this might well be his last.

"Perhaps when this war is won, your Grace. William Heron was the only man I ever told it to."

"Mr Heron was unmarried, are there any nephews or nieces to continue the line?" Not that he cared one way or the other.

"It appears William was the last Heron," Crowe said. Perhaps a little evasively.

Redfort sipped some wine, forcing himself to put it down. "These are difficult times. For two hundred years you have dwelt here independently of Lord Fisher, only now deigning to become part of his House. A House besieged by its previous master, one of the Fallen."

Crowe's face betrayed no reaction. He had not survived so long by being stupid, and Redfort prayed he would see the opportunity in what was being offered.

Or Redfort would not leave this club alive.

"I sense you are working up to a proposition, Bishop," Crowe said.

Redfort took a long drink from his wine, trying to calm the tremble in his hand. *Time to play my hand and pray it is a good one.* "Niall Fisher's days look to be almost done. In half a year he has been betrayed by one Elder and lost another. His House has suffered heavy losses, and the secret society his regents have ruled the city through has been crippled. Whether we wish it or not, Fisher's time is over, and Erik Keel's is fast returning. And he would invite you to join him."

Crowe regarded him, his pallid face betraying neither approval nor outrage. "An interesting offer." He motioned his hand, signalling Redfort to continue, which was heartening. Or at least suggested he was not going to immediately rip off Redfort's head.

Redfort raised his hand, and Erik Keel himself soon joined them at the table and sat down. A risk, but if Crowe killed his Vessel, Josiah could simply Summon him into another.

"Good evening. It has been many years, Mr Crowe."

"Hundreds, Mr Keel," Crowe said. "Or do you prefer *Arakiel*?"

"I prefer Erik Keel, for now, until I reclaim my true flesh and become *Arakiel* again in truth," the demon said.

"As you wish," Crowe said.

"Redfort has relayed my offer?" Keel asked.

"He tells me you wish me to defect to your side. Why I should do so, he did not say," Crowe said.

"I have taken the Bothwell Street Crypt from Fisher. His possession of my House is in its dying days," Keel said.

"Fisher is a *Dominus Nephilim*. Margot Guillam is an Elder. Between them, those two alone could defeat you. You were *Grigori*, and I assume you wish to capture Fisher alive in order to take his heart to restore yourself as *Grigori*. How do you think to take a *Dominus* without even one Elder?" Crowe asked.

"A plan has been set in motion." Keel sounded confident, at least. "You need not concern yourself with Niall Fisher."

"What you should concern yourself with is the score of Templars newly arrived in Glasgow," Redfort said, as arranged.

"I understood Steiner to have only brought one with him," Crowe said.

"He did. My understanding is that Steiner returned to Glasgow without permission. His master sent more Templars, from Edinburgh and London, and Steiner has been relieved of his duties," Redfort said. A pity his brother Templars had not simply shot him and dumped his body in the river. *I must do everything myself, it seems.*

Crowe looked at him. "You're very knowledgeable with regards to the Templars in this city. Have you a foot in their camp too?"

Redfort ignored the jibe regarding his loyalties. "Recall that it was I who masterminded the fall of the Templars in the spring. They have long memories and will doubtless seek me out. They also, as you said, well remember that much of the Heron Crowe Bank's early capital was once theirs. My source reports that your bank is among their targets, Mr Crowe. To be robbed once is a misfortune; twice would be a calamity."

Crowe looked reflective. "We should attend to them, as the Sooty Feathers did earlier this year."

"They are in contact with Lady Delaney, but most of them are not lodging with her," Redfort said. "We must lure them out."

"If I have the Templars dealt with, will you pledge your loyalty to me?" Keel asked.

Crowe hesitated. "Deal with the Templars, and I will provisionally follow you. Deal with Fisher and restore yourself to your old form, and you will have my open fealty."

The demon nodded once. "We have a deal, Mr Crowe."

"As you say."

Redfort watched as the pair shook hands, relieved that there would be no bloodshed tonight. At least, not in this restaurant.

Keel raised his hand briefly. "As a sign of good faith, I would like you to meet someone."

There was cold murder in Crowe's eyes as one of his

bank's directors, Walter Herriot, approached the table and stood next to Keel. "Mr Herriot. What a surprise seeing you here tonight."

"Cast no blame towards Mr Herriot, *Gadriel* has Possessed him for some time. You recall the attempt to abduct William Heron? Had that succeeded, *he* would have become *Gadriel*'s Vessel, ruling the bank and soon to sit on the Sooty Feather Council." Keel clasped his hands. "Instead, you prevented that abduction, Heron died at Dunkellen, and *you* were given the Seat on the Council. And Mr Herriot became *Gadriel*'s Vessel."

"You expect me to permit this demon to continue to spy on my bank?" Crowe asked.

"For now. I have another purpose for him that will benefit us both."

*

Steiner watched Lady Delaney's guest with a sceptical eye but kept his opinions to himself. Lt Millen had allowed him to observe this meeting, leaving it unsaid but understood that should Steiner overstep his bounds, he would be returned to Lady Delaney's cellar.

"To be clear, you are an employee of the Heron Crowe Bank, Mr Herriot?" Lady Delaney asked once her visitor had sat down. Steiner was curious – and suspicious – as to what had brought the banker here, to the home of one who opposed that bank. And presently entertained the scions of the Order that bank's founder had betrayed and stolen from.

"I am one of the bank's directors, Lady Delaney," the middle-aged man clarified.

Delaney studied him. "An unfortunate timing for you, Mr Herriot. Messers Millen, Steiner and Gray, and Miss Jackson, are Templars and have no love for your bank."

"You'll be showing us the vaults of your bank, Mr Herriot," Millen said with a menacing air of confidence.

"I do not have access," Herriot said. "Since the death of Mr Heron, only Mr Crowe has access, save for certain staff given a Warded token during the day."

"What brings you to my home, Mr Herriot?" Delaney asked. "My accounts with your bank were closed many years ago. And I have no wish to open another."

Herriot looked around the room. Seated, like everyone else. "Since the Dunkellen incident, Mr Crowe has tied the bank further to the Sooty Feather Society. He has a seat on their Council. I and most of the other directors believe that was a mistake, that our aligning ourselves with one faction risks us being destroyed in this war."

"My sympathies," Delaney said, not sounding particularly sympathetic.

"Why are you here?" Miss Knox asked.

Herriot leaned back in the chair. "I am a director of the Heron Crowe Bank, which exists to make money. In the last six months, many of our investors have died and their heirs have closed their accounts with us. Our bank was robbed, and the last Heron was killed. Speaking on behalf of myself and the other mortal directors, we want this war ended."

"Who is your favoured candidate to win?" Delaney asked dryly.

"Who do I believe will win, or who do I *want* to win?" Herriot looked at Lady Delaney. "The first, I could not say. The second, whichever 'candidate' will return this city to 'business as usual' again. Or perhaps … I wish for neither side to win."

"You wish both sides to lose," Steiner said. Were Herriot's motives truly as he claimed? Was he even human, or did a demon lurk inside him, seeking to use the Templars against whichever faction it opposed?

"Aye. An end to the undead controlling this city. It is … bad for business."

"How do you propose for a score of Templars to end it, Mr Herriot?" Lady Delaney asked.

"Despite recent losses, Niall Fisher's House is still the dominant. I can tell you where to find his regent, Margot Guillam," Herriot said.

There was a glint in Millen's eye. "Where is her Crypt?"

This was an opportunity, Steiner knew. Killing an Elder

vampyre and her undead attendants would be a great victory, even if Herriot was leading them into a trap – so long as the Templars proceeded cautiously.

Herriot hesitated before pushing aside whatever fear or lingering loyalty still held his tongue. "Dumbreck Castle. You can find Margot Guillam in Dumbreck Castle."

*

Kerry Knox listened as the others discussed what to do next, Walter Herriot having been allowed to leave. Margot Guillam had helped Knox and Luc … *Lord Ashwood* … save some of the people in this room, but if any harboured thoughts of gratitude, they were not enough to prompt them to speak against hunting down and killing the Elder *Nephilim*.

"I will lead the attack," Millen said, not that there had been any doubt. "Sergeant Jefferies will be my second."

Steiner stirred slightly but offered no complaint. The 'knight' appellation to his inquisitor rank was a recognition of his experience fighting the undead, and Millen would be wise to have named Steiner his second, regardless of his current disgrace.

"Gray, you will remain here to continue your recuperation," Millen said. A recognition of his wounds, or a rebuke for him following Steiner to Glasgow?

"You could use a marksman to cover your attack, and to offer cover should you need to flee," Gray said.

"There will be no flight," Millen said.

"What of me?" Steiner asked. "I would make myself useful."

Millen looked at him, but it was Caroline who spoke first. "A *knight*-inquisitor is not an ally a wise leader would quickly dismiss, Mr Millen. Mr Steiner is a veteran, and you would do well to include him."

"I would rather he remain here and attend to Gray," Millen said, doubtless aware of the insult he offered by reducing Steiner to the role of nursemaid.

Caroline looked at Steiner for a moment. "I will attend

to Gray's needs, thus freeing Steiner to accompany you."

Knox noted the surprise on Steiner's face, both appreciating what it cost Caroline to not be a part of this mission.

"I had intended for you to act as guide, Lady Delaney," Millen said.

"I can do that," Knox said. "I know the city as well as Lady Delaney."

"Fine. Steiner and Miss Knox will come, Lady Delaney will remain here with Gray," Millen said after a moment. To insist otherwise risked him looking churlish, or worse, threatened by the veteran Steiner's presence. "And the day after the attack, Steiner will return to London to answer to Grandmaster Maxwell."

Caroline did not look happy at missing what promised to be the most significant action taken against the undead since the attack on the Necropolis, but she kept her disappointment unvoiced. "Slaying an Elder vampyre will be no simple endeavour, least of all one in its own Crypt, likely attended by allies. What is your plan, Mr Millen?"

"We should acquire plans of the Dumbreck Castle," Knox said.

"That would be wise, but we should act quickly, attacking tomorrow during the day," Millen said.

"Such haste?" Caroline asked.

"To delay risks our banker 'friend' having a further change of heart," Millen said. "I am confident twenty-five of us can meet any threat we will find there."

"A fair point," Caroline conceded. Knox suspected she was referring to the risk of Herriot betraying them rather than twenty-five being necessarily sufficient; this war had seen many casualties. Steiner kept silent, perhaps knowing his own opinion would not be welcomed by Millen.

"We will need ink, pens and paper," the Templar leader announced.

This would be a long night, Knox knew.

Followed by a longer day.

Chapter Twenty-Six

Dumbreck Castle lay in the Pollokshields area, a formerly independent burgh that only two years prior had become part of the city of Glasgow. Steiner accepted there was no time to conduct a surveillance of the castle or check council records for plans, but Lady Delaney's library, at least, contained a book telling a little of the castle's history.

The castle had been built by the MacInesker family in the 16th century to replace an older castle, in turn replaced by Dunkellen House about a century later. According to Lady Delaney's book, Dumbreck Castle was an L-plan tower, standing four storeys tall and having been restored in recent years for use by the MacIneskers' factor.

If Walter Herriot was to be believed, the castle was now home to Margot Guillam and likely other undead. Perhaps, even, the reclusive Niall Fisher.

The day was cold and cloudless, an ineffectual autumn sun shining brightly overhead. It was eight minutes shy of ten o'clock, Lieutenant Millen having dispatched a handful of Templars to scout the castle grounds while the main force waited nearby. The daylight meant there was no risk of there being any undead outside the castle – indeed, most if not all would be partaking in whatever passed for sleep – however at best there would be gardeners and servants to contend with, and at worst armed guards protecting the undead while they slumbered.

Habit compelled Steiner to keep an eye on the rest of the Templars, on their disposition and movements, by dint of his extensive experience leading men and women in battle. Today, he was acutely aware that he was neither in charge nor second, and so kept his own counsel. Lieutenant Millen was young and less experienced than he, but Sergeant Jefferies had joined this war decades before. His battles against the undead of Edinburgh preceded his service with the Templars, and he had aided the Order's expedition there in its successful efforts to free that city of its scourge.

Steiner wondered at Grandmaster Maxwell's decision to not dispatch the eighteen London Templars under the command of an experienced knight-captain. Millen would make an acceptable second-in-command, but to have him lead men and women he had never before met, many of whom were more experienced, was … odd. Perhaps the grandmaster was trusting Millen to listen to his sergeants, but all the same Steiner wondered what was going on in London.

Such answers might have to wait. Steiner recognised most of the London Templars, however this was their first meeting in Glasgow, and he knew better than to antagonise Millen by associating with them unduly. For now, he would keep quiet and follow orders.

And if Millen proves inadequate for the great task before him? Steiner would remove the young lieutenant, should such prove to be the case, by gun or by knife, if need be. The mission was all. *Deus Vult*.

The London Templars had brought a small arsenal of weapons, everyone armed with a revolver and either a shotgun or rifle, every bullet forged from silver. Likewise, silver knives had been issued to everyone.

"You two, stay by the doors," Millen said to Schumacher and Ralle as the group congregated by the main entrance. "If this is a trap, we will need to leave quickly."

Steiner was heartened by the pragmatism in Millen's voice. Everyone here was willing to die in this war against the undead, but not to be needlessly sacrificed. Millen led the twenty-two others inside the castle.

*

Delaney stood in front of her dressing table as her maid, Ellison, arranged her hair. By now Kerry and the Templars should have reached Dumbreck Castle, and her absence from that mission pained her. Steiner had privately assured her that he would keep an eye on Kerry, but Delaney knew that should he have the choice between saving Kerry or killing Margot Guillam, he would choose the latter.

Kerry was well-trained, at least, and Delaney had quietly told her, should matters turn dire, to abandon the Templars and return home. Delaney was not alone in her discontent at being left behind; Terrance Gray was likewise unhappy at missing the battle. He was in a spare bedroom, slowly healing from his mistreatment at the hands of the demon *Maridiel*.

"Are you going somewhere nice, ma'am?" Ellison asked as she finished.

"I am taking Mr Gray out for luncheon." His dark skin would doubtless draw looks, but that was of no concern to her. Better to have the pair of them out of the confines of the house than to remain within all day, brooding in discontent over their exclusion from the attack.

Steiner was to be sent back to London tomorrow, though Delaney suspected that would depend on how today's attack went. Should Millen fail or fall, it might land on Steiner to seize the reins of command and recover the situation, and if so, he would stay. Ben Jefferies had the look of a sergeant, a man who would take command, if necessary, but preferred to follow than to lead. He would not contest Steiner's usurpation of command.

There was a knock on the bedroom door.

"Enter," Delaney said.

The door opened to reveal the butler, Smith, who entered. "Lady Delaney."

"What is it, Smith?"

A heavy sigh. "I have bad news, ma'am."

"So long as no one has died, Smith." The venerable

butler had proven to be a disappointment. Either *Lord Ashwood* had low standards where his staff was concerned, or age had withered Smith's abilities.

"Not yet, ma'am. But imminently."

Delaney looked at him. "Explain."

Smith raised his hand to reveal a derringer which he aimed at Ellison, the gunshot echoing round the bedroom.

"Ellison!" Delaney cried out as her maid fell to the ground. She knelt next to her but the blood frothing from her mouth made it clear the bullet had struck Ellison's lung, the poor woman starting to drown from her own blood.

"Why?" Delaney spat. Ellison had been her lady's maid for years, as close to a friend as she had enjoyed until Kerry's arrival.

"Be glad I never doused her in lamp oil and set her alight," the butler said.

Those words sent a chill down her spine as Smith revealed who he was, in truth. "*Beliel*." His name was like acid in her mouth.

He smiled as he loaded a fresh bullet into the gun's single chamber. "A *pleasure* to meet you again. Last time, our reunion was so short." He stepped forwards. "And painful."

Delaney pushed aside fear and grief, and an overwhelming hatred, forcing herself to find the cold calm that might allow her to survive.

Beliel stepped closer, Delaney noting that he kept a distance. Two deaths at her hand had taught the demon caution. *Perhaps a third will teach him to stay in Hell.*

"When did you Possess Smith? Upon his employment here?" she asked, seeking to purchase time. Had Gray heard the gunshot?

"Shortly before. *Arakiel* Summoned me to keep watch on Lucifer and his spawn after the failed attempt on the younger Hunt," *Beliel* said. "However, Lucifer showed no interest in involving himself in the war, and on seeing your advertisement for a butler, I seized the opportunity to re-enter your household." There was a dark promise in his smile.

"You have made for a poor servant."

"*Arakiel* might disagree. Thanks to me, he learned of your involvement with the Templars. A pity *Maridiel* failed to have you all killed after your arrest, but no matter."

A pit formed in Delaney's stomach. "You told *Arakiel* of today's attack."

Beliel's smile widened. "Only the timing of the attack, he already knew it would happen. *Gadriel* played his part well."

"*Gadriel?*" The pieces fell into place to reveal a dreadful picture. "Walter Herriot. Your master seeks to have the Templars kill Margot Guillam."

"And then deal with the Templars. In a matter of hours, one enemy will be gone, and another mortally wounded. Leaving me to attend to you, my dear Caroline." *Beliel* drew a knife and pocketed his derringer. "This will not end quickly."

A tide of fear washed over Delaney as the demon Unveiled, stalking her with knife raised. She raised her hands and prepared to defend herself.

Perhaps overconfident because she was unarmed, or perhaps fearing the commotion might alert the convalescing Gray, *Beliel* wasted no time before attacking. Delaney jumped aside at the last moment and drew her hair pin, in truth a short silver poniard that she stabbed into the demon's side.

Both fell to the ground, Delaney losing grip on the hairpin. *Beliel* cried out and stabbed with his blade. She grabbed hold of his wrist with both hands, and they wrestled for control of the knife. Smith had been an old, increasingly frail man; Delaney released her right hand's grip, making a fist and smashing her hand down on his face several times, feeling the cartilage of his nose shatter.

Blood exploded over his face, and Delaney pulled the knife from *Beliel*'s bony hand, stabbing it down into his abdomen. Again and again, she stabbed, the demon howling its agony. Part of her wanted to keep stabbing but another part thought it preferable to let the hellish thing suffer.

The bedroom door swung open again and Gray dashed inside. “I heard noise, what is–”

Delaney got to her feet, noting the American Templar stare in shock at the grey-haired butler bleeding out over her bedroom floor as she tried to catch her breath.

“I’m guessing he did more than fuck up your darjeeling tea,” Gray said upon finding his voice.

“Mr Gray, meet the demon *Beliel*.” She forced herself to assume a casual air, but had the demon prevailed…

“It does not look to be a long acquaintance,” Gray said. He doubtless saw the tremble she couldn’t quite suppress but he was good enough not to comment on it.

“It will not be,” Delaney agreed as the demon died slowly, face twisted in agony. “There is no time to waste. Our friends are walking into a trap. The banker who visited us with the location of Margot Guillam is in truth Possessed by a demon serving *Arakiel*.”

Alarm crossed Gray’s face. “The enemy will be waiting for Steiner and the others?”

“Not quite. It seems this trap is intended to snap shut on Guillam as well as your brethren and Miss Knox.”

“What can we do?” Gray asked.

“We need allies,” she decided. “Are you well enough to fight?”

“I’ll manage. Just where will we find allies with so little time to spare?”

Delaney grimaced. “I have an idea, and not one you will like any more than I do.”

*

Knox had rarely felt so alive or so scared as she and the Templars crept through Dumbreck Castle. The word ‘castle’ had put her in mind of something massive, with forbidding towers, but in truth it proved little more than an old large country house that had been added to over the years. The MacIneskers’ newer home, Dunkellen

House, was a grander affair, though with less thought for defence.

If Margot Guillam and other undead did live here, they would likely be found in the cellar, 'asleep' and vulnerable. Even if the undead awoke, there were over twenty armed men and women ready to slay them with silver.

And after? Millen had written to London about the presence of Lucifer as well as the existence of his son. If the Templar leader far away in London commanded it, they would attack the Hunts – would attempt to kill Lord Ashwood and Wilton Hunt. Knox was unsure how she felt about the young man she had first met in the theatre all those months ago, where he had played Lucifer in *Faustus*. She felt betrayed, yet Hunt had been given no say in his nature or parentage. He had stood against the undead and the demons, and the *zombis*.

Even Lucifer had done so.

"How long have you trained under Lady Delaney?" Miss Jackson asked quietly. There were four women among the group, the other two looking no less proficient than Jackson.

"Since April," Knox answered.

"Have you seen any action?" Jackson asked.

"Some," Knox said in self-deprecation. "Together we hunted vampyres haunting the streets. With Dr Sirk, we destroyed the Imperial Mill that the Sooty Feather Society was using as a Crypt for ghouls, letting them feed from orphans housed next to the mill."

"A fair start," Jackson said.

"I was also at Dunkellen House where we faced hundreds of *zombis*," she said, wanting the respect of these damned people.

"What is it like to fight *zombis*?" Jackson asked. If she was impressed, it didn't show.

"Like fighting ghouls, a bit, except that the only thing that works is damaging their brains. At least with ghouls, you can kill them with a shot or stab to the heart," Knox said. "A necromancer broke my ribs, but Lady Delaney killed him."

"I hear what happened at Dunkellen was bad," Jackson ventured. Caroline had written to the Templars of that dreadful day.

"Bad? A whole village died, rose from the dead, and killed dozens at Dunkellen House. Who then also rose from the dead and attacked the rest of us. Very few of us survived." She glanced at the Templar. "Hunt, his parents and Singh fought alongside us. Hunt's mother died saving her son."

That was met by silence.

"Sergeant Jefferies, take five with you and go room to room upstairs," Millen ordered. "We'll secure the kitchen and then go down into the cellar."

"Aye, sir. Parker, Jackson, Waite, Fleishmann … Knox. With me," Jefferies said.

Knox followed the others up the large staircase that led to the main hall, part of her relieved to be going upstairs rather than down into the cellar where the undead waited. She held a shotgun in both hands, knowing its poor range would be offset by the devastation it could cause in close quarters.

*

With two Templars standing outside the castle, six sent upstairs to secure the upper levels, and two left to guard the entrance hall, that left fifteen Templars to venture down into the cellars where, if Walter Herriot spoke truly, the undead dwelt.

Steiner had half-expected to be left in the entrance hall, but Millen was wise enough to recognise the folly in not fully using a man who had fought the undead for two decades. Not that any of the others, even those he knew from London, had spoken to him, his disgrace known to all. Though had it not been for his disobedience, they would not now be positioned to cleanse a castle of undead, including an Elder vampyre. Possibly even Glasgow's lord of vampyres, though Steiner privately feared that Niall Fisher would prove a foe beyond them, if he were present. *Unless we attack him unawares.*

A handful of servants were found in the kitchen while preparing luncheon, offering no defiance as two Templars led them into the pantry, ordered by Millen to bind and gag them. Two footmen had been with them, likely waiting to take the food upstairs once ready.

"Food for maybe fifteen, servants included," Anna Moir commented on surveying the kitchen. She had been a kitchen maid as a girl, Steiner recalled.

"Sergeant Jefferies should be able to deal with them," Millen said, more interested in the cramped stairs leading down to the cellar. How many enemies waited below, they had no idea, for the kitchen did not cater to the undead.

"Light the lanterns," Millen told Sergeant Sand. Templar doctrine said that when attacking an undead Crypt below ground, every third soldier should carry a lantern to ensure sufficient light.

"You brought just two lanterns?" Steiner asked Millen uneasily, taking care his voice did not carry beyond the two of them.

Millen glared at Steiner but not before he saw a flicker of chagrin. "Two will be enough. More lanterns mean more of us who can't shoot a gun."

Those carrying a lantern could still fire a pistol, and besides when battle was joined, they were trained to put the lanterns down and form a circle. But Steiner said nothing, knowing it would serve only to embarrass Millen and would likely see him sent back to the entrance hall.

"Sergeant, take three men down with you and report back on what you find," Millen said. A sensible precaution.

Sergeant Sand led three men down the stairs, the remaining Templars standing in the kitchen with grim faces and readied guns. The four men scouting the cellar should be gone for no more than five minutes, but it would be a long five minutes for the others.

*

"Hurry!" urged Redfort as he followed Neil MacInesker down the hidden passage's stairs. A soldier accompanied them as bodyguard, ostensibly to protect them both but Redfort knew the guards garrisoning Dumbreck Castle were there chiefly for MacInesker's sake.

The remaining guards had stayed behind to hold the main hall and slow down the attackers. It would have been a surprise attack had the intruders not broken Magdalene Quinn's Wards surrounding the castle and its grounds, and so given the defenders a little time to prepare.

"We're nearly there," MacInesker said, having some familiarity with the castle. "We'll be away before Keel's people take the hall."

"Aye." Though Redfort knew the invaders to be Templars, not mercenaries sent by Keel. Regent Guillam had hosted the Council here last night, most leaving early in the morning, but some remained. Fisher was probably not here, but today's slaughter might prove to be a mortal blow against his House. Albeit not one that the Templars would live long enough to savour.

"Won't the enemy be waiting for us?" the guard asked.

"This exit is secret," MacInesker assured him. "But we'll need to keep low when we leave the castle, in case they've left a guard outside."

*

"Someone comes," Arthur Hopper warned, followed by a chorus of breaths as everyone prepared for the worst.

"Ease your trigger fingers," Steiner said from habit. "Do not panic and fire at our comrades."

Lt Millen did not look happy at Steiner's brief usurpation but neither did he protest.

"It's Sand," a voice said, the sergeant taking a precaution lest someone panic at his reappearance at the top of the stairs. The tension broke and a moment later Sand and the others climbed back into the kitchen.

"Report," Millen said.

"Quiet as a grave down there, sir. We didn't go too far in but we saw a number of coffins and long wooden boxes," Sand said. "Bigger than I expected. They've extended it, I reckon."

"Excellent work, Sergeant." Millen looked around. "Follow me. The undead down there have seen their last night."

The Templars quietly descended down into the cellar, the undead seemingly unaware that their doom had arrived. Coffins and boxes lay scattered around, the Templars' lack of lanterns meaning Steiner could not tell how many, nor could he see fully into the depths of the cellar. They had indeed extended the cellar beyond the footprint of the castle.

"Orders, sir?" Sand asked as the Templars milled around, the lieutenant hesitant to direct them now that they were finally in Margot Guillam's Crypt.

Millen answered. "Sand, take four men to the other end and start attending to the undead. I will take four to the other side and kill those there. Work quickly and quietly. Steiner, with me. Those not with myself or Sergeant Sand, remain here."

Their lack of lanterns worked against them; had they another three lanterns, they could have divided into five groups and dealt with five undead at a time. Instead, the lack of light meant they must work slower, increasing the risk of the undead awakening.

That aside, their mission was clear; open each coffin or box and impale its occupant with a silver spike through the heart. Should any awaken, a bullet to the head would suffice, though then they must fight the remaining undead in the relative darkness.

Steiner walked with Millen, Moir, Jameson and Weber, Moir carrying the lantern. A wine rack sat against the nearest wall, holding only a few bottles draped in cobwebs. The cellar was separated by walls and pillars, built to support the castle and ground above. It lay mostly empty, the undead no doubt 'living' in the castle above once the sun had set. Empty, save for some scattered debris. And the coffins where the undead lay.

Millen led them to the nearest coffin, an old battered looking box of wood. It was said that the undead rested better where they Transitioned from corpse to undead, in many cases a coffin. There was speculation that the Transition exuded an aura of some sort that the surrounding material, such as coffin wood, absorbed. Where the undead were concerned, there was a large grey area where gathered intelligence met folklore and superstition, so Steiner lent it little credence. What was known was that where possible, the undead had their coffin moved from grave to Crypt.

The five Templars gathered round the coffin silently. Moir stood with the lantern in one hand and her pistol in the other, her job to provide light and shoot the undead if it attacked. Millen held a hammer, electing to kill the first undead himself. Weber's job was to watch for other threats, for any sign that the other undead were awakening. Jameson produced the first silver spike, his task being to hold it steady over the undead's heart for Millen to strike it.

Again and again this must be done, until the last undead lay truly dead. One mistake risked them all awakening and attacking the Templars en masse.

Steiner's job was to lift the coffin lid and thereafter stand ready for trouble. He looked from face to face, his comrades nodding in turn. It was time.

He knelt next to the coffin and slowly took hold of one edge and lifted, taking care that the lid did not clatter to the cellar floor. His pistol sat in his jacket pocket and his silver hunting knife lay on the ground, and so he must trust Moir to shoot the undead if it awoke and attacked him.

He slid the lid next to the coffin and prepared to move back to let Millen take his place. Jameson was already squatting on the other side of the coffin, ready to place a silver spike over the undead's heart.

Except the coffin was empty.

Millen barked a nervous laugh. "It must be this

vampyre's lucky day," he said quietly. "Onto the next."

Steiner tore his gaze away from the empty coffin and looked around, pricked by a sudden unease. *It is said that empty ships make the most noise. Perhaps it is the same for coffins.* "Lieutenant, I–"

Something flickered out from the cellar's shadows, enveloping them in darkness as Moir and her lantern fell to the ground.

"Welcome to my home, Mr Steiner," a woman's voice said from the darkness.

"You know me?" Steiner called back as he drew his gun.

"You were brought before the Council when you were our prisoner. I see you have brought more Templars for us to kill."

"Miss Guillam, I assume." So much for killing vampyres as they slept. They were awake and ready, and that fool Millen had brought too few lanterns. A cold sweat drenched Steiner at the thought of fighting vampyres – an Elder among them – in the dark.

"Miss Newfield is here also, eager to discuss you shooting her in the chest. You should have stayed away, Steiner." Her tone held a note of finality.

"Defend yourselves!" Steiner roared, not caring that it was not his place to do so. Shouts echoed round the cellar, swiftly drowned out by gunfire. A dark shape rushed at Steiner who fired his revolver, half-blinded by the flash. Experience told him that he had likely as not failed to strike the heart and so he leapt aside to evade the charging undead.

The cellar descended in chaos as the undead attacked the now-blinded Templars. Somehow, they had learned of the Templar attack and concealed themselves, letting Millen lead them into a trap. One flung itself at Jameson, Steiner hearing what sounded like someone striking a bloody slab of meat and knew his comrade was being stabbed to death. He fired at what he hoped was the undead's head.

Jameson was alive but not for long, and so Steiner

returned his attention to the carnage. Templars were firing, succeeding mainly in blinding and deafening themselves and those around them. The undead were darting shadows, none apparently armed with guns, relying on knives, fists and fangs. That told Steiner that any warning the undead had of the Templar attack could be measured in minutes.

In-between the screams, shouts and gunshots, he could hear Millen shouting out ineffectual orders, trying in vain to rally the Templars. Steiner knew to fight here was suicide, and so he moved to Millen's side.

"We must withdraw to the entrance hall and make our stand there!" he shouted.

"We will not flee, Steiner! We fight here!" Millen shouted back.

So be it. "You are relieved of command, Lieutenant. Go with God."

Steiner stabbed Millen in the chest.

"Templars!" he roared, ignoring what small regret he felt at killing Millen. "Retreat to the entrance!" God alone knew how many remained to carry out that order.

There was a bloody scramble as the surviving Templars fled to the stairs leading back up to the kitchen, pursued and butchered by the undead. Steiner knew if they could only get outside, the undead would be powerless to follow them into the daylight.

Guns fired though Steiner knew that barring luck, few of the undead would be slain.

He ran up the narrow stairs, relieved to see some light from the kitchen. Not much, as the windows were mostly shuttered, and he knew that either he or Millen should have had them opened to allow in enough sunlight to make the undead wary of continuing the pursuit.

Steiner reached the entrance hall, disquieted to witness what should have been an orderly retreat reduced to a panicked rout. Fifteen Templars had ventured below, almost half failing to return.

"Outside!" Sergeant Sand shouted at the two gaping Templars left guarding the entrance hall. No small number had dropped their rifle or shotgun fleeing the undead, Steiner was displeased to see, but they had drawn their revolvers, at least.

"Hold," Steiner said to three Templars with him. Upon the first undead entering the entrance hall, he gave the order to fire.

Perhaps the undead believed every Templar was in flight, or perhaps the bloodlust was upon them, but they were not prepared to be shot at. Two undead fell while others lingered in the kitchen.

"Do we hold here and regroup, and then go back down after them?" Weber asked.

Steiner briefly considered it, knowing Ben Jefferies and five other Templars were upstairs. If they could find lanterns and return to the cellars with order and discipline, they might snatch victory from disaster. "No," he said, the words bitter in his mouth. "Go upstairs and tell Sergeant Jefferies to join us."

"The vampyres have no guns," Weber said.

"Our fallen comrades had guns aplenty, and by now the vampyres will be arming themselves," Steiner said. *Arming themselves and gorging on the blood of our fallen.*

"Inquisitor!" someone shouted from outside.

"Hold here," Steiner said as he went outside to investigate. "Weber, do not go upstairs until my return." Two might not be enough to hold the entrance hall; better to keep Weber here than send him upstairs now and risk the undead cutting them off.

"Sir," John Sand said urgently as Steiner walked out into the blessed sunshine.

Steiner saw a crowd surrounding the entrance, rotted and lifeless. Undead, he thought at first, but the sunlight did not trouble them. They carried knives and clubs and made no sound, and as one they advanced. The two Templars who had been stationed outside lay dead on the grass.

"Fire at will!" Sand shouted, most of the Templars obeying before Steiner could countermand that order. A ragged volley of gunshots echoed off the castle wall.

The bullets barely slowed the approaching mob of dead, Templar training guiding them to aim for the heart. Some of the corpses had been torn bloody by discharged shotguns but silver did not hinder them, nor did they show any signs of pain. *Zombis*, Steiner knew, and he knew that just as Millen had walked them into a trap beneath Dumbreck Castle, he had led them out into a second trap here.

*

"This is your carriage, your Grace?" MacInesker asked as they exited the grounds out onto the road. Dark curtains covered its windows.

"I arranged for it to convey me home," Redfort lied smoothly.

The guard opened the door, only to be yanked inside with a cut-off scream.

MacInesker swore and stepped back, finding Redfort's derringer aimed at him. "Bishop Redfort, what is this?"

"Someone wishes to speak to you regarding the location of Niall Fisher," Redfort said.

"How would I know that?" MacInesker said, that name sparking panic in his eyes.

"You're of his line. MacInesker means 'son of the fisher'," Redfort said.

The guard's body fell from the carriage.

Redfort kept his gun trained on the trembling young man. "Climb inside or die here."

MacInesker chose the former and climbed into the carriage.

"Just him, Bishop," a voice said as Redfort made to follow him inside.

The carriage left, leaving Redfort on the street. He looked around with a growing discontent as he realised he had a long walk ahead of him.

Chapter Twenty-Seven

"Lady Delaney, Mr … Gray. For what do we owe the pleasure?" Father asked dryly as Singh showed the pair into the sitting room. "Tea?"

"We did not come for refreshment, but for … for your help." Lady Delaney looked as though she had eaten something bitter.

Hunt saw a flicker of surprise on Father's face. "I helped you once before and was almost shot for my pains upon you learning my identity."

"You are the Devil," Lady Delaney said. "Were you expecting a more convivial reception?"

"We don't have time for this," Gray said to Lady Delaney.

"Take a seat," Father invited them, to which the pair did so.

"Very true, Mr Gray." She looked at Father, Hunt and Sirk with pursed lips. "Mr Steiner's return to Glasgow was against orders, however that aside, over a score of Templars were later sent here from Edinburgh and London."

"What might have changed the Templar grandmaster's mind?" Sirk asked with a rhetorical air. "Steiner wrote to him of Lord Ashwood's identity, yes?"

"Yes," Gray admitted. "Steiner was to be sent back to London in disgrace tomorrow."

"We can discuss this later. What is important is that we were visited last night by a Mr Herriot of the Heron Crowe Bank, claiming an eagerness to free the bank from the Sooty Feathers and undead. He told us we might find

Margot Guillam and other undead in Dumbreck Castle," Lady Delaney said.

"I assume these Templars decided to call upon Dumbreck Castle?" Hunt asked.

Delaney nodded. "Today, yes. Mr Gray and I remained behind. Earlier, your old butler, Smith, killed Ellison, my lady's maid." There was anger and grief in her eyes. "He revealed himself to be *Beliel*."

"Smith was Possessed by *Beliel*?" Father asked in surprise.

"With the original intention to spy on you, but my advertisement for a butler proved an opportunity the demon could not resist," Delaney said. "He murdered Ellison and told me that Herriot is also Possessed by a demon working for *Arakiel*, and that a trap has been set to destroy the Templars and any undead in the castle."

"What happened to *Beliel*?" Singh asked.

"I killed him."

Three-Nil to Lady Delaney. Hunt shivered a little as he recalled all the times he had seen Smith silently performing his duties in Lady Delaney's house, a malevolent presence betraying them at every turn.

"You intend to help the Templars and wish our help in doing so. The same Templars sent here to kill me," Father said. "You have yet to provide a reason for us to do so."

Lady Delaney looked at Hunt. "Miss Knox is with them."

Fear for Kerry Knox flooded Hunt. "You let her go off alone?"

"It is not for me to 'let' Miss Knox do anything," Delaney said. "Mr Gray was to remain behind due to his injuries from our time in police custody. Miss Knox is capable, and Mr Steiner assured me he would watch over her."

"Except now she is walking into a trap," Hunt said. Regardless of what his father decided, he would go with Delaney and Gray.

"An old friend of yours is also in danger, Dr Sirk. A Mr Ben Jefferies?"

"Jefferies?" Sirk blinked in surprise. "I knew he was a Templar, but I thought him too old for such adventures."

"Well, he's here and in danger," Gray said. "If you want to tell him you think he's too old, you'd best come with us."

Sirk eyed Gray. "Are you not too injured?"

"I can't run or fight hand to hand, but I can shoot," Gray said confidently.

"He can cover our approach and escape," Father said.

"'Our'?" Delaney asked. "Are you willing to help us?" There was a rekindled hope in her eyes, but ambivalence too.

"What's your price for helping us?" Gray asked.

"Not your souls, if that is your worry," Father said with a cold smile. "No price. *Arakiel*'s necromancer killed my wife. The necromancer still lives, so I will not suffer *Arakiel* to win this war." He met Hunt's eyes. "And besides, my son is doubtless feeling chivalrous towards Miss Knox."

"We'll need weapons and transportation, and soon," Gray said.

"We may already be too late," Sirk said.

"I have guns and ammunition within the house. And a carriage nearby, which Singh is proficient at driving," Father said.

"Then let us waste no more time," Sirk announced. "I will drive Foley's wagon and let us hope that there are Templars enough to fill it."

"Are you coming, Singh?" Father asked.

"Gratitude may not be enough to keep the Templars from killing you. It may require my presence to convince them otherwise," Singh said.

"They know what you are, Singh, and who you serve," Lady Delaney assured him.

"Then let us make haste," Father said.

*

"You kept your head, Miss Knox," Jefferies said

grudgingly. Three men armed with guns had been waiting for them in the main hall, all dead now along with Fleishmann and Parker. Had the three gunmen been better coordinated they might have killed more, but instead two of them had shot Fleishmann and the other Parker. Rhonda Jackson had shot one with her rifle, and while Jefferies and Knox gave covering fire, Waite had snuck down one side of the hall to flank and kill the last two.

They checked the small room at the back of the main hall and found no one else. There were still two floors above.

"Sounds like the others have found a fight too," Jefferies said as muffled gunshots could be heard from the floor below.

So much for quietly killing the undead in their sleep, Knox thought but did not have the gumption to say aloud.

"Someone's coming up the stairs," Jackson called out, the other three joining her in the hall with their guns ready.

The relief Knox felt on recognising the first one up the stairs as a Templar died on seeing the panic on his face.

"Weber, report," Jefferies said.

"Get ready!" the man roared out as more Templars followed behind him, Steiner the last. All faced the stairs, fear written on almost every face. Knox belatedly realised only five Templars had come up, and their expressions suggested that the next face to appear would not be friendly.

"Is it undead?" Jackson asked.

"Worse. *Zombis*, I believe," Steiner said between breaths.

"I shot one in the heart but it kept coming," a man said, his eyes wide. Others nodded.

"They come." There was iron in Steiner's voice, but it was a brittle metal that would break before it would bend.

Fear made Knox's chest hurt as her heart pounded. Not so far from here she had fought *zombis* before and nearly died.

Three lurching corpses reached the top of the stairs, decayed and stinking. Knox took a breath and cocked her revolver, aware that the panicked Templars would waste what ammunition they had on these three unless she acted.

"Watch and learn," she managed to say with hollow bravado as she stepped forwards and levelled her revolver. The first *zombi* was maybe a metre away when she fired, her bullet penetrating skull and brain. By the time it fell to the floor, she had already re-cocked her gun and taken aim at the second *zombi*. In small numbers they were no great threat so long as one kept one's head.

Her second shot 'killed' the second *zombi*. She stepped back and let Steiner deal with the third.

"Your lesson is well heeded, Miss Knox," Steiner said. The nods from the surviving Templars told Knox that, finally, she had earned their respect.

"Aim for the head every time, or the spine at the base of the skull," she advised. "Forget the heart, these are not undead. A necromancer controls these corpses."

*

"Where's the lieutenant?" Jefferies asked when it became apparent the necromancer would send no more *zombis* against them just yet.

"Dead," Steiner said, not mentioning that Millen had died by his hand. "The undead ambushed us in the cellar. Those of us who survived escaped outside where *zombis* awaited. More of us, including Sergeant Sand, fell to them and to the undead. We were left with no choice but to return inside the house and fight our way up here."

He recalled the surprise on the faces of the undead trading shots with Weber and the others as the Templars ran back inside. The *zombis* had followed them into the house, attacking the undead as well as the Templars. Their indiscriminate attack was the only reason Steiner and the rest had survived to climb the stairs. God willing, the *zombis* and undead below were destroying each other.

Someone swore as another gunshot rang out.

"What do you think you're doing?" Waite demanded of Knox who had just shot the fallen Parker in the head.

Eyes older than those Steiner remembered her having half a year ago regarded the remaining Templars. "The necromancer can Raise the dead as *zombis* and send them against us. I suggest you shoot every corpse you see in the head unless you want it trying to kill us, later."

A sound precaution, Lady Delaney has taught you well. "Do so," Steiner instructed.

"You were relieved of your position, which puts me in command," Jefferies said quietly as the other corpses were dealt with.

Steiner looked at Jefferies. "If you wish command, I will not argue with you. Or you can be my second."

Jefferies seemed to mull it over for a moment before blowing out a breath. "Knight-Inquisitor Steiner, your orders, sir?"

The others heard and none offered any argument. "We must check this floor for other staircases, and post sentries. We must also check the upper floors lest there be more enemies hiding from us."

"And then what, sir?" Jefferies asked. "Even if we can hold off the *zombis*, when night falls the surviving undead will come after us."

"We must fight our way out before the sun sets," Steiner said. "Ensure the curtains are open at every window you find." The undead would not have to wait until nightfall. Soon, the sun would pass behind trees or another building, and the undead would creep up those stairs. Unless the *zombis* overran the undead first, and then the Templars would be attacked before sunset.

*

Newfield watched as Miss Guillam tore the head from the last of the *zombis* in the cellar. None had followed them down, but the dead Templars had risen and attacked with their silver knives, killing Bart Knowles and wounding

Harold Fowler. After fighting both Templars and *zombis*, only Newfield, Guillam and Fowler still lived of Dumbreck Castle's undead.

"What of Mr MacInesker?" Newfield asked. Had he been killed by the Templars, by the *zombis*, or had he escaped or hidden himself away?

"There is nothing we can do for him right now," Miss Guillam said, a sour expression on her face. "When darkness falls, we will hunt down the Templars. For now, the *zombis* are keeping them trapped on the first floor. Let the Templars exhaust their strength and bullets on the dead."

"I hope Miss Quinn still lives. And Bishop Redfort," Newfield said, though in her opinion the magician was more trustworthy than the bishop. She was confident she could look down on Redfort's corpse without a jot of regret.

"Miss Quinn can take care of herself. As can Redfort."

*

Time passed, dragging by in a haze of fear and death as Knox and the remaining Templars battled to survive. The necromancer sent his *zombis* against them en masse. Nine lived to fight against them, winning but at the expense of the last of their ammunition.

After, as more *zombis* climbed the steps, the survivors fought with knives and used their shotguns and rifles as clubs, beating down the approaching dead. Knox had watched helplessly as Weber and Waite were pulled down, screaming as they died. Knox recognised Templars among the *zombis*, Raised by the necromancer to replace those 'killed'.

Losing ground and numbers, Steiner had shouted for them to retreat, and so began a game of cat and mouse. The survivors separated in an attempt to divide and lose the slower *zombis* among the narrow halls and staircases of the castle. Steiner's last order had been to draw as many of the dead away from the main hall as possible before returning, their last desperate gamble being to then flee down the stairs and pray the undead were not waiting.

Part of her wanted to enter one of the rooms and close it behind her, to hide under a bed until the threat was gone, but she knew dusk would bring the undead up from their cellar. One small mercy was that unlike Dunkellen, where the necromancer had unleashed all of his *zombis* and Raised their victims, here he or she was limited in how many they could control.

Her gun empty, she had only her silver knife, and resolved that should there be no escape, she would cut her own wrists before enduring the slow agony of being bitten and torn apart.

She fought the urge to succumb to panic and run blindly, instead moving from hall to hall, spying each one for any sign of *zombis*. Chipped floorboards creaked beneath her weight as she moved, the wallpaper faded and peeling. Knox had imagined castles to be grand affairs, but clearly the MacIneskers had been stingy in maintaining this one. Few pictures decorated the walls, only a little furniture lay in the rooms she had seen, the best having been moved from this carcass of a home to the newer Dunkellen.

This castle was home to the undead, invaded by the actual dead who now stalked the living within. How many Templars would join her in the main hall, she dared not guess, instead focusing on getting there herself.

A shuffling sound behind her warned of approaching *zombis* and so she quickened her pace, breaking out into a mad dash towards what she hoped was the main hall, where waited the stairs leading down to the entrance and the slim chance of safety.

The dead were in pursuit, slow but relentless. She bounded down the stairs leading to the first floor and found herself in the main hall, where Steiner, Jefferies and Jackson waited. Either the others were dead or behind her.

“Let’s go!” she shouted.

Steiner shook his head mutely, and Knox felt fresh despair on seeing four *zombis* blocking the door leading to the stairs. More were approaching from behind as the necromancer guided them to the main hall, where Knox and the Templars would make one last futile stand.

She looked at the window, daylight still pouring through. To jump out meant death or serious injury, and if she was to be killed by the dead or undead, she would rather do so fighting than lying crippled on the ground below.

"It has been my honour to fight alongside you all," Steiner said.

"I've fought demons and the undead for three decades, and I knew this would be my end one day," Jefferies said, knife ready. "God wills it."

"You're saying you survived thirty years fighting the undead in Edinburgh, but died after less than a week in Glasgow?" Knox managed to tease, drawing a few short laughs.

A grimly determined look settled on Jackson's face. "God wills it, Inquisitor. Undead died this day."

"They did, Jackson," Steiner assured her.

A handful, from what Knox had gleaned, and Margot Guillam not among them. The presence of *zombis* attacking both Templars and undead told her they had been used, the demon *Arakiel* luring them here to weaken both its enemies. *But what point in saying as much aloud?*

Gunshots echoed up the stairs, growing closer. The *zombis* turned to face this new threat, and Knox wondered if impatience had driven Margot Guillam to move before dusk, daylight be damned.

The tension that had gripped her chest since arriving here eased as she recognised the new arrivals entering the main hall, forcing her to blink back tears of relief. Lord Ashwood and Singh led the way, devil and angel firing with cool precision into the heads of the risen dead. Lady Caroline Delaney joined them, likewise armed. Wilton Hunt and Dr Sirk were at the rear, brandishing revolvers of their own, firing down the stairs at *zombis* Knox could not see.

Within a minute, the last of the *zombis* haunting the main hall were down, the acrid smell of gunpowder having never smelled so welcome to Knox.

"Lady Delaney!" Jefferies said. "God bless your timely arrival!"

Jackson managed a smile. "Your reputation is well earned, Lady Delaney. My thanks to you and your associates."

"Perhaps expressions of gratitude can wait until we're safely away," Lord Ashwood suggested.

"Jefferies, your talent for survival remains undiminished," Sirk said.

"Jesus! Sirk, you got old!" Jefferies said, taking the doctor's hand.

"As did you. We never thought that would happen, did we?"

"For most of us, it never did," Jefferies said.

Sirk looked down. "No. It did not."

"We should be leaving." Lady Delaney eyed the corpses surrounding them.

"Margot Guillam and some undead are below," Knox said.

"We're in no state to attack her. More *zombis* will be heading this way," Hunt said.

"Where did so many corpses come from?" Caroline wondered. "There was no plague like last time."

Sirk stared down at one of the bodies with a frown. "I believe I can answer where our necromancer got some of his corpses from."

"Where?" Hunt asked, anger in his eyes as always at the mention of the necromancer.

Sirk looked at him. "Do you not recognise this fellow?"

Hunt walked over and looked down at the large man. "Should I?"

"This is Mr Henry. Do you not recall us … recovering and delivering him recently?"

Hunt hissed out a curse. "That bastard. He must have

been laughing at us the whole time. We'll discuss this later."

"With the others?" Sirk asked.

"My father and Singh. The others … We'll see."

Knox wondered what they were talking about, but she had more pressing concerns than the implication Hunt had returned to bodysnatching. The group descended the stairs down to the entrance hall, Knox and the Templars having been given a little ammunition.

*

Hunt spied the door ahead as they reached the entrance hall, relieved to be leaving the castle – more relieved that Kerry Knox still lived – but aware also that *zombis* still infested the grounds.

A gunshot rang out, and he spun to see Ben Jefferies fall, Margot Guillam standing at the far end of the hall with a rifle in hand and a baleful look on her face.

Father faced her, a warning look on his face. Sirk knelt next to his old friend and looked up with a pained look on his face. Jefferies was dead or as good as. Singh shot the Templar in the head, either to prevent the *Nephilim* from Making him undead, or to prevent that fucking necromancer from Raising him as a *zombi*.

Regardless of reason, Sirk voiced no complaint, and they fled the hall into the daylight, where more *zombis* waited.

*

"With me!" Singh shouted, the *Seraphim* firing at the closest *zombi*. Everyone followed him, those with still loaded weapons firing at the attacking dead. Knox ducked past the nearest *zombis*, alarmed to see more of them standing at the gate Singh was leading them to.

The distinctive *crack* of a rifle rang out, a *zombi* falling over. Moments later it fired again, the rifleman she assumed to be Gray aiming true again. On they ran, a figure standing up from the bushes ahead with a rifle, Knox unsurprised to see that it was indeed the American. He climbed onto the driver's platform of a carriage parked on the street outside the castle's garden and reloaded before firing again.

"I understood you to be too injured to attend to your duties, Gray," Steiner said between breaths as the survivors reached the carriage.

"Still limping, but my hands and eyes work just fine, Inquisitor," Gray said with a pained grin. Knox guessed that the rifle's recoil had done his bruised or fractured ribs no favours.

"That carriage isn't big enough for all of us," Knox said, fearing some of them would have to escape on foot.

Wil thumbed towards a nearby wagon. "We brought that."

The survivors – Knox, Caroline, Gray, Wil, Sirk, Singh, Lucifer, Jackson and Steiner – quickly boarded either the wagon or carriage, Gray taking the reins of the latter as Sirk took control of the former.

Carriage and wagon rolled swiftly away from the castle, leaving behind Dumbreck Castle and twenty-two dead or dying Templars.

"Thank you for your aid," Rhonda Jackson said to Lord Ashwood between breaths as the carriage battered along the rough road. "Your name, sir?"

This might prove awkward. Knox cleared her throat. "Miss Jackson, this is Lord Ashwood. Lord Ashwood, Miss Jackson of the Templar Order."

Her hope that Jackson would not remember that name proved a forlorn one, the Templar's eyes widening. "Satan!"

Lucifer ignored her last imprecation. "You are most welcome, Miss Jackson."

Jackson pushed back against the carriage seat, her face gripped by panic. "Someone shoot him!"

Caroline hissed out a breath. "Do calm yourself, Miss Jackson. One might think you had never encountered a demon before. Lord Ashwood has been good enough to assist me in your rescue and calling for his death smacks somewhat of ingratitude."

"He's the Devil!"

Caroline's face twisted in a rare loss of control. "I *know* he's the *fucking* Devil! A demon! Like *Asmodiel*, whom I sent back to Hell with poison in his wine. Like *Beliel*, whom I have killed *thrice*. Do not talk to me of demons, Miss Jackson, when this is your first and they have done naught personally to you. And do not let superstition drive you to hysteria. Lucifer is a demon like any other, killable like any other." Caroline leaned back and closed her eyes.

That last statement drew a smile from Ashwood, one that failed to reach his eyes. An invitation daring anyone to try.

A fraught silence fell over the carriage.

*

"You are aware that the main hall is littered with bodies. Here, too, I see."

Newfield looked round to see Magdalene Quinn descend the steps down to the entrance hall.

"I thought you must be dead, Miss Quinn" Newfield said.

"I hid in a small room on the top floor and Warded the door to 'encourage' the eye to miss it," the magician answered. "Remind me to lift the Ward, or this castle's servants may spend a lot of time wondering where their mops and brooms have gone."

"Well done," Regent Guillam said. "Where is Mr MacInesker?"

Quinn paused. "He was not with me. I alerted him and Bishop Redfort, and then came down to the cellar to awaken and alert yourself. When I returned to the hall, he, Redfort and a guard were gone."

Guillam's eyes fixed on Quinn. "MacInesker and Redfort are gone?"

"This castle belongs to the MacIneskers. Perhaps the young man knew of a secret way out?" Quinn said.

"Perhaps." The Regent did not sound convinced.

"Redfort is a survivor," Newfield said.

"I care not about Redfort. If Neil MacInesker is dead, then…"

Newfield understood. MacInesker was Lord Fisher's last heir. "Where is his contingency?"

"In this castle, thankfully." A sample of blood from every Councillor was kept, sufficient for a Diviner to use to track down any Councillor who went missing. Guillam looked at Miss Quinn. "Are you skilled as a Diviner?"

"No, I'm afraid that's not one of my Talents, Regent."

"It is still daylight. You must leave here and find a Diviner. Mr Keane, if available. By the time you return here, it will be dark enough for myself, Miss Newfield and Mr Fowler to leave."

"I'll return as soon as I am able, Regent," Miss Quinn said.

"Be fast and nimble," Newfield advised. "There may still be *zombis* haunting the grounds."

Chapter Twenty-Eight

Whatever their private thoughts, no one had argued as carriage and wagon conveyed survivor and rescuer alike back to Father's house rather than to Lady Delaney's. Singh had made the point that *Beliel*'s infiltration of Lady Delaney's household had likely prevented a further assault upon it, but that impediment's removal meant there was no longer any reason preventing *Arakiel* from attacking.

And the Templar attack on Dumbreck Castle meant that sunset could see a vengeful Margot Guillam leading an assault on Lady Delaney's house, known ally of the Templars.

"I would return home. Ellison's body still lies within," Lady Delaney said, her voice brittle. The exhausted survivors sat within the sitting room, Rhonda Jackson continuing to stare at Father as if he were a venomous snake who might bite at any time.

"And the remains of Smith." Father sighed. "Not the retirement I had in mind for him, after his long years of service to my family."

"Would it be safe?" Kerry asked.

"While it is light. We have proven ourselves stalwart opponents, and neither faction will risk an understrength assault," Father said.

"Miss Jackson, are you sure I cannot get you a drink? Whisky helps," Hunt offered.

"You've certainly drunk enough in recent times to attest to its effectiveness," Father said with a dry disapproval.

Her head jerked in a shake.

"My thanks to you all," Steiner said with a stiff reluctance. "This has been a dark day for the Order."

"I'm sorry for your losses," Lady Delaney said quietly. "But you were not in command and so are not responsible."

"I came here against orders. I wrote to London telling Grandmaster Maxwell of Lucifer's presence in Glasgow. That is why he dispatched so many. All dead save for Miss Jackson." There was a bitter melancholy on Steiner's face, and the ease with which he gulped down his whiskey and made no complaint when Singh poured more suggested the Templar was teetering on the edge of despair.

"Then let us discuss how we may strike back," Lady Delaney said, her own fire undimmed.

"With what army, now that a score of trained Templars have fallen?" Steiner looked around the sitting room with contempt. "Three Templars, one of whom limps, and one who has been relieved of his duties. A middle-aged lady and her young protégé. A grey-haired doctor who has hidden from this war for decades. The Devil and his son. And an angel who serves as the Devil's valet." A harsh laugh issued from his lips. "A company of heroes, indeed."

"We are what remains," Singh said. "I have fought and died more times than I care to remember. I will die and be reborn time and again, long after your bones are dust."

"How many victories and how many defeats?" Steiner asked him through twisted lips.

"It is the cause we fight for, not the result," Singh said.

Miss Jackson's head jerked up. "You are familiar with the writings of Jeanne de la Byar? She aided the Templars in France until her death almost fifty years ago."

"Very familiar, Miss Jackson," Singh said with a wry chuckle. "I was Jeanne de la Byar in my previous life."

"Well damn me," Gray said with a whistle. "Were you anyone else we might have heard of?"

"Have you heard of Sir Galahad?"

Gray sat upright. "Yes!"

"Well, I wasn't him."

"Mademoiselle de la Byar was murdered by the undead, her work undone within months," Steiner said.

"Enough," Kerry said. "This serves us not at all. We must decide what to do next." Lady Delaney had opened her mouth and now closed it, a similar comment perhaps on her lips. She gave her pupil a small nod of approbation.

What this remnant of resistance did next was a lesser concern of Hunt's. What burned his guts was that at last he knew who the necromancer's Vessel was: Professor Mortimer. *That bastard had Sirk and me digging up corpses for him to turn into* zombis. Kerry and Delaney had passed on Bishop Redfort's warning that the necromancer had Possessed another body, but the revealing of his father's identity – and his own unnatural origin – had fractured Hunt's relationship with the pair, and so he had said nothing to them.

The avenging of Mother will be a private affair.

"That was a grim business." Steiner looked at Lady Delaney. "I understand now what you faced at Dunkellen House."

"You begin to understand," Delaney corrected. "At Dunkellen, we faced many more *zombis*. Today, for a reason beyond my ken, the necromancer sent its *zombis* after us in smaller numbers rather than all at once."

"At Dunkellen, the necromancer inflicted a sorcerous plague on the village of Kaleshaws, unleashed through a dark ritual that gave him the power to Raise and control so many at once. Each death thereafter acted as a sacrifice that further powered the spell. Today, whatever spell the necromancer worked was on a smaller scale, limiting the number of dead he or she could control," Father said.

"We must find this necromancer and kill it," Steiner said.

Hunt gave Sirk a warning shake of the head.

"First we must identify the necromancer's current body," Sirk said. "And to date we have enjoyed no success in that regard." He was a fair liar, on occasion.

"Until then, let us focus on the enemies we have identified," Gray said. "That demon *Arakiel* played us and Fisher's faction against one another, weakening both of us."

"Will either group attack, finishing us off lest Mr Steiner calls for more Templars?" Kerry asked.

"More Templars? The Order has lost too many in this damned city," Steiner said.

Gray nodded. "The Edinburgh chapter has been gutted. It doesn't have enough to protect Edinburgh against an undead incursion, never mind send any more here."

"The Grandmaster will not send any more from London. That would compromise our operations there," Steiner said. "That the London Templars were led here by a sergeant rather than an officer tells me they are busy."

"We're on our own, then," Kerry said.

"We're a capable group," Gray said. "As George Rannoch could attest, if Mr Hunt hadn't killed him."

"Our enemies will be aware of that too. To return to Miss Knox's question, can we expect one faction or the other to finish us off?" Lady Delaney asked.

"Your home is no doubt being watched, with ill intent in mind," Father said. A look of discontent crossed his face. "I suggest you all remain here."

Steiner barked a laugh. "Accept the hospitality of the Devil? At what cost?"

"The hospitality of a demon." There was venom in Lady Delaney's voice.

"Put aside your superstitions," Singh said. "Being in *Samiel*'s presence will not imperil your souls. If I can tolerate it, so too can you. My death by his hand in Heaven saw me cast out of that realm to here, while he has never done harm to any of you."

Jackson stared at the valet, still stunned at being in the presence of demon and angel.

"You can stand against both *Arakiel* and Fisher?" Kerry asked.

"I have no great powers, but I have separate agreements with both Fisher and *Arakiel* that we will not meddle in one another's business," Father said.

"Agreements you have not exactly adhered to," Sirk said. "Nor have they."

"True. *Arakiel* has assured me he will not move against me."

"Why?" was Lady Delaney's blunt question.

A frown furled Father's brow. "A good question and one I do not know the answer to, Dunkellen House aside. After that misadventure, he apologised for the death of my wife and assured me there would be no repeat."

"Did he?" Hunt spat.

Father looked at him. "The necromancer was directly responsible, and at the time I believed he had been dealt with."

"So just why is *Arakiel* content to risk you attacking him?" Gray asked.

"I do not know," Father admitted. "As Lord Ashwood I have wealth and position, but few resources to turn against him. If he attempts to assassinate me and fails, he knows every resource I *do* have will be deployed against him."

"He has been Summoning demons to aid him, such as *Asmodiel*. Perhaps he fears you working against him in Hell," Singh said.

"Perhaps. Though I am not exactly loved there," Father said with wry understatement. His failed rebellion was the reason the demons had Fallen there.

"Not loved but feared."

"Regardless, you will all be safer here," Father said.

"We accept your hospitality," Lady Delaney said reluctantly.

Steiner managed a single, stiff nod.

"What time is breakfast served?" Gray asked with a grin.

"Early," Singh replied.

"I will not be staying here," Miss Jackson announced.

"What are your intentions, Jackson?" Steiner asked.

"I will return to the house Lieutenant Millen rented for us and destroy anything that might incriminate the Order. In the morning I will take the first train to Edinburgh and report to Captain Barker."

"Direct to London would be better," Steiner said.

"You were relieved of your duties, Mr Steiner, and so cannot order me anywhere," she said.

"It was a suggestion, Miss Jackson, not a command. I *suggest* you report directly to Grandmaster Maxwell. If you agree and will remain here an hour longer, I will write a report for you to convey to the Grandmaster in person."

A grudging nod. "As you *suggest*, sir. London it is."

"Our pantry is insufficiently stocked for our additional guests. Might *I* suggest, Lord Ashwood, that you make alternative arrangements for dinner?" Singh said.

"As you say, Singh." Father looked around the room. "We are not far from the Albert Club. You are all invited for dinner. Yes?"

"I fear we are improperly dressed, Lord Ashwood," Lady Delaney said. "Let us take this opportunity to return to my house and pack some trunks."

"A fine idea, so long as you do not tarry overlong," Father said. "Miss Jackson, will you be joining us for dinner?"

"No. I will accompany Steiner, though, and await his letter to the Grandmaster."

"A pity." Father smiled. "We will meet again, I am sure. In time."

"*Samiel*," Singh chided as Jackson turned pale at the implication. "He is teasing you, Miss Jackson. What will happen to you after death is unknown to either of us."

Once the others had departed, leaving just Father, Singh and Sirk, Hunt cleared his throat. "Father, we know who the necromancer is."

Father regarded him with a surprise that quickly turned to a cold simmering anger. "Who?"

"Professor Mortimer, the Senior Professor of Anatomy at the university. We recognised one of the *zombis* as a corpse we … ah … knew to be in Mortimer's possession," Hunt said. He preferred not to mention the bodysnatching.

"Then we will attend to Mortimer very soon. I think it best if tomorrow, we call upon Bishop Redfort," Father said.

"Redfort? Why? What need have we for a corrupt clergyman?" Hunt asked.

"It was he who revealed to Lady Delaney that your mother's killer survived the death of Essex's body. I suspect the man we knew as Dr Essex is Khotep, a necromancer from antiquity," Father said, his eyes alight with rage.

"The 'good' bishop plays his own game," Sirk warned. "He told Lady Delaney but manipulated events to bring you together, guessing that she would pass on the information."

"I am done with games," said Father. "We will meet Redfort and see if he might be of use."

"And tonight?" Hunt asked.

"Tonight, we have a dinner engagement with our new guests. Do try not to vex the Templars further. I am due to attend London next month to be introduced to the House of Lords, now that I have received my writ of summons, and I would rather not have to contend with assassins."

"I'll mind my manners," Hunt promised.

*

"That's unfortunate," Regent Guillam said, and Newfield was relieved it was not her who had to deliver such news to Miss Guillam given her present mood.

"I'm sorry, Regent, but I could not find any Diviners in the Under-Market. Mr Keane has not been seen in over a week," Miss Quinn said upon her return to Dumbreck Castle. "I did come across Bishop Redfort on the road to Glasgow, and he said he saw Neil MacInesker being taken by the enemy."

"Templars?" Miss Guillam asked.

A shake of the head. "Bishop Redfort said that Mr MacInesker had led him and a guard outside via a secret passage. Armed men attacked them, killing the guard and dragging MacInesker towards a curtained wagon, which thereafter left."

"They did not attempt to take or kill Redfort?" Guillam asked sharply.

"He said that he ran and that they did not pursue, their priority being MacInesker. I left Redfort where he promised to send reinforcements here," Miss Quinn said. "The *zombis* are gone too. Only the dead remain."

Night had fallen, allowing Newfield, Guillam and Fowler to leave the castle, but without a Diviner, they had no means of tracking down Neil MacInesker and so they remained within. "What now?" Newfield asked. Harold Fowler looked at her curiously, doubtless having heard the fear in her voice. A *Nephilim* close to three centuries old, the fate of Neil MacInesker was of no interest to him. But then, he didn't know the truth of MacInesker's relationship with Lord Fisher.

Miss Guillam looked at Quinn and Fowler. "Neil MacInesker is privy to a secret worth more than his life. He is protected from Possession by the Ward tattooed onto all Councillors, but if Keel has him, they will torture him. If we cannot rescue him then we must ensure his silence."

"If we cannot find him then how can we kill him?" Newfield harboured no illusions about MacInesker's ability to withstand torture. *And how will Fisher react?*

"What does he know?" Mr Fowler wanted to know.

"He knows the general location of Lord Fisher's Crypt." Miss Guillam said after a moment.

Surprise showed on Fowler's face. It was known that MacInesker had met Fisher, but Regent Guillam had made it clear that he did not know where the Crypt was. "I thought he *didn't* know?"

"I suspect he may have an idea, whether he knows it or not," Guillam admitted. "Keel will torture every last detail out of him."

Newfield thought back to her visit to Fisher's Crypt but could recall no detail that told her its location. Perhaps there had been something there relating to the ancient family both Fisher and MacInesker came from?

"I can kill him, but I'll need his blood," Miss Quinn said with a slow reluctance.

The Regent picked up a small bottle of blood from the table. "I had hoped a Diviner would use this to find him, that we might rescue him. But we have no choice. Work your sorcery, Miss Quinn."

"How will Lord Fisher react to this?" Newfield asked quietly as Quinn began mixing various ingredients with Neil MacInesker's blood in a small bowl. Fowler had been sent out to the stables to fetch straw and sackcloth. A few strands of MacInesker's hair had been carefully removed from his pillow.

"I do not know," Miss Guillam confessed. "Keel and his followers will answer for it, have no doubt. But will punishing them sate Fisher's wrath or will he hold us to account? We shall see, Miss Newfield. And once Miss Quinn has cast her spell, we must inform him."

Fear grew in Newfield's gut. She had thought today's danger passed, but it seemed a potentially greater peril still awaited. Templars and *zombis* had failed to kill her – now she must survive her own master.

Fowler returned with the straw and sackcloth, which Miss Quinn soaked in MacInesker's blood and fashioned into a rough doll, adding the strands of his hair last. She stared at the bloody thing and began whispering to herself, the words alien to Newfield. And then she stabbed it in the chest with a knife.

"MacInesker is dead?" Guillam asked. Newfield had felt nothing.

"If my spell worked, and they usually do, Regent." Quinn's voice was heavy.

"Very well. Miss Quinn, return to your people and find out why there was not a single Diviner available. It can be no coincidence."

"I will look into it," said Quinn.

"Do so. And now Miss Newfield and I have some bad news to deliver."

*

"Mr Keel, what a surprise." The necromancer Khotep had settled into his new role as Professor Mortimer. "What brings you here? I admit that my *zombis* accomplished less than I had hoped, but only due to interference from Lord Ashwood and Lady Delaney. You have been most insistent that no harm befalls the former."

'Here' was the university's medical school. "I am not displeased with what transpired today. Neil MacInesker was taken, and I had no expectation that Margot Guillam would die. Indeed, her survival better suits my purpose." *For now.*

"Ah, Fisher's last heir. Will he need much 'encouragement' to talk?" Mortimer leaned back in his chair, a glass of something smelling of alcohol on the study desk.

"I should say so, since he is dead," Keel said.

"That was careless. And the reason for this visit, I presume."

Neil MacInesker's body was brought inside and lain on the floor, Mortimer casting a critical eye over it. "I see no evidence of torture. Was the threat alone sufficient to stop his heart?"

"One of Fisher's magicians helped him along, as I hoped. When his body is found absent signs of torture, Guillam and Fisher will believe he died before betraying Fisher's location." Keel was banking on Margot Guillam being no less ignorant regarding a necromancer's capabilities than she had been in his day. A fair assumption, given that Fisher had continued Keel's edict that necromancers be slain without exception.

Mortimer laid a hand on MacInesker's head for a moment. "I do believe I can sense the residue of such a spell. No matter, I can recall his soul and you can ask your questions."

"Then do so."

Mortimer removed a small bottle containing a liquid so dark it was almost black, though Keel knew it contained *Nephilim* blood reluctantly donated some weeks ago by Richard Canning. "The taste never improves," the necromancer complained as he drank it down. He placed his hand on MacInesker's head and began muttering the incantation.

"Do you not need to inject *Nephilim* blood into the brain?"

"Not so soon after death, the soul has not long left the body," Mortimer said upon finishing his spell.

Neil MacInesker's corpse jerked, and Keel knew his soul had been snatched back from whatever realm it had travelled on to.

"Mr MacInesker, welcome back. My associate here has some questions for you," Mortimer said.

"Where am I?" the corpse rasped. There was no fear in his voice. No emotion whatsoever, such humanity now beyond the shade of Neil MacInesker.

"In my study." Mortimer looked at Keel. "The spell compels him to answer, and to answer truthfully. Ask your questions."

Keel did, and the corpse answered.

Chapter Twenty-Nine

Kerry Knox walked through the restaurant of the Albert Club as if she owned the place, a successful method, she had found, of disguising her nerves at being in places that normally wouldn't let her darken their doors. Waiters in starched shirts and black waistcoats moved from table to table, the guests dressed in their finest evening wear. Mr Gray drew a few looks owing to his skin colour, which he reciprocated with an insolent grin.

A forced grin, Knox sensed. Everyone was still shaken by the day's events, by the loss of a score of allies, balanced only by the guilt-tinged exhilaration of having survived. Perhaps it would have been more decent to have suggested to Lord Ashwood that they dined quietly in his house, but everyone here tonight had escaped Death's bony grasp, and Knox suspected she was not alone in wanting to embrace life and its pleasures.

For now. Mourning could come tomorrow.

Ellison, you poor soul.

The *maître d'* led Knox, Caroline, Steiner and Gray to their table, the others already present. Singh was absent due to his position as Lord Ashwood's valet. Miss Jackson had declined Ashwood's invitation, returning to wherever the Templars had been staying. Lord Ashwood, Wilton Hunt and Dr Sirk stood as Knox and the others arrived at the table, polite greetings exchanged to maintain appearances.

"You look very nice, Miss Knox," Hunt said to Knox with an air of hesitation.

"Thank you, Mr Hunt." She wore a pale blue evening

dress with an open neckline, its sleeves puffed. The skirt almost touched the ground, an increasing irritation thanks to a wet autumn, and her chestnut hair was worn up in a bun. Knox and Caroline had attended to each other's hair, opting for simplicity over elegance: Knox had spied unshed tears in Caroline's eyes throughout.

Once again *Beliel* had taken someone from her.

Steiner and Gray each wore black trousers and black tailcoats over formal white shirts. Their shoes had been bulled and polished. Steiner had brought his own evening wear from London, whereas Gray had been forced to borrow from Caroline, the clothes belonging to her late husband. Mr Foley had worn them the night he and Caroline had infiltrated Dunclutha House to rescue Hunt from the Sooty Feathers in the spring.

"You look very dashing, Mr Hunt," Caroline observed. While Lord Ashwood wore traditional black tails, his son wore a less formal tuxedo jacket.

"Thank you, Lady Delaney. Most of my clothing burned with Mr Foley's flat and shop, requiring me to procure replacements."

"Requiring *me* to pay for them," Lord Ashwood said. Lucifer, Knox reminded herself.

Dr Sirk's attire had seen better days, and Knox suspected they had spent a decade or two hanging forgotten in a wardrobe, perhaps only taken out and dusted off for formal occasions at the university.

Everyone sat, a young waiter attending the table to take the drinks order.

"Very fine place," said Gray as he looked around. The walls were covered in a dark-grey wallpaper and adorned with various landscape paintings. Light came from candles on the tables and walls, making for an intimate atmosphere.

"I've been a member for many years, and never had cause to regret my patronage," Ashwood said.

"I let my own membership lapse some years ago," Caroline said. "It has changed a little."

The drinks arrived – bottles of red and white wine –

and food orders taken, Knox deciding on a salmon dish. She would have quite liked the steak, which the men all ordered, but if the meat was tough then she would look less than ladylike tearing it apart. Ladies were expected to eat little and daintily. *I'm so damned hungry, I'll struggle with that!*

"So, gentlemen … Miss Knox … this has been a dark day, indeed," Caroline said.

"The darkest for the Order in many years," Steiner said heavily. Thirty-two Templars had died in Glasgow this year. In the spring, Steiner at least had some victories to show for his losses. Today, twenty-two had been lost for nothing, save for several slain *Nephilim*. *Arakiel*'s *zombis* counted for nothing.

"What of Smith and Ellison?" Hunt asked.

Caroline looked at him, weighed down by grief. "Both obviously died by violence, so if their bodies are found, then questions will be raised. We must dispose of them by some quiet means. Neither had family, at least."

"We know of some empty graves," Hunt said. "Perhaps we might bury them, at least."

Emptied by you. It was rare for Hunt to allude to his bodysnatching days.

"More respectful than tying them in weighted sacks and dumping them in the river," Gray said.

"If you can identify the closest graves, I would be grateful," Caroline told him. No one mentioned the twenty-two dead Templars and all those *zombis* strewn within and without Dumbreck Castle. Cleaning up that mess was Margot Guillam's problem.

"I would strike a blow against this demon *Arakiel*," Steiner said.

"Bravo, Mr Steiner. And what, pray, do you have in mind?" There was mild sarcasm in Ashwood's tone.

Steiner stared hard at the Devil. "That is what we are here to discuss, yes?"

Knox was here chiefly for the food, but she took his point. "You don't favour a return to Dumbreck Castle?" she asked. She allowed Hunt to pour her some red wine and took a sip, her eyes widening at the strength and fullness of flavour.

"To your taste, Miss Knox?" he asked.

She gave him a nod and smile. "I can taste the Spanish pine."

Surprise flickered over Hunt's face, his cheeks reddening at the memory of their illicit summer swim.

"Spanish pine?" Lord Ashwood enquired. "I had thought Lady Delaney better prepared you for society. Wine is stored within casks of oak."

"A joke, Father," Hunt said. He briefly met Knox's eyes, that look enough to convey understanding and gratitude as he correctly interpreted her reference to that day as a step towards reconciliation.

Lord Ashwood returned to her question. "As much as it would please me to burn Dumbreck Castle to the ground, *Arakiel* has proven himself the more dangerous of our enemies. I would see his faction weakened first."

"Having a necromancer who can turn the dead into an army does give him an advantage," Caroline said in reluctant agreement.

"I will deal with the necromancer." There was an iron promise in Lord Ashwood's voice. But doubtless he had told his followers in Heaven as much when he led a rebellion in Heaven. That ended with them in Hell.

"I killed him in the summer, and that has not impeded him greatly," Caroline pointed out.

"We will take steps to ensure that his next death will be his last," Ashwood said.

"What do you need from us?" Gray asked.

"This matter need not concern you," Ashwood told the table.

"That necromancer killed many of my brethren," Steiner said harshly.

Ashwood met that fanatical stare. "He killed my wife. He dies tomorrow. By my hand."

"God willing?" Gray dared to tease. Steiner gave his fellow Templar a disapproving look.

Ashwood's mouth twitched. "By my will."

The waiter returned to their table with some starters, ending all further conversation for a time.

*

"This might not end well for us," Miss Guillam warned as she pulled off the hood covering Newfield's head.

They stood underground, next to the door to Lord Fisher's Crypt. Newfield felt like Miss Guillam looked; sick at the thought of having to tell Lord Fisher that his last known mortal heir was dead.

Regent Guillam knocked on the door. After perhaps a minute, it creaked open.

Little more than yellowed skin stretched over bones and tendons, Niall Fisher beckoned them inside. "Welcome, Miss Guillam, Miss Newfield. I was not expecting you."

The crypt looked unchanged since Newfield's last visit, a stone sarcophagus lying in shadows at the far end, a wooden desk sitting against a wall with a candle burning thereon. Old tomes adorned three bookcases against the opposite wall.

"That bookcase is filled with books too precious to entrust to the MacInesker library," Fisher said. "The other two contain my own written works, philosophical musings mostly."

"You've written a lot, Lord Fisher," Newfield said, to make conversation.

"I have a lot of time on my hands." His voice was raspy, and as dry as paper of the books he cherished.

She wondered how he could endure an existence such as this, an eternity hidden away from those craving his power. Unmanned by his own strength, for two hundred years.

"What brings you here, Miss Guillam?" Fisher asked. "News from the war?"

"Yes, my Lord," Guillam said. "Ill news, I regret."

"When I entrusted the regency to you, I did so in the expectation you would crush any challenges to my rule.

Instead, I find my House much diminished in less than a year."

"The Bothwell Street Crypt has fallen." Miss Guillam did not add honey to the medicine, as Newfield's grandmother would have said.

Fisher's rotted visage stared at Guillam, capable of no expression. "I trust the enemy paid dearly for it?"

"They suffered losses, yes, my Lord. But that was not the only attack we faced. More than a score of Templars raided Dumbreck Castle."

"My senior *Nephilim* dwell there, you among them! You do not dare tell me that the Templars seized the castle?"

"No, my Lord. Miss Quinn's Wards alerted us to the trespass and bought us time to prepare for them. We routed them, however we were unable to pursue past the entrance hall due to daylight. Keel's necromancer was in the area with many *zombis*, who attacked both us and the Templars. The Templars held out upstairs for a time. I suspect Keel manipulated the Templars to attack the castle, intending for his *zombis* to slay the survivors from both sides."

"Continue."

"Lucifer and Lady Delaney led a small troop to help the Templar survivors escape. There were many bodies, making it impossible to say just how many were Templars and how many *zombis*, but I would say no more than five Templars escaped. Fewer."

"Neil MacInesker was staying in the castle, as I believed it safe owing to the presence of yourself and other veteran undead. What of him?" Fisher asked, dread in his voice. *Now we come to it.*

"He was upstairs during the attack, but he and Bishop Redfort escaped the castle, while Miss Quinn hid herself away. Some of Keel's men waited outside and took Mr MacInesker away. Miss Quinn could find no Diviners in the Under-Market, and so I told her to use her magic to kill him, lest they torture him for your location." Miss Guillam said her piece and awaited the consequences.

"He is dead?" Fisher's voice was like a coffin being dragged over a stone floor.

"Miss Quinn assures us he is," Guillam said.

The *Dominus Nephilim* said nothing for a time.

Miss Guillam dared speak again. "Of the *Nephilim* using Dumbreck Castle as a Crypt, only myself and Harold Fowler survived."

"This is a day I vowed to never see pass. The near-end of my line, save for the demon and the abomination."

Newfield wondered at the 'abomination' but sensed a rage growing in the undead lord and decided it might be best to avoid his notice.

"We had no choice." Guillam held firm. "Had we found a Diviner, we might have tracked MacInesker while he lived, but such was not to be. Killing him was our only means of protecting your location, should he have realised it."

A pause. "You say Lucifer took a hand in this?"

"Not as such. He attended later with his son and others, to help what remained of the Templars escape."

"My earlier command still holds. Neither Lucifer nor his son are to be harmed," Fisher said.

"Have they not interfered enough?" Miss Guillam asked.

"I have my reasons and you have your orders. Ensure this command is carried out: the Hunts are to be left alone." Fisher paused. "The time has come for me to finish this war, personally. Gather every undead and what remains of the Council at Dumbreck Castle in seven days, I will address them there."

A rare look of surprise showed on Miss Guillam's face at this instruction. For two hundred years Fisher had hidden himself away here, relaying his orders to Regent Edwards and the Council via Miss Guillam. On the very rare occasions Fisher had met Edwards – perhaps to reassure the then-Regent that he still lived – it had not been in his Crypt, that location known only to Guillam.

Who had feared that Neil MacInesker may have discerned it, suggesting to Newfield that the Crypt was somewhere in the Dunkellen estate. Not Dumbreck Castle, but not too far.

"It will be done," Miss Guillam said.

"I will need more blood. A lot more blood," Fisher said. Guillam personally delivered victims for Fisher to feed from, and Newfield knew that he would need a lot to regain his full strength and power.

"You wish me to bring twice as many people here?" she asked.

"More. Many more. I will be ending this war personally."

Guillam's mouth opened. For Fisher to meet the undead of his House for the first time in two hundred years was unprecedented, but for him to personally lead his House was a shock. "It will be done. Though as I must do it alone, it will take some days for me to bring all you require."

"Be about your business, then," Fisher said. His dusty dry voice was absent emotion, but Newfield sensed a rage growing within him.

Newfield and Guillam left the Crypt with some alacrity, a bag once again put over Newfield's head. They were 'alive', and it might be best to leave before Fisher decided to change that.

Chapter Thirty

"I will receive them in here, Hendry." A thrill of uncertainty went through Redfort as his butler left the drawing room to show in these unexpected guests.

He took a calming breath and hoped he looked suitably nonchalant about their arrival. In truth, he had slept poorly, fearful that Fisher or Guillam might suspect his involvement in Neil MacInesker's abduction. There had been a risk in telling Miss Quinn that he had seen it, but to do otherwise might have led to a suspicion that he had abandoned his fellow Councillor.

Hendry returned, not alone. "Your Grace, Lord Ashwood and Mr Hunt."

"Come in, gentlemen. Be seated. Hendry, have tea brought in." Redfort glanced at his clock. Ten minutes past nine. "What occasions this early visit, Lord Ashwood?"

Lucifer and son sat. "We have identified Dr Essex's … replacement, your Grace." There was a hard grimness to the Devil's face.

"That … is excellent news, Lord Ashwood. I assume Lady Delaney passed on my information. Are you here as a courtesy, or do you wish my aid in dealing with him?" Or her, Redfort supposed. "Who is the necromancer now?"

"Professor Mortimer, of the Glasgow University medical school," Hunt said.

"You are quite certain?"

"You are aware of what happened at Dumbreck Castle yesterday?" Lucifer asked.

"I am." He saw no point in denials. Nor in admitting he had been there.

Hunt spoke. "At least one of the *zombis* came from the medical school mortuary. A body Mortimer arranged to be taken there."

The furtive expression on Hunt's face suggested there was a little more to that story, but Redfort was more interested in the revelation that the necromancer's identity had indeed been discovered. "After the Dunkellen incident, I investigated Dr Essex. He left London rather abruptly in the summer, moving to Glasgow with no post in place. No family, just him and a valet called Eustace Yates."

Hunt straightened. "Yates? Mortimer's valet is called Yates!"

"Then we can assume that you are indeed correct, and the necromancer Possessed Professor Mortimer after Lady Delaney slew Dr Essex's body," Redfort said. *Finally, this thorn in my side can be pulled.*

The excitement left Hunt's face, replaced with a look of frustration. "How, then, can we send the bastard to Hell, if his soul simply Possesses another body?"

"Simply? Not at all. Upon the body's death, the necromancer's soul returns to a prepared Soul-Repository. Should some unfortunate person touch the Soul-Repository, then the necromancer's soul Possesses that person, evicting their soul," Lucifer said, saving Redfort from having to reveal his own knowledge on this forbidden subject.

He assumed a thoughtful look. "That sounds an uncertain business, the necromancer having to hope that someone will happen across this Soul-Repository. But at the same time ensuring it is kept safe. Perhaps this Yates is fully aware of just what his master is, and upon the necromancer's death ensures that the Soul-Repository comes into contact with an appropriate victim?"

Lucifer gave him an approving look. "Well reasoned, Bishop. That would mean that this Yates is fully trusted, knowing what the Soul-Repository is and where it is hidden."

"Can we not just kill Mortimer and Yates?" Hunt asked. He blinked slightly, perhaps surprised at his own callous words, at how comfortable he was becoming with murder.

"If we kill Mortimer, his soul will return to his receptacle. If we kill Yates too, we will have no way of knowing what or where it is, and eventually someone will stumble across it, and Khotep will return," Lucifer said.

"Khotep?" Redfort asked.

"Our necromancer's original name. He hails from what is now Arabia. I knew of him when I was still *Grigori*," Lucifer said.

"He is *that* old?" Redfort asked, startled. *The possibilities…*

"He is."

"Then it sounds past time for him to go to Hell," Redfort said. *My own ultimate destination, I fear. All the more reason to befriend Lucifer.*

"How?" Hunt clearly chafed to end, once and for all, his mother's killer.

"I have an idea," Redfort said, most of a plan already in his head. *An opportunity beckons.*

*

"Mr Hunt, what a surprise. And I assume this gentleman is your father?" Professor Mortimer asked as he sat behind his study desk.

Hunt stared at the professor for whom he had exhumed bodies for maybe ten weeks, all the while not knowing he was the bastard responsible for Mother's death. *You must have laughed, thinking me a fool.*

"Yes, Professor, this is Lord Ashwood, my father." It was a struggle for Hunt to keep his voice even. They stood in Mortimer's study, the same one once occupied by the late Professor Miller. It was Miller who had introduced Hunt and Foley to bodysnatching, ultimately being tortured to death by Richard Canning.

If all went well, the university would once again be seeking a new senior professor of anatomy.

"A pleasure to meet you, Lord Ashwood," Mortimer said, standing to shake his hand.

Father's smile could have frozen water. "The pleasure is entirely mine. Khotep."

Hunt was gratified to see Mortimer's eyes widen in fear, shocked at the use of his original name.

"Don't move," Hunt said, pulling a derringer from his pocket and aiming it at Mortimer's chest.

Mortimer ignored the gun, his eyes fixed on Father. "You know who I am, then. I'm flattered you recall that name."

"Few mortals defied my kind as successfully as you did after the Fall. But in the end, death found your kingdom and your apprentices. And now you."

"Mr Keel tells me you are Lucifer. The first of your kind to create the undead."

"By accident," Father said modestly. Miss Guillam had briefly told how Lucifer's long-ago encounter with a woman called Lilith had led to her becoming the first undead, and Father had confirmed it.

"You are aware, Mr Hunt, that your father has been Possessed by the Devil?"

"My father *is* the Devil. He was Summoned into Lewis Hunt's body before I was born," Hunt said. A secret scant few knew, but Mortimer would soon be in no position to share it.

"I was led to believe that a man or woman Possessed by a demon could not conceive," Mortimer said, the revelation energising him, despite his predicament. "How?"

Father leaned down on the desk that had once been Miller's. "I am *Samiel*."

As if that is an answer. But Hunt knew it might be all the answer he ever got. Certainly, it was an event memorable enough for a *Seraphim* to be sent to watch over father and son.

"You intend to kill me." There was a certain smugness about Mortimer, death no more than an inconvenience.

"You killed my wife. I am not known for my forgiving nature."

"All I ask is that you do not harm my valet, he is entirely innocent," Mortimer said.

Innocent, my backside. But neither Hunt nor Father objected, happy to let the necromancer believe his minion would be left unscathed. In truth, Singh and Sirk should be taking him prisoner even now.

*

"You're alive, praise God!" Redfort exclaimed as he 'found' Yates tied up in the pantry. He cut the man's bonds and removed his gag. "You are Professor Mortimer's man, yes? I am Bishop Redfort."

"I'm his valet. My thanks," Yates said with only a grudging gratitude, rubbing chafed wrists and ankles. "Two men confronted me at gunpoint and left me tied up in here hours ago! An older man called Sirk and an Indian. The swine!"

"You're lucky. A police inspector still loyal to Mr Keel reported to us that Professor Mortimer's body was found in Kelvingrove Park, still warm," Redfort said.

Yates' eyes widened. "The professor is dead?"

"Undeniably," Redfort said. "But Mr Keel required his services as a matter of great urgency and sent me here to find you."

Suspicious eyes regarded Redfort, who knew that Yates was wondering if he was genuine. "Urgency?"

"Mr Keel plans to assault another enemy Crypt and requires reinforcements typically arranged by your master. He instructed me to find you, if still alive, to see to the arrangements." Redfort feigned ignorance, hoping that the necromancer had not revealed to Yates that Redfort was also a practitioner.

Understanding dawned on the valet, a hint of cruelty in his smile. "I understand Mr Keel's meaning and intention. Follow me, Bishop."

He thinks the demon has sent me here as a lamb to the slaughter, to become the necromancer's next Vessel. Redfort maintained an innocent façade as Yates led him out of the kitchen, afire to learn what item Khotep used as a receptacle for his soul. The risks the necromancer faced, keeping it both safe yet not so hidden that it might be lost forever.

Redfort's own talent with necromancy was poor indeed compared to Khotep's, but then, Khotep had spent thousands of years mastering it. Cheating death and surviving the rise and fall of empires. After the execution of his mentor, Redfort had struggled for years to master necromancy, rarely using it save as a useful tool to be employed with the utmost discretion. Learning what a true master was capable of had renewed his interest.

He followed Yates into the ground floor study, seeing a number of dusty medical books on the bookcase shelves. There was nothing obvious to Redfort's eye that might hail from antiquity, but he was mindful not to show too much interest in the room or its contents.

Yates unlocked and opened a wooden case lying on the desk to reveal an old bronze lamp. Khotep's Soul-Repository? Redfort believed so, staring at the item that might be capable of containing a man's soul. Or Yates might have revealed a decoy to test Redfort. The sight of it brought to mind old stories of genies and their lamps, and he wondered if Khotep had inspired those ancient Arabian legends. Or perhaps he had heard the tales and simply chosen a lamp as his Soul-Repository as a joke of sorts.

The English valet regarded the lamp with an air of trepidation, making no move to touch it. Then he turned to face Redfort, holding out the small case. "Bishop Redfort, an artifact from Arabia. Would you care to hold it?"

"I would," Redfort said, reaching out and removing the lamp from within, blackened with age. He raised it up and studied it, aware he was touching something pricelessly historical. And capable of casting his soul to Hell in the right circumstances.

Yates watched him expectantly, doubtless waiting for the Possession to take hold, for Khotep's soul to usurp Redfort's own.

"A magnificent piece." Redfort said as he reached into his jacket pocket.

Yates' eyes narrowed as whatever he was expecting – Khotep's soul leaving the lamp to usurp Redfort's body, no doubt – showed no obvious signs of happening. The valet had doubtless been the one who had delivered the lamp to an unsuspecting Mortimer following the death of Essex. "Sir?" Yates asked hesitantly.

"Yes?" he asked innocently, knowing the valet was addressing the necromancer.

Yates spoke hesitantly in an unknown language, an agreed-upon phrase between the pair, no doubt. Redfort answered it by pulling out his derringer.

"I fear I'm still Redfort, Yates."

Eyes widened. "Not possible! It should have worked immediately."

"I am sure it would have, had Professor Mortimer actually been slain," Redfort said with a smile, victory over the necromancer literally in his hand. The one man who knew of Redfort's dabbling with necromancy would soon be in no position to tell anyone of it.

Yates launched himself at Redfort who calmly aimed and fired, blood appearing on the valet's upper chest as he collapsed to the study floor. Blood bubbled from the Englishman's lips as death approached, and Redfort placed the lamp back in the box, lest the Hunts become impatient and kill Mortimer prematurely.

He looked around the study and spied a large silver and gold bowl on Khotep's desk, which he took. *Now to find a furnace hot enough to melt metal.* The Chemistry Department seemed like the best place to look.

*

Footsteps echoed off the mortuary's tiled floor. "The task is done, gentlemen."

Hunt recognised the voice as Redfort's, the Bishop sounding particularly pleased with himself. The room was cold by necessity and stank of bleach and formaldehyde, another necessity to disguise the stench of blood and rot. Hunt had delivered a number of bodies here, first to Miller and then Mortimer. *I'm done with this place.*

Holding a necromancer prisoner in a mortuary containing the medical school cadavers struck Hunt as an ill-advised idea, to say the least, but Father had warned Mortimer that should any corpse so much as twitch, he would be swiftly killed. So far, the necromancer had been content to sit quietly in a chair. For the first few hours, they had remained in his study, necromancer and Devil passing the time by reminiscing over that long-dead age where the *Grigori* Fell to earth and warred with humanity and each other. As the time neared for Redfort to 'rescue' Yates, Hunt and Father took Mortimer to the mortuary.

"Bishop Redfort, we meet in person, at last," Mortimer said, somehow recognising him. He showed little concern at his imminent death, believing it would prove no more lasting than when he died as Dr Essex. *If Redfort has done his job, then our necromancer will be in for a surprise.*

"The pleasure will soon be all mine," Redfort said.

"It is done?" Father asked.

Redfort dropped three pieces of melted metal onto a table. "His Soul-Repository, destroyed as promised. A bronze lamp, which I first smelted and then separated into several pieces. Sufficient, I should think, to deprive his soul of a sanctuary."

The look of consternation that passed over Mortimer's face seemed to confirm Redfort's assessment. Hunt felt a cruel pleasure on at last seeing fear on the face of his mother's killer.

"Yates betrayed me?"

"I told him you were dead and let him believe Erik Keel had sent me here to become your next Vessel," Redfort told him. "He's dead now."

"The idiot," Mortimer hissed.

"You can take him to task soon, when you join him in Hell," Hunt said.

"The world is well rid of you," Father said. He aimed his gun at Mortimer's head and pulled the trigger without ceremony, sending blood and brains over the floor. With the Soul-Repository destroyed first, death had finally claimed Khotep.

"Someone will need to clean this up and dispose of Mortimer's body," Redfort said with a hesitant remonstrance.

"We'll leave that in your capable hands, Redfort," Father said as he pocketed his gun. "Come, Wilton. Our business here is done. Good day, your Grace."

"Good day, Lord Ashwood, Mr Hunt," Redfort said as he surveyed the carnage. He did not look pleased at being left with cleaning up the mess, but Hunt cared not at all for his inconvenience. For a supposed man of God, the Bishop of Glasgow seemed more interested in worldly matters, and he served the dark powers fighting over this city. Had Steiner been here, he would have left Redfort lying next to Mortimer.

Father and son emerged out into the daylight. "Your mother can rest, now, her killer dead in truth," Father said after taking a long breath of air.

"Yes." There had been no joy in watching Mortimer … *Khotep* dying at last, but there had been much satisfaction. For thousands of years the necromancer had been a blight on the world, cheating death and stealing lives. And today, finally, he was dead and gone.

Chapter Thirty-One

"Damn the Council! Damn the Sooty Feathers, those rich bastards who placed their heels on our throats and make us serve them!" Bartholomew Ridley stood atop a box and ranted to the crowd gathering around him. "And damn our own who help them!"

He means me, Magdalene Quinn thought. A few weeks ago, neither he nor anyone else would have dared say such things publicly in the Under-Market. None of the magicians and non-magicians who frequented it would have dared listened to him. They would have hurried past, eyes averted.

Now a crowd openly congregated to listen. A pale-faced man and woman stood silently behind Ridley, *Arakiel*'s undead there to protect the rebel magician from the Sooty Feathers. The massive railway bridge overhead allowed the undead to browse the market's wares even in daylight, though coming and going presented a problem while the sun was up. Most lingered until sunset, perhaps making use of the dull-eyed men and women who loitered in shadowed corners selling their blood and risking death should an undead's Thirst exceed the seller's surplus.

Others made use of the decrepit tenements that pressed against the bridge, either knowing of a covered route that would return them to their Crypt or lying low inside until dark.

The burned-out shell of one tenement remained, it and the cellars below once a Crypt for the undead. Templars had seen it burned, its undead slain in a bloody slaughter.

Market traders and patrons had been caught in the middle, some struck by stray bullets, others killed by loosed ghouls lost to the Thirst. The Crypt had never been restored, and the magicians who frequented the Under-Market were increasingly split between Fisher and Keel.

For several years, Magdalene Quinn had been among the more respected magicians of the Community, a voice listened to even if not always heeded. Her elevation to the Sooty Feather Council had made her the de facto leader of those magicians still loyal to the Council. Regaining the loyalty of the magicians as a community would fully restore control of the Under-Market to the Sooty Feathers, and thus allow the Regent to re-establish a Crypt here. One thing she always kept in mind; among the Sooty Feathers, one was only as valuable as one's latest contributions.

She watched from a distance, recalling Ridley's Puppet; an attack she had barely survived.

Now he strove to recruit more magicians to Keel's side, and no longer in secret. Now he stood openly on a box and denounced Lord Fisher and Regent Guillam, denounced the Council and what remained of the Sooty Feather Society. And in particular he derided Quinn and the other magicians who still served the Council.

The loss of the Bothwell Street Crypt had emboldened Keel's followers, who were ironically unaware of the Necropolis Crypt, which stood closer and hosted most of Fisher's surviving *Nephilim*.

Eyes darted between Quinn and Ridley, many no doubt wondering if she, *Quinta*, the Council's Fifth Seat, would challenge Keel's senior magician. Ben Gould, a Tattooist, tilted his head as his eyes met hers, one of the few bold enough to do so. His expression seemed to query if she would stand by while Ridley defied the Council.

If I don't act, then we will have lost the Under-Market. That revelation sent a cold chill down her spine. Defeat the Puppeteer and win back the magician community. Otherwise, he would simply claim it, her lack of challenge seen as concession. Regent Guillam would not accept that.

How to kill him? Had she some of his blood and a sacrifice, she might accomplish that goal with the same spell she had used to kill Neil MacInesker. But she did not.

"There she is! Miss Quinn, the Council's lapdog magician, skulking among us," Ridley shouted. Any inclination Quinn had to leave the Under-Market died, heat rising in her cheeks. *One of us will die tonight.*

She was damned if it would be her. Facing Ridley, she walked towards him and forced down her fear. As she slowed, she dropped a Warded stone onto the ground.

"Mr Ridley, if you have something to say to me, here I stand before you," she said.

Ridley paused, clearly not expecting her to answer his defiance. "You heard my words, Miss Quinn. You serve Fisher and Guillam."

"You serve the demon, *Arakiel*. Tell us how that serves our people better."

Everyone in the Under-Market came to witness the confrontation. A pale, gaunt young man wearing stained rags almost tripped on the uneven, mossy cobbles, a *Nephilim* beside him, her lips red and cheeks pink. Twin top hats bobbed above the crowd as two well-dressed gentlemen pushed their way to the front. Mr Wheran and his current lover, Quinn realised. Further along wearing a tweed frock coat and flat cap stood Mr Chandler, once known as Lady Ruth Chandler, years since disowned by his family. He had moved from Dundee to Glasgow and now made a living selling herbs and potions to the Community.

The cream of society stood next to outcasts and the forgotten, all gathered to watch. It was these people she must win over to reclaim the Under-Market, and to do that she must kill one man.

Bartholomew Ridley.

Anticipation showed on most of the surrounding faces, wagers no doubt being made as to who would win if this confrontation turned violent. There was ambivalence on the faces of those who were known to support either Quinn or Ridley, a fear of reprisals should the wrong magician lose.

They sparred verbally back and forth, Ridley seemingly distracted.

Which was not unanticipated.

Quinn felt an itch as the Ward behind her was breached, and she turned in time to see Ridley's puppet heading towards her, a knife in its hands aimed at her back.

Which was not unanticipated.

She grabbed the puppet as it leapt at her, muttering her spell as quickly as she dared. Too slow, and the puppet would either kill her or distract her long enough for Ridley to do so directly. Too quick, and a mispronounced word would ruin the spell, and with the same dire result. She uttered the last word and felt her strength drain as the spell struck the puppet.

Among the less palatable branches of magic was the ability to inflict harm on someone by making a construct to represent that person, linking them with hair or suchlike. Ridley had linked himself to the puppet by placing some of his blood inside it, perhaps some hair too. Quinn held the thrashing puppet with one hand while her other drove a needle into its chest. With one spell, the puppet was transformed from Ridley's weapon to his doom, and he jerked as Quinn's magic reached through his puppet and attacked his heart.

Bartholomew Ridley fell dead to the ground, Quinn dropping his now-limp puppet onto the damp cobbles. Whispers ran back and forth across the crowd as they stared at Ridley's corpse.

"Witness the fate of traitors," Quinn said as she straightened her jacket. "The Under-Market is now solely the domain of the Council. Does anyone … anyone else … dispute this?" *That was too close!*

Several of the surrounding magicians bobbed their heads in acknowledgement. Most said nothing but no one vocally disagreed. Ridley's undead companions had slipped away, no doubt to inform Keel that he had lost what influence he had over the magicians.

Quinn had in mind another means of communicating that fact to the demon.

*

Screams roused Canning from his reverie, his hand knocking off the lid of the wooden box he rested in during the day. He craved blood, the Thirst something he must always contend with, though since Transitioning to *Nephilim* it no longer overcame his reason as it had when he was a ghoul.

Other undead rose, some from coffins, others from wooden boxes like Canning's, confused expressions turning to alarm as the shouts and screams continued. Barking and growling too, as if a horde of dogs had descended upon the Crypt beneath Bothwell Street.

"We are attacked," a ghoul said, stating the obvious. Anthony Halsey, he was called, Made two months ago by Bresnik. He had mastered his Thirst sufficiently to no longer require confinement with the newly Made ghouls who were locked away.

Canning drew his long knife, his feelings conflicted. Part of him hungered to kill, but if Margot Guillam was here, then she would have brought enough force to win back the Crypt. By herself she might be enough to win it back…

Jana, one of the Eastern European *Nephilim* from the Carpathian Circus, led the undead towards the main part of the Crypt where the mercenaries lived. Where the screams were coming from, and gunshots – though fewer than Canning expected. Already he could smell blood and shit, the perfume of battle.

Carnage awaited them. Whatever Canning had expected to see, it wasn't this. There were no enemy undead or soldiers. Instead, a large pack of dogs had somehow got inside the Crypt and taken it upon themselves to attack everyone within. They had the look of street dogs about them, lean and feral, and utterly fearless. Yet oddly directed. Man after man was pulled down and had his throat ripped out. The few mercenaries who managed to arm themselves fired wildly, killing some of the dogs but immediately becoming the next target.

One emptied a shotgun into one scarred beast only to be hamstrung by another before a third savaged his face and neck.

"Kill them!" Jana shouted, an old sword in hand. A dog gave a brief yelp as she cut it down, and Canning found himself wishing he had something larger than his knife.

*

Quinn sat in a circle with eight other magicians, feeling a flash of pain as the last dog she was linked with died. "I am done."

The others offered similar comments, confirming that their attack on the Crypt was over. Having established her control over the magician community, Quinn had directed them to acquire dogs. Strays had been rounded up and dog fight organisers had been visited, 'persuaded' to part with their animals.

She and the eight magicians had then travelled to Dumbreck Castle to demonstrate their worth to Regent Guillam.

"That was brutal," Jacob Farran said, one of the younger magicians present.

"But effective," Julia Kerr said.

"How effective?" Regent Guillam asked, a bite of impatience in her voice as she stood over the circle of magicians seated on the floor.

"Every mortal in the Crypt was killed or wounded. Many undead suffered severe injury, though we did not kill any," Quinn said.

"And with no loss to us," Guillam said, approval in her voice. "Excellent work, Miss Quinn. All of you."

Quinn basked in the vampyre's praise. Ridley's death had convinced most of the magician community to return to the fold, and if they continued to deliver victories such as this, their value would rise.

*

"What happened here?" A cold rage hardened Keel's face as the demon surveyed the slaughter, dead men and dogs littering the Crypt, the ground stained with blood. Bishop Redfort had arrived shortly after.

"A pack of wild dogs attacked," Canning said.

"The magicians did this." There was a look of distaste on Redfort's face. "Somehow they got the dogs inside and unleashed them."

"Bring Mr Ridley to me, to explain why he permitted the magicians to carry out this outrage," Keel said, his voice like frozen steel.

"Mr Ridley was slain this afternoon by Miss Magdalene Quinn of Fisher's Council. It appears this was how she chose to celebrate," Redfort said.

"Our losses?" There was murder on Keel's face.

"The mercenaries are either dead or wounded. Those few who were able to have fled," Canning said. "We lost no undead, however many are wounded and are in need of a lot of blood to heal." He himself had suffered gruesome bites to his arms. *Bastard dogs!*

"Give *Nephilim* blood to the wounded mercenaries, and then have the wounded undead feed from them," Keel ordered.

"Aye, Master," Canning said. A neat solution, one that would hasten undead healing while creating new ghouls.

"What of Miss Quinn?" Redfort asked.

"I'll hunt her down," Canning said, looking forward to ripping out Quinn's throat.

"I have another task for you, Canning. But be assured that they will pay for this," Keel said.

"'They'? You mean Fisher's faction?" Redfort asked.

"Them too, but the magicians first. They have chosen

their side, a choice they will rue." Keel turned to Canning. "Bresnik returned to Glasgow last night and reports that he left the Carpathian Circus camped near Lanark. The driver and wagon who transported him will convey you to the circus in his place, for I have a message I want you to deliver."

Canning listened as Keel spoke. He had no fondness for the Carpathian Circus, having been hidden there upon being newly Made. The undead among them had locked him in a trunk for many days as punishment for failing to kill Hunt and Foley. Hunt would have suffered more than a few scars had Foley not intervened with his damned gun.

"I will go."

He was loathe to miss the coming battles, but Keel gave orders not suggestions.

Keel must have sensed his reluctance. "Be assured, Mr Canning, that the key to victory awaits in the circus and you will be at the final battle."

A very powerful key, Canning hoped, since to win, they must defeat a *Dominus Nephilim*.

Chapter Thirty-Two

A Very Long Time Ago

Memories came to Lilith as she walked towards *Samiel*, sitting atop her throne in the large tent set aside for her and her attendants. The young Lilith who had died almost six hundred years earlier was long gone, replaced by the undead night-killer who had risen in her stead, mindless and thirsting for blood. She had killed her son. Her mother and father.

Curiosity had compelled *Samiel* to let Lilith live. The *Grigori* had made others drink her foul blood and killed them. Most had become undead, depending on how they died. Her small army of undead had fallen on one of *Yomiel*'s camps at night, and Lilith had killed again.

Horror had routed those men and women who had once been Lilith's tribal kin but were now her enemy by dint of what she had become. Because of the *Grigori* she now reluctantly followed.

Those who did not flee were divided into three; the prisoners, who became *Samiel*'s warriors. The badly wounded, who were made to drink *Samiel*'s blood. And the dead, whose cooling blood sustained *Samiel*'s macabre army.

A year or so had passed. Before battle, *Samiel*'s most favoured warriors would drink of her blood so that if they fell, they stood a chance of returning as undead. Most of her maddened mob of undead perished each battle owing to a lack of anything resembling tactics or discipline. But always there were enough mortally wounded warriors from both sides for the *Grigori* to Make new undead.

For that year Lilith had been notable simply due to being the first of *Samiel*'s undead, and her continued survival –largely due to the *Grigori* keeping her close by. Until that one night when she fed from yet another faceless victim and had *changed*. Her four sharpest teeth had lengthened, as *Samiel*'s did, allowing her to better feed. Her strength had increased tenfold, as did her ability to control her Thirst, and she could now Unveil, making mortals and undead quail before her.

She could even force her will upon the mortals in the manner of the *Grigori*, making them forget what she willed them to, if to a far lesser degree.

Samiel had been close to destroying her; Lilith could see her life being weighed in those cold, dark eyes. Instead, the *Grigori*'s curiosity compelled her to spare Lilith once again, to see what other changes would manifest themselves within her.

Other undead Changed as she had, the cowed subjects of *Samiel* calling them the Children of the *Grigori* – the *Nephilim*. *Samiel* was alone among the *Grigori* in knowing how to create the undead, and as her ranks of *Nephilim* grew, so did her capacity to Make more undead, trusting in the growing numbers of *Nephilim* to control them. As *Samiel*'s new domain grew, encompassing cities, her subjects were commanded to deliver tithes of people. The eldest and weakest were fed to the undead, and the fittest joined the mortal armies of *Samiel*. *Nephilim* Made the rest.

Yomiel fell to *Samiel* in single combat, a spectacle watched by many awed *Nephilim*. Any who thought to match their strength against the *Grigori* thought again, Lilith included. As *Samiel* intended, no doubt. She advanced west, taking *Yomiel*'s former lands surrounding the Nile.

Years passed, rival *Nephilim* taking Lilith's place by *Samiel*'s side. Not that she showed any open signs of holding a grudge, content to feed and survive, and to rule the towns *Samiel* assigned. *Arakiel*, *Ramiel* and *Batariel* had continued their alliance against her, their greater numbers offset by their lack of undead. They would dispatch their armies to fight during the day, relying on mortal leaders as did all the *Grigori*. They might win a battle, only for the undead to leave their tombs and caves at night to fall upon them.

In time, most of the other surviving *Grigori* learned how to create their own undead, but by then *Arakiel*, *Batariel* and *Ramiel* had retreated to their lands in the south and west, and an uneasy truce came about more or less by default, save for border skirmishes.

Other threats had distracted the *Grigori* from resuming their war. Mortal kingdoms resisted, aided by those claiming to be kin to the *Grigori*. They were born in mortal bodies but could Unveil. The *Seraphim* they called themselves, fighting and dying, and being reborn to fight again. Heroes such as *Zerechiel*, *Seraphiel*, *Uriel* and *Kariel*.

The ancient necromancer known as Khotep reappeared, harassing the *Grigori*-controlled lands with his armies of the dead, before being defeated and slain. *Samiel* had wryly spoken of Khotep's first death, some decades after the Fall of the *Grigori*, and did not expect this death to prove any more permanent. Somehow the necromancer had the means to defy death and reappear in another body.

Other human magicians emerged. Some could Summon the spirits of slain *Grigori* into mortal bodies. *Arakiel*'s armies were led by demons such as *Asmodiel*, *Gadriel*, and *Maridiel*. Unbodied kindred to the *Grigori*, similar to the *Seraphim* only they were never reborn; they must be Summoned.

Once again Lilith had Changed, becoming what her once-dismissive fellow undead now called Elder. For many years she had been the only Elder, surpassing her fellow *Nephilim* in strength and power, repaying those who had usurped her position with death.

It had taken her three hundred years to become Elder, and as expected other *Nephilim* became Elder in turn.

Another three hundred years passed, with Lilith

disappointed to show no signs of further ascension. With a score of Elders, five hundred *Nephilim*, and four thousand lesser undead, *Samiel* had decided now was the time to strike at her enemies. She had dispatched her armies against *Ramiel*, *Arakiel* and *Batariel*, and Lilith was given command of one army.

Arakiel's army had broken, the *Grigori* fleeing to the north and west with what little remained of his undead, leaving his mortal followers as a sacrificial rearguard. *Batariel* had retreated early and in good order, abandoning her allies. Lilith and most of her fellow Elders had attacked *Ramiel* personally, almost all dying to the *Grigori*'s fury. In the end, he had fallen to Lilith's sword.

Lilith ended her reverie as she reached *Samiel*, prostrating herself before the *Grigori*.

"Welcome, Lilith. I hear the enemy is in rout."

"Yes, *Samiel*."

"Our losses?" *Samiel* asked.

"Heavy. I am among your few surviving Elder. Most fell against *Ramiel* before I slew him."

"I was made aware that some of our assaults were planned and executed poorly. Can you explain?"

"I can," Lilith said, fear and anticipation battling within her.

"You appear to have carelessly sacrificed much of my army, destroying the forces of *Arakiel* and *Ramiel*, yet allowing *Batariel*'s army to escape largely unscathed."

"Carelessly? No. With the greatest of care … Lucifer," Lilith said slowly. The young woman Lilith had once been was long dead. But the desire to make *Samiel* pay for what she had made of Lilith, what she had inflicted on that long-forgotten village remained. *My child.*

Distant shouts echoed out as *Batariel*'s army fell on what remained of *Samiel*'s, as per the arrangement Lilith had made with the rival *Grigori*.

Samiel was a moment too slow in recognising the danger she was in, just starting to rise as Lilith kicked her down and stabbed a bronze dagger into her gut.

Stunned by the power of the blow, it took the *Grigori* a moment to respond. "You have grown stronger, Lilith. Another Change?"

"Of a sort," Lilith told her. "I ate *Ramiel*'s heart and so now stand your equal, more or less."

She had heard of lesser undead eating the hearts of the *Nephilim* to hasten the Change, or *Nephilim* eating the heart of an Elder to become Elder, and so she had decided not to wait hundreds or thousands of years in the vain hope of becoming like a *Grigori*.

She had slain one and eaten his heart, inheriting his strength and power.

Samiel stared up at her, eyes wide with surprise and a growing rage. "You will pay for this betrayal!"

"*You* will pay for the death of my son, my village," Lilith told her. "I deliberately sacrificed your Elders, and many of your *Nephilim* and undead tonight, and save for myself, your line will end before the sun rises."

Samiel's remaining defenders rushed at Lilith, who was pleased to find herself able to withstand their attempts to slay her. Able to predict and recognise every intended attack by the tensing of muscles, the glancing of eyes, Lilith made short work of *Samiel*'s bodyguard. Two Elders were among them, two who had never treated Lilith with much respect. She took a great pleasure in seeing the shock in their eyes as she tore them apart with little effort, aware that the wounded *Samiel* was fleeing the tent.

Ramiel's heart had given Lilith the power of a *Grigori*, and she permitted herself a moment to revel in it, bask in her ascension to near-godhood.

Samiel had fled but Lilith would follow, content to leave the destruction of *Samiel*'s kingdom to *Batariel*'s army. *Batariel* herself should be nearby, and Lilith went forth to meet her. *Samiel ...* Lucifer … had been defeated once before only to return even stronger, with an army of undead – *Batariel* would not make the mistake of allowing Lucifer to escape again.

Chapter Thirty-Three

The air of triumph that had pervaded Keel's Council was gone, dispelled by the magician attack two days earlier. That seemed to be the way of the war now – one side would win a battle, only to lose the next. Little was accomplished save for more dead as both sides exhausted themselves.

Redfort knew Keel had a plan, but the demon had so far failed to share it. Tonight, he had summoned what remained of his Council to his house, along with a few other trusted followers. Richard Canning was absent, off to Lanark on some mission, and Redfort was not displeased by his absence. He had been bad enough when alive, and death had done nothing to cure his murderous nature.

Redfort was relieved Keel was not holding this meeting beneath Bothwell Street. Every way in or out of the Crypt was guarded, but Redfort was not hopeful that the defenders could withstand an attack of undead led by Margot Guillam herself, let alone Fisher. Of Keel's army, only the undead remained, most of them recently Made ghouls.

Edmund Crowe was present, persuaded to change sides owing to the destruction of the Templars. Whether the magician attack on the Crypt left him regretting his choice, Redfort could only wonder.

Keel surveyed those sitting around his table. "Our company has diminished in recent weeks."

"As has Fisher's Council," an undead unknown to Redfort said, his accent foreign.

"Indeed, Bresnik. And two of Guillam's eight now sit among us," Keel said, pointing to bishop and banker. "This is Bishop Redfort and Mr Crowe. Gentlemen, meet Bresnik, among the very few of my *Nephilim* to remain loyal after my death."

"And the only one to still live," Bresnik said.

It jarred to see his diffident former secretary giving orders. Bresnik sat next to him, the greyish hue to his skin suggesting he was in need of blood.

The Demonist, Josiah, spoke only when addressed, clearly intimidated by the company he kept. The only time he was ever seen, these days, was in Keel's company at meetings such as these. Perhaps the last surviving Demonist in Glasgow, Keel needed Josiah to Summon his demonic allies. And if Keel somehow captured Fisher, he would need Josiah to complete the ritual to restore his *Grigori* flesh.

Gadriel, currently Possessing the banker Walter Herriot, was Keel's last remaining demon, the other four cast back to Hell upon the deaths of their Vessels; Keel was unforgiving of failure. Bartholomew Ridley was dead, ending Keel's influence in the magician community. Redfort and Crowe were the latest additions to Keel's Council, both still on Fisher's diminished Council. *It is hard to lose when one is on both sides.*

"These past weeks have been eventful," Keel said, after savouring a large mouthful of wine. Redfort did not spend much time with Keel, but he had noted the demon eating and drinking more. Was he making the most of these last – probable – days in a mortal body? Perhaps soon, *Arakiel* would either be once again *Grigori*, or in Hell.

The demon continued. "We have lost our influence over the courts and the police. More recently, thanks to *Gadriel*, the Templars were manipulated into attacking Margot Guillam and the other undead at Dumbreck Castle. As Templar fought undead, the necromancer Khotep's *zombis* attacked both. The Templars were all but wiped out, and many of Guillam's strongest *Nephilim* were slain. Bishop Redfort delivered Neil MacInesker to us, and Khotep ensured that even death could not prevent me questioning him."

His tone darkened. "Unfortunately, Khotep has since been slain, and we must do without *zombis* in the last battle with Fisher."

"Will he not return as before?" *Gadriel* asked.

"His servant was also killed. As Khotep has not yet contacted me, I assume that his Soul-Repository was either destroyed or is hidden somewhere. If it is the latter, it could be months or years before it is discovered, so for now we will count him as dead," Keel said. He spoke again, barely able to master his anger at these setbacks. "Two nights ago, magicians sent dogs into the Bothwell Street Crypt, killing the last of our mercenaries." Some had survived the dogs, but Redfort thought better of mentioning that, as those survivors were now Transitioning to undead.

"Do we delay? Lie low until our ghouls are ready and more mercenaries have been recruited?" Crowe asked.

"There will be no delays. The final preparations are underway and once complete, we will attack Niall Fisher."

The others exchanged looks, no doubt sharing Redfort's concern. How exactly could a handful of undead overcome a *Dominus Nephilim*, to say nothing of an Elder and many other undead? And magicians, capable of sending beasts and puppet-like constructs against Keel's remaining forces?

Bresnik alone nodded at Keel's words, and Redfort wondered what the foreign *Nephilim* knew that the others did not. He considered Keel's words, suspecting the demon was keeping secrets. Just where had Bresnik been for all those weeks? And where had Keel sent Canning?

He shifted restlessly. He liked secrets; just not when they were kept from him.

"What of the magicians?" Bresnik asked. "Next time they send dogs, might also send ghouls, followed by *Nephilim*, followed by Guillam. Or Fisher." He said that last name quietly. Margot Guillam was an Elder vampyre, a threat no one took lightly. But Fisher could take back the Bothwell Street Crypt alone and with ease.

Crowe tapped the table before Keel could answer. "If I may, it should be borne in mind that the magician community is centred around the Under-Market. To preserve it, the land and the surrounding tenements were owned by a few Sooty Feathers. Hence why they have not been demolished like similar decrepit properties off High Street."

"I fail to see the relevance." Keel gave Crowe a cold look.

Crowe spoke again, his voice like a pen being scraped across dry paper. "Those Sooty Feathers have died in recent months. Their heirs must pay hefty Death Duties. The land in question is valuable – in theory – but restrictions put in place by the city council prohibit its redevelopment, and so the families sold me the land and all that stands upon it without hesitation."

"Are you telling us that you own the Under-Market?" Redfort asked, his astonishment making him speak out of turn.

"Most of the land, yes. Though I am prohibited from demolishing the slums thanks to old rules put in place by the city council per instructions from the Sooty Feathers."

"How does this help us eliminate the magicians? Do you intend to charge them to operate beneath the bridge?" Keel made no effort to hide his sarcasm.

"If the buildings presented a clear danger to public safety, then the city council would have little choice but to permit redevelopment," Crowe said, as unruffled as ever.

"And just how do you propose to accomplish this?" Keel asked, his interest piqued.

There was a ruthless simplicity to Crowe's answer.

*

Two raps against the outside of his box told Canning that

they had at last arrived. He pushed the lid off slowly, ensuring that the sun had indeed safely set before shoving it aside, climbing out the box and jumping off the wagon. The circus woman tasked to transport Bresnik from the circus to Glasgow, and to return to the circus with Canning, had no reason to betray him … that he knew of.

It was late in the evening, Canning finding himself in a Lanarkshire wood. The Carpathian Circus, whose arrival in Glasgow in February had sparked this war, was much smaller than it had been back then. Most of its men and undead had died during the spring, its folk reduced to women, children and a handful of men. Two hundred years had passed since Marko, Lucia and Bresnik – the fleeing remnant of Keel's loyal undead, save for George Rannoch – had found the circus, made themselves part of it and subverted it for their own purposes.

For all those years the circus had travelled Europe, the three *Nephilim* Making more undead and feeding from the unwary wherever they went. Now only Bresnik remained of the original three *Nephilim*, and only four remained of their circus-Made undead.

There were fewer caravans than Canning remembered. Perhaps there had been too few circus-folk to maintain them, or more likely their mission demanded speed and so they were abandoned. Led by Bresnik, they had travelled south to fetch something, something Keel had ordered Canning to return to Glasgow with, as fast as possible.

He walked through the camp while the woman who brought him here attended to the horses and wagon. The people stared at him, broken by loss. And by something else, perhaps. There was a new fear about them, but not of him, Canning sensed.

"Who is in charge?" Canning asked loudly. This was his first visit to the circus while there was no vampyre leading it. He wondered why they simply hadn't fled. Perhaps after two hundred years, they could imagine no other life beyond service to the undead.

Those who heard him looked at one another until

finally an older woman stepped forwards. "I am." Her words were slow and heavily accented.

"There is no man among you willing to lead?" Most had died, but there were a few here and there.

A shrug, followed by a word he did not understand. One of the other women lifted up an empty dark-glassed bottle and mimed swigging from it. *So, the men are all drunk.*

"Mr Keel has sent me to hasten his cargo's arrival in Glasgow. Bring it to me," he said, wondering just what this cargo was. Keel would only tell him that he would learn soon enough.

The woman in charge said something in her own tongue, a look of relief passing over her face and the faces of the others. Evidently this cargo was not a source of joy to them. A magical weapon perhaps?

A younger woman appeared, small and black-haired. "Who are you?"

"I am Richard Canning. Sent here by your master. Where is what I am to bring to him?"

"It is already before you," the woman said with an air of mockery that offended him.

Time to give these foreign vagabonds a lesson in respect. "Lead me to it or I'll rip your head off."

"Will you? Erik Keel would not like that," the woman said, amusement in her voice. Her accent was different to the others, her English better.

Anger torched his self-control, and he lunged at her, intending her to be a pointed lesson in courtesy to the others. Instead, he found himself bent to one side, the woman holding his right arm. After a moment's shock, he tried to shake himself free, only to find that she held him tightly.

"Who are you?" Canning managed to ask, shocked to find he could not break the woman's grip, chagrined to find himself once again underestimating an opponent. Belatedly he realised that he had no memory of ever seeing this woman in the circus during his stay with them.

"I am the 'cargo' your Mr Keel wants," she said.

Canning forced down his rage. If she was indeed what he was to bring to Keel, then the demon would not thank him for killing her. And he was not sure he could, her iron grip beyond his strength to break. "You are *Nephilim*." An Elder, probably.

A smile. "I am. The circus is proceeding to Glasgow. Why did *Arakiel* send you here?"

"His affairs in Glasgow are progressing faster than expected, and he wants you there as soon as possible. Sooner than the circus can manage."

"What of the circus?" she asked, releasing him.

"He made no mention of it."

"If he has no further need of it, then I will make use of it. Feel free to indulge yourself, Mr Canning," the woman said as she faced the circus women to her rear. Their eyes widened in fear as the *Nephilim* attacked without warning, killing the closest. She made no effort to feed just yet, moving from victim to victim with a supple speed.

She did invite me to join in.

Screams echoed around the camp as Canning and the mysterious vampyre attacked everyone in sight, killing and hunting down one victim after another. Women, men and children died, and once the slaughter was done Canning and the woman sated their Thirst with blood. Some may have escaped, but Canning cared not. If they spoke to anyone of vampyres and demons, they would be sent to Bedlam.

They fired the caravans, the burning wood providing a thick cloud of smoke. Canning and the woman mounted a horse each and rode towards the road, leaving the caravans to burn, a funeral pyre for the Carpathian Circus, and good riddance.

Why had Keel gone to such an effort to bring her to Glasgow? "Where do you come from?"

"I was in Marrakesh when *Arakiel*'s invitation reached me. From Casablanca I took a ship to Liverpool, where the circus awaited me." The blood she had drunk had darkened her complexion from pale grey to light-brown.

"Why did Keel go to so much effort to bring you here?" Canning asked. Surely there were *Nephilim*, even Elder *Nephilim*, closer to home happy to help bring down Fisher.

"He did not tell you?"

"He did not even tell me your name."

Away from the burning circus, he could not see her face, but the amusement in her voice was plain to hear. "My name is Lilith."

Her name answered both questions. Canning had little interest in vampyre legends and history, but the other undead had spoken of Lilith. The first human *Nephilim*, Made by Lucifer Himself.

"*Arakiel*'s letter claimed that Lucifer lives in Glasgow, Possessing a human. Did he write true?" she asked.

All of a sudden, the demon's insistence that Lord Ashwood be left unharmed, that Wilton Hunt also be left unharmed lest it enrage the father, made sense. According to legend, Lilith was the one who brought Lucifer down, her hatred for her Maker eternal.

Canning smiled.

Chapter Thirty-Four

John Grant stared at the man who had knocked on his front door, a man he had not expected to see again. "Foley!"

"In the flesh, Grant. It's good to see you. I'm sorry to turn up unannounced, hope it's not a bad time." There was a wry smile as he said that, surely not deaf to the muffled sounds of one child shouting and another crying, and Agnes trying to calm them both.

"The Struan Bar's five minutes down the road, let's talk over a pint. Give me a minute to get my coat and tell the missus."

Foley peered past him. "You're a brave man, leaving her to deal with the two weans."

"I'll tell her it's to do with work." Which was not entirely a lie. What he had to discuss with Foley did indeed touch on his work. "I'll explain it's part and parcel of me being an inspector."

"Congratulations on the promotion."

Maybe ten minutes later, Grant led Foley into the Struan's snug, a closed-off area of the bar habitually used by those shy of being seen drinking. Grant had no such concerns, but it offered some privacy for their conversation.

"Slainte," Foley said as he and Grant touched glasses. The snug was dark and dingy, save for what little light a lone candle on the table provided. Apt for what they were to discuss. Grant had been due to meet others here later, and Foley's presence might prove fortuitous.

*

Foley sipped his ale, the taste familiar even after months away from Glasgow. The people he had stayed with near Inverarnan had not mixed much with the other locals, and so Foley had spent little time at the inn there.

He could not recall having been in this bar before, and it was not one he would be rushing back to. The tables and stools were chipped and uneven, and the floor was sticky from spilled ale.

"Have you been back to your pharmacy and flat yet?" Grant asked.

"What's left of them. Wil Hunt sent a letter explaining what happened." Both were insured, so at least he would get compensation for their loss. Had Roddy McBride contented himself with the arson, Foley would have let it pass glad to be no longer tied to the city. But his brother had led men to Inverarnan and brought death to Foley's new family. That he would not let go unanswered.

Grant looked rather relieved that Foley knew. "Mr Hunt said he had written to you, but letters can get lost. I did not expect to see you back here. Your friend told me that Roddy McBride wants you dead."

"I'll settle things with McBride. Speaking of Hunt, where is he? His first letter said that he was staying with Lady Delaney, but her house is deserted. He mentioned you in his second letter, so I thought you might know where he is."

"It's not just Roddy McBride. He has brothers," Grant warned.

"One fewer now." Foley took a gulp of ale. Another dead brother the bastard could blame on Foley, though in truth it had been the Templar Paul Carter who had cut Eddie McBride's throat.

Grant pretended he hadn't heard that. "Mr Hunt, Lady Delaney and her other guests are currently staying with Lord Ashwood."

"Hunt's father? Are you sure? I know where the house is." Unless Grant was mistaken, it seemed Hunt had reconciled with his father. *The Devil…*

"I'm sure, unless they've moved again. Mr Hunt, Lady Delaney, Miss Knox, Mr … Steiner and a Mr Gray."

"Steiner and Gray?" That *was* a surprise. Foley knew Steiner and Gray were back in Glasgow but had expected Hunt to keep his distance from them. He was surprised to hear that Hunt had not only reconciled with his father, but also with Steiner, given the man's attempt to execute Amy Newfield in cold blood. And he had seen what Delaney did to demons; if she learned that Lord Ashwood was really Lucifer, it would be a race between her and Steiner over who attacked Hunt's father first. Hunt had left out most of this from his second letter.

"A hard pair. And that Lady Delaney too," Grant said. "You sound surprised."

Foley considered his next words carefully. "Hunt and Steiner had a bit of a falling out."

"Because Steiner shot Amy Newfield? Hunt and Steiner made their peace. Newfield and a Miss Guillam even made a brief truce with Lord Ashwood to rescue your friends."

Newfield and Guillam were not names Foley expected to hear come out of Grant's mouth. "You've met them? How the hell do you know of this?"

"I've met Miss Newfield a couple of times." Grant's face twitched slightly.

"How did you get dragged into this."

"I was under the command of a Superintendent Kenmure, who turned out to be Possessed by a demon." Foley listened as Grant calmly told him of the Possessed policeman recruiting thugs and killers into a company sent against *Arakiel*'s enemies, and who arrested Hunt, Lady Delaney and the others, save for Miss Knox. Knox and Lord Ashwood had then formed a brief alliance with Margot Guillam and Amy Newfield to rescue them, and Grant had witnessed first-hand the carnage resulting from Guillam's thorough cleansing of Kenmure's police station.

"I knew something unnatural was going on," Grant continued. "And so I girded my loins and visited Lady

Delaney's house, where I learned about all this." He shook his head. "Demons and vampyres…"

"Must have been a shock to hear."

"Aye, but for years myself and my colleagues have known *something*'s wrong in this city. Strange deaths and injuries, disappearances. Senior officers ensured that we didn't look too closely into things, and those constables who did suffered accidents. I told you some of this earlier in the year, remember?"

"Aye."

Grant looked at him. "You mentioned Amy Newfield when we met in March, and when all this started, I remembered the name."

"You need to be careful. If you say any of this to the wrong person, you might end up floating in the Clyde."

"I'll hold my tongue. In any case, Kenmure's death seems to have ended *Arakiel*'s control over the police. Some of my colleagues are asking questions, and for once no one is telling them to shut their mouths." Grant looked as if he might add something but didn't.

"When one side or the other wins, that will change," Foley warned. "That damned secret society will resume its control over every important institution in this city."

"Unless both sides lose."

"That would be grand," Foley said, though for now his priority was in making Roddy McBride pay for the murder of his friends up north.

"What will you do now? And just what brought you back here, besides your pharmacy getting torched? I'd let that one pass if I were you, rather than tangle with the McBrides. That damned family is involved in something almost everywhere in the city now."

"Roddy McBride sent his brother Johnny and a gang of thugs to kill me up north. They murdered some of the people who took me in, and so I'm here to make Roddy pay for that. I've no choice. Not with another of his brothers dead."

Grant nodded his understanding. "He'll chase you to the ends of the earth."

"First, I'll go to Lord Ashwood's house and let Hunt know I'm back in the city. If I know Lady Delaney and that maniac Steiner, they'll be planning another attack."

"Maybe have another pint or two," Grant suggested.

Foley squinted at him. "What are you hiding?"

"Some friends of mine are due here soon, and I'd like you to meet them."

*

The situation at Lord Ashwood's home, Knox decided, was proof that any situation could become normal as time passed, no matter how incredible it was. Both Niall Fisher and *Arakiel* seemed content to leave Lord Ashwood and his guests alone, and so everyone slowly settled into a new routine.

Mostly. Every so often she felt a start on recalling she was guesting with the Devil, and suspected she saw similar reactions from the others. Wolfgang Steiner refused to stay in a guest bedroom, instead taking an empty servant's room. He had tried to browbeat Terrance Gray into doing likewise, but the American had pointed out that Steiner had been relieved of his Templar duties, and as such Gray was the senior Templar in Glasgow. And he would damned well continue to enjoy a comfortable bed.

Caroline said little. Her antipathy towards demons approached obsession, and here lived Lucifer, King of Hell. Twice now she had fought alongside him and once he had even rescued her, yet still she regarded him with a simmering mistrust, and Wilton little better. The presence of the angel *Kariel* was perhaps what weighed her decision to stay here and not send Lucifer back to Hell.

There was an unspoken truce between Knox and Wil, their renewed friendship forged over morning tennis and walks in the Botanical Gardens. Walks chaperoned by Caroline for the sake of propriety, of course. Lord Ashwood's library had books enough to entertain her in the evenings.

She entered the drawing room to find Caroline sitting alone, a glass of white wine on the table before her. "Caroline."

"Kerry. An excellent wine, do help me finish the bottle lest I find myself intoxicated." A sardonic smile. "Had Lucifer tempted Christ with the contents of his wine cellar, he would not have needed forty days, and I suspect there would have been a different outcome."

Caroline's casual blasphemy left Knox briefly at a loss for words, but she managed a smile. "You'll give Steiner a fit, saying things like that." She accepted a glass of wine and took a sip, finding it to her taste.

"He is well aware of my opinion towards God and religion. He was not there for my family, and so I will have naught to do with Him. *Beliel* murdered my children, and yet despite my returning him to Hell three times, there is nothing preventing *Arakiel* and his Demonist from Summoning him back yet again."

Knox chose her words with care. "And yet you are content to live with Lucifer. With his son, who may very well be the Antichrist." *Wilton Hunt, a man, who, God help me, I think I'm in love with.*

"Lucifer has done naught to me or mine. It was the Sooty Feathers who had my husband Possessed by *Beliel*, it was George Rannoch who brought *Beliel* back, and it was *Arakiel* who had the demon freed from Hell yet again to infiltrate my household and kill Ellison. An angel keeps watch over Lucifer, I shall content myself with that."

"And what now for us?" Knox asked.

"That is what we wish to discuss in the sitting room," a man's voice said, Knox looking over to see Lord Ashwood standing in the doorway. "We would welcome your thoughts."

Caroline poured herself and Knox some more wine. "Do feel free to join us."

Lucifer managed a tight smile. "This was my wife's room, where she entertained our guests. It reminds me of her, sometimes so much that I avoid it."

After a small hesitation, Caroline stood. "Then we will join you and the gentlemen in the sitting room." Knox noted that she did *not* say, 'the *other* gentlemen,' but Lucifer either did not notice the small insult or chose to ignore it.

Wil, Steiner, Gray and Sirk were in the sitting room, a tension still lingering in the air. Singh was absent, either attending to his duties or in bed. The valet had an early rise each morning, directing the cook and housemaids to ensure breakfast was ready in time for Lord Ashwood and his guests.

"Lady Delaney. Miss Knox. I trust we did not interrupt anything important?" Steiner asked, his voice heavy with sarcasm.

Neither Caroline nor Knox deigned to reply.

"What would you care to drink, Lady Delaney? Miss Knox?" Ashwood asked as he stood next to the drinks cabinet.

"This excellent wine will suffice, Lord Ashwood," Caroline said, a sentiment Knox echoed.

"Now that we are all gathered, perhaps we might discuss how to proceed with this war?" Steiner asked.

"As I recall, your last adventure accomplished precious little, save for a handful of slain undead and a score of dead Templars," Ashwood said. "Are you so keen to see the rest of us dead?"

"Do you find amusement in the deaths of my brethren? I was not in command that day, but had I been so–"

"You would not have needed my help in escaping?" Ashwood suggested. "Or would you have all been dead by the time I arrived?"

"Enough," Wil said in a firm but weary voice.

"I agree with Mr Hunt. Our pressing concern is how to defeat both Fisher and *Arakiel*," Caroline said.

"What do you suggest, Lady Delaney?" Gray asked, uncharacteristically dour. Did he feel guilt that he had not been with his fellow Templars when they died?

"I suggest we take a breath and identify an opportunity," she said.

"Against which enemy?" Knox asked. Both had caused them hurt in recent days.

"Whichever presents a vulnerability," Dr Sirk said. "But I would recommend caution, lest one side seeks to play us against the other." He gave Steiner a reproachful look, which was not entirely fair given that the Templar inquisitor had not been in command.

"Miss Jackson should have reported to Grandmaster Maxwell in London. Might be we'll get some reinforcements," Gray said. The doubt in his eyes belied the optimism in his voice, which to Knox's ears sounded forced.

Steiner was not a man for such comforts. "No more Templars will be sent to Glasgow. Thirty-two have been lost to this city alone in less than a year. For years the Edinburgh chapter has kept vigil over that city, keeping it largely free from the undead. Any soldiers that can be spared will be sent there to ensure that does not change."

"We're on our own, then," Wil said. "Protected – for now – only by Fisher and *Arakiel*'s orders not to risk vexing the Devil." He looked furtively to his father, who said nothing.

"I have been on my own for twenty years, Mr Hunt. We will manage," Caroline said.

"What of you, Mr Steiner? Will you stay and fight, or will you return to London?" Lord Ashwood asked.

As always when Steiner's gaze fell on Ashwood, his eyes narrowed, and he gave the smallest of starts. Knox recognised his reaction for what it was; the same as her own. "I will stay and fight. To leave now will mean that my brothers and sisters died in vain, and that I will not permit."

"I'll stay too," the American said. He looked at Ashwood with little of the hate and fear shown by some of the others. "Lord Ashwood, who do you believe will prevail, Niall Fisher or *Arakiel*?"

Ashwood rested his chin in his hands. "That is difficult to say. A year ago, I would have not believed any enemy could have brought down Fisher's House and the Sooty

Feather Society, not without a large force. But Rannoch inflicted much damage from within, and Khotep's *zombi* attack killed many Sooty Feathers."

He sipped his whisky. "More recently, *Arakiel* has pushed hard against Fisher, owing to his control of the police and the use of *zombis*. Those two advantages are now gone. He has weakened Fisher's House and left the Sooty Feather Society all but dormant, but does he have enough resources remaining to make a meaningful attack? Even if he wins, losing too many of his followers will leave him unable to control the city."

"So, the short answer is, it is too soon to tell," Sirk said.

"The war may pause if neither side is confident that they have enough undead to both win and control the city," Ashwood said. "They may wish to lick their wounds, regroup and reinforce."

"That would give us an opportunity to strike," Caroline said.

Knox nodded. "Keep *them* from regrouping."

Wil raised a cautioning hand. "We must be cautious, or we risk handing victory to one enemy."

"Do we sit here and do nothing? What about after we've drunk all of Lord Ashwood's whisky?" Gray wanted to know, leaning back.

"Finish off the wine?" Knox suggested with a smile, raising her wine glass.

"I have a number of rare and expensive vintages, I would prefer we take action before you deplete my cellar entirely," Ashwood said with a faint smile.

There was a knock at the door, causing everyone to freeze, fear crawling down Knox's back.

"Are you expecting visitors?" Gray asked.

Ashwood had stood, staring at the door. "No, I am not." He left the room to answer it. Unarmed, but Knox knew there was a shotgun hidden beside the door with its barrels sawn off.

There was a rustle as those in the room with a gun on their person or hidden nearby armed themselves.

Knox turned to Gray. "Of all of us, save perhaps Mr

Hunt, you seem the least affected by being with … with Lord Ashwood. Were you raised in some pagan African faith, Mr Gray?"

The American laughed. "I was born and raised a Christian, Miss Knox, thank you very much." The mirth left his face. "Born and raised in the state of Alabama. I saw evil there, Miss Knox, you can scarce imagine. Slavery might be over in America, God be praised, but it didn't end easily, and some folks would be happy to see it back."

His brown eyes stared into his glass. "I saw evil, Miss Knox, and saw the folks who did it." He looked up into her eyes to reveal a pain he kept hidden behind laughter and a quiet sardonic wit, pointing to Lord Ashwood. "I didn't see *him* there, much as the preachers liked to blame evil on him every Sunday – all the while preaching to the *good people* who oppressed and murdered my people during the other six days. I *did* see him in that police building when you, he and Singh rescued us from the demon *Maridiel*."

The frown on Steiner's face suggested that rescue or not, he was not willing to judge Lucifer solely on his recent good works, but he said nothing. Caroline considered the American speculatively. Before, the others had largely regarded Gray as an extension of Steiner, a mostly quiet man excellent with a rifle and dependable in a fight.

We all have a past, and it seems there's usually pain hidden at the heart of it.

Lord Ashwood returned in the company of a pale, gaunt stranger, a tension in him Knox had not seen before. "Ladies, gentlemen, please put away any guns that might be near to hand."

"This gentleman is a friend?" Caroline's expression was sceptical.

"No, but if anyone raises a weapon, we may all die."

Often contrary, Caroline raised her derringer – and as she did so, a bone-deep chill seemed to fall over the room, a fear like nothing Knox had experienced before.

"Vampyre!" Steiner roared, but like everyone else, fear seemed to have rooted him to the couch he sat on. The apparent undead sprang forward, his hand whipping out to disarm Caroline before she could shoot.

"Good evening. Do not be alarmed or make any more foolish movements. If I wished you dead, I would have not bothered knocking," the stranger said, Scottish but with an odd accent. "Will you introduce me, *Lord Ashwood*?"

Ashwood cleared his throat. "Ladies and gentlemen, may I introduce Mr Niall Fisher. Mr Fisher, this–"

"Spare me, I am here to speak with your son. And then I will be leaving."

Niall Fisher, the vampyre lord who had ruled Glasgow from the shadows for two hundred years. What had brought him here if he had *not* come to kill everyone within?

"Me?" The *Dominus Nephilim* no longer Unveiled, but the fear on Wil's face deepened upon hearing he was the reason for Fisher's visit.

"We have matters to discuss, Mr Hunt. In private." He stared at Wil, and so Knox took the opportunity to study him. His hair was thin and grey, his almost yellow skin stretched against his skull. A film seemed to cover his eyes though he showed no sign of being blind. His grey tweed suit was not an exact fit, but from what she recalled, the master of Glasgow's undead had been a recluse for the best part of two hundred years. *Just what does he want with Wil?*

"Wilton, we will take Mr Fisher to the drawing room." Ashwood's emphasis on the word 'we' was lost on no one.

"As you wish," Fisher said as Ashwood led the three of them out the room.

Singh entered the sitting room moments later. "I was told to make sure none of you did anything stupid."

Steiner was incredulous, barely containing his rage. "You expect us to let a … a *vampyre lord* just walk out the door? There are guns and silver bullets in this room, sufficient for us to write an end to this abomination! He does not look to have even fed. If you believe I will let you and your *master* dictate–"

Singh raised his hand. "Enough."

Knox was impressed. Steiner was not a man easily interrupted, and the Indian valet had managed it with one word and a gesture. But of course, he was also an angel, something that had perhaps briefly slipped Steiner's mind in his eagerness to assassinate the lord of Glasgow's undead.

"My *master* in this case is *Mikiel*, which you would do well to remember, Mr Steiner. Now let me explain why attacking Niall Fisher would accomplish nothing save for our deaths." The *Seraphim* walked into the centre of the room, ensuring he had everyone's attention.

"First, Fisher is a *Dominus Nephilim*, but the many generations separating him from a *Grigori* means that he is … inefficient … where blood is concerned. He must drink much and often to maintain his full strength and a human appearance. *Samiel* spoke of meeting him once, almost thirty years ago, and reported that Fisher was almost skeletal. To have restored his appearance by as much as he has tonight means that he has drunk a lot of blood.

"He is not at his full strength, but he is no mere Elder like Margot Guillam. He would know your intentions by where you looked, the flush of your skin, the increased beating of your heart, the tensing of muscles and the shifting of balance. He would *know*. And he would move with a speed and lethality you have never seen before. You and all of us in this house would die." Singh – or *Kariel*, as seemed more appropriate – took a breath.

"He is among the most powerful beings in this world."

Chapter Thirty-Five

"What do you wish from me?" Hunt asked, a question he wasn't sure he wanted to hear the answer to.

There was an odd possessiveness in the *Nephilim*'s manner as he studied Hunt. "Neil MacInesker died recently."

"I didn't kill him, and if I did, why would you care, Mr Fisher?" Hunt asked.

"He was the last of the Glasgow MacIneskers," Fisher said.

"So the lawyers will fatten themselves while distant relations fight over his estate," Father said. "I have guests, kindly get to the reason for tonight's visit. I do not believe you left seclusion after two centuries simply to tell us a young man we barely knew has died."

Fisher's lipless gash of a mouth managed a smile. "Your 'guests', aye. Templars and meddlers, plotting more violence against me and mine."

"And against *Arakiel*," Father said.

"You went to Dumbreck Castle to save the Templars."

"To save Miss Knox, chiefly. That attack was a Templar folly, though one manipulated by *Arakiel* in the hope of weakening both the Templars and you, by killing anyone left with *zombis*," Father said. "You may not be aware, but the necromancer is dead. A *Jinn*, truth be told, but with his soul's receptacle destroyed, he will trouble the world no more."

"Young MacInesker was taken from Dumbreck Castle," Fisher said, evidently uninterested in Mortimer or his fate. His voice was raspy.

"Not by us."

"No. By Keel's people." Fisher looked between Hunt and Father. "And this is not the first time I have left my Crypt, though even Miss Guillam may believe such is the case. On occasion I leave and drink enough blood to restore my appearance, and then I wander my city to see how it has grown and prospered in the two centuries since I became *Dominus*. The six centuries since I lived and died as Sir Neil MacInesker. The first Neil MacInesker of many."

"Ahh," Father said slowly. "MacInesker – 'son of the fisherman'. You became undead and anglicised your name. And your family prospered under your watchful eye."

"Mostly prospered. Since I slew Erik Keel, my line has been plagued by deaths. I suspect, now, that George Rannoch was quietly killing the MacIneskers to ensure the tree did not grow outward too much, while letting the line continue."

"What does this have to do with me?" Hunt challenged.

Surprisingly, it was Father who answered. "Recall the Hunt family history. In the mid-eighteenth century, a Neil MacInesker married a June McKellen. Their elder son, also Neil, was the heir, from whom the recently deceased Neil MacInesker is descended. A younger son, Cullen, took the mother's maiden name."

Hunt nodded as the memory returned. June McKellen was the granddaughter of the chief of the Kail'an sept slain by the English Sir Geoffrey Hunt and his soldiers after the 1719 Jacobite Rebellion. The surviving Kail'an son escaped and anglicised his name from mac Kail'an to McKellen, and the family's hatred – deserved, in fairness – of the Hunts was passed down the line.

June McKellen was evidently wise enough to leave her elder son ignorant, instead educating Cullen in the blood feud. Cullen MacInesker had become Cullen McKellen, seeking out Harold Hunt, the 3rd Baron Ashwood. A notorious gambler, Ashwood had managed to lose most of his inheritance, finally losing the Dunlew estate and castle to Cullen McKellen, never learning that both had once belonged to McKellen's great-grandfather.

Not content with regaining Dunlew Castle, Cullen McKellen had continued gambling with Harold Hunt, and when the impoverished baron could no longer settle his debt, Cullen killed him in a duel. Hunt suspected that as Harold Hunt had lain dying, his killer had quietly told him who he was and why he had targeted him.

Regardless, a cousin of the childless Harold Hunt inherited the title of baron and what scraps remained of the Ashwood estate in Loch Aline. As descendants of the hated Sir Geoffrey Hunt still lived and held title and land in what had been the Kail'an ancestral lands, the McKellens married a daughter to Hunt's grandfather, thus connecting the two families. She later drowned her husband and faked her death, her return years later resulting in Lewis Hunt's Possession by Lucifer.

And now Hunt understood why Niall Fisher – the original Sir Neil MacInesker – had come here. Through his paternal grandmother, Hunt was a Kail'an … and a MacInesker.

"I'm descended from you," he said numbly.

"Distantly, but aye," Fisher said. "You're not a MacInesker, but you are the last of my blood, aside from your father."

"What do you want of me?" Hunt asked. "If you want me to become a MacInesker and sit on your damned Council, I won't. I'm no Sooty Feather."

"What I *want* is for you to stay out of this war. If Erik Keel realises your relationship to me, he will have you killed, regardless of who your father is." Fisher paused. "The MacInesker estate is in a poor financial situation, owing to Death Duties relating to the late Sir Neil MacInesker last year, his wife in the summer, and now his son. Lady Delaney's destruction of the Imperial Mill as well as the loss of the Kaleshaws village textile industry to the necromancer's plague means that I will be selling the Dunkellen estate.

"I will hold onto Dumbreck Castle, but as Lord

Ashwood is the nearest identifiable male relation to the late Alasdair McKellen, arrangements have been made for Dunlew Castle and its estate to pass to him. And upon his death, it will go to you, Hunt."

Hunt stared at Niall Fisher, a distant ancestor of his. "You're giving us a *castle*?"

"I would have the last of my blood away from this city. Go north and live in peace," Fisher said. "The necessary paperwork has been drawn up, and I will leave it here for you to look over." He placed an envelope on the table. "You were a lawyer, Lord Ashwood, so you can verify that it is all in order."

"Very generous," Father murmured.

"You can thank me by leaving Glasgow. By rights I should have had you both killed months ago for your interference in my affairs, but I suspected young Neil might not survive. Be gone, and if you value any of your guests, take them with you." Fisher's raspy voice hardened. "This war has tried my patience long enough, and I mean to end it. I sent Keel to Hell once, and I will do so again. I will see an end to all my enemies. Do not be among them."

Hunt felt a chill as he realised what Fisher was telling them: go north and live in Dunlew Castle or stay here and die.

"Thank you for your visit, Mr Fisher. I will see you out," Father said, a thoughtful expression on his face.

*

The first time Redfort had entered Walker's Bar, one of McBride's men had attempted belligerence, forcing the late Sid Jones to put a knife to his throat. Since then, Redfort had made several visits, and McBride's men knew better than to treat him with anything bar the utmost respect. Which was well, since Redfort was yet to recruit a replacement for his erstwhile bodyguard.

In any case, tonight he came with company. One of McBride's men silently led the trio to the pub's back room where Roddy McBride still held court despite his rising eminence.

"Bishop Redfort, back again, I see," McBride said, not bothering to rise. "And Mr Crowe, this is a surprise. Are you here for an impromptu Council meeting?" He squinted at Redfort's second companion as if trying to place him.

Redfort had been looking forward to this introduction. "Mr McBride, this is Mr Erik Keel." He relished the look of shock on the brute's face, the widening of bloodshot eyes.

"What the hell is this?" McBride asked, looking between bishop and banker.

"Leave the gun beneath your desk be, Mr McBride. I assure you, you will not be fast enough," Edmund Crowe said.

"Mr McBride. We finally meet," Keel said, a sharp edge to his voice. McBride was about to learn that it was an edge pressed against his throat.

"Mr Keel," McBride acknowledged carefully. Redfort could guess where the man's thoughts were running to; if he killed or captured Keel, he would accrue much favour with Miss Guillam and the reclusive Lord Fisher. But how to execute such a coup when the demon in question was flanked by two fellow Councillors, one of whom was an Elder *Nephilim*?

"Mr Keel is here to make you an offer, McBride," Redfort said.

"Our collaboration in the past proved beneficial to you," Keel said.

"What bloody collaboration?" McBride looked trapped.

Crowe spoke. "It was Mr Keel who approved and arranged for you to be in a position to hunt down Thomas Foley. It was a demon ally of his who infiltrated the Delaney household and marked Hunt's letter with Jimmy Keane's blood, allowing the Diviner to follow it."

"Has your brother returned yet with news of Foley's death?" Keel asked. The intention had been to recruit him slowly to Keel's side, but circumstances demanded a more direct approach.

“No, not yet. He sent a few letters from Inverarnan. The last was brief, saying only that he had found Foley and that they would kill him that night. I’m expecting him back any day now,” McBride said. “Bastard’s probably gone on a five-day drinking binge to celebrate Foley’s death.”

“Miss Guillam has known all along that Foley survived, yet did not tell you,” Redfort said.

“My thanks for the information,” McBride told Keel stiffly. He was a brutal thug, but no fool. He knew where this was going and was in no hurry to get there.

“You are welcome. As you can see, two of your fellow Councillors now serve me. A third Councillor, Neil MacInesker, is recently dead. Join me, Mr McBride. See an end to secrets, to thwarted vengeance.”

“Oh, aye, and you’ll be fully honest with me, Mr Keel? No secrets and the like, eh?”

“I need you, McBride. Or to be exact, I need your enterprise and the men you command. This war will end within the next few days. Join me,” Keel said.

“Or?” McBride asked.

“Or Mr Crowe will remove your head from your shoulders.”

Roddy McBride’s face paled as he realised he had no choice after all.

*

Hunt sat on what had been his usual stool in the Old Toll Bar, part of the late afternoon crowd. Being here brought back memories of living with Foley a few doors up the road. Simpler times, when his decision to study the natural sciences had alienated him from his parents and all he had to worry about was a lack of money. A deficit he had attempted to solve through bodysnatching, figuring the dead were no threat. *Oh, how I learned my lesson there.*

“I’ve not seen you here in a while,” the publican, Eoin McCoy said in his distinctive Highland brogue.

"I lived in Tam Foley's flat, which burned down," Hunt reminded him.

"Oh, aye. Good to see you back, Mr Hunt."

"It's good to be back, Mr McCoy." The Old Toll was a 'palace' bar, one with fancy expensive fittings intended to lure patrons in and away from cheaper bars or indulging at home.

"You got my message, then," a familiar voice said over Hunt's left shoulder.

"A pint of ale for my friend and one for yourself," Hunt said to the landlord. "Yes, I got it this morning."

"Sorry to hear about your shop and home, Mr Foley. You're looking well," McCoy said as he left to get their drinks.

"I can't leave you alone for two minutes without you burning down my pharmacy and flat," Foley said.

Hunt turned to face him, surprised to see his friend look younger and healthier than he had for as long as Hunt had known him. "McBride did it. Must have learned you were still alive."

"Oh, he did that. He had someone mark one of the letters you sent to me and had that Diviner Jimmy Keane lead Johnny McBride and a bunch of killers to my new home." A sense of dread fell over Hunt as Foley spoke, the bitter rage in his voice warning that there was tragedy to follow. "A lot of my friends died that night."

"You survived," Hunt said by way of scant consolation. Survival was sometimes a prison rather than a freedom.

A nod. "Bastards had no idea what we were, but they fucking learned. Elder werewolves can transform at will and can keep a sense of self."

"You killed Johnny McBride?" Hunt was pleased his friend had found people like him who had made him welcome, but guilty that once again innocents had been caught in the middle of this damned war.

"Him, his men, and that prick Jimmy Keane. But it was Roddy McBride who sent them, Roddy McBride who put two bullets in my gut in the summer, and I'll see him dead."

"He's grown more powerful since you left Glasgow," Hunt warned. "He's expanded from the south side into the rest of Glasgow."

"He's a Sooty Feather now?"

"Yes, not that there's much left of the society these days. What kept him mostly in check was that *Arakiel* largely controlled the police, hounding his criminal enterprises where they could."

"I know. I paid John Grant a visit last night and he caught me up on current affairs. I was surprised to learn just how much he knows; seems Lady Delaney saw no harm in telling him everything."

"Not quite everything, he doesn't know about … my parentage. And you visited him before me?" Hunt feigned a hurt expression. Mostly feigned.

"I didn't know where you were living, or if you *were* still living. My flat's a burned-out ruin and Lady Delaney's house is deserted. Your prior letters suggested you weren't talking to your father, and your last was lean on details. Had you not mentioned John Grant, I wouldn't know you were at your father's."

"Well, in the near future I may be back in the Loch Aline area," Hunt said.

"Aye? A nice area, but your house needs a lot of work."

"Builders are set to start work on Ashwood Lodge in the spring, but that's not where I'll be staying – if I go." Hunt leaned on the bar, affecting a casual air. "You remember Dunlew Castle? It's now my father's."

Foley whistled. "That must have cost a pretty penny! What possessed … sorry, poor choice of words … what *made* your father buy that place? Last time we were there some of the locals tried to have you Possessed."

"He didn't buy it. Niall Fisher gave him it. Turns out my father and I are his last descendants, and he would rather we were away from the city. Essentially, giving us the choice of a castle in the Highlands or a grave in Glasgow, since we insist on interfering with his business."

"I'd need to give that offer some thought, but I think I'd pick the castle," Foley said with an exaggerated thoughtfulness. “Thanks, Mr McCoy,” he said as the publican placed a pint of ale before him.

“You’re welcome, Mr Foley. ’tis good to see you back again.”

“His profits have probably halved since we left,” Hunt said quietly.

Foley smiled. “I admit, I’ve missed this. Sitting in a fine pub with a good friend, I mean.”

“You weren’t far from the Drover’s Inn, don’t tell me you didn’t skulk off there for an ale or five every few nights.”

“I didn’t! By necessity the folks I stayed with don’t … didn’t … mix too often with the other locals, so I never spent much time there. Maybe a pint or two once a week when I went to the post office to see if I had any mail. There was whisky in the estate where I lived, but farming is hard work, and the others wouldn’t have looked kindly on me stumbling around at dawn half-drunk.”

“Your liver will be in shock,” Hunt said, uncomfortably aware that his own drinking had increased greatly in recent weeks. At least he had stopped taking laudanum, knowing Lady Delaney and Father would disapprove of it in their respective homes.

“I do feel better.”

Hunt glanced at the clock above the bar. “It’ll be tight, but there’s room at Father’s house if you’re needing somewhere to stay.”

Foley shook his head. “Thanks, but I’m staying with a friend of John Grant’s for a few nights.”

“Do you want to come by the house and say hello to Dr Sirk, Lady Delaney and Miss Knox? Mr Steiner and Mr Gray are there, too. And Singh and my father.”

“I’ve business to attend to,” Foley said with a furtive air. He downed his pint and stood. “Good to see you. If you need me or want to give the McBrides a bloody hiding, send a message to John Grant. Here’s his address.” He left a slip of paper on the bar and extended his hand.

Hunt gripped it tightly. “It was good seeing you again too. Take care, and I’ll let you know if we plan to do anything stupid.”

Chapter Thirty-Six

"Miss Newfield, walk with me," Magdalene Quinn said on spying the young ghoul in the Under-Market. A wave of nods, half-bows and curtsies followed as many among the patrons and traders recognised Quinn, her star risen in recent days. Killing Bartholomew Ridley on these very cobbles and leading a pack of wild dogs into the Bothwell Street Crypt had removed any doubt as to who now led the magicians.

"Miss Quinn." Amy Newfield was no magician – and indeed her status as undead, her own seat on the Council, and her being a protégé to Regent Guillam made her at least an equal to Quinn – but there was still an automatic deference in her tone. Likely the result of their age difference. At the turn of the year, Miss Newfield had been a sixteen year-old girl raised to respect her elders.

Now she was undead, a killer and drinker of blood. But some shadow of that girl remained, albeit another part had died with the murder of her parents. There was little doubt that Erik Keel had ordered the killings in revenge for her role in the attack on Kenmure's station.

"What brings you here?" As the Regent's favourite, Newfield had no need to prowl the Under-Market, paying the desperate for their blood.

"Regent Guillam sent me here to look around and report back. She is concerned Keel may seek to tempt another magician to his cause, preferring that the magicians remain wholly loyal to the Council," Newfield said.

"I have agents of my own keeping an eye on the nooks

and crannies of this place, rest assured," Quinn said. "The only magician I know of who serves the demon is Cornelius Josiah, who has not shown face in months."

"Is it true that demons cannot use magic, even if Possessing a magician?" Newfield asked.

"Yes. I do not know why, but the Art is beyond them." Quinn gave her a sideways glance. "It is also true that a magician who becomes undead loses the ability to use magic. Perhaps for the best."

"For the best?"

"I am an accomplished magician, if I may say so, and expect to further hone my powers in time. Imagine how powerful I might become if I were immortal, with hundreds of years to study every school of magic."

*

Newfield slowed slightly, having failed to consider that. "For the best, indeed, Miss Quinn."

"That is largely why necromancy is forbidden. There are legends of the necromancers of antiquity seeking to defy death. Such a magician would truly be a master of the Art."

"As well that Lady Delaney and Lord Ashwood slew the last two necromancers to trouble Glasgow," Newfield said as their stroll took them to the edge of the bridge. As night had fallen, she had no need of the vast bridge's overhead protection.

Miss Quinn failed to respond to that, her pace slowing as something caught her eye.

Newfield followed her gaze to a man standing next to a wagon loaded with barrels, struggling to strike a match. He appeared agitated, dropping spent match after spent match to the ground as they failed to light properly.

The man turned, suddenly aware of their scrutiny, freezing for a moment before running away.

"We should catch him," Newfield said, starting to run, the man's flight stirring the predatorial hunger within her.

"The wagon first," Miss Quinn said, her face paling as if struck by some dreadful suspicion.

Newfield looked the wagon up and down, parked as it was next to one of the bridge's pillars. There was no livery, but it was familiar. "This looks like one of Mr McBride's wagons."

"You are sure?"

"It is nearly identical to the wagons he used to transport spirits to the Thistledown Tavern." Newfield reached out to open one of the barrels.

"Careful," Miss Quinn warned, pointing to what looked like a long piece of thick black string dangled from a barrel.

"What is that?"

"A fuse," Miss Quinn said. She tried and failed to prise the lid off the barrel.

"Allow me." Newfield jammed in her knife and attempted to jemmy it up, the lid slowly yielding to her undead strength. The barrel was filled with black powder.

"Gunpowder. Check another barrel," Miss Quinn suggested quickly, a sick look on her face.

A thick black liquid filled the second barrel Newfield opened.

"Oil. If one of those matches had properly lit that fuse…" Miss Quinn said in a horrified whisper.

"Enough to destroy the Under-Market?"

"No, but the oil would have ignited into flame and the gunpowder would cause a terrible explosion," Miss Quinn said. She glanced at the pillar the wagon sat next to. "Significant damage would have resulted."

Newfield remembered something. "What if there were more?

"More?"

"I've seen several wagons in and around the Under-Market tonight." She saw her own growing dread mirrored on Miss Quinn's face. *If those wagon drivers were tasked to light their fuses at the same time…*

Miss Quinn spun on her heel to face the Under-Market, candles and lanterns lighting up the space beneath the bridge, the market crowded with people. "Get out! All of you, get–"

Newfield was hurled backwards as the world exploded into fire, bludgeoned by a shower of shrapnel. How long passed, she did not know, as her broken body struggled to do what her mind commanded of it. Eventually, she managed to pull herself up to look upon the Under-Market.

It was gone, fallen into Hell. Barrels of exploding gunpowder had shattered the pillars supporting the bridge, half of it collapsing onto the Under-Market. The oil had ignited, pools of flame spilling across the cobbled ground and setting fire to those slums that had survived the explosion and collapsing bridge. Poorly built and crammed tightly together, the flames spread quickly from crumbling tenement to crumbling tenement.

Magdalene Quinn lay motionless on the ground. Other bodies were scattered around, some stirring, others still. Had they not chased off that man before he ignited the wagon here, the devastation would have been worse, hard as that was to imagine.

Her ears still ringing from the explosion, Newfield could barely hear the shouts and screams that filled the night as flame and death stalked the narrow wynds of the rookery. Many had died, and many more would die before this night was done.

*

This Council meeting should have had an air of triumph.

Instead, an air of shocked despondency lingered over the Councillors and other Sooty Feathers as they arrived at Dumbreck Castle for tonight's meeting. All knew of the destruction of the Under-Market. The entire city knew of it, and Newfield suspected that newspapers around the whole country would be reporting on the disaster.

She joined the Council – what remained of it – at the main hall's long table as the other undead and Sooty Feathers stood before it. There should have been chairs to seat the non-Councillors, but there were none. Perhaps Regent Guillam had removed them, an expression of her anger at the progress of this war.

The Regent sat in the middle seat of the table, a severe expression on her face. Her cheeks and lips were ruddy, telling Newfield that she had fed recently and fed well.

"Miss Newfield, you were at the Under-Market at the time."

"Yes, Regent." Was that an invitation to speak, an observation, or an accusation?

"Tell us what you saw." *And what I did not act upon, such as wagons filled with gunpowder and oil.* Perhaps she was being paranoid or perhaps the Regent wanted a sacrifice.

Newfield duly spoke of her visit to the Under-Market, her meeting with Miss Quinn, and their success in preventing one of the wagons from being blown up. Silence fell over the hall, save for the crackle of coal burning in the large marble fireplace.

"If you had realised sooner the threat presented by these wagons, Miss Newfield, could you have prevented this disaster?" Miss Guillam asked.

Aware that all eyes were on her, filled with speculation as to her fate, she considered her words carefully. "I might have saved more people, perhaps prevented one or two of the wagons from exploding … but no, it was inevitable. The wagons bore no livery but I recognised them as Mr McBride's." Roddy McBride was conspicuously absent from this meeting, and Newfield pointedly turned her gaze to that empty seat.

"Has anyone seen McBride lately?" the Regent asked the others on the Council.

Those who remained. Bishop Redfort sat in the Second Seat to the Regent's right, his fingers clasped together. To her left sat the undead banker, Edmund Crowe, now the Council's *Tertius*.

Magdalene Quinn was now *Quarta*, the Fourth Seat, promoted after her recent successes. She sat burned and bandaged, but Newfield suspected other wounds assailed her worst. She had said nothing so far, letting Newfield do the talking. Tonight should have been her triumph, a celebration of her recent accomplishments. Now ashes in the wind.

Neil MacInesker was dead, Roderick McBride absent and suspected of treachery. Newfield still considered herself *Octavia*, sitting in the Eighth Seat until directed otherwise.

It was as if the Regent read her mind. "Miss Newfield, you are in the wrong seat."

She rose and took a chance, sitting in the Fifth Seat. *Quinta*. For now. The Regent offered no comment or correction, confirming that unofficially, at least, McBride was the chief suspect in her mind.

The main door creaked, footsteps sounding on the stone floor as another entered the hall. Roddy McBride, perhaps? It occurred to Newfield that perhaps suspicion was being pointed at him deliberately, that Keel had simply taken McBride's wagons and used them to turn the Council against its own. Given the Regent's mood and the murderous look on Miss Quinn's face, he would have to talk very quickly indeed to stay either woman from killing him on sight.

"Regarding Mr–"

"I heard there was an incident at the Under-Market. Miss Quinn, would you be so good as to correct my ignorance regarding this situation?" A stranger approached the Council, unfamiliar to Newfield, though something about him did spark a fearful recognition.

Ailsa Kerris and Jonah Murray blocked his path. "Who are you to interrupt the Regent?" Miss Kerris hissed. Both *Nephilim* revealed their fangs, prepared to kill this intruder.

"Do you serve Erik Keel?" Murray demanded, a knife in hand.

"I did, once," the stranger admitted.

Murray lunged at him, only to be flung effortlessly to the ground. Kerris drew her own knife and half-crouched, as if ready to lunge, Unveiling.

The man smiled. And Unveiled too, drenching the hall in fear. Newfield half-heard the gasps of terror from the mortals in the room, her eyes fixed on this man. Because she knew him now.

"Enough." Miss Guillam said loudly. She recognised the new arrival, as would Mr Crowe. Harold Fowler did, too, standing wide-eyed to one side and having made no move to confront him.

"Miss Guillam?" he invited.

She rose, wrong-footed for once. "Ladies and gentlemen. It is my honour to introduce you all to … Lord Fisher."

A chorus of gasps filled the hall. All knew of the reclusive *Dominus Nephilim*, though only a few of the older *Nephilim* had seen him before, and not in the last two hundred years. Newfield suspected most had not expected to ever see him again.

The last time she had seen Fisher, he had been a bony thing of yellowed skin and patches of thin, white hair. Now he stood in the fullness of his power, thick brown hair reaching his shoulders, cleanshaven and pink-cheeked, looking like a man of thirty in the prime of health. He wore trousers, shirt and a frock coat that looked to still be in fashion. *How much blood must he have drunk to have restored himself so fully?*

And what does he intend now that he has done so?

"Margot Guillam. Regent of my House and *Prima* of my Council. Edmund Crowe, an old friend and now a member of my House." Fisher slowly looked around the room, the relative darkness no obstacle for him. "Harold Fowler! Still here, I see. I recognise so few of you now, the *Nephilim* of my House. But then, this has been a bloody year."

"Yes, my Lord," Fowler whispered.

"Miss Newfield! It is good to see the most promising of my ghouls again."

"You honour me, my Lord." So long as he did not blame her for the Under-Market's destruction.

"I believe I asked a question?" When no one saw fit to answer it, he asked again. "The Under-Market. Tell me of its condition, of our losses."

Miss Quinn spoke. Either brave or no longer caring about her own life, she showed no fear of the *Dominus Nephilim*, the wounds to her face making her speak slowly. "The Under-Market is gone, buried beneath the bridge." One eye was gone, a bandage covering what remained. The other contained enough rage for both. "Fire destroyed most of the surrounding slums, the few buildings still standing deemed unsafe and have been abandoned."

Newfield recalled the rapid spread of the flames, those unable to escape the narrow wynds snaking around the tightly packed tenements screaming in fear and pain; the lucky choked by smoke, the unlucky burned alive.

It had horrified her, but less than expected, perhaps because she had died once herself – or perhaps because she was now undead, and had taken lives herself.

"Casualties?" Lord Fisher asked.

"Hundreds, certainly. We may never know for certain, as there were no accurate records as to who stayed in that rookery," Redfort said.

"I care not about the scum. How many magicians died?" Fisher snapped.

"Between market traders and patrons, and those who just liked to mingle, I would say we have lost most of the magician community," Miss Quinn said slowly. She looked like she might be sick.

"And those responsible?"

Newfield spoke. "The wagons were owned by Roderick McBride, who has not attended here tonight."

"Despite being no true Sooty Feather, McBride was raised to the Council. His interests suffered under Keel's attentions, so what drove the man to treachery?" Fisher asked.

Newfield saw surprise on some of the faces upon hearing how familiar Fisher was with his House, but Miss Guillam had kept him well-informed.

"He serves his own interests first. Perhaps he was bribed or perhaps he was threatened," the Regent said. "What matters is his apparent betrayal. He must be found."

"If he is indeed behind the destruction of the Under-Market, then he will not be sitting at home waiting," Redfort said.

"He may be hiding, but he cannot hide forever. He rules an empire of thugs, thieves and killers, and he must be seen and heard, or another will seize what he has built," Miss Guillam said. "He has family in the Gorbals, that is his home. Start there. Question every wretched soul who crosses your path until he is found."

Miss Quinn stirred. "I would be the one to kill him. He murdered many friends and acquaintances."

"I would have him brought here *alive*," the Regent said with a quiet but unmistakable emphasis. "I would know why he betrayed us and learn what he knows of Keel's plans."

"And after?" Miss Quinn asked, her lone eye fixed on the Elder *Nephilim*.

"After that he is yours. A reward for your excellent work in the Bothwell Street Crypt," Lord Fisher answered before the Regent could. Miss Guillam did not look overjoyed at his presence, but she kept to herself any objections.

Fisher addressed the hall. "Two hundred years ago I led this House against its founder, Erik Keel, whom we now know is the demon *Arakiel*. I have been content to keep my own company and entrust the day-to-day ruling of this House to my regents since becoming Master of the House. And for almost all that time, our control over Glasgow has strengthened. But George Rannoch's treachery brought *Arakiel* back, brought *war* back to this city.

"I had trusted in Regent Guillam to bring a swift end to this war, but such has not proven to be the case. And so, I have returned to write an end to this demon-led insurrection personally. Let us stop naming this creature 'Erik Keel'. He is the demon *Arakiel* so we will name him as such."

"I stand by your side, as always, Master," Miss Guillam said. Not that she had any choice.

"I would see you take back the Bothwell Street Crypt, Margot," Fisher said.

"As you command." It was dangerous. To attempt it might also see Miss Guillam dead, despite Miss Quinn's excellent work, but to refuse would certainly see her dead.

"I would accompany the Regent," Mr Crowe said to Newfield's surprise. Elder or not, he did not seem one to put himself in danger. "With Mr Murray."

"As you wish, Mr Crowe," Fisher said absently. He risked his two Elder *Nephilim* but perhaps in his mind if they died, then they were of little use anyway. Not that Newfield expected they *would* fail. The guards killed by the magicians may have been mortal, but they were mercenaries with experience of fighting undead. What remained were ghouls and a handful of *Nephilim*.

"I would go too," she said hesitantly, feeling she should support her mentor.

"That will not be necessary," Miss Guillam said sharply. "It would not do to risk three Councillors." Fisher offered no comment.

"You spoke of ending this war," Mr Crowe observed. "After the retaking of the Crypt, what then?"

"McBride will be dealt with. *Arakiel* has been deprived of the constabulary and magicians. Deprived of his necromancer and *zombis*, and now he has been deprived of his mercenaries." Fisher looked around. "I am gathering most of our forces here. Miss Quinn has re-established her Wards here and around the Dunkellen estate. Should *Arakiel* strike at either, we will know and move against him in force."

The return of Niall Fisher gave Newfield some trepidation, but with him leading the House and Sooty Feather Society against the remnants of the demon's faction, this war should be over soon.

Chapter Thirty-Seven

Hunt sat on a stool next to the bar, taking his time over a pint of ale. Risky, yes, but he needed respite from his father's house. The fragile civility still held, Steiner and Delaney refraining from attacking Father. But the atmosphere was taut and tensions high, and Hunt wanted away from it all for an evening. Decamping to Dunlew Castle next to Loch Aline appealed to him, there being little anymore to tie him to this damned city.

The necromancer who murdered his mother was dead, for good this time, and the war between the two undead factions showed every sign of entering an exhausted stalemate. The talk of a shocked city was the destruction of one particular slum off High Street, that Hunt knew had surrounded the Under-Market. All gone.

To attack one side now risked the other rising to dominance over Glasgow, and in truth Hunt and his companions hardly presented as a unified force.

Foley's return was a welcome surprise, albeit one due to terrible circumstances. The McBrides had inflicted heavy losses on Foley's fellow werewolves, and the former pharmacist seemed grimly intent on avenging those losses. Maybe Hunt could help him kill Roddy McBride, and then the pair could go to Loch Aline where Dunlew Castle awaited. Foley might even invite his packmates, or whatever they called themselves, making a home for themselves in the vast Lewswood.

Maybe Hunt could invite Kerry. Maybe. The distance that had grown between them upon her learning of his true paternity had lessened of late, but if she learned of his growing feelings for her, she might reject him. It was one thing to be cordial to the son of the Devil, another to consider marriage and children. Besides, she seemed committed to fighting alongside Lady Delaney in Glasgow.

A shadow fell over Hunt as someone approached and sat on the stool next to him. "Have you tired of drinking my wine and whisky, Wilton? Between you and your friends, my drinks cabinet and cellar are *much* diminished."

Startled upon recognising his father, it took Hunt a moment to shake off his reverie. "What are you doing here? Have you decided upon a change of scenery, Father?"

"I saw you leave and decided to keep an eye on you. Some time has passed since our last father-and-son visit to a public house, and this establishment looks as good as any. Smaller than the Ashwood Arms, alas." He motioned to the bartender to bring another two mugs of ale.

"The Horned Lord, the locals call it. And the late landlord's daughter told me that she used to spit in your ale." Hunt drank heavily from his glass. It occurred to him that he and his father had rarely talked of anything significant. Mother had taken the lead in raising him, as she had in most matters, and Father had spent a lot of time working in London. Father and son had largely spent the years either exchanging pleasantries, or latterly, discussing demons and the undead.

"Did you love her?" Hunt blurted out.

"The Ashwood Arms' landlord's daughter? No, she is too young for me, and she spat in my ale," Father replied with a straight face.

"Very funny."

"I admired and respected your mother greatly, she was a remarkable woman." A laugh escaped his lips. "Who else would marry the Devil and insist upon reading that dreadful *Paradise Lost* time and again? She used to quote passages at night, feigning ignorance when I challenged her about it. 'I must have talked in my sleep,' she would say."

"You didn't answer the question."

"You speak of concepts alien to me and mine. And I speak not just of the Hellish angels but of the Heavenly ones too." He rubbed his chin. "Yes, I loved her, as much as I could."

Hunt had to force himself to say what came next. "What of me? Was I a freak accident? Singh claims that *Seraphim* and demons cannot bear or sire children, yet here I am."

"We cannot, yet an … exception was made in your case. Your mother always wanted children, and so I arranged for that to happen," Father said.

"A favour, then, to her." Hunt drank again from his ale.

So did Father, until he slowly placed the mug down. "No. The time for lies and lies by omission are at an end. I did not sire you just as a favour to your mother. Nor were you an accident."

Hunt said nothing, waiting for him to continue while part of him dreaded to hear what might follow.

Father half-smiled mirthlessly. "My motives were not so laudable. I sired you in the hope that when you died, the part of me within you would reach Heaven. That part of me would at last return to Heaven, and I might…"

"You might what?"

Father looked him in the eye. "Use that essence to pull the rest of myself into Heaven. End my exile."

You sired me to get back into Heaven? "And then resume your rebellion against God?"

Father laughed. "If I ever succeed in returning to Heaven, rest assured I will be living quietly. Even should I be so inclined to rebel, the only angels remaining are those who refused me the first time around. I daresay the dire consequences faced by my followers served only to convince them that they chose the right side. Secondly, I have met God no more than you have. My dispute was with *Mikiel*."

A disquieting revelation came to Hunt. "Why am I still

alive? Should you not have killed me years ago, lessening the risk of my sins sending me to Hell?"

"Your mother might have taken that amiss, firstly. Secondly, *Mikiel* knew of you before you were birthed, arranging for a *Seraphim* to visit the morning you were born. Had it been so easy as to simply kill you and then kill myself to return to Heaven, the *Seraphim* would have ensured you were never born, so I daresay there are complications to my plan. And thirdly … I wished to see *you*. None of my kind has ever had offspring. I was curious as to how you would be."

Tears stung Hunt's eyes. "I hope I was not too much of a disappointment."

Eyes identical to his own stared into their reflection. "I am almost as old as time. In the smallest fraction of my existence, I have watched you … a piece of myself within you … grow from a squalling babe to a self-aware being. I feel … awed … and privileged … to have witnessed your growth. The fourth reason I have not simply killed you is … there is no rush. I … you … will die in time, inevitably. And I am confident that one day, you will reach Heaven, and I can content myself with that knowledge."

Hunt stared into his father's shining eyes, a lump in his throat. "Singh believes I may be more akin to the *Seraphim*."

Father drank from his mug. "He may be right. Heaven and Hell may be denied to you, dooming you to being reborn again and again."

They drank thereafter in a companionable silence for a time.

Hunt spoke. "Mother is avenged. I wonder if, once my studies are complete in early summer, I should move to Dunlew Castle. With your permission, of course." Both the Dunlew and Ashwood estates would belong to Father until his death, and then they would be Hunt's.

"Whatever you wish, my castle is your castle," Father said carelessly. "A quiet life until matters settle here might prove wise."

"Assuming the locals don't have me dragged off to a

pagan shrine in the forest again," he said dryly. A student of the natural sciences, he would certainly find much more of botanical interest up north than he would in the city.

"I see you are not alone among my guests in seeking a quiet pint," Father said, looking over Hunt's shoulder.

Hunt turned to see Wolfgang Steiner sitting alone at a small corner table, a pint of ale before him.

Hunt finished his own ale. "Shall we return home? Help the others further empty your wine cellar?"

"You go ahead," Father said, his gaze fixed on the Templar.

*

Steiner sipped from his ale, surprised by its quality. His scant experience with the ales of this city had not left him with a favourable impression, but this public house served a better brew. Not as good as the ales and lagers of his native Switzerland, but a wealthier clientele patronised this public house, and so the publican stocked his cellars accordingly.

Someone sat across from him, and he looked up with a scowl to encourage the intruder to sit elsewhere. Surprise and a shiver of fear went through him on recognising the interloper as Lord Ashwood. *Lucifer. The Devil Himself.*

"Good evening, Mr Steiner." Lucifer placed his half-done mug down on the table. "They serve a good ale here."

"Tolerable." He doubted the Devil had sat across from him to discuss ale.

"For some days now, you have guested at my home, and it occurs to me that we have not talked. Remiss of me, as a host," Lucifer said.

"I forgive the lapse," Steiner said stiffly. Having the Devil bid him a good morning at the breakfast table was bad enough. He had no wish for conversation in a pub.

"Good of you," Lucifer said carelessly. "Do you have a family?"

Steiner felt his chest tighten. "Once. No longer."

Immediate understanding showed in those blue eyes, older and harder than his son's, but otherwise identical. "Disease, accident, or the undead?"

"The undead. In Geneva."

"Dare I say, you have spent your days since wishing you might turn back the clock and be with your family on their last day, with the lethal skills you possess now? That you would do anything to save them?"

"I would." *I was a tailor in those days.*

"Then understand, Mr Steiner, that I will do likewise to protect *my* son from any who mean him harm. I trust you will make that clear to your grandmaster?" The amiable Lord Ashwood was gone, replaced by Lucifer in that moment.

Part of Steiner bristled at the bared threat, a primitive part urging him to defy Lucifer. But another part of him recognised the father in the Devil, and understood where that threat came from – and bitterly envied that Lucifer still had a living child on whose behalf he could levy such ultimatums.

"Ask your question," Lucifer said.

Steiner frowned. "What question?"

"The question I see in your eyes whenever you look at me, when curiosity has gotten the better of your hate for me. Or rather, the hate you bear for the devil you believe me to be."

"What is Heaven like?" *And what possessed you to risk exile? Pride?*

Lucifer spoke slowly, his brow furled. "I do not know. It is a realm utterly unlike this one, and while in this realm, I find myself limited by this mind, by your words. It is a place of … creation. To call it a paradise is to do it an injustice."

"And yet you rebelled."

"Yes. But not for the nonsense your religions talk of. God did not appear and order us to bow to you. We were unaware of you until two hundred demons Fell here, and several thousand *Seraphim* were cursed to be reborn here again and again."

If Steiner had suffered discomfort being hosted by the Devil, the one salve to his scourged soul had been the presence of the angel *Kariel.* That alone had convinced Steiner to live beneath Lucifer's roof, had reassured him that this world had not been entirely abandoned.

"What was the Fall like?" he asked, driven by curiosity.

"I cannot describe it. One moment I was in Heaven, the next I was on this world, cloaked in flesh that looked like the primitives who dwelt here, vulnerable to the sun."

"You claim that you cannot fully recall Heaven when in this world. Do you remember Heaven when you are in Hell?"

Steiner almost flinched as eyes haunted beyond measure met his own.

"Yes. All of it."

To recall paradise while trapped in damnation ... "Another ale?" Steiner asked, feeling a rare pity for the creature before him.

"Yes, that would be appreciated."

*

Hunt staggered down Byers Road, half-minded to visit another pub on his way home. Tonight had been good, he and Father finally clearing the air. There had been no sign of Father following him, and Hunt wondered if he had joined Wolfgang Steiner. How might Steiner react to such a presence. *Maybe they'll get drunk and brawl?*

Something sharp jammed hard against his back as he walked past a black-curtained carriage. "Don't move."

The carriage door opened, and Hunt was alarmed to see Roddy McBride sitting inside with a look of twisted satisfaction on his face. "Evening, Mr Hunt. Climb inside." It was not a request.

Hunt was careful not to make any moves that the man behind him with the knife jammed against his back might misinterpret as an attempt to fight or flee. "Mr McBride. You're making a mistake. Niall Fisher attended my father's house, and an agreement was struck. He will not be pleased to hear about this." Which was putting it mildly. If McBride killed Fisher's last heir, then he would find his own life ending painfully.

McBride's smile was ugly indeed. "I no longer work for Niall Fisher or Margot Guillam. Mr *Keel* told me to take you, and I told him it would be my fucking pleasure."

Hunt's chest tightened, nausea flooding his belly and sending bile up his throat as memories of his time as a prisoner of the Sooty Feathers crowded his mind. He was numbly aware of McBride and the thug with the knife to his back manhandling him into the carriage, and the door shutting.

It moved off with a sharp jolt, hooves and wheels clattering off the cobbled road.

"You should know, I learned that your friend Foley somehow survived my two bullets to his guts, so I sent my brother Johnny – you remember Johnny? – and some of the lads to kill him. Inverarnan, aye?"

Hunt would normally have kept his mouth shut, but the leer on McBride's face goaded him to speak. "I remember Johnny. He's dead and so are your 'lads'."

McBride's face reddened. "You're a fucking liar."

Hunt managed a smile of his own as he tried to dig into the darkness within him. "You thought I lied when I told you and Walker that I killed his son, Gerry. I wasn't lying then and I'm not lying now. Your brother is dead. Foley and his new friends used him and his men to decorate trees before having them buried in anonymous graves."

McBride looked like he very much wanted to murder Hunt.

"You don't believe me? Lady Delaney's butler was Possessed by the demon *Beliel* who saw a letter I wrote to Foley, addressed to a post office in Inverarnan. The envelope was marked with Jimmy Keane's blood, so that he could use his magic to follow it. Keane led your brother and his men to the farm where Foley was staying. Foley survived, your brother did not. Keane's dead too."

"Bastard!" McBride clenched his fists, his face boiling red.

"Boss! You said this Mr Keel wants Hunt alive," the thug said.

It looked a struggle, but eventually McBride got control of his temper. "That's two of my brothers your friend has killed. I'll spend days fucking killing him!"

"He's back in Glasgow. Sends his regards." Even as he spoke, he knew it was a mistake to let McBride know Foley was in the city, but let the bastard know fear. "It wasn't Foley who killed your other brother … Eddie? … A Templar called Carter did that, and Carter's been dead for months. You lost a second brother trying to avenge the first killed by a man who's already dead."

"I hope Keel lets me be the one to kill you."

Hunt met McBride's eyes. "You know who my father is. What he is. If you kill me, he'll kill *you* in this world, and will make sure you spend eternity in the next one wishing you hadn't."

"Shut your mouth or I'll cut your tongue out. Same if you Unveil."

The rest of the journey passed in silence.

Where is he taking me? He prayed that his father and friends found him quickly.

*

"This city's a bad influence on you, Inquisitor. You're keeping bad company," Gray observed, Kerry evidently not alone in being surprised to see Ashwood and Steiner returning home together. There was a smell of ale about them though neither appeared drunk.

"I did not ask your opinion, Sergeant Gray," Steiner snapped, clearly somewhat embarrassed at having been caught drinking with the Devil.

"Neither you did, Mr Steiner. And need I remind you, until the Grandmaster decrees otherwise, you've been relieved of your duties, making *me* the senior Templar in this godforsaken city."

"You both drank together? And the evening did not end

in fisticuffs or murder?" Caroline asked in mock-amazement as she continued with her embroidery.

"Mr Steiner and I shared a cordial drink or two together and cleared the air," Ashwood said. He looked at their visitor. "I see we have a guest. Welcome, Mr Foley."

"Lord Ashwood," Foley said, already on his feet. "Mr Steiner."

"Mr Foley." Steiner gave a sharp nod of his head. "You look to be in good health."

"Wilton mentioned you had returned to the city. To stay, or will you be leaving again once your business is complete?" Ashwood asked.

"Leaving, I think. Once McBride is done. Did Hunt return with you?" Foley asked.

Ashwood's face went still. "He has not yet returned? He left the pub some time before us."

"Perhaps he attended another public house on his way home?" Caroline suggested. But already a tension had risen in the room, everyone well aware just how dangerous the streets of Glasgow had become, even for those without the enemies this household had accrued.

*

Almost one hour had passed since Steiner had returned to the house in the less-than-reputable company of Lucifer, whose son was still absent. The sitting room had been mostly silent, save for the sounds of Lady Delaney's embroidery and the dry rasps of paper as Gray had turned the pages of his book.

And then the demon arrived.

Arakiel stood in the sitting room, wearing the body of Bishop Redfort's secretary and showing no fear of what might befall him here. Steiner was tempted to shoot him then and there but decided to see what he had to say for himself.

"We struck an agreement, you and I," Lucifer said. No one else dared speak, the atmosphere as sharp as a blade as both demons Unveiled, heedless of the effect it had on the others present. They might have been the only two in the room, so intent they were on each other.

"We did. And then I divined the reason for you siring a child, Lucifer. And I vowed that you would fail," *Arakiel* said.

"You do not know why or how Wilton was born. And I would warn you against harming him." The Devil spoke those words quietly, but who he was shouted them loud and clear.

"Say what you have come here to say, *Arakiel*, and then begone," Singh said.

Arakiel glared at the valet, and then his eyes widened in shocked recognition as Singh Unveiled. "*Kariel*! You follow Lucifer, now? A third of our kind followed him once, straight to Hell."

"I follow *Mikiel*," the *Seraphim* corrected. "And you know less than you think. Release Wilton Hunt. I know what you fear, and rest assured that if it were possible, the birth of *Samiel*'s son would not have been permitted."

Arakiel studied *Kariel* for a moment, then turned his attention back to Lucifer. "If you want to see your son again, follow my instructions. I will have an address delivered here tomorrow. Be there at midnight."

Steiner spoke. "Why should we not send you back to Hell here and now, demon? And end this war."

Arakiel's smile was not pleasant, sending a chill of fear down Steiner's spine. He was used to dealing with the undead, once-people turned into abominations. But this being had once been an angel of Heaven, now a demon of Hell. "Kill me, and my Demonist will Summon me into Wilton Hunt."

"Let him go, Mr Steiner," Lucifer said. "We will resolve this matter tomorrow."

"Jesus, Mary and Joseph, but that was something!" Gray said with an explosion of breath after *Arakiel* had left. "Three angels exiled from Heaven in one room!"

Foley walked to the door. "I have some friends who may be able to help. I'll return tomorrow, if I can, to learn where the hell this demon wants us to go."

"Wants *me* to go," Lucifer corrected. "But you will be welcome, Mr Foley. Unless you must leave immediately, you are also welcome to stay for dinner."

Foley hesitated. "It's not an imposition?"

"We appear to have an empty seat at the dining table," Lucifer said heavily.

Foley nodded. "Thank you. But if I am to stay, I would hear about the origins of the werewolves. You claimed some months ago to know about it."

"As you wish, Mr Foley." Lucifer grimaced.

Chapter Thirty-Eight

Northern Europe
A Very Long Time Ago

For several moons *Samiel* had fled, knowing Lilith remained in perpetual pursuit, aided by some of *Batariel*'s Elders. On occasion they had clashed, the last time seeing an Elder fall while *Samiel* lost an arm, struggling to lose her nemesis. Also struggling to find somewhere to escape the sun as each dawn approached. With middling success. Her flesh was burned from those days where she had found just enough cover to survive but not enough to fully protect her from that blazing fire in the sky.

North, she had gone, the nights lengthening. Days had passed since she had last drunk blood and she still bled from a stomach wound. If she could just reach a village, she could feed from enough mortals to restore her strength and heal.

A chorus of howls rung out, meaning more than one wolf, *Samiel* knew, and it was not a fight she would survive unscathed should they attack. Desperately she Unveiled, attempting to breach the barrier separating this realm from Heaven, to either return home or at least access enough power to restore this body. Every *Grigori* had tried as much, she suspected, many times since the Fall, but why not try again…

The wolves fell upon her, teeth tearing at flesh as she fought back. With her remaining hand she held off one wolf, but the others savaged her. She kicked one wolf, hearing a startled yelp and the crack of its spine. She released the wolf she held and with a rock she crushed its skull. Finally, she succeeded in forcing an imperceptible breach between this foul realm and Heaven, a stray tendril of that power touching the full moon shining in the sky overhead.

She could sense the bliss of Heaven through the breach, but she had no means of moving through it, tormented by that glimpse of *home*. Some of the surviving wolves howled, *Samiel* sensing a change in them as her blood – coursing with a power she could do nothing with – altered those who had ingested it, similar yet different to how her blood had Made undead of the humans. She had in the past experimented with different beasts, feeding them her blood and then killing them, but death had proven final for them.

Samiel sank her fangs into one wolf that got too close, ripping out its throat. Its blood only sated her Thirst a fraction of what human blood would, a fraction of what she needed to heal, but enough to give her the strength to fight off the remaining beasts.

The surviving wolf fled, driven mad by the changes wrought upon it by the power of Creation it had ingested through *Samiel*'s blood, charged by her brief connection to Heaven. She had won but at the cost of a leg. Trees surrounded her but too few to offer cover, and the sun was rising.

She crawled as fast as she could with only one arm and one leg, finding no sanctuary from the rising fire, feeling her flesh start to burn. There would be no return to Heaven, and soon she would join the rest of her kindred in Hell, her only hope of respite being the possibility that a human magician might Summon her back.

Pain…

*

For hundreds of years, Lilith had feared and hated *Samiel*, her Maker.

Now she stood over her pitiful remains, the

Lightbringer reduced to a charred, two-limbed corpse. Despite her relief that this hunt had finally ended, she felt a bitter disappointment at not having personally killed *Samiel*, at not having watched the life leave those eyes as the *Grigori* left this world for Hell.

She was both the first and last of *Samiel*'s *Nephilim*, the others dead by her hand or by *Batariel*'s army. *Batariel* had expected her to take over *Samiel*'s kingdom, but she had no interest in ruling *Samiel*'s legacy, only in destroying it.

"It is over," said Havid, one of the two surviving Elders *Batariel* had sent with her to hunt *Samiel* down. *Samiel* had been thought beaten once before only to return, and so this time the *Grigori Batariel* wanted to be certain.

"Yes. Return to *Batariel* and tell her," Lilith said.

"What of you?" he asked cautiously.

Lilith had wondered if her escort had been ordered to kill her once *Samiel* was dead, but neither Elder moved to attack. They might have, had more of them survived this endless running battle with *Samiel*.

"I will wander," she said. They parted ways, the surviving Elders taking *Samiel*'s remains with them.

Her revenge finally accomplished, Lilith chose to explore this world, regretting that she would see it only at night. Her first stop was at a village where they celebrated hunting down a maddened wolf that had attacked many, leaving only a handful of survivors.

By the next full moon, that village would again suffer as wolves tore themselves free from those survivors, killing in an indiscriminate rage until dawn when the men and women would in turn burst free from their wolf selves. Those who survived being bitten by the man-wolves would also carry the curse. Most were killed, others managed to hide their condition, being confined every full moon by family.

As the millennia rolled on, Lilith learned much on her wanderings. Of the two hundred *Grigori* exiled to earth, only a scant few remained. Some were slain in battle, others had their hearts eaten by an Elder who took over their kingdoms. A few wearied of the world and just disappeared, such as *Batariel*. Many years later, Lilith met Havid again, who told her that *Batariel* had built herself a tomb and intended to remain inside, letting herself wither into a state of near-death. Perhaps she preferred that to the risk of death and Hell. Her subjects brought wealth and human sacrifices to her tomb every year. In the hopes that if they did so, *Batariel* would feel no need to return.

Batariel's kingdom soon fell apart as her Elders squabbled for power. The more the *Grigori* and their undead fought to rule this world, the less of it they controlled, and in time the undead would be remembered across the world as little more than myth as the living became ascendant.

Ambitious Elders hunted Lilith down, eager to eat her heart to take her power, dying one and all. By that time, only a few *Grigori* remained, most factions ruled by either a *Dominus* or *Domina Nephilim*. Lilith's reputation grew, the ruling *Nephilim* tolerating her presence in their domains, hoping she would not linger.

Arakiel fought in lands that would in time be called Greece and Rome, eventually being driven into the wild north with a small surviving remnant.

Lilith heard nothing more about *Arakiel* until she received a letter from him in 1893, the once-*Grigori* now a demon reduced to Possessing a human. He invited her to Scotland, claiming *Samiel* had returned likewise as a demon, and offered her the opportunity to send her Maker back to Hell, this time doing the deed herself.

And so she had left Marrakesh on a ship bound for Britain.

Chapter Thirty-Nine

Dumbreck Castle had been the main residence for the MacInesker family from the late 16th century until the late 18th, often lying empty after Dunkellen House's construction about a hundred years ago. And from what Newfield had gleaned, Dunkellen House was built near the site of a MacInesker castle preceding Dumbreck; indeed, most of Dumbreck Castle's bricks and stones had come from that earlier estate.

No longer was Dumbreck Castle abandoned. Lord Fisher had decided to consolidate what remained of his House here, bringing in the *Nephilim* who had once dwelt in the Crypt beneath the Necropolis. The few other remaining Crypts around Glasgow, including those housing the newly Made ghouls, had been closed for now, those undead summoned also.

There was a risk in consolidating the entire House here, but one mitigated by the presence of the newly emerged Niall Fisher. A *Dominus Nephilim* alone could defend this castle against whatever *Arakiel* had left to throw against it. The demon had lost the police, his necromancer and his mercenaries. Though he may have gained McBride's thieves, thugs and cutthroats.

Lord Fisher still had some mortal soldiers remaining to him, sent out to snatch up those living on the streets of Glasgow and bring them here to feed the undead. What remained of Newfield's humanity felt guilt at those imprisoned in the castle's cellars, being fed from by *Nephilim* and bled to feed the ghouls. But the Thirst was all, and she drank their blood all the same.

Regent Guillam and the Messers Crowe and Murray were absent, gone forth to reclaim the Bothwell Street Crypt. Newfield felt a lingering fear that it was a quest doomed to failure, Fisher's way of punishing Miss Guillam for their losses in the war so far. But then, to risk the House's last two Elder *Nephilim* on a venture with little hope of success was beyond foolish, and so Newfield had to hope that Fisher, Guillam and Crowe knew better their capabilities.

Magdalene Quinn insisted on staying here, the maimed magician caring for little now save revenge against *Arakiel* and Roderick McBride. McBride's blood was missing, someone having removed his contingency, further proof of his suspected treachery.

Quinn sat in a chair in the main hall, gazing into the blazing fireplace. And then she stirred. "Fetch Lord Fisher!"

"And tell him what?" Mr Fowler asked with a sneer, the seniormost undead in the hall.

Miss Quinn rose and met his gaze with her last eye. "Tell him the Wards he ordered me place around the Dunkellen estate have been breached."

Fowler duly advised Lord Fisher, and within half an hour the *Dominus Nephilim* had mobilised his retainers, every undead and mortal armed and hastening towards Dunkellen House.

Newfield was among them, wishing that Regent Guillam was present, and wondering how the Regent fared against *Arakiel*'s undead holding the Bothwell Street Crypt.

*

"Not what I expected," Margot Guillam said quietly as she moved carefully through the underground tunnels and basements that lay below Bothwell Street.

"You expected more resistance?" Mr Crowe asked softly, his underling, Mr Murray, lurking behind him.

"I expected *some* resistance," Guillam said. Not that

she was complaining, precisely, but she had hoped to at least present Niall Fisher with a pile of bodies upon the recapture of the Crypt. The war had not gone well, and she knew Fisher would be tempted to lay the blame at her feet before killing her. Here was a chance for her to secure a victory and silence those who doubted her as Regent.

"I hear no one," Crowe said. Like her, he was an Elder, albeit one new to Fisher's House. For two hundred years, Guillam had been one of three elders. Edwards had been regent, now dead; she had been Fisher's contact, now moot with his return; Rannoch had been least favoured and untrusted, with reason. She had long suspected that Fisher had allowed him to remain in order to strike a balance – to ensure his Elders were too busy eying one another to ever unite and overthrow him as he had once overthrown Keel.

Now Guillam remained the last survivor of those Elders, slightly resenting the presence of Edmund Crowe. Always a presence in Glasgow, the banker had been aligned with, yet never part of, the House before. Now he was, providing necessary monies to fund this war. *A rival?* She doubted it; Crowe had never before demonstrated such ambitions.

The Crypt was deserted. "Perhaps Miss Quinn was more successful than she believed, inflicting such losses as to convince Keel to abandon this Crypt," she suggested. A pity. She had looked forward to slaying his undead. "I wonder where they have gone?"

"The Dunkellen estate," Crowe said.

"Why do you say that?"

"Because that is where Niall Fisher's Crypt is, where he keeps the remains of *Arakiel*, and where *Arakiel* has led what remains of his army. Leaving me to deal with you, Miss Guillam."

It took a second for the full meaning of Crowe's statement to sink in, and she turned just as thunder roared within the cramped confines of these tunnels. Flesh centuries dead screamed in agony as silver tore it apart.

She fell to the ground, catching sight of Crowe looking down at her, his man Murray having fired his shotgun.

"Traitor," she gasped, trying to muster the strength to rise and answer this betrayal, but thwarted by the silver shrapnel buried deep within her. Murray hastily reloaded both barrels of his shotgun, a precaution in case she did indeed rise.

"I serve myself and my bank. I care for stability, not the name of whoever rules this city," Crowe told her.

"Kill me, then."

"I am afraid not. Mr Rannoch, it seems, made certain promises to the undead of the Carpathian Circus, and Mr Keel has agreed to honour them," Crowe said. "Mr Bresnik?"

"Just Bresnik," a new voice said, his accent foreign. Guillam recognised the name, having met him briefly in Bucharest when he had been new among Keel's undead. The night *Arakiel* had been slain.

She tried to move, to escape, but too much damage had been done, damage that would not heal so long as the poisonous silver remained within her. The *Nephilim* known as Bresnik approached with knife in hand, stabbing it down into Guillam's chest, careful to avoid her heart. Riven with fresh agony, she knew he would rip free her heart and eat it, and so become Elder himself while she died.

"Tell me why," she gasped. "Why … so sure … Fisher will lose…"

Crowe told her as Bresnik took hold of her heart and started to rip it from her chest.

Darkness fell.

*

"Spread out and find the Crypt's entrance. But do not enter, lest Fisher still be within," Keel ordered. He had brought everyone he could muster, and Canning knew that the war would be decided here tonight. Dunkellen House lay in darkness, deserted, but Keel had no interest in the house. Tonight, his servants were to search the grounds for the entrance to Niall Fisher's Crypt.

This much had been gleaned from the dead Neil MacInesker: The Crypt was within the Dunkellen estate, on the site of an older castle that had once sat on these grounds. MacInesker had visited the Crypt on at least one occasion and had seen the family seal on the Crypt door, knowing only that it was underground. That castle had been torn down, its materials used to build Dumbreck Castle, but its cellars and dungeon likely remained, buried and forgotten. Some of the old castle had been turned into the newer house's stables, making that a good place to start. There were also the remains of a 12th century motte within the gardens.

Canning was eager to find this Crypt, but he spared a moment to glance at the prisoner, taking pleasure in the drawn, fearful face of Wilton Hunt, hoping Keel would allow him to kill the son in front of the father. But for now, Keel had made it clear that the Hunts were to be left alone. Canning was among the very few to know why, and he looked forward to seeing how tonight ended. How this war ended.

Shouts rang out, and to Canning's ear they did not signal victory.

*

Redfort froze as he heard scouts raise the alarm, a spike of fear going through him.

"Rally!" Keel shouted, calling back his scattered forces. For months both sides had skirmished back and forth, a victory here and a loss there, but tonight would prove decisive one way or the other. Given that he still sat on both Councils, Redfort was confident he would prosper regardless of who prevailed, but that meant keeping out of sight. With luck, should any of Fisher's lot see him, they would simply assume he had travelled here with them.

Gunshots rang out as battle was joined. Eager to avoid

it, Redfort crouched down. Some served a cause they were willing to die for. Redfort served two, and preferred to die for neither.

*

"Did *Arakiel* invite *everyone* here tonight?" Knox asked as they entered the grounds. She had believed that the demon had picked this place because no one would dare go near it, given its recent history, but instead she and her companions found themselves facing a pitched battle.

Lord Ashwood surveyed the shadowed grounds with a look of biting impatience. "It would seem he wishes us all present, perhaps hoping for a clean sweep of the board. No matter. Our priority is to rescue Wilton."

Steiner stirred, perhaps wishing to suggest an alternative priority, but the grim look on Ashwood's face and the lack of argument from Singh stilled any opposition. When angel and demon were in agreement, who dared dissent?

Knox had come here with Ashwood, Singh, Caroline, Steiner, Gray and Foley – the latter now claiming to be a werewolf! Having a companion turn into a ravening beast had its advantages, but for the moment Mr Foley was unable to transform save by the light of a full moon, and he cautioned that as a wolf he was uncontrollable.

Foley's a werewolf, Wil's half-demon, Singh's a Seraphim*, And Lord Ashwood's Lucifer.* Humanity was in danger of becoming a minority among her companions, but she found herself not minding so much, facing as she was two warring undead factions.

Gunshots pierced the night, and screams followed. The grounds and gardens surrounding the house were extensive, partitioned by brick walls and tall hedges in need of pruning. Lawns that Knox remembered as immaculate in the summer had grown long and wild.

"We're outnumbered," Foley said.

"Let us hope they do not put aside their enmity with each other and make common cause against us," Steiner said.

"We should find my son quickly while our foes are distracted by one another," Lucifer said.

"Our strength will be in our unity," Caroline said.

Gray hefted his rifle. "And in our marksmanship."

The group was small but well-armed; Gray, Sirk and Lucifer bore rifles, the rest barrel-shortened shotguns. Everyone also carried a revolver, a knife and the silver ammunition Lord Ashwood had hidden in his cellar.

Knox's faint hope that everyone else would be too busy killing one another to bother with them died a swift death as a band of hard-looking men shouted a challenge and opened fire. McBride's men, she thought, aware of Steiner cautioning the shotgunners among them to hold fire. Two men fell, dead or wounded, as Gray, Steiner and Ashwood fired, followed by a third and fourth as Gray and Ashwood swiftly reloaded and fired again.

The thugs ran off in search of easier pickings.

*

"Lucifer is here," Redfort told Keel, having spied the Devil's arrival on the estate through his telescope. He had not lingered to renew their acquaintance, instead sending some of McBride's men to slow them while he made his way to Keel. His last experience with a battle on this scale had been the *zombi* attack on this very estate, and he was not comfortable being in another one, risking a stray bullet or being savaged by a ghoul. Any ghoul; *Nephilim* on both sides would be tasked to control their lesser kindred, but once battle was joined and blood spilled, many would be lost to the Thirst and the frenzy of battle.

"Excellent." Was that *relief* in the demon's voice? Redfort had warned him beforehand that Magdalene Quinn had Warded the estate grounds, but that seemed to encourage rather than discourage Keel from coming here.

"He did not come alone," Redfort cautioned. As well as the risk of dying to random violence, there were also people here who would happily go out of their way to kill him, Wolfgang Steiner chief among them. To say nothing of Fisher's undead if they realised that he had betrayed them. He had met Fisher at the Council meeting, and it was not an encounter he was keen to repeat. *I would happily have stayed at home. Damn this demon for insisting upon my presence.*

Keel shrugged that off as unimportant. "So long as Lucifer is here."

Redfort pulled his hood down lower, relying on the cowled robe for anonymity. The victor was undecided, and Redfort would straddle both sides as long as he could.

"Make yourself useful and find the entrance to Fisher's Crypt," Keel told him.

"You are confident it is here?" Redfort asked. "Fisher did not appear when the *zombis* attacked in the summer."

"The late Neil MacInesker visited the Crypt. He saw enough to suspect it was on the site of the keep that preceded Dumbreck Castle. Fisher would not have been aware of the *zombis*, and even if he were, that attack happened during the day and so he could not have left his Crypt."

"Young MacInesker might have lied."

Keel smiled. "The summoned dead cannot lie."

"He might have been in error."

Keel ignored that, dismissing Redfort with a wave.

Fine. I will wander around the stables in search of a vampyre's Crypt. At least he need not worry about meeting Niall Fisher should he find it, the *Dominus* having taken up residence in Dumbreck Castle.

*

Newfield tried to hide her fear as she approached Lord Fisher at the front of Dunkellen House, having been appointed his aide in this battle. "Master, the battle is underway."

"I expect victory to be swift. We have taken them by surprise and should outnumber them," Fisher said with an air of confidence.

Newfield was no tactician but from what she had spied

of the enemy, it did not look like it would end quickly or easily. "There are a lot of undead and no small number of men armed with guns and knives. I recognised some as McBride's." *And I recognise some of the others ... but how to tell Fisher?*

"He was raised to the Council from the gutter, and treachery is how he repays me. He will regret it." There was a hesitation in his voice. This might have been Newfield's first battle on this scale since the one in spring in the Necropolis, but it was Fisher's first battle since Bucharest, two centuries earlier. "Miss Guillam and Mr Crowe's task to retake the Bothwell Street Crypt will prove unexpectedly simple."

Miss Guillam. She had half-forgotten her mentor, and her last bit of news did not bode well for the Regent. If she was wrong, she was making an accusation she might not survive. "Not all of the mortals are McBride's, I recognised some other ones. They are led by Arthur Wallace."

"And he is?" Fisher asked with a biting impatience.

"Mr Wallace works for the Heron Crowe Bank, he is in charge of its security. And its company of guards."

Fisher's voice was quiet, shouts and gunfire sounding nearby. "So, Roderick McBride is not alone in his treachery. Crowe will have warned *Arakiel* of Miss Quinn's Wards here and that is why he has brought everyone he has."

"What of Miss Guillam?" Though she suspected she knew.

"In a fight, I would wager on Miss Guillam prevailing. But Crowe is a banker, prudent and cautious, and he will attack without warning, if such is his intention."

Margot Guillam. Elder *Nephilim* and Regent. Newfield's mentor. Probably dead. There was an echo of grief, but merely an echo. "We have more *Nephilim* than *Arakiel*, we should prevent him from taking Dunkellen House, Master."

"He is not here for the house. My Crypt is here, and he has come for his remains. It is time for me to join the battle and be done with this war once and for all," Fisher said with a grim and growing rage.

*

"Excellent shooting, Mr Gray," Lucifer said with a grudging admiration.

"Practice makes perfect, Lord Ashwood," Gray said. Steiner hoped the American did not forget just what 'Lord Ashwood' was.

"Which I am out of," Dr Sirk said with an air of self-admonishment, being the only one not to score a hit.

"I believe, Doctor, that tonight will give you ample practice and no shortage of targets," Lady Delaney said. For the moment, the battle was little more than a series of skirmishes as small groups from either side ran into one another across the expansive estate. Steiner knew that, soon, captains from both sides would rally their forces, and a decisive battle would be fought.

"I had anticipated *Arakiel*'s forces, but not Fisher's," Lucifer admitted. "We are greatly outnumbered."

"There is little point in wishing for more companions when none were available," Delaney said.

Steiner keenly felt the loss of his brethren, wishing Sir Thomas Maxwell had sent more Templars. With fifty disciplined soldiers, he knew he could end Glasgow's war tonight.

Foley opened his mouth and paused before speaking. "Let's get a move on." Steiner suspected the former soldier had intended to say something else but thought better of it.

"Mr Gray, might I suggest you find a perch providing a good overview of the estate, so that you can better target the undead and give covering fire upon our withdrawal?" Lucifer suggested.

"I'll see what I can find," Gray said, keeping low as he left the group.

Onwards they moved, shooting only when they had to, avoiding fights where they could.

"Ready arms!" Singh said as his shotgun swung up. Two packs of rival ghouls were rushing at one another, and they were about to be caught in the middle.

Rifles fired and Steiner raised his shotgun. He hoped that his less experienced companions such as Miss Knox would not lose their nerve and discharge their shotguns before the enemy was in range. Their lives depended on efficiency.

Only rifles fired, doing nothing to dissuade the maddened charge of undead. And then they drew close enough for Steiner to see their pale, wasted faces, hands stretched out like claws, and he fired the left barrel and cocked the right. Silver shot flayed two ghouls, dropping both. More undead fell as the others fired too.

Five shotguns. Two barrels. Ten discharges. There would be no time to reload, and so they must turn to their revolvers.

And if the undead persisted, knives.

Chapter Forty

The Crypt was surprisingly easy to find. A small staircase led down to an unassuming door at the bottom of worn, loose steps on the outside of the stable courtyard wall. Redfort had expected it to be better hidden, but on reflection decided there was little need. The door was heavily locked, and staff of the MacIneskers would have been warned not to enter it.

Anyone who did would have found a *Dominus Nephilim* waiting for them, angry at the breach of his privacy.

Dynamite had dealt with the door, and Niall Fisher was absent from the Crypt. Redfort entered gun in one hand nonetheless, a lantern in the other.

There was an earthy smell to the Crypt, despite flagstones covering the ground, and it was certainly spacious. Two unlit lanterns hung from the walls while melted wax stained the desk at the far end. Three sagging bookcases lay against one wall, filled with books, most old, others surprisingly recent. Niall Fisher, it seemed, passed his time reading and writing.

A heavy stone urn caught Redfort's attention, and a look inside confirmed its contents to be what he hoped it was. A large pile of ash and burned bone lay at the bottom, most likely the remains of *Arakiel*'s *Grigori* body, slain and then burned two hundred years ago.

He hurried back the way he had come, climbing the steps leading up to the outside of the stable, keeping low as he returned to Keel. The fighting sounded closer.

"Sir, I have found the Crypt and *believe* I have found

what you seek within. An urn, containing what I believe to be your remains," Redfort said breathlessly.

Keel's chin lifted, a look of relief on his face. "Excellent, Redfort, excellent!" He turned to a small foreign-looking woman standing beside Canning. "Return here with the urn. Redfort will lead the way."

"I would join the fight," Canning said, licking his lips.

Keel glanced back at him. "Go."

The *Nephilim* left in a run, and Redfort led the woman to the Crypt, wondering how she would manage to lift the heavy urn, even being undead.

*

Newfield watched as the two 'armies' clashed on Dunkellen House's rear lawn, Fisher's force having gone round the servant wing and kitchens. Distant shouts and gunshots told her smaller skirmishes were taking place elsewhere throughout the grounds but here the bulk of both forces had come together. Fisher should have held a numerical advantage after his magicians slaughtered Keel's mercenaries, however treachery had evened the odds; the bulk of Fisher's mortal soldiers – McBride's thugs and Crowe's guards – now served the enemy.

Armed with a mismatch of guns, fear of the approaching *Nephilim* spurred McBride's men to fire wildly with pistols and shotguns to little effect. The handful of *Nephilim* in Keel's service unleashed their 'fresher' ghouls, a mob of blood-starved undead charging towards Newfield and her comrades. Older ghouls from both sides were entrusted with guns.

Muzzle flashes from atop the wall ahead caught Newfield's eye, and she realised that Crowe's ex-soldiers had rifles, and the advantage of height and cover. The one disadvantage Crowe's men might have suffered was the darkness, but there was a bright moon tonight, and both sides had brought lanterns.

She fired her pistol at the enemy ghouls closest to her, recognising many from the Bothwell Street Crypt. Keel had far fewer *Nephilim*, but he had successfully turned many of the mortal and newly Made undead to his cause, using them as fodder in tonight's battle. Fisher's *Nephilim* should be more than a match, but already some were falling – swarmed by ghouls and torn apart, or shot by silver.

And then he arrived.

The razor-sharp coldness of his Unveiling alerted Newfield to Fisher's presence before she saw him, enough to halt the enemy advance. He carried a large sword, and Newfield knew that any who went against him would fall.

She was not alone in reaching that conclusion, she realised, upon seeing a figure break away from the small band of ghouls he had been leading. Despite the dark, her undead eyes were good enough to make out his features, to recognise him from the photograph the newspapers had published of him months before.

A cold anger caressed her still heart.

*

Canning was quickly regretting his enthusiasm to join this battle. He was only too happy to kill for Keel, but would rather not die for him. The enemy was pushing them back towards the river path and ultimately the stable, and Canning had caught sight of the man leading the enemy tonight. Surely this must be Niall Fisher, for who else was capable of such effortless slaughter? Canning stared for a time, mesmerised by Fisher's brutal power.

McBride's gutter-rats were running back towards the stable, having just enough sense to know that deserting entirely would not go down well with either their boss or Keel. Crowe's men were also retreating, but in a more orderly fashion, alternating between moving back and offering covering fire. Canning's ghouls were all lost, but Jana had succeeded in wrestling control over her survivors and getting them to fall back with her.

Vladimir, another circus *Nephilim*, had been cut down by Fisher. Tessa, the ghoul Canning had rewarded with a *Nephilim* heart, still lived but at least one other *Nephilim* had fallen.

Fisher had taken losses too, most of the few mortals he commanded run down by ghouls. Some of his *Nephilim* had been killed or wounded by silver bullets, but Canning suspected the *Dominus Nephilim* would sacrifice every undead in his House to end this war and count it a good trade.

One day I will be a Dominus Nephilim*, a god among the undead, a fresh terror to haunt the living.*

Longsword in hand, Fisher still hacked through ghouls and men, restoring the morale of his followers. Canning had no intention of facing such a foe, and instead looked for easier prey. Movement to the right caught his eye.

Ahh…

*

Knox stumbled through the bushes, breathing heavily and clutching her pistol tightly. She was alone, separated from her companions during that frantic running battle with the undead. Shotguns had slain the foremost of the enemy, but there had been no time to reload, and so they had relied on revolvers.

The undead had been too many, forcing the group to flee, Newfield finding herself on her own. Her last bullets had slowed the ghoul chasing her, but still it had kept coming, forcing her to run. At least here she might find a minute to catch her breath and reload before finding her friends.

Or not. A shadow stood waiting for her, knife in hand, "Well, looks like it's just the two of us."

Near panic, Knox backed away, drawing her knife as the shadow came towards her.

"You must be Miss Knox. Made quite a nuisance of yourself in recent months. My name's Richard Canning, and it is my *very great pleasure* to make your acquaintance."

Richard Canning, the Glasgow Ripper, infamous for his horrific murder of several women. And that had been *before* he had been hanged and Made undead. She had seen the scar on Wilton's chest, Canning's handiwork. The only reason Wil had lived was Foley's intervention. Canning had survived at least one bullet by jumping out a window one floor up, according to Wil.

And now it was just the two of them. Caroline had taught Knox how to kill with a knife, but Canning had been a butcher in life and had a surplus of experience in killing with a blade. *Stay calm, panic will kill you.*

"I've killed undead before," she told him. "Including vampyres, so a ghoul like you shan't trouble me." Bravado, but it might goad Canning into a rage and doing something stupid.

"I've killed vampyres too, Miss Knox, including one fellow whose heart I ate."

Fear caught her throat as Canning Unveiled, his way of confirming that he was indeed *Nephilim*. "Let's get this over with," she managed, feeling sick.

"In a rush to die? Rest assured, I'll take my time killing you and drinking your blood." There was a hateful confidence in Canning's voice, and Knox knew she was outmatched. *One last trick left.*

She expected him to lunge, but he walked over to her slowly, knife extended. It was too dark to make out his features, though his undead eyes could probably make hers out. Holding her knife in her right hand, she reached into her coat pocket with her left, drawing and cocking her derringer in one motion.

Canning jumped at her, reflex making her finger pull the trigger, the flash blinding her for a moment. She blinked, dismayed to see that while the bullet had struck Canning, it had missed his heart. The *Nephilim* hissed in pain as the silver burned inside him.

"I'll kill you even slower now. And not with this." There was a thud as he dropped his knife. The dark mocking humour was gone. He had been a monster in life, and death had only made him worse.

Panic screamed at her to run, but her training warned that he would simply chase her down, untiring. He lunged at her, hands reaching out for her. She lashed out, stabbing at him several times in quick succession but to little result.

Something hammered into her head, and she felt herself hitting the ground.

She tensed, her nerves on fire as she expected him to fall upon her and tear out her throat with his teeth.

"Do you expect me to share?" Canning said, Knox assuming not to her.

"You murdered my mam and dad," a woman said, cold iron in her voice.

"Ah, Miss Newfield! We're siblings of a sort, did you know that? Both Made by George Rannoch, who was Made by *Arakiel*. Grandchildren of a Fallen angel, in a sense."

"We're not family."

"Mr Keel ordered your parents' deaths, not that I didn't enjoy myself tremendously. He wasn't happy about you killing *Maridiel*. He had little love for the demon but losing the police was a blow."

"I'll kill *Arakiel* too."

"Best be quick, because very soon he'll be beyond your ability to fight. I showed your dear parents what I am, by the by, and I told them you were like me. Well, almost. Told them you were a thing of the night, a killer and a monster. And then I killed them."

Knox struggled to get up as the two undead fought. Amy Newfield was a ghoul, and Knox suspected she would not last much longer against Canning than she had. This was her opportunity to escape.

*

Driven by rage and guilt, Newfield only now realised her error in confronting her parents' killer. Better to have simply shot him while he was busy with Kerry Knox. She tried to rectify that mistake by firing as he charged her, but he was too fast and neither of the shots struck him.

He knocked the revolver from her hand, and she ducked to avoid being grabbed.

Her strength was greater than most humans, but Canning was a fully Transitioned *Nephilim*, on top of which he had a height and weight advantage. He weathered her blows and kicked out at her, knocking her back against a wall. She was only stunned a moment, but that was long enough for him to grab hold of her.

"Pity you won't live long enough to see *Arakiel*'s ret–" he started to say, before his face twisted in agony.

Newfield broke free of his grasp and saw Kerry Knox standing behind him, blood on her knife. Canning collapsed.

*

The small silver bullet in his chest still burned, and now his back was aflame too. Inwardly he cursed his lack of concentration, failing to kill Knox before attending to Newfield. Had she struck him a few inches to the left, he would be dead.

He tried to stand, to rip the bitch's head off, but his legs would not respond. The pain was in the centre of his back, and with a dawning horror he realised she had stabbed him in the spine. Time and a surplus of human blood would heal such a wound, but the grim expressions on the two young women standing over him suggested he would have neither.

"Fucking bastard!" Kerry Knox spat, a tremor in her voice.

"Leave him to me, Miss Knox," Newfield said, looking down him with unblinking eyes. "You owe me that."

"I owe you?"

"I helped rescue your friends from *Maridiel*. In response, *Arakiel* sent this creature to kill my parents."

"I'm sorry." Knox held out her knife.

"I have my own. And for this, I need iron, not silver."

Canning lay helpless on the ground, praying that allies would arrive and chase off the two women intent on his death. He had murdered many young women, and he had no desire to die to one, much less two.

"Take your time with him, Miss Newfield."

"Once I start, I must be quick," she replied.

Canning realised her intent a moment before her knife plunged into his chest, outrage swelling within him. "You can't!" *I was to be immortal, to feed and kill forever!*

The knife cut through ribs, Newfield taking care to avoid his heart, awakening a fresh agony within him. The knife she threw away, reaching into his chest and pulling apart his shattered ribs. A bitter rage consumed him as he felt his heart being ripped free, an anticipated eternity of joyful slaughter being reduced to a mere six months.

His last fading sight was of Amy Newfield biting into his heart, dark blood smeared around her mouth. *Fucking...*

*

She felt something growing within as she ate every bit of Richard Canning's heart, reducing her Transition from ghoul to *Nephilim* by at least half a year. It tasted as foul as the bastard whose chest she had ripped it from, but it would be worth it. Canning's dead eyes stared up at her, frozen in hateful outrage. Her parents' killer.

Already she could feel the Transition begin, the power awakening within her. Miss Guillam would be proud of her for vanquishing Canning and taking his power. If she lived, which Newfield doubted. More likely she was dead, betrayed and slain by Edmund Crowe.

She finished her grisly feast, aware of the disgust on Miss Knox's face.

The two women stared at one another, the corpse of their mutual enemy between them.

"I would not have survived had you not stabbed him in the back," Newfield said. "For that, I suggest a brief truce between us, Miss Knox."

"Agreed. For now. I cannot speak for later, Miss Newfield."

Power *thrummed* through her. "Nor can I."

Miss Knox hastened away.

*

Foley entered this thick of the fight, uncaring, driven to rescue Hunt and kill that bastard McBride. He had left Glasgow to learn more about his lycanthropic curse and to escape this war, only for it hunt him down and destroy his new home.

And now they had taken his friend.

He had run into a skirmish, shooting any who got in his way, not knowing or caring whose side they were on. His friends had to be ahead, and so he fought on, mindful of threats on his periphery while firing his revolver at those in his way. He had no time to study the men he fought, but he was fairly sure that none were undead. Fortunately, neither had they much, if any, experience with guns, as evidenced by their ineffectual firing.

The birds are in more danger than me.

His training and experience as a soldier, married with instincts heightened since he became a werewolf, saw him safely through the bloody chaos. He had become separated from the others, but what he lost in numbers he made up for in stealth. It looked like Fisher was having the best of the night, his people forcing *Arakiel*'s back towards the stables. Unsurprising, since Fisher had joined the fight.

Foley had caught a glimpse of the *Dominus Nephilim* wielding what looked like a claymore against any who stood in his way. A few hacked up bodies later, and *Arakiel*'s thugs and undead were in full rout. If *Arakiel* was in the stable courtyard then Hunt was probably there too. And hopefully alive.

"Foley!" The whispered shout made him turn, movement catching his eye. A figure was perched on the wall, and it took him a moment to recognise who it was.

"Miss Knox!"

"I got separated. Please tell me you're not all that's left

of the others." She hopped off the wall, her head darting around in search of danger.

"Not so far as I know," he assured her. Gunfire and screaming owned the night, sounds all too familiar to Foley.

"Then let's find them!"

"Fisher's advancing on the stables. If Delaney and the others are still set on rescuing Hunt, they'll be heading there too." He paused. "Probably keeping close to the river and sneaking past the sawmill. If we hurry, we should catch them up."

"Then let's hurry."

They might be heading into danger, but she sounded keen to share it with the others.

Foley agreed wholeheartedly.

*

Hunt sat on the courtyard cobbles, his hands and feet bound. He had not been mistreated – which was to say he had been fed, watered and otherwise ignored. *Arakiel* had visited him often, saying little but staring at him. Staring at the impossible made flesh, Hunt knew. The spawn of a demon.

Arakiel seemed oddly unbothered despite his night not going well. His ragtag army of ghouls and thugs, led by a handful of *Nephilim*, had retreated to the stables in much diminished numbers, many wounded. Richard Canning had been among his captors, regularly taunting him, though he was not among the survivors rallying in the stables. Dead, Hunt hoped.

He had other concerns beyond the Glasgow Ripper. A small foreign woman had visited him in the company of *Arakiel*, the hatred in her eyes enough to terrify him. She had wanted to kill him then and there, but the demon had stopped her, warning that to do so risked Lucifer gaining an anchor in Heaven.

The woman scared him. But the look in *Arakiel*'s eyes had scared him more; relief. The demon had relied on reason alone to stop this murderous, mysterious woman.

Gunshots and shouting drew louder as Fisher's faction attacked the gatehouse leading into the stable courtyard, Hunt recognising the leader as Niall Fisher himself. One swing of his sword cut a man in half, one of McBride's. Relying on a *Dominus Nephilim* for rescue, even one who was sort-of family, was not Hunt's preference, but he was in no position to be picky.

"Skulking as always, Keel," Fisher called out. "You should have fled."

"You should have found a new place to hide," *Arakiel* replied. The hatred between the pair was palpable. The fighting had stopped for now, the surviving remnant of the demon's army gathered around him on the courtyard cobbles. Hunt was forgotten for the moment, and he quietly hoped that this would continue until Fisher had won. He had no love for Fisher but at least the vampyre lord was minded to protect the last – for now – of his line.

"I am disappointed young Neil talked before he died."

"He talked after he died," *Arakiel* said.

"I see. Perhaps you should have hidden your necromancer better. Had you an army of *zombis*, you might have fared better in this battle."

"Khotep was a useful ally, but I will not mourn his loss."

Fisher's gaze now searched the courtyard, his face dark with anger. "Will you mourn McBride when I kill him?" The criminal patriarch was absent from the courtyard, luckily for him. Hunt had not seen him at all tonight, though most of his men were here. And most would not be leaving alive.

"For betrayal? Rest assured you will answer for your treachery first," *Arakiel* said. The small woman entered the courtyard from the rear entrance, carrying a stone urn, a slow smile appearing on the demon's face at the sight of it. "This has been an interesting match but one whose endgame has arrived."

"Keeping your remains was a mistake, but one I will rectify when I take that back," Fisher promised. "After your death I will have them emptied down a sewer. You, woman. Come here."

The woman took a few steps forward. And smiled. There was no fear on her face, just anticipation. "Is my enemy here yet?"

"He is on the grounds. He will be here for his son anon," *Arakiel* said.

"Excellent. Do introduce us." She gestured in the direction of Fisher.

"This is Niall Fisher the usurper. Fisher, it is my great pleasure to introduce you to … Lilith."

Fear was not something Hunt ever expected to see on the face of a *Dominus Nephilim*, but he saw it now on Fisher's face. He recalled Margot Guillam relating the origins of the undead months before, of the two hundred or so Fallen angels who became the *Grigori*, the first vampyres. Of the first human to be Made undead.

Certainly, Fisher's reaction suggested that he believed this Lilith to be the one from legend, the first *Nephilim*. Hunt remembered something else; the identity of the *Grigori* who had Made Lilith undead and had in time been brought down by her.

My father.

Chapter Forty-One

While Fisher led a charge against the gatehouse entrance to the stables, Lord Ashwood had led them round the side, by the sawmill, as yet unnoticed by their enemies. Knox had never seen him shaken before, and as much as she was loath to admit it, she had drawn strength from the quiet, boundless confidence exuded by the Devil no matter what they faced.

His eyes, now, were wide with shock as the small woman was named as Lilith. Wilton was tied up on the other side of the courtyard, seemingly unharmed, but Ashwood's attention was fixed on this Lilith.

Steiner, too, had noticed his reaction. An expression of satisfaction flickered across his face on seeing the Devil finally put out, before concern showed in his eyes; now was not the time for doubt, now was the time for confident action.

"This is the Lilith you spoke of?" Caroline asked, a bite of impatience in her voice.

"Yes," Ashwood breathed. "*Arakiel* must have invited her here to aid him against Fisher."

"Why would she accept? What could tempt the world's oldest *Nephilim* to Glasgow of all places?" Foley asked.

"Me. *Arakiel* has revealed to her my escape from Hell, and she has come to send me back."

"That explains his prohibition against harming you or your son," Singh said.

"Quite."

"Let's shoot her. A volley of silver bullets will deal with any *Nephilim*," Foley said.

Caroline pointed to the carnage. "Some have tried, to no avail." Sure enough, someone fired his rifle at Lilith, a shot she evaded with inhuman quickness. She ducked to pluck up a stone from the ground and threw it at him, cracking his skull open. Blood and brains oozed between the cobbles as he fell, and no one else looked willing to face her after that, guns or no guns.

"Let's just free Hunt and then decide what to do next," Foley said.

"We'll need to fight through *Arakiel*'s remnant," Singh said.

"I didn't come to this stable for riding lessons." Foley cocked his shotgun.

*

"Send that damned demon back to Hell!" Fisher roared as the battle resumed. Redfort hid in one of the houses that was part of the compound, peeking out an upper window. Fisher had the advantage of numbers, but the revelation that he fought a dark legend, the first *Nephilim*, had sown fear and confusion among his ranks. Edmund Crowe's remaining gunmen fired from the upper windows into Fisher's people below.

Fisher hacked through Keel's ghouls absently, a mere inconvenience standing between him and the demon. There was no sign of Margot Guillam, meaning she was likely dead at Crowe's hands. Save for Fisher, the last of Keel's betrayers was gone.

Redfort recognised Harold Fowler among the melee, perhaps the oldest *Nephilim* in the city not an Elder. A strong and powerful vampyre, two ghouls had already fallen to his blade. He was expected to Transition to Elder within the coming decades.

Which would never happen. He grabbed at Lilith, who stood several inches shorter than him, and in response she punched through his chest and ripped his heart out through shattered ribs, throwing it carelessly to Keel's ghouls who squabbled over it until one raised the bloody meat to his mouth and ate it.

Lucifer, Steiner and Lady Delaney had come too, with a few others among their little band. Come for Wilton Hunt, unaware he was the bait in a trap. They moved as a group, blasting their way through any undead or thug in their way with brutal efficiency. But even they were not foolish enough to face either Fisher or Lilith.

Redfort glared down at the Templar who fought with a revolver in one hand and a drawn swordstick in another. The grievous threats and insults delivered by that man to Redfort some months before had been neither forgotten nor forgiven.

He had intended to stay out of the way, taking care that Fisher did not learn he also served Keel, a prudent precaution lest this night not end the way Keel expected.

But this was too good an opportunity to miss.

*

There was no time to reload his shotgun so Foley dropped it, relying on his revolver. Sirk had stayed outside the courtyard, to shoot any stragglers approaching the stables and to help Gray, the pair tasked to cover the group's retreat upon Hunt's recovery.

Aside from the guns being fired by Foley and his companions – and a few shots from the windows – most of those still fighting did so with knives and clubs, or hand to hand. Ghouls on both sides had gone mad, tearing apart the flesh of fallen men and women to drink blood heedless of the battle still ongoing.

Foley looked for Roddy McBride but there was no sign of him. He wanted to kill the bastard himself but if an undead ripped his throat out, he'd not complain.

Miss Knox's mouth and eyes were wide open with fear, but Lady Delaney had trained her well, and she held panic at bay. Lady Delaney herself carried a revolver in each hand, double-action so that she need not re-cock them after each shot, sacrificing accuracy for extra firepower and double the available bullets.

Lord Ashwood and Singh fought back-to-back. *Samiel* and *Kariel*, demon and angel. Singh stabbed an enemy in the chest while Lucifer clubbed another with his rifle. Steiner fired his revolver and dropped it into his pocket, switching his swordstick to his right hand as he coolly stabbed a feral ghoul in the chest. He stumbled and clutched at his right shoulder with his left hand, his back bowed, his injury coinciding with a rifle shot from one of the upper windows. *Shit!*

"Can you walk?" Foley asked, slipping his left arm under Steiner's right as he helped him towards Hunt.

"Yes," the Templar said tightly, his teeth clenched.

"How bad do you think it is?" Sirk was a doctor, but he wasn't here. In any case it was unlikely there would be a chance to tend to the wound.

"Painful but not mortal," Steiner said through gritted teeth.

"Try being shot twice in the guts," Foley told him. *Where are you, McBride?*

"I would prefer not to."

*

Hunt wasted no time with gratitude or pleasantries as he was freed and handed a revolver. "We need to get out of here now!"

"You're welcome, Wil," Kerry said dryly.

He ignored her. "Father, the reason *Arakiel* won't let his people kill us is because–"

"Because sending me back to Hell is to be Lilith's reward for defeating Fisher," Father said. "Yes, I realise that."

"Lucifer! Welcome," a voice shouted.

"*Arakiel*," Father said coolly. The demon hid within his people. "I believed we had struck an honest agreement."

"I had intended to honour it. But the existence – the impossible existence – of your spawn troubled me. I pondered it long and hard, and I came to realise your abominable intent."

Father's mouth tightened.

"Part of you is within your son. When he dies, you hope that that part of you will ascend to Heaven, allowing you to claw your way back." The demon spoke hot, angry words. "And that I cannot countenance. Cannot permit."

"If that is the case, then why does Wilton still live?" Father asked quietly. "Why would I not kill him as a babe, what do I wait for?"

"Perhaps you fear that your grand plan might not work? Perhaps even the hope of success is enough to sustain you, the dream of returning to Heaven while those of us who followed you into that doomed, damned war are forever condemned to Hell."

"If there was a chance of *Samiel* defying this exile, then *Mikiel* would have acted," Singh said. "Instead, he has sent me to watch over both *Samiel* and Wilton. Step back, and trust that *Mikiel* will never permit *Samiel*'s return to Heaven."

"*Mikiel* has seen fit to abandon you and the rest of the *Seraphim* to these worlds. Your faith is misplaced. As misplaced as mine was," *Arakiel* said.

The fight was all but done, the living almost all killed or wounded, and most of the undead fallen too. Fisher and Lilith now fought, the survivors on both sides drawing back to watch this titanic clash. Two centuries of George Rannoch's plotting, weeks of *Arakiel* quietly infiltrating the Sooty Feathers, and more weeks of open warfare between both factions now came down to this duel.

"We need to get out of here," Foley said quietly as he pressed his hand hard against the wounded Steiner's shoulder, ignoring the Templar's scream.

Leaving while most eyes were fixed on the *Dominus* and *Domina Nephilim* fighting it out seemed like a good plan, so the group moved back towards the sawmill entrance.

Hunt dared to look back at the fight, almost mesmerised by the fluid, brutal beauty to it. Lilith stabbed Fisher in the leg, who in turn revealed a derringer which he fired into her chest.

They moved with a darting quickness, Lilith's face

screwed up in pain as the bullet, presumably silver, burned her from within. As she still stood, Hunt assumed it had missed her heart. They circled one another, knives cutting flesh as their hands moved in a blur, two of the most powerful beings in the world fighting with unparalleled strength and speed. Hunt found himself hoping that his ancestor would prevail, despite all the evil done by him and his House.

The intense tempo of the duel and the wounds suffered took its toll on both, but Hunt noticed that Fisher seemed more fatigued than Lilith. *Too many generations separating him from a* Grigori. Meaning he was 'inefficient', requiring a lot of blood to maintain his full strength. Whereas Lilith had been Made by a *Grigori*, meaning she needed so much less blood. *She is letting him exhaust himself.*

They were halfway across the courtyard.

"Stop there, Lightbringer, or my men in the buildings will fire upon your son and companions," *Arakiel* shouted. The group halted.

If Fisher won, then they could leave. If Lilith won, then they would have a battle getting out of the stables alive.

Fisher cried out as a foot cracked against his knee. He was moving slower than before, Lilith's knife scoring deeper and deeper cuts, driving him back. Her blade sliced across his belly to spill his guts out, and a second slash cut his throat to the bone.

Lilith's hand punched into his ruined abdomen, and the *crack* that followed suggested she had broken his spine. Fisher fell to the blood-stained cobbles. A silence fell over the courtyard.

"Mr Josiah, attend us if you please," *Arakiel* shouted, and sure enough the Demonist emerged from the safety of a building. Had Hunt a rifle, he would have shot the magician to end *Arakiel*'s plan to return as *Grigori*.

The demon stood over the crippled *Dominus Nephilim* who had betrayed and succeeded him. He said no words to his archenemy, his smile speech enough. "Do it, Lilith."

The ritual proceeded quickly, Lilith pulling out Niall Fisher's heart and dropping it into the urn containing *Arakiel*'s ashes as Josiah began his chanting.

"Now," *Arakiel* commanded. Lilith took his head between her hands and broke his neck. A minute later the Demonist stabbed one of the wounded thugs in the chest, sacrificing him so that his soul's passage to the afterlife would briefly thin the barriers enough for Josiah to reach Hell where *Arakiel* had just returned.

Josiah and those gathered around him began chanting, "*Arakiel. Arakiel. Arakiel.*"

The hairs on Hunt's arms and neck stood stiff, a cold chill going through him as this horror of a ritual continued. An empty horse trough was dragged over, the urn's contents tipped into it. Wounded people were hauled over, an artery cut so that they could bleed out into the pile of ash, Fisher's heart on top. It filled with blood.

The gory mess formed into a man's shape and solidified. A cold pit formed in Hunt's stomach as *Arakiel* slowly returned, not as a demon trapped in a man's body but as a *Grigori*. His own flesh as it had manifested here upon being cast out of Heaven. Miss Guillam had believed the *Grigori* were either all dead or content to hibernate in long-forgotten tombs buried beneath distant lands, yet one now returned.

A man emerged from the trough, naked save for the blood smearing his body, and hairless for the moment. He was tall, taller than any man Hunt had seen, and he understood now why his primitive ancestors had worshipped these beings.

"Mr Keel?" Josiah asked tentatively.

It took the *Grigori* some time to find his words. "At last, I am returned. Mr Josiah, you have my gratitude. But you are in error. I am Erik Keel no more. I am *Arakiel* in truth, and never again will I suffer the name that I took all those years ago."

"Yes, master," Josiah said hastily.

"My work is done, where is my reward?" Lilith asked.

Arakiel faced her. “Lucifer is there. Do with him as you please.” He pointed to Hunt and his companions.

“What of the enemy?” an undead asked, his accent revealing that he was one of the circus vampyres.

“Enemy, Timot? You see before you the House of Keel.” *Arakiel* faced the shocked survivors. “I do not know how you demonstrated your fealty to Margot Guillam, Thomas Edwards, and Niall Fisher…”

The remnants from both sides took the hint and knelt before the returned *Grigori*.

He looked around with a look of satisfaction on his beautiful, bloody face. “Excellent. Now bring Lucifer to Lilith. Keep Wilton Hunt alive but you may do as you wish with the others.”

“Run!” Steiner barked. Even that fanatic entertained no notions of attacking a *Domina Nephilim* and a *Grigori*, to say nothing of the other undead gathered around them.

Hunt and his companions fled the stables, the faster Kerry leading them along the riverbank towards the bridge. The enemy were too many and they were too fast, outpacing Hunt and his weary or wounded companions. Some were formerly loyal to Niall Fisher and now eager to impress *Arakiel*, Hunt guessed.

Rifles fired, panicking him until he realised the shooters were Gray and Sirk, both standing on the bridge and attempting to hold off the undead pursuing them.

Father cursed, clutching his leg as he sank to one knee.

“Are you shot?” Hunt stared at the growing blood stain on his father’s trouser leg that answered that question.

“Yes.” Father grimaced, looking back towards the distant stables. Hunt could see Lilith lowering a rifle in the distance.

“As well she is not the best shot,” Hunt said.

“Had she intended to kill me, she would have,” Father said through gritted teeth. “I believe she intends to have words with me first.”

“We can carry you,” Hunt said, kneeling next to him.

Father shook his head. “No. You must go.”

Despair and frustration clawed at him. "We can't leave you here!"

"It must be done," Steiner said, his face pale by the lantern light.

"You'd happily leave him even if he were not wounded," Hunt accused.

"I will be staying also, Hunt. I am slowing you all down. With us holding back the enemy for as long as we can, the rest of you can escape," Steiner said as he reloaded his revolver.

Father took Hunt's hand and met his eyes. "It has been a good life for me, with you and your mother."

"I hope I wasn't a disappointment." A lump formed in Hunt's throat. This was the Devil before him, but also his father, and without him the world would feel less safe. Not that he had been free from danger ever since he had exhumed Amy Newfield back in March, but still he lived despite the odds, despite being captured on several occasions.

Father managed a crooked smile. "Not entirely. Go, with my blessing, for whatever that may be worth. *Kariel*!"

"*Samiel*?" The *Seraphim* looked impassively down at his one-time enemy.

"Watch over my son, if you would be so good."

"I will." He managed a faint smile of his own. "A task given to me by both you and *Mikiel*? How could I refuse?"

"The rest of you made for stalwart companions," Father said to the others. "You are good people, so I doubt we shall meet again."

Lady Delaney regarded him. "If you meet *Beliel* in Hell, give him my regards, and make him suffer."

"As you say, Lady Delaney. Now all of you, go." He gave Hunt's hand one last squeeze before letting go.

"I'll linger behind and help out," Gray said as he left some rifle bullets next to Father.

"Go with the others, Gray," Steiner said.

"You keep forgetting you're not my superior no more,

Steiner," Gray said, a smile in his voice. "I'll leave when the enemy get too close."

Lady Delaney led Hunt, Kerry, Sirk and Foley across the bridge towards the ruins of what had once been the village of Kaleshaws. Hunt looked back once, watching as his sitting father raised his rifle and prepared for one last battle.

Chapter Forty-Two

Steiner heard Lucifer chuckle briefly. "Our situation amuses you?"

"It just occurred to me that the last time I died in battle, it was during Lilith's rebellion against me. The time before that, it was alongside *Arakiel* as we rebelled in Heaven, fighting *Mikiel* and his angels, *Kariel* dying by my hand. Now I face both Lilith and *Arakiel*, and *Kariel* escorts my son to safety."

Steiner could think of no reply to that, and so watched as Lucifer and Gray fired their rifles at the approaching undead. His wounded shoulder precluded him from taking Sirk's rifle, but he held a revolver in his left hand and waited, trying to ignore the burning pain. The enemy were closing.

"You are a good soldier, Gray, a fine companion in this war. The Order has lost too many men of quality this year, do not sacrifice yourself for so little gain." He gave Gray's hand a quick shake.

"Go with God, Knight-Inquisitor Steiner." A glance at Lucifer. "Once you've parted ways with this one."

"Your wit's as droll as your shooting is sharp, Mr Gray," Lucifer said.

Gray responded with his rifle, resuming fire at the approaching enemy. Lucifer joined him, and Steiner waited patiently with his revolver, knowing those who survived Gray and Lucifer's aim would soon be upon them.

"I'm out," Gray said tersely, no small number of undead having fallen. Ghouls, probably, sacrificed to spare the *Nephilim*.

"As am I," said Lucifer.

"Depart, Gray, and rejoin the others," Steiner said.

"Die well." And then Gray was gone.

The leading ghouls closed to within several feet, Lucifer and Steiner firing until the last round was spent.

"This is it, then," Lucifer said, pain straining his voice. "How it ends."

"*Deus Vult*," Steiner said, unable to resist.

"You think to even begin to know the faintest edges of God's will? Your ignorance is matched only by your arrogance."

Steiner had no chance to respond. The enemy approached, led by Lilith and *Arakiel* now that Steiner and Lucifer had exhausted their ammunition. Bishop Redfort stood among them. He lifted his rifle and grinned at Redfort, the gesture a claim to have been the one who shot him. Ever had that false cleric been a serpent in the grass.

"Lucifer, does envy prick you, seeing me dressed in my old flesh?" *Arakiel* asked. "Do you lie awake at nights wondering where your own remains might be?"

Steiner was not about to die as an afterthought. "Fallen one, will you fight me?"

"The Templar." *Arakiel* looked irritated at the interruption, but perhaps he also feared being seen to refuse a challenge, and one issued by a wounded mortal. "I can spare a moment to give you the martyrdom you so desperately seek."

A sword was tossed to Steiner, which he took in his left hand, his right arm useless. Once upon a time he would have prayed to God, even dared to hope that God might strengthen his arm to smite this abomination.

No longer. His battered faith still held, but it was something he clung to now rather than used to pull himself up. But still, he would try.

The sword he had been given was pure theatre. A *Grigori* had the speed and strength to avoid any strike he made until his arm wearied. Should he block a strike made by *Arakiel*, his would find his own blade hammered down into his flesh.

His death was assured regardless of what happened next. There was no defeating this *Grigori* in a duel, but perhaps he could cheat.

He lunged and swung his sword wildly at *Arakiel*, who evaded each strike with insulting ease. And then, standing near the Fallen angel, he threw his sword at *Arakiel*'s face and reached into his pocket. The thrown sword was battered away, and Steiner lunged low with his newly drawn and cocked derringer swinging up towards *Arakiel*'s head…

*

Samiel watched as Steiner's head fell from his shoulders, a small pistol falling unfired to the ground. The Templar had died well, which seemed important to him. For *Samiel*, death simply meant the horror of returning to Hell.

Lilith kept her eyes fixed on him as she approached. Hatred or caution? Both had kept her alive for countless years. "Lucifer. It has been some time."

"Thousands of years, Lilith."

"I met your son tonight. *Arakiel* convinced me that killing him risked you returning to Heaven, so for now he lives. But I will kill him in time, if no one else saves me the trouble."

"You may do as you wish," *Samiel* said with a forced calm. To show concern for Wilton to this woman would surely doom him. Her mortal death had seen the birth of the *Nephilim*, and her bloody revenge had led to the birth of the werewolves.

"I was so disappointed that wolves beat me to you all those years ago." She hauled him up with one hand, opening her mouth to reveal her fangs. "This time, I will have the pleasure of sending you to Hell myself."

Teeth ripped into his throat to unleash a fresh agony on *Samiel*, and agony he would prefer to what awaited when it was done. Death might not have been painless, but it took him swiftly, too swiftly, returning him to–

*

A grim air lingered over the burned, blackened remnants of Kaleshaws, the site where Khotep's foul sorcery had begun, killing many of the villagers with an unnatural plague. The dead had risen and killed the rest of the villagers and most of the residents, staff and guests of Dunkellen House. Foley and Sirk both bore a grim expression as they entered the eerily silent ruin, but then, they had been here when the plague had reached its climax.

"More of them ahead as well as behind," Lady Delaney said between heavy breaths. Maybe a dozen cloaked figures waited in the centre of what had once been a prosperous textile village. Father, Gray and Steiner had delayed the undead at the bridge, but others must have splashed across the river in a bid to catch the fugitives before they could escape.

"Outflanked, with enemies to the front and rear," Singh said grimly. "Sell your lives dearly."

"Maybe not," Foley said. He whistled twice, once short and once long.

Someone in the group ahead responded with two sharp whistles, and Foley grinned. "Friends ahead, so don't be shooting at them."

Sure enough, the strangers began firing at the undead approaching from behind, armed with shotguns and revolvers, by the sound. The undead faltered; many fell, the others retreating. Some of the fallen got up and limped away, a few managing to escape despite being repeatedly shot as they fled.

"Non-silver ammunition," Lady Delaney said with a shake of her head.

"If it's who I'm expecting, it's their first fight against the undead, and they just saved our lives," Foley said, "so let's not judge them too harshly."

"Let's not wait until Lilith and *Arakiel* arrive," Singh said. The group increased their pace, Hunt's lungs burning from the exertion.

He stumbled, feeling as if part of himself had been cut away.

"Are you okay?" Kerry asked, her eyes running over him in case he had been shot. Singh watched him, a knowing look on his face.

"My father is dead."

"You felt it?" Lady Delaney asked.

He managed a nod, almost dizzied by the shock of it.

"Keep moving, or he and Steiner died in vain," Foley said, more interested in the group ahead.

"Foley," the apparent leader called out.

"Good to see you and damned bloody glad you came!" Foley said. "You should remember most of these people."

"Inspector Grant, a surprise seeing you here," Lady Delany said, the first to recognise the leader.

"You brought friends," Kerry noted. "Hope you're not here to try and arrest us again."

"Fellow malcontents from the constabulary," John Grant said with a grin. "Foley told us what we needed to know. What some of us have maybe suspected for some time. Too many strange deaths and too many powerful people covering them up."

"I didn't believe him, really," someone confessed. "Until just now when I saw someone shot twice get up and run away!"

"Aim for the head or heart next time," Kerry advised. "And get some silver bullets if you can."

"I sent a message to Grant telling him where we'd be and what we'd be facing. Wasn't sure he'd come, so I didn't want to raise hopes," Foley said. "I'd met some of his colleagues down the pub a couple days ago, but again, maybe they thought me insane, or maybe they believed me and were smart enough to stay away from this mess!"

"We're not that smart, Mr Foley," someone called out to the laughter of others. Hunt recognised the giddiness in them, the result of adrenalin and relief over having survived their first contact with the enemy.

Lady Delaney surveyed the fallen undead. "The others will regroup and be upon us soon, so let us hasten away."

They escaped, thanks to Inspector Grant and those he trusted to follow him into an illegal action firing guns at the stuff of penny dreadfuls and the darker parts of the Bible.

Hunt said nothing as they scrambled through the darkened trees towards the road, hoping to lose any remaining pursuers. He had lost both parents to this dreadful place and wanted nothing more than to be free of it.

*

"They escaped, Master," Redfort heard one of the undead tell *Arakiel.*

"A ragged band of less than ten mortals managed to escape my 'fearless' undead?" *Arakiel* asked quietly, his expression fierce. Being his subject might prove only marginally less perilous than being his enemy.

"We were ambushed by an unknown group as we caught up with Hunt and the others in Kaleshaws," the undead was quick to explain.

"More of Fisher's survivors?"

A shake of the head. "I do not think so. They made no attacks upon Hunt or his companions."

"It is of small import," *Arakiel* decided after a moment. "Lucifer is back in Hell, and Wolfgang Steiner of the Templars is dead too. Where is Amy Newfield, I would have her pay homage to me. She was Made from blood of my line."

"She disappeared after Fisher's death," someone said.

"Have her found and brought before me."

"What of Wilton Hunt, Lady Delaney and whoever else of their group survives?" Redfort asked. *Wilton Hunt, the new Lord Ashwood.*

"For now, we have matters of greater import to attend to. My return has necessitated the compromise of this House's control over Glasgow. But we are now whole again, and so we must regain our influence over those mortals with power and influence," *Arakiel* said.

"You wish to restore the Sooty Feather Society?" Redfort asked. *The old lord is dead, long live the new.*

"Yes. Fisher did well in establishing it. A pity he could not find contentment serving me."

Redfort kept his mouth shut as Lilith approached. Apocryphal elements excised from older versions of biblical material suggested she was Adam's first wife, who had been forsaken and became a demon. The reality scared Redfort more.

"*Arakiel*, our business is done?" Lilith asked. As if killing a *Dominus Nephilim* was little more than a difficult chore.

"It is done. Fisher is dead and you sent Lucifer back to Hell. I trust you are as satisfied as I am by the conclusion of our arrangement?" *Arakiel* asked.

"It was a pleasure to look into his eyes again, and this time to see the life leave them. Regarding his son, I must give that some thought."

"Whatever you wish. I bid you a safe voyage home, Lilith," *Arakiel* said carelessly.

She laughed a little. "Safe for me, yes. It is a long voyage from Liverpool to Casablanca, I foresee many of my fellow travellers succumbing to a mysterious illness."

*

Newfield descended into the cellars of Dumbreck Castle, knowing she had little time. Her fellow survivors had bowed to *Arakiel*, whose rule was absolute and uncontested now that Niall Fisher was dead, and Margot Guillam, too, probably.

She should have sworn fealty to him too; he was after all the original master of the House of Keel, but she could never forgive him despatching Canning to murder her parents, purely to hurt her for her role in sending *Maridiel* back to Hell.

Invigorated by her Transition to *Nephilim*, she had decided to forsake the House, but whether she stayed to defy him or fled, she must remove the jar containing her blood from this place – the 'contingency' supplied by every Councillor lest they go missing. If *Arakiel* got hold of it, he could use a Diviner to track her down, assuming any survived the destruction of the Under-Market.

She jerked to a halt, surprised to find someone already at the safe holding the contingencies. Had *Arakiel* been so sure of victory he had sent someone here early?

It was Magdalene Quinn. "Miss Newfield. I thought you would be fawning over your new lord and master. Did he send you here to secure the blood?" There was a resignation to her. A powerful magician, yes, but one wounded.

"I came here to remove my own blood. You believe I would 'fawn' over the one who sent that monster Canning to kill my parents?" Newfield asked.

"I have long ceased being surprised at what some will accept, Miss Newfield. You plan to flee here?"

"You too? I assume you are equally opposed to serving *Arakiel*, after what he ordered done to the Under-Market?"

Half of Miss Quinn's mouth curved upwards. "Flee? I will make the *Grigori* pay for that act of slaughter. I will see him back in Hell, if I can, and this time there will be no remains kept as a trophy allowing someone to bring him back."

"You are removing your own contingency."

"That, and I was hoping to find Roddy McBride's, to make him pay for his own involvement. Alas, his blood is gone. As is Edmund Crowe's and Bishop Redfort's," Miss Quinn said.

"All traitors then?" If three of Regent Guillam's Council were really serving *Arakiel*, small wonder the now-*Grigori* had won the war.

"Crowe and McBride, certainly. Redfort? Perhaps, or perhaps he simply had his blood removed as a precaution. He has always been a slippery one," Quinn said as she removed one further small jar of blood. "Yours."

"Thank you." Newfield came to a decision. "If you are staying to oppose *Arakiel*, then I will aid you."

"A singed magician and a ghoul. How will he manage to sleep during the day knowing he faces such a foe?" Quinn asked with a wry smile.

"A singed magician and a new *Nephilim*," Newfield corrected. "I ate Canning's heart."

"That is excellent news. Most unexpected. Later, you must tell me how you managed to slay the Glasgow Ripper."

"Later, Miss Quinn, as you say. We should take our blood and be gone before *Arakiel* arrives."

"Let us hope we can find more likeminded folk."

Newfield recalled her fight with Canning. "I may have a suggestion."

Chapter Forty-Three

"It is a sacrilege, holding this here," Father Patrick Finnigan whispered to Redfort as *Arakiel* hosted his House and the Sooty Feathers within the Glasgow Cathedral at midnight.

"Appalling," said Redfort, who had offered the site's use to the *Grigori*. Finnigan, a rising star in Glasgow's Catholic community, was a relatively new addition to the Sooty Feathers – one Redfort was keen to keep an eye on lest he prove particularly useful or competent, and thus risk Redfort's own position as the Society's pre-eminent cleric. Finnigan probably believed the cathedral being home to the protestant Church of Scotland was likewise a sacrilege.

Lit candles were spread across the cathedral floor. Every surviving undead sworn to *Arakiel* was present within, which was pretty much all of them in the city save for the elusive Newfield.

Arakiel stood at the altar in a white robe, flanked by his two Elders, Edmund Crowe and Bresnik. The latter was one of two surviving circus *Nephilim*, having been with Crowe while they laid Margot Guillam low and fed her heart to Bresnik, making him Elder.

Canning was dead and mourned by no one.

No magicians attended the cathedral, their leader Miss Quinn having also disappeared. So far, the surviving magicians had been silent, having lost their centre of power.

It was gone, it and its surrounding fire-wrecked slums scheduled for demolition to make way for new tenements, the land owned by the Heron Crowe Bank.

That bank looked to make a lot of money from the calamity.

Redfort had taken a particular pleasure in seeing Wolfgang Steiner killed, pleased that he had helped by wounding the Swiss fanatic. With his death so too died the Templar ambition to take Glasgow. From what Redfort had gleaned, the Templar Order would be hard-pressed keeping Edinburgh free from the undead, and so Glasgow could rest free from any further interference.

There had been much nervous speculation from those who had been loyal to Fisher as to how *Arakiel* would rule. Would he reconcile the two factions into one, populating his new Council with people and undead from both sides? Or would he hold a grudge, Fisher's loyalists quietly disappearing as the months passed.

Redfort also wondered how Fisher's surviving loyalists would manage to serve *Arakiel*, knowing he had spent months trying to have them killed. So far, there had been no trouble, in part because it was easy to disassociate the elusive demon Possessing the body of Henderson, Redfort's former secretary, with *Arakiel* the *Grigori*, a being who had until two centuries ago survived millennia of war and intrigue.

And in part because they feared the *Grigori*. No longer a demon trapped in the flesh of a mortal, now he wore the flesh of an exiled angel; divinity tarnished was still divinity, a being who had lived in Heaven.

"Welcome." *Arakiel*'s voice echoed out across the cathedral. "Welcome to the House of Keel … *Arakiel*. The House I established thousands of years ago in what is now Egypt, enduring victory and defeat. The House whose remnant I led to Ancient Greece and Rome. After the fall of Constantinople, a House I led across Europe until we reached Glasgow and found our new home, a town we could nurture to greatness."

The *Grigori* paused for a moment to take in faces around the cathedral before gesturing to his left. "Mr Crowe is now an Elder of the House, an ally from long ago."

To his right. “Bresnik is the last *Nephilim* of this House to have seen my previous rule, albeit confined to Bucharest where he was Made. He was rewarded with the heart of Margot Guillam to ascend him to Elder, my right hand.”

“Will Mr Bresnik be your regent, Master?” Sir Kenneth Jasper asked, a tremor in his voice. The Black Wing Club had reopened and was seeking new members. At its heart lingered the Sooty Feather Society, as before, recruiting from the club those of power, wealth and influence who might have the moral flexibility to serve the undead.

Silence fell over the cathedral. “I am not Niall Fisher. I have no intention of hiding myself away while another rules in my stead.”

“What should we call you?” someone else asked, more brazen than most.

“I am *Arakiel*.”

“Lord *Arakiel*? Master *Arakiel*?”

A cold smile. “It is an angelic name. ‘Lordship’ is assumed in the name itself.”

“What of your Council?” Roddy McBride asked. It was well known that he was unhappy at the losses he’d suffered at Dunkellen House. Most of his thugs had died there and good riddance. He was clearly after reassurance and recompense.

“The Council is disbanded. Tonight I am establishing my court, the Court of Rooks, after the bird that once flew as the sigil of my House. I will have Councillors to advise me, but my word alone is law. Bresnik and Crowe, of course, will be first among my councillors. Cornelius Josiah brought me back first as demon and later as *Grigori*, and so he is a Councillor, as is *Gadriel*. Bishop Redfort and Roderick McBride sat on Fisher’s Council until wisdom turned them my way, and they are appointed Councillors. If Miss Newfield presents herself by tomorrow night and swears fealty, she too may serve. If not, she is declared outlaw.”

“She is a mere ghoul, Master,” Jonah Murray said, perhaps daring to do so as he was in high favour having helped Edmund Crowe and Bresnik assassinate Margot Guillam.

"That may no longer be the case," Redfort dared to say. "Richard Canning was found dead the night of our master's return, missing his heart – such as it was." No one missed Canning, least of all *Arakiel*, who was probably pleased to see the back of the murderous lunatic.

"You say Newfield beat Canning and ate his heart?" Bresnik's eyed crinkled. "Canning was cold bastard and *Nephilim*. Newfield a ghoul. She maybe killed him, if she sneaked up and shot him in head or heart, but beat him down long enough to cut out heart?"

Ailsa Kerris, a *Nephilim* from Fisher's 'stable' spoke up. "I last saw Miss Newfield near the area where Canning's body was found. There was blood on her knife and around her mouth. One of the women in Lucifer's company was with her, each going their separate ways and both looking the worse for wear."

"You believe Miss Newfield and this woman defeated Canning together, after which Newfield cut out his heart and ate it?" *Arakiel* asked. He kept his own opinion on this theory to himself.

Redfort cleared his throat. "Miss Newfield was most unhappy at Canning for killing her parents. I believe she would hold no love towards you for ordering it. That would explain her hunting Canning down and failing to call upon your own good self."

"Find her," *Arakiel* decreed, to Redfort's lack of surprise. The *Grigori* had just returned after two hundred years in Hell owing to one act of betrayal, he was unlikely to let a fresh treachery fester in his city.

"Miss Quinn has also not been seen since that night," Crowe said.

"Many of her fellow magicians perished with the Under-Market. She will remain a thorn in our side unless we pluck her out," Redfort said.

"Aye," Roddy McBride said with a firm nod of his head.

"Aside from *Arakiel*, she particularly blamed you, Mr McBride." Redfort couldn't resist needling the jumped-up thug.

"She's one bloody woman, what can she do?" McBride said with a mocking bravado.

"Let us ask those here who were present in the Bothwell Street Crypt when she and her fellow magicians unleashed a pack of wild dogs under their control," Redfort said. "Or the late Bartholomew Ridley."

Bresnik glanced at *Arakiel* before speaking. "Add this Quinn witch to the list. Bring her before us if you can. If not, kill her."

"If we're adding names to lists, what about Tam Foley and his fucking friends?" McBride asked.

"Mind your coarse tongue." *Arakiel* spoke softly, but it was enough to make McBride shift his feet.

Redfort spoke. "Lucifer is back in Hell. Wolfgang Steiner is dead. Our friend in the Browning Shipping Company reports that one of their smaller ships was ordered to take the company's owner, the new Lord Ashwood, to Tobermory in Mull. Aside from his father's valet, he was accompanied by four others. We can assume Thomas Foley and Lady Delaney were among them."

"Tobermory? What is there for them?" someone asked.

"The ferry to Kirkaline, a village at the mouth of Loch Aline," Crowe said.

"Hunt has an estate there, now that the Devil's dead," McBride growled. "A half-derelict house not too many years from collapsing, from what I saw."

"Leave them be," *Arakiel* commanded. His eyes fixed on McBride. "Unless they return to Glasgow. My order forbidding any to harm Wilton Hunt is rescinded. It was in place to prevent Lucifer from being goaded into a confrontation before Lilith's arrival. I enticed her here with news of Lucifer's return, and killing his Vessel in person was her price for Fisher's heart."

"I understand," McBride said. He didn't sound happy about it, but he was not foolish enough to defy *Arakiel*, even to avenge two brothers.

"Should they return by way of a Browning Shipping Company vessel, we will learn of it," Redfort said. A most dissatisfied young man working for that company had been recruited into the Black Wing Club and was even now poised to become an Initiate of the Sooty Feather Society.

Arakiel addressed the cathedral. "Winter will soon fall upon us, the days dark and the nights long. The Sooty Feathers will recruit those of wealth and power. Those few of its older surviving members who remained loyal to the Society are to be offered the gift of my blood. My House has endured war and exile for thousands of years. It has endured even my loss and the losses suffered in this war. We will rebuild and regain power. I want control of the newspapers. Control of the police and the courts. Control over the hospitals. I want this city." He stepped forwards and raised his hands. "I will have it all."

*

Redfort descended the steps leading to his cellar, carefully carrying a locked wooden box. What he intended carried great risk, but the necromancer Khotep had re-awoken his interest in that dark and forbidden branch of magic, and while he had learned much from the ancient grimoire inherited from his late mentor, neither its original author nor any subsequent possessor had described how to create a receptacle for his soul.

Such a creation would allow him to cheat death as Khotep had for millennia, Possessing body after body so long as the Soul-Repository remained safe. Redfort had humbly declined *Arakiel*'s offer to Make him undead. As Fisher, Guillam, Canning and Rannoch had learned, undeath offered but a respite from death, which had claimed each of them this year.

To become a *Jinn*, however, was to defy death so long as one's Soul-Repository was intact, and Redfort was resolved to become such a creature. But help was needed, help only one could provide.

He studied the old woman tied to a chair in the centre of the cellar and unlocked his box, carefully opening it. Using tongs, he removed the bronze lamp from the box and placed it on top of her bound hands, ignoring her gagged attempts at screaming. He then shuttered the lantern so that it only let out a little light.

She spasmed once, every muscle seeming to tense. And then she went limp for a short time before speaking. "Who is there?" There was fear in the woman's voice – in Khotep's new voice. *He wonders if he has gone to Hell.*

"Do calm yourself, Khotep." Redfort opened the lantern fully, the woman now hosting Khotep's soul blinking rapidly.

"Redfort? I assume that you did not destroy my Soul-Repository after all. My gratitude. Lucifer will not be pleased if he finds out." Khotep spoke slowly, still adjusting to his new Vessel.

"Lucifer is dead. Well, his Vessel is. The Devil, we can assume, is back in Hell, long may He stay there."

"That *is* good news." Khotep paused. "How much time has passed since Mortimer's body was killed? How fares the war?"

"A number of days. Niall Fisher and Margot Guillam are dead. Erik Keel is *Grigori* once again, is *Arakiel* once again, served by the remnants of both factions."

"Excellent, let us hope *Arakiel* remembers my contributions. Who is this woman you chose as my Vessel?"

"I do not know. She lived on the streets, a prostitute I imagine, one who was grateful at my offer of a bowl of soup," Redfort said. The look in the woman's eyes had suggested she believed the Bishop of Glasgow had another motive than feeding the poor when he invited her to his home. And she was correct, albeit it was depravity of a different sort he had in mind.

"Not to sound ungrateful, but I think you could do better." Khotep sounded cautiously critical, clearly wanting a Vessel that would allow him back into the higher echelons of society but concerned about offending Redfort while in his power.

"Speaking of gratitude, let us discuss how you might demonstrate it. Had I destroyed your Soul-Repository as I told Lucifer, you would in truth be dead. But I spared you." He had smelted down some other metallic pieces recovered from the study, showing them to Lucifer and His son.

"You wish to learn more about necromancy," Khotep guessed.

"I wish to master it. I wish to become a *Jinn*, like you, with my own soul anchored to an item in this world so that I might escape whatever awaits after." Even if it only delayed the inevitable.

"I will take you on as my pupil, but first you must release me. And locate a more suitable Vessel. Someone in medicine, preferably. I do like to keep my hand in."

"You misunderstand. You are my prisoner. You will teach me down here. If I am satisfied, you will be kept prisoner in better quarters, with luxuries. And when I have learned everything, your Vessel will be killed and your lamp kept in storage for, shall we say … fifty years? It will then be released so that some unwitting fool can become your new Vessel."

"Unacceptable!"

"I had expected as much." Redfort sighed. "We will discuss this again tomorrow night. And the two nights that follow. If you still find my terms unacceptable, then I will have your lamp melted down and your Vessel killed."

"Wait…!" Khotep cried out as Redfort stepped forwards and raised his derringer, firing it into the woman's skull. He had expected Khotep to answer as he had, which was why Redfort had expended only a little effort in acquiring a Vessel. *I must do the same again tomorrow*.

He was confident Khotep would submit. After all, as an immortal, what was a few years teaching? And yes, it would be disorientating to emerge half a century hence, but better that than to truly die.

And so Redfort would serve *Arakiel* well and – more or less – faithfully, making himself useful while learning everything Khotep had to teach. He would find a suitable second or third son from a wealthy family, one bound for the church. That child would be given every advantage, mentored by Redfort to gain influence and respect within the church, groomed to become a future bishop.

And when Redfort died, that young man would be gifted a legacy in his Last Will and Testament.

Redfort's Soul-Repository. *My soul. And for me, the game will begin again.*

Chapter Forty-Four

Kerry Knox stood in silence next to Caroline as the piper standing post by the Hunt family mausoleum played *Flowers of the Forest*. A sombre melody composed in remembrance of the defeat of the Scottish army at Flodden, and the fall of King James IV, pipers played it only at funerals and the like, or to instruct new pipers. Knox had heard it only once before, at Lady Ashwood's funeral within the Glasgow Necropolis as a carriage took her across the Bridge of Sighs.

Now it played again as her husband's coffin was slowly carried into the small private cemetery partitioned away from the main churchyard by a crumbling wall, reserved for the Hunt family. The lords and ladies were entombed in the rough marble mausoleum, surrounded by the graves of those Hunts who never carried the title of Baron or Baroness Ashwood.

Wilton Hunt and Tam Foley were the lead pallbearers. Dr Sirk, Mr Gray and Mr Singh also bore the lead-sealed coffin, with the undertaker making up the sixth. The piper continued his mournful dirge as the pallbearers passed between the mausoleum pillars and down into the tomb.

After a while everyone exited save for Wil. Now the 7th Baron Ashwood, Knox reminded herself, though Lady Delaney had told her that by tradition, he was not to be called such until after the last Baron's funeral. *Went down Mr Hunt, comes back up as Lord Ashwood.*

A damp drizzle lingered in the air. Foley seemed restless, probably impatient to get to the Ashwood Arms, the local inn nicknamed the Horned Lord. No one seemed eager to go back into the tomb, so after giving him another five minutes of privacy, Knox hesitantly went in after him.

"Wilton," she said quietly, an irrational part of her not wanting to disturb the dead. The mausoleum smelt musty and was filled with a number of stone sarcophagi. She knew that only nine were occupied, as the 3rd and 5th barons had died unwed, and Wilton's mother had been buried in Glasgow.

"Yes?" Wilton stood before his father's sarcophagus, the lead-sealed coffin having been placed inside and covered with a heavy-looking stone.

"Are you coming, or do you want us to give you more time alone?"

His face was lost in the dark but she heard a hint of humour in his voice. "Are Foley's feet itching to take him to the pub?"

"It is raining," she said diplomatically.

"Do the heavens weep for my father? I doubt it, somehow. I thought of having a service, for the sake of Lewis Hunt, but his soul has long since gone to Heaven or Hell. Having his body buried here will have to suffice. Listening to Reverend Harcourt drone on about what a good man my father was and how he's sitting next to Jesus would have been a joke. We all know where my father is."

In Hell.

"Will you have your mother brought up here to lie beside him?" Knox asked.

"No. She wanted to lie with her parents and brother, and I will honour her wishes as my father did. That one will be mine."

"What?"

"That sarcophagus is for the 7th Baron. The 2nd Baron, my great-great-something-grandfather picked out my final resting place about a century and a half before I was born when he had this mausoleum excavated and built." He pointed to an empty sarcophagus lying against the wall, one down from Lucifer's.

A chill went through Knox upon seeing it.

He then pointed to one lying beside it. "That one's earmarked for my future wife, should I have one."

"Lovely." *Hope that wasn't his idea of a proposal.* "What woman could say no to a stone coffin?"

"What woman could consent to marry the son of the Devil?"

Knox wondered if he was indirectly asking if she still liked him, but his cold, distracted tone suggested the question might be rhetorical. She was tempted to speak, but part of her feared he might believe she was only after him for his money and title, and so she said nothing.

A heavy silence lingered in the tomb.

"I think we've made Foley wait long enough." Wil rested a hand on his father's sarcophagus for a moment before turning and walking out of the tomb, Knox hurrying to keep up with him.

*

In a remote village that saw few visitors, the small procession of strangers approaching the Horned Lord drew every eye, and Foley saw some narrow as they recognised the young man leading them. Behind him and Foley were Lady Delaney, Miss Knox, Dr Sirk, the black Mr Gray and the Indian Mr Singh. An eclectic group, to be sure.

Some of the villagers, crofters and farmers were descended from the Kail'an sept who had originally settled this area, and Wilton Hunt was a figure to inspire no small degree of ambivalence among them.

He was the last known descendent of the 'Black Hunt', Sir Geoffrey, later titled the 1st Baron of Ashwood as reward for all but destroying the sept. But Wilton Hunt was also descended from the Kail'an chiefs, and furthermore was the son of Lucifer, whom the sept had worshipped as Lugh and Cernunnos. Many Kail'ans – the more fanatical – had died in the Lewswood, no small number dying to Foley as a wolf.

All told, Hunt might not be any safer here than in Glasgow. Foley knew from bitter experience that killers had no qualms about committing mayhem and murder in places of rural tranquillity.

Upon their arrival three days ago, Miss Knox had looked around with wide-eyed curiosity at the mostly white-washed sandstone houses and cottages of the village, the young woman having rarely left Glasgow. A cramped carriage had conveyed Hunt and his guests to Ashwood Lodge, and so her view of the village as they passed quickly through it had been restricted. Today her eyes darted around as she walked its streets, the novelty still fresh.

While the others had made themselves at home in Ashwood Lodge, Hunt had busied himself arranging his father's funeral and visiting Dunlew Castle with Singh, perhaps to learn the state of the castle while awaiting the estate to be legally transferred to him. Given the state of Ashwood Lodge, the sooner they could move to the castle, the better.

"What's that tower?" Knox asked, pointing across the loch to the east.

"Ardtornish Point Lighthouse," Hunt said as the group walked down the road. "At night, its beacon is lit to warn passing seacraft away from the rocks."

Shops that Foley remembered from his last visit were still present on the main street, including a general store, a butcher's shop and a post office. He smelled the fishmongers before he saw it, though it had a new sign above the door. Maybe the last fishmonger had been a Kail'an who died in the Lewswood.

The weaver's shop and the bakery were open, though the cold wind blowing through the rain-flecked streets meant scant few villagers were out and about, and those who were did not linger, contenting themselves with a quick gawp before continuing with their business.

There was a smithy next to the inn, and Foley had pitied its workers during that hot, long summer, having to endure the scorching heat from the forge while pounding metal into shape all day long. Now, as the autumn wind and rains lashed at him, he envied the smith and his young apprentice.

*

A silence fell over the inn as the group entered, Wil and the rest of the gentlemen removing their top hats, everyone removing their coats. The tap room was large and dark, lit only by candles sitting on most of the tables and a large fire in the fireplace. The few windows were small, the glass thick and misted so that the inn was likely gloomy even in summer. Knox loved the taste of the clean, fresh country air, though hungry as she was, the smells of cooking food were no less welcome.

Assuming the locals did not drive them out. Most of the patrons looked to be villagers in for an afternoon ale, joined by a smattering of farmhands and fishermen.

Once, Wil would have been hesitant, a young man overshadowed by his formidable parents. Now that shadow was gone from Wilton Hunt, and Lord Ashwood stood in his place.

"Singh, if you would," Knox heard Wil say quietly. Most stared at the clearly foreign Gray and Singh, but Knox noted a few staring at Wil.

"As you say, my Lord." Of the *Seraphim*, *Kariel*, there was no trace, today there was only Lord Ashwood's valet.

Singh stepped into the centre of the room and spoke loudly and clearly. "Lord Ashwood has today buried his father, the 6th Baron. He would invite you all to drink to the late baron's memory, and as such will be buying a glass of whisky for everyone here."

There was a murmur of appreciation at that, the tension dissipating somewhat. Knox was not blind to the hostile looks some still gave the group, tinged by fear in many cases.

"Must be nice being rich, being able to buy a round of drinks for everyone," Foley said quietly.

Wil's smile was tight. "I can afford it." And he could, having inherited the Browning Shipping Company. Whether he intended to take a personal hand in the running of the company or merely offer a broad direction and take the money, he had not so far indicated.

"I won't accept a drink from a damned Hunt," a burly fisherman declared, getting up from his stool and standing belligerently several feet from Wil.

"I may be a Hunt, but I also have the blood of the Kail'an chiefs in my veins, from my paternal grandmother," Wil said quietly.

The man backed off a few steps, mouth open as an oppressive chill fell over the taproom despite the blazing fire. *Wil's Unveiled!*

Wil continued. "As for my father, I suggest you speak to some of your … kin regarding who and what he was. Who and what I am."

Cowed, the man walked quickly out of the inn, the chill leaving with him as Wilton Hunt Veiled himself once more.

Wil approached the bar where a young dark-haired woman waited, a dark expression on her face. Maybe she just wasn't looking forward to the prospect of having to pour drinks for a score of impatient men at the one time. Knox followed him.

"Miss Kyle, you're looking well. I see you decided to keep the inn, after…"

"After my father's death. Lord Ashwood." She said his title mockingly.

"At the hands of one of his own. And as he and you had come to the Lewswood to witness me become the avatar of Lugh, I must confess to a lack of sympathy," Wil said. "Cousin."

Her answering smile was bitter.

"Miss Kyle," Foley said as he joined them.

There was fearful recognition on her face. "Mr…?"

"Foley. And do not worry, I won't turn into a beast and kill your customers. Today."

"You'll all be wanting food, I assume?" she asked Wil.

"Indeed we will. Untampered with. I recall you telling my father you used to spit in his ale," Wil said.

"That was before I knew what he was. What you are. There will be no repeat of that, I promise you."

"Excellent. My friends and I will take a seat while you serve your patrons."

"A fine place," Gray said as the party sat around a large rough-finished table. "I'm guessing these folks ain't seen too many brown people before."

"Indeed not, Gray," Hunt said.

"Or the son of a god, more than once," Sirk said. "I recognise one or two faces from the Lewswood."

"The barmaid's welcome seemed lacking," Caroline said. "I saw little of that famed Highland hospitality."

"Kayleigh Kyle is the landlady, after her father died in the summer. Her feelings towards me are somewhat … mixed," Wil said.

"I remember her flirting with you in the summer," Foley said with a grin.

Once, Wil would have blushed at such a comment. Now he ignored it. "She is a distant cousin. We are both descended from the last Kail'an chief to hold this land."

"Who owns the land now?" Gray asked.

"Me, mostly. At least, once the legalities are dealt with. My family held the Ashwood estate, for what little that's worth. Mostly income from some farms and crofts. The 3rd Baron lost most of the lands to various people, though it turns out that the McKellens bought most of them after winning Dunlew Castle and thus expanded the Dunlew estate back to what it had originally been, save for the Ashwood estate."

A tray of small glasses filled with whisky arrived, one for everybody seated.

Wil picked his up. "I won't ask you to toast the Devil, but between us we have suffered many losses lately, and I think a toast to the fallen is appropriate."

Everyone took a glass.

"To absent friends," Wil said.

"Absent friends," everyone said quietly. Knox thought

of Steiner and the Templars who had died, doubtless as did Gray, Caroline and Sirk. One of those dead Templars had been Sirk's old friend, Ben Jefferies. Singh had lost his employer while *Kariel* had lost an ancient enemy. The McBrides had killed many of Foley's new friends. Wil had lost his father less than three months after burying his mother.

Food and drinks were ordered, ale for everyone except Caroline who asked for a glass of white wine. Fish was served along with potatoes, and the conversation turned to the future.

*

"When will you be moving into Dunlew Castle? Dare I say, some stout walls and tall towers might dissuade enemies from knocking at your door," Gray said.

"Soon, I hope. Lawyers are scrutinising the transfer of the castle and estate from Fisher to my father, and his Will. There will also be Succession and Legacy Duties to be dealt with, and I've tasked Singh to see about staffing the castle prior to taking up residence," Hunt said. He would be living in Ashwood Lodge for a while longer.

"And what do you plan for the future, Lord Ashwood?" Lady Delaney asked. It still felt odd being addressed as such. Prior to the spring, 'Lord Ashwood' had been Great-Uncle Thomas. Then it had been Father. *Now it is me.*

"I am still to decide, Lady Delaney. And at the risk of presumption, my friends, I think we can dispense with the formalities?"

"Do you intend to play lord of the castle and hide up here forevermore, or will you be returning to Glasgow to finish our business there?" she asked.

"Meaning what?"

"Meaning, will you sit up here while *Arakiel* terrorises Glasgow, or will you be coming back to help us kill the bastard?" Kerry asked.

"*Arakiel* had my father killed. His necromancer was

responsible for the death of my mother. I am not yet done with this war," he promised coldly.

"Have you all lost your minds?" Sirk asked. "We barely survived against two weakened enemies more interested in killing one another than us. Now you propose we battle a fallen angel who has returned in the fullness of Its power, a *Grigori* who now rules Glasgow and the entirety of its undead. The war is lost."

Hunt looked him in the eye, enveloped in that welcoming coldness that he had embraced ever since his father had died, taking strength from it. "My war has not yet begun."

"I assume you will not be joining us, Doctor?" Lady Delaney asked.

"I am sorely tempted to stay up here and concentrate on my studies, but you lot will be lucky to survive the first day without my help."

Delaney smiled. "It would not be the same without you."

"What of you, Mr Gray?" Hunt asked. "We could use a man of your courage and skills."

"By rights, I should return to Edinburgh. But too many of my fellow Templars have died in Glasgow for me to let that be in vain. I'm with you," Gray said.

"Foley?" Hunt asked his friend. He had left once already, only for trouble to follow him.

"Roddy McBride still lives. I'll need to see what I can do about that," Foley said. "But once we're done, I'm returning to my friends. It's because of me they lost their home, so I need to help them rebuild, wherever they decide to do that."

"Bring them here," Hunt said, an idea forming. "I'll need people I can trust here. If you accept the post of estate factor, you can live in Ashwood Lodge. Your friends lived in a farming hamlet, so they can live here too. And when it's that time of the month, you can all roam around in the Lewswood and hunt rabbits."

Foley lifted his chin. "A generous offer. In a day or two I'll leave here and visit them."

"Excellent. My parents made arrangements for the house to be renovated in the spring. You are all welcome as my guest for as long as you wish."

"Will you then be abandoning your studies, Hunt?" Sirk asked, an air of disapproval hovering over that question.

"Not as such. If you are willing, I would have you tutor me in the subjects you consider yourself knowledgeable enough in. I will acquire the necessary books for those subjects you do not."

"I would be pleased to, though you may have cause to regret it," Sirk answered with a slight smile. "And your examinations next spring?"

"I'll sit them, assuming I still live. I have obtained an agreement from the university in this regard," Hunt said.

"And what did you need to bribe them with?" Foley asked with a smirk.

Hunt gave him a look of mock chastisement. "I assure you, Foley, that money had no bearing in my conversation with the university. My offer to establish and fund the 'Ashwood Library' was entirely unrelated."

"Entirely unrelated," Singh echoed with a straight face. "When I passed on the offer, at no point was there any mention of quid pro quo."

"Did they even wait a day before agreeing to your requests?" Sirk asked.

"A day and a half, Doctor. Everything is above board," Singh said with a smile.

"Above board," Hunt echoed. Once *Arakiel* had been dealt with, he was resolved to visit other lands and put his botanical, zoological and archaeological studies to good use.

"I'm sure it was," Kerry said with a knowing laugh.

"When do you expect to receive your Writ of Summons?" Lady Delaney asked.

"Writ of what now?" Gray asked.

"A Writ of Summons, Gray, summoning me to the House of Lords to be introduced to my fellow peers and to take my seat there," Hunt said. "Soon, Lady Delaney. My petition and the relevant documents and proofs have been submitted. My father was to appear in late November, but my lawyer is hopeful that the relevant formalities can be completed before then, and that I can attend in his stead."

"Did you go through all that, Lady Delaney?" Gray asked.

"I am no peer, nor was my husband," she explained gently to the American. "My husband, Sir Andrew, was knighted. As his wife, I became Lady Delaney."

"Let us finish our drinks and return to my house," Hunt said, suddenly impatient to be gone from this inn. "We have much to discuss."

"Killing Roddy McBride," Foley said. "John Grant and those constables of his he assembled to fight the undead can help us."

"Returning to Hell any demons brought back by *Arakiel*," said Lady Delaney.

Gray raised his half-empty pint mug. "Avenging my brother Templars and freeing Glasgow of the undead scourge."

"Freeing Glasgow," said Sirk.

"Hunting down every bastard Sooty Feather working for the undead," said Kerry.

"Sending *Arakiel* back to Hell," a woman said, joining them uninvited.

"Who are you?" Hunt challenged. One of the woman's eyes was covered with a patch and her face showed burn scars.

"I am Miss Magdalene Quinn, formerly of the Council," she said.

"Should you not be currying favour with *Arakiel*?" Foley asked. No one drew a weapon, but Hunt knew fingers were reaching for derringers hidden in pockets or purses.

"He killed many of my friends and colleagues when he ordered the destruction of the Under-Market," she said. "This I cannot forget or forgive."

"You a magician, then?" Gray asked once introductions had been made.

"I am."

"Not a necromancer, I hope," Hunt said.

"I specialise in setting Wards and enchanting artifacts," she said.

"Kirkaline is far from Glasgow, Miss Quinn. What brings you here?" Singh asked.

"I seek an alliance. You have proven to be a formidable group, but you now face a *Grigori*." She looked from face to face. "Or do you intend to stay here indefinitely?"

"We are not yet done with Glasgow," Lady Delaney said. "Can you provide information on what is happening in the city?"

"Somewhat, Lady Delaney. The Black Wing Club has reopened and is recruiting once more, as is the Sooty Feather Society at its heart. But the destruction of the Under-Market killed many magicians, and those who survive are either lying low or have fled Glasgow altogether."

"You have few contacts, then," Sirk observed.

"There are a few magicians among the Sooty Feathers who will not forgive what happened to our Community. And Miss Newfield remains in Glasgow. So long as I am here, she will keep me abreast of developments."

"*Arakiel* will not take her because she killed Richard Canning?" Kerry asked in surprise.

"She will not serve *Arakiel* because he sent Canning to murder her parents," Miss Quinn said. "She is now a *Nephilim*, and thus not an ally to be dismissed lightly."

"Letters are only collected and delivered here once a week, via the Oban ferry," Hunt said. "Correspondence between you and Miss Knox will not be quick."

"I have a quicker means of communication than the post," Miss Quinn said.

"Magic?" Kerry asked.

The magician managed a slight smile. "Telegrams, Miss Knox. Lord McKellen arranged such a service to ensure that while staying in Dunlew Castle, he could be swiftly contacted in the event of an emergency."

Kerry pouted. "No crystal balls or scrying with water?

Your magic is something of a disappointment."

The smile on Miss Quinn's face took on a harder look. "I assure you, Miss Knox, that when I employ my magic against our mutual enemy, you will be suitably impressed."

"We can use this telegram service to stay in contact with … our friends," Foley said.

"The mysterious group who aided your escape from the Dunkellen estate?" Miss Quinn asked. "They are the subject of much speculation. Some believe them to be Templar reinforcements, others that they were devil worshippers. Or criminal rivals of McBride, or scouts from another undead House."

"Those are some interesting theories," Lady Delaney said, offering no denials. If it became known that they were in fact rogue policemen, then Sooty Feather retribution would be swift and merciless.

Hunt considered himself no friend to vengeful magicians or undead, but he was also short on allies. Magdalene Quinn and Amy Newfield could be useful. He raised his glass.

"Welcome to the war."

Epilogue

The City of London
Late November 1893
The Day of Lord Ashwood's Introduction
to The House of Lords

Jebediah Kane stood sentinel near Queen Victoria as the aged monarch sat at the head of Earl Easdale's ballroom, content to watch the other guests dance and make merry. Musicians played, ladies and gentlemen danced, and the earl almost shook with excitement at being honoured with royal attendance. He loitered nearby lest Her Majesty require anything, perspiration beading his forehead.

Queen Victoria raised her glass with a trembling hand and took a sip. "Which one is he, Kane?"

There was no need for Kane to ask to whom she referred, nor did he need to search the room for the new Lord Ashwood, fresh from his introduction to the House of Lords that day. "The young man with the reddish hair, Your Majesty. Talking with Sir Thomas and Lady Maxwell."

"Ah, yes, we see him." She stared at him for a while. "Not what we imagined."

"No, Your Majesty. Nevertheless…"

"We would speak with him, Kane." She sounded insistent, though he noticed she took another shaky sip from her glass, a mixture of red wine and whisky.

"Yes, Your Majesty." Kane walked towards the man, surreptitiously checking his derringer was present within his pocket. 'Foolish' was not how one normally described the seventy-four year old queen who had reigned for so many years, but this act was a notable exception. He approached the two gentlemen and the lady.

"Excuse me, but Her Majesty wishes a word with Lord Ashwood," he said.

Sir Thomas' eyes narrowed slightly, doubtless having hoped that the Queen would have decided against demanding this. "A great honour for you, Lord Ashwood."

"Yes." Ashwood extended his hand, Sir Thomas hesitating before shaking it. "Grandmaster Maxwell."

Kane felt his heart quicken, his hand reaching into his pocket in breach of etiquette.

Sir Thomas Maxwell, Grandmaster of the Order of the Poor Knights of the Temple of Solomon stared at him, his granite face looking close to cracking.

"Calm yourself, Sir Thomas. Steiner mentioned you by name, and I assumed there were not two Sir Thomas Maxwells. He wrote to you of me, I understand."

Sir Thomas jerked a nod. "He did, and of … your father. What madness took Steiner, we can never know, first deserting his post and then failing to send you and the Enemy to Hell."

"He died well, choosing to fight an enemy greater than a lawyer-turned-lord and his botany-studying son. My father lived peacefully for years, even in this city. I assume Her Majesty's footman here is one of your Templars? With a gun in his pocket?" Lord Ashwood sounded amused rather than alarmed. If he believed Kane would hesitate before shooting him dead in front of the Queen and these eminent guests, he was mistaken.

"What are your intentions, Lord Ashwood?" Sir Thomas asked.

"I came here to take my seat in the House of Lords, as Lord Durford can attest. He is also one of yours, yes? Spent the ceremony this afternoon almost soiling his robes every time he looked at me."

"He is a friend of the Order," was all Sir Thomas would say regarding the baron currently seated not far away and drinking his way through Lord Easdale's scotch. "And after?"

"After, I return to Dunlew Castle. And in time, to Glasgow, where a Fallen angel rules. For the moment." Kane saw a flash of it then, the fear and rage hidden behind those icy blue eyes, and suddenly Lord Ashwood was as Wolfgang Steiner had described: a frightened young man out of his depth.

"You will fight him?" Lady Maxwell asked.

"I tried to avoid this damned war of yours, but it keeps finding me. Yes, I will fight *Arakiel*. He can pass on my regards to my father, in Hell."

"Including Steiner, thirty-three Templars died in your damned city this year, with little to show for it. What do *you* expect to accomplish?" Sir Thomas asked.

"Send more men, and we can free the city," Ashwood said, his blue eyes fixed on Sir Thomas's.

Sir Thomas sneered. "Send soldiers of God to fight alongside the spawn of Satan? I think not."

"Terrance Gray is with me."

"Gray will answer for his failure to return here in time," said Sir Thomas.

Ashwood paused. "Did Miss Jackson reach here safely?"

"She did and has since returned to Edinburgh."

"Her Majesty grows impatient," Kane interrupted quietly.

"I would tell you to go with God, Lord Ashwood, but I fear you will not find Him on the path you walk," Sir Thomas said heavily.

"A good evening to you, too, Sir Thomas. Lady Maxwell." Lord Ashwood gave them the briefest bow before following Kane.

"Give me a moment," Ashwood said as they walked, not waiting for an answer as he diverted from their path to the Queen.

*

Sir Thomas watched as Kane led the Devil's son to be received by the Queen, after briefly losing sight of them. Upon reading Steiner's letters, he had been tempted to dismiss them as the ravings of a madman, the Swiss inquisitor pushed into insanity by his many years of battle.

Rhonda Jackson had confirmed the letters, and that Terrance Gray had apparently been seduced into following Lord Ashwood. The one in Hell, though Gray's failure to return after Steiner's death confirmed he now followed the younger one. An American of African origin, perhaps it was not a surprise his loyalty had been so easily subverted.

A turban-wearing Indian man approached. "Good evening, sir."

"Yes?" he answered brusquely, keeping an eye on Queen Victoria as she talked with Ashwood. He trusted his men to protect Her Majesty should 'Lord Ashwood' attempt anything but all the same he had a gun in his pocket just in case.

"I am Lord Ashwood's valet. Just now he instructed me to pass on this."

Sir Thomas turned, staring at the Indian. "What?"

The valet held up a cane. "This was Mr Steiner's. Lord Ashwood brought it tonight to give to Lord Durford, confident that his Lordship would see it returned to Templar hands. But as you are here, he thought it best to return it directly."

Sir Thomas recognised the cane, the one Steiner had brought back from Glasgow. A gift from Lady Delaney, containing a hidden swordstick. He accepted it. Steiner might have faltered at the end, but he had died in battle, and he had served faithfully for many years before that.

This valet had spoken familiarly of the Templars, arousing certain suspicions. "You have been Lord Ashwood's valet for long?"

"I served his father first. My name is Singh."

"You know who his father truly was?" Sir Thomas asked. Perhaps this Singh might be persuaded to spy on Lord Ashwood for the Order.

Singh's mouth turned. "I know."

"I would have you watch the Devil's spawn for us, Singh. Help the Order, and you may reach Heaven. Serve Lord Ashwood, and you will surely be damned to Hell with him."

Singh laughed, making no effort to hide his mirth. "Firstly, I was raised a Sikh. Do not offend me with your nonsense, you speak of matters you cannot comprehend. And I worked with your Order once before."

Anger at being addressed in such a way by a servant, and a foreign one at that, sparked fury in Sir Thomas. "Address me in such a tone again and I'll have you whipped! Be damned to Hell, then!"

He expected Singh to cower back, but the insolent knave stood his ground, no give in his dark eyes. "There will be no return to Heaven for me, I fear. And as for what fate awaits Lord Ashwood upon his death, it is beyond my ken and yours. I serve Lord Ashwood for now and watch him on behalf of another."

The intensity in Singh's voice made Sir Thomas cold. "What are you? A demon?"

"Not a demon. I followed *Mikiel* in Heaven and now here on Earth."

Sir Thomas let out a breath as he stared at the valet. "*Mikiel* … you mean the Archangel Michael?"

"As you say."

"You are *Seraphim*," he said, feeling cold all over.

"I am."

Sir Thomas was aware that his mouth had fallen open, standing as he was in the presence of an angel condemned to live and die and live again on Earth – spared Hell but forbidden from Heaven in perpetuity.

"You spoke of working for the Order before, but I do not recognise your name," Sir Thomas managed to ask.

"I was Jeanne de la Byar."

Jeanne de la Byar. A Templar legend who fought undead in the catacombs beneath Paris half a century ago; never joining the Order but always a stalwart ally.

Staggered by this, on top of meeting the Devil's son,

Sir Thomas could only nod when an amused Singh bowed his head and left him standing there, holding the cane of the late Wolfgang Steiner.

*

"You know I am armed," Kane quietly warned Hunt. "And I am not alone."

The hard stares directed at Hunt from two of the other footmen ostensibly waiting on Queen Victoria confirmed that to be no bluff. "I mean Her Majesty no harm. It was she who summoned me," he assured Kane.

He complied with the correct protocol when approaching and addressing Queen Victoria, making the necessary deferential small talk. Not long before, he had been selling the dead to make a living, and now he was speaking with a queen. *What a hell of a year it has been.*

Queen Victoria regarded him with an air of wary speculation. "It was suggested to us that we should decline Lord Easdale's invitation. That you are a dangerous man, Lord Ashwood. The very Devil, it seems."

Hunt had not expected her to know of such matters, and certainly not to address them so openly. "Ah, that was my father, Your Majesty."

"We were raised per the Kensington Protocol, giving us a most … isolated childhood. But we can scarcely dare to imagine being raised by Satan himself. Was he a strict and tyrannical father, or did he let you run wild, encouraging you to indulge in all manner of debauchery?"

A smile came unbidden to Hunt's face as he recalled his upbringing. "Neither, Ma'am. I was raised with a strict hand, but that hand belonged to my mother. I knew nothing about my … heritage until the summer."

There was a flicker of disappointment in her eyes. "Can you tell us nothing of Heaven or Hell? Did your father not speak of his time as God's Most Favoured Archangel? Of his rebellion and Fall? Of the horrors of Hell?"

"No, Ma'am." He considered his next words. "He said that while in our world, he had only a faint recollection of Heaven and Hell, that to attempt to describe them was an exercise in futility, that there were insufficient words or points of reference. And that he had met God no more than you or I."

"But people are in Heaven, yes?" she pressed.

"I do not know. I don't believe he knew, either, though it pleased him and his fellow demons to hint as much to those they wish to manipulate."

Disappointment was etched on the Queen's lined face. She was in her seventies, and with death approaching, perhaps she sought reassurance that a life awaited beyond this one.

"It was … interesting to meet you, Lord Ashwood." A small gesture from her brought Kane over.

Hunt took the hint and bowed. "Your Majesty." Kane led him away from the troubled monarch.

"I understand your family estate is in the Highlands," Kane said. "Is it beautiful?"

"It is, yes."

"Good. You would be well advised to stay there and visit London only sparingly."

Hunt Unveiled a little, taking pleasure in the fear he saw in the Templar's widening eyes. There was no need for words as they parted.

"That was foolish," Singh chided him a short time later as they left the ballroom after Hunt had bidden his host a good night. They were to spend the night in Lord Easdale's house and then return to Scotland in the morning by train.

"If they must threaten me because of who … what I am, then I will *show* them what I am," Hunt said.

"You don't know what you are. And if *Mikiel* does not like what you are, then–"

"You will hand in your notice, Singh?"

It was *Kariel*'s time to Unveil, and Hunt was reminded that the *Seraphim* had lived countless lives on this world. "Let us say I will be in need of a new employer. My Lord."

“I’ll bear that in mind,” Hunt said to placate his valet.

“What do you intend to do next? Return to Glasgow?”

“Not yet. We return to Loch Aline, to prepare for the arrival of Foley’s fellow werewolves. Part of the Lewswood must be set aside for them during every full moon. I will not have the locals killed or injured, or their livestock slain. There should be ample game in the forest for them to hunt.”

“You begin to sound like him.”

“Foley?”

“*Samiel*.”

“Thank you.”

“I did not say whether that was a good thing,” Singh said. “Do not lose yourself to grief and anger and become him.”

“I do not know what you are talking about.” Which was a lie. Since his father’s death … Lucifer’s death … Hunt had embraced the coldness within, the demon within.

They reached the stairs. “The servants’ quarters are in the attic, so I will leave you now.” Singh paused. “Once your business is done in Loch Aline, what then?”

“Then? Then we return to Glasgow and finish this war, finish *Arakiel*,” Hunt said. “Good night, Singh.”

“Good night, my Lord.”

My Lord. Wilton Hunt the natural science student and body snatcher was gone. In his place stood Lord Ashwood. His mother and father’s son.

The Baron is dead. Long live the Baron.

Lucifer is dead.

Long live…?

THE END

Acknowledgements

As always, thanks are owed to my wife, Dana, for her unceasing love and support.

Thanks also to Peter, Alison and Sofia for their work vastly improving this book and creating its cover.

Elsewhen Press

delivering outstanding new talents in speculative fiction

Visit the Elsewhen Press website at elsewhen.press for the latest information on all of our titles, authors and events; to read our blog; find out where to buy our books and ebooks; or to place an order.

Sign up for the Elsewhen Press InFlight Newsletter at elsewhen.press/newsletter

Sooty Feathers by David Craig

David Craig's *Sooty Feathers* series is a masterful gothic tale about a supernatural war for control of the Second City of the British Empire, and the struggle of flawed characters of uncertain virtue who try to avert it. It is set in a late 19th century Glasgow ruled by undead – from the private clubs, town houses and country manors of the privileged to the dung-choked wynds and overcrowded slums of the poor. Undead unrest, a fallen angel, and religious zealots intent on driving out the forces of evil, set the stage for a diabolical conflict of biblical proportions.

1: Resurrection Men

Glasgow 1893.

Wilton Hunt, a student, and Tam Foley, a laudanum-addicted pharmacist, are pursuing extra-curricular careers as body snatchers, or 'resurrection men', under cover of darkness. They exhume a girl's corpse, only for it to disappear while their backs are turned. Confused and in need of the money the body would have earnt them, they investigate the corpse's disappearance. They discover that bodies have started to turn up in the area with ripped-out throats and severe loss of blood, although not the one they lost. The police are being encouraged by powerful people to look the other way, and the deaths are going unreported by the press. As Hunt and Foley delve beneath the veneer of respectable society, they find themselves entangled in a dangerous underworld that is protected from scrutiny by the rich and powerful members of the elite but secretive Sooty Feathers Club.

Meanwhile, a mysterious circus arrives in the middle of the night, summoned to help avenge a betrayal two centuries old…

ISBN: 9781911409366 (epub, kindle) / ISBN: 9781911409267 (400pp paperback)

2: Lord of the Hunt

June 1893.

Undead prowl the streets of Glasgow at night hunting for blood. They, in turn, are hunted by the formidable Lady Delaney and her apprentice Kerry Knox, whose fight against the secret society ruling Glasgow will lead them into the city's industrial heart where the poor toil in miserable conditions. Children have been exploited in mills and factories for decades, but the Sooty Feather Society has refined its cruel disregard in service to the undead.

Delaney and Knox are not the society's only problem. The elusive demon Arakiel employs murder and necromancy in his campaign to seize control of Glasgow, avenging betrayal and reclaiming what was once his.

Wilton Hunt and Tam Foley are lying low in the Highlands where Hunt's father has recently inherited title and estate. The blue skies and clear waters of Loch Aline may seem a tranquil sanctuary to the city men, but its forbidding forests and shadowed glens conceal dark secrets pertaining to Hunt's family, and a diabolical revelation will change Wilton's life forever.

Demons walk the crowded, cobbled streets of Glasgow, and a necromancer's debt is called in. Knox will learn what joining this war might cost her; Hunt and Foley will learn they can't escape it. Their diverged paths will meet again when dark magic unleashes a horror not everyone will survive…

ISBN: 9781911409762 (epub, kindle) / ISBN: 9781911409663 (416pp paperback)

By David Craig

Thorns of a Black Rose

David Craig

Revenge and responsibility, confrontation and consequences.

A hot desert land of diverse peoples dealing with demons, mages, natural disasters … and the Black Rose assassins.

On a quest for vengeance, Shukara arrives in the city of Mask having already endured two years of hardship and loss. Her pouch is stolen by Tamira, a young street-smart thief, who throws away some of the rarer reagents that Shukara needs for her magick. Tracking down the thief, and being unfamiliar with Mask, Shukara shows mercy to Tamira in exchange for her help in replacing what has been lost. Together they brave the intrigues of Mask, and soon discover that they have a mutual enemy in the Black Rose, an almost legendary band of merciless assassins. But this is just the start of their journeys…

Although set in an imaginary land, the scenery and peoples of *Thorns of a Black Rose* were inspired by Egypt, Morocco and the Sahara. Mask is a living, breathing city, from the prosperous Merchant Quarter whose residents struggle for wealth and power, to the Poor Quarter whose residents struggle just to survive. It is a coming of age tale for the young thief, Tamira, as well as a tale of vengeance and discovery. There is also a moral ambiguity in the story, with both the protagonists and antagonists learning that whatever their intentions or justification, actions have consequences.

ISBN: 9781911409557 (epub, kindle) / 9781911409458 (256pp paperback)
Visit bit.ly/ThornsOfABlackRose

You might also like

The Avatars of Ruin series by Tej Turner

Book 1: Bloodsworn

"*Classic epic fantasy. I enjoyed it enormously*" **– Anna Smith Spark**
"*a stunning introduction to a new fantasy world*" **– Christopher G Nuttall**
"*This is epic fantasy with a touch of the mythic to it. There were villains I loved to hate, and a queer protagonist I loved rooting for. Action, magic, a world in peril…what more could you ask for?*" **– Trip Galey**

It has been twelve years since the war between the nations of Sharma and Gavendara. The villagers of Jalard live a bucolic existence, nestled within the hills of western Sharma, far from the warzone. They have little contact with the outside world, apart from once a year when Academy representatives choose two of them to be taken away to the institute in the capital. To be Chosen is considered a great honour… of which most of Jalard's children dream. But this year, their announcement is so shocking it causes friction between villagers, and some begin to suspect that all is not what it seems. Where are they taking the Chosen, and why? Some intend to find out, but what they discover will change their lives forever and set them on a long and bloody path to seek vengeance…

ISBN: 9781911409779 (epub, kindle) / 9781911409670 (432pp paperback)
Visit bit.ly/Bloodsworn

Book 2: Blood Legacy

"*a nuanced, smart high fantasy novel with intelligent, complex characters, good LGBT rep and some killer twists*" **– Joanne Hall**
"*an exciting book which ups the stakes, mixing traditional fantasy with an element of possession horror*" **– David Craig**
"*a journey into Fantasy, only it's not quite the journey you expected, and it's all the better for it*" **– Allen Stroud**

The ragtag group from Jalard have finally reached Shemet, Sharma's capital city. Scarred and bereft, they bring a grim tale of what happened to their village, and a warning about the threat to all humanity. Some expect sanctuary within the Synod to mean an end to their hardships, but their hopes are soon dashed. Sharma's ruling class are caught within their own inner turmoil. Jaedin senses moles within their ranks, but his call to crisis falls mostly on deaf ears, and some seek to thwart him when he tries to hunt the infiltrators down.

Meanwhile, Gavendara is mustering its forces. With ritualistically augmented soldiers, their mutant army is like nothing the world has ever seen.

The Zakaras are coming. And Sharma's only hope of stopping them is if it can unite its people in time.

ISBN: 9781911409991 (epub, kindle) / 9781911409892 (474pp paperback)
Visit bit.ly/Blood-Legacy

You might also like

The Avatars of Ruin series by Tej Turner

Book 3: Blood War

"*Smoothly throttles up a gear from the previous two books. The diverse and fleshed out characters face the desperate horrors of war, leading to a thrilling climax. An excellent addition to a gripping series.*" – **David Craig**

Sharma stands on the precipice of destruction as Gavendara's army of shapeshifters surges towards the Valantian mountains. A mutant invasion leaving terror and death in its wake and whose victims rise again, swelling its ranks.

Yet still the Synod dithers, its leaders fractured as they plot and scheme against each other. Jaedin is now a fugitive, Bryna's powers are waning, and Rivan grapples with the consequences of his resurrection – as well as the ominous entity that now lives beneath his skin. Whilst Miles, torn between loyalties, faces an impossible choice that could reshape the fate of nations.

Meanwhile, to the east, Elita seeks sanctuary within the enigmatic depths of Babua's jungle. The people who dwell there are distrustful of her, but for a good reason. She indeed has secrets, and it seems that trouble has followed her.

ISBN: 9781915304360 (epub, kindle) / 9781915304261 (450pp paperback)

Visit bit.ly/Blood-War

Book 4: Blood Ruin

Coming soon

Tej Turner is an SFF author and travel-blogger. His debut novel *The Janus Cycle* was published by Elsewhen Press in 2015 and its sequel *Dinnusos Rises* was released in 2017. Both are hard to classify within typical genres but were contemporary and semi-biographical with elements of surrealism. He has since branched off into writing epic fantasy and has an ongoing series called the *Avatars of Ruin*. The first instalment – *Bloodsworn* – was released in 2021, and its sequel *Blood Legacy* in 2022. The third – *Blood War* –was published in early 2024.

He does not have any particular place he would say he is 'from', as his family moved between various parts of England during his childhood. He eventually settled in Wales, where he studied Creative Writing and Film at Trinity College in Carmarthen, followed by a master's degree at The University of Wales Lampeter.

Since then, Tej has mostly resided in Cardiff, where he works as a chef by day and writes by moonlight. His childhood on the move seems to have rubbed off on him because when he is not in Cardiff, it is usually because he has strapped on a backpack and flown off to another part of the world to go on an adventure.

He has so far clocked two years in Asia and two years in South America, and when he travels, he takes a particular interest in historic sites, jungles, wildlife, native cultures, and mountains. He also spent some time volunteering at the Merazonia Wildlife Rehabilitation Centre in Ecuador.

Firsthand accounts of Tej's adventures abroad can be found on his travel blog at https://tejturner.com/

About David Craig

Aside from three months living on an oil tanker sailing back and forth between America and Africa, and two years living in a pub, David Craig grew up on the west coast of Scotland. He studied Software Engineering at university, but lost interest in the subject after (and admittedly prior to) graduation. He currently works as a workforce planning analyst for a public service contact centre, and lives near Glasgow with his wife, daughter and dog.

Milton Keynes UK
Ingram Content Group UK Ltd.
UKHW031834290724
446271UK00001B/8

9 781915 304667